WILL

WILL

by Paul Steinmann

Will

Windy City Publishers
2118 Plum Grove Road, #349
Rolling Meadows, IL 60008
www.windycitypublishers.com

Published in the United States of America

ISBN:
978-1-941478-56-1

Library of Congress Control Number:
2017960337

WINDY CITY PUBLISHERS
CHICAGO

Dedicated to my wife, Stephenie

And an old friend,
Pete Prince of Kinloch, Missouri

ACKNOWLEDGMENTS

MANY THANKS TO DR. SHIRLEY Crenshaw, Alison Allman, and Nancy Wagner for time spent editing and providing constructive criticism. To Karen Hulwick and Keith Kehlbeck for putting me in touch with the folks at Windy City Publishers. To Janet, Shelly, and Dawn at WCP for their help and suggestions. For friends kind enough to read preliminary drafts and provide suggestions: Julie Kindle, Jim Boedeker, Arthur Silverblatt, Joanne Barkley, Lou Birenbaum, Bob Kindle, Paul Penick, and Pat Menzel. And to my wife Stephenie for telling me how much she looked forward to reading the next chapter—even if it meant passing on quality time with Alex Trebek and *Jeopardy*.

Will is a fictional story.
Some incidents, dialogue, and characters are based on historical fact.

INTRODUCTION

AUGUST 13, 1831, A PARTIAL eclipse caused the sun to turn bluish green; Nat Turner believed it was a sign from God that his revolution was to begin. On August 22, he led a band of slaves, armed with guns, knives and axes, through the Virginia swamps. By nightfall, over fifty white men, women and children were killed along the Nottoway River.

The news of Turner's rebellion spread quickly, and fear of another revolt haunted white slave owners. A popular verse intensified those fears.

> "You might be rich as cream,
> and drive you a coach and a four-horse team.
> But you can't keep the world from turn'n round,
> and ole Nat Turner from gainin ground."

Newspaper headlines announced, "SLAUGHTER OF WHITE INNOCENTS." Two months later came another report, "NAT TURNER CAPTURED." In October of 1831, Turner was taken to the courthouse and tried. On November 11, he was hanged. His body was dismembered. Trinkets and Talismans were made from his skin and bones.

Hundreds of miles away in a military garrison, Colonel James Pritchard read newspaper accounts of Turner's uprising. He held Virginia authorities in high regard for the manner in which they brutally punished Turner and the other slaves involved. He believed severe retribution was the only way to deal with mutinous slaves.

Twenty years after the Turner rebellion, Pritchard gained control of a lucrative Mississippi plantation known as Mary Dale. A slave on the plantation, Will Douglas, knew the Colonel obtained the property illegally. He found proof. The only way he could avoid the Colonel's wrath and certain death…was to run.

1

WILL STOOD IN THE SHADOWS watching the Colonel smoke his cigar and stroll along the veranda. The orange glow on the tip of the cheroot changed intensity and finally disappeared from view. He bit his lower lip and approached the cabin where slave meals were prepared.

He had tried once before to find a strongbox containing items the previous owner wanted preserved. Shortly before his death, Ben Douglas instructed a trusted female servant to carefully hide the box and its contents.

Pritchard was aware objects of value were stored somewhere on the plantation. He was not aware two house servants knew about the items or that the two slaves could read and write.

Before the Colonel sent her to auction, Teeny tried to slip a note to Will revealing where she hid the contents. In her haste, the fragile paper separated.

Will pulled what remained of the message and read it one more time.

Will
I have taken the moneybox
Master Douglas
kept papers
and put them
look in the cook
Pritchard knows
miss
please don't forge

1

The location of the box had been lost. He hoped the missing last part of the message said something about how much she would miss him. He folded the scrap of paper and stuffed it in his trouser pocket.

Will took a deep breath, ready to begin a new search. He moved through a maze of utensils and supplies, making as little noise as possible. He lifted floor planks and examined dirt below, looking for marks left by a hoe or shovel. He peered inside storage bins, then tipped a large barrel to one side and ran his hand through corn meal. The only place he hadn't searched was the small attic above, a room used to store bowls and dishes.

Diagonal rays of moonlight filtered through a small window and provided dim light on the first floor, but the attic was ominously dark. Will peered into the stairwell and started to climb. His heart began to pound.

He ran his hands and fingers over every item. Anything that was in the box could easily have been moved. Fifteen minutes spent fumbling in the dark revealed nothing; the dingy storeroom was another dead end.

Will was backtracking when he saw a folded cook's apron atop a barrel. Running his hand along the dense fabric he found two large pockets, both sewn shut with thick string. His fingers touched items that felt like bundled paper as he reached inside. Just as he started to pull the strings apart, the cabin door creaked.

Someone carrying a grease lantern entered; an eerie glow filled the cabin. Will noticed the shadowy outline of a large man wearing a wide-brimmed hat. It was Blackstone, Pritchard's overseer. The lantern cast enough light for Will to discover something else: two eyes peering down at him. Sam, the large cat kept in the shed to keep rats and mice out of supplies, lay sprawled on a shelf above him.

Sounds of pots and pans being moved about came from below. The light moved erratically and came to rest in different locations. Will wondered whether he and Blackstone were looking for the same thing. Will glanced back; the cat was still stretched out, unfazed.

The lantern moved again. This time it stopped at the stairwell. Blackstone's heavy boots on the wood stairs became louder. Will was trapped. The burly overseer hovered now just a few feet away. Will braced his body against the wall. His mind raced; given an opening, he would make a mad dash to the nearby woods.

Blackstone stood at the top of the stairs. He saw something move on the shelf and raised the lantern. The flame inched closer. The cat began to pant heavily. Suddenly it arched and sprang from the shelf. Claws sliced through Blackstone's shirt and dug into his chest. There was a barely audible, "God damn you," as he stumbled backward.

Will heard a series of heavy thuds, which ended with a loud groan. Remains of the flickering lantern illuminated a sprawled body below. Will grabbed the apron, bolted down the stairs and vaulted over Blackstone. As he ran, yells, curses, and Sam's high-pitched shrieking pierced the calm night. He jumped the fence surrounding the vegetable garden and raced frantically to his cabin. Will stuffed the apron under the mattress, crawled into bed, and pulled the threadbare blanket to his chin.

Will's cabin mate lay awake. "Wha da hell ya up to, an' wha's goin on oud'side?"

Will tried to calm himself. "If anybody comes down here, you've got to tell them I've been here all night."

"You gonna get us whupped or kild! Prob'aly both!"

"I found something in the cook shed; it might be what Teeny took from the big house."

Loud shouts rang out in the distance.

Tom rolled to his side and hissed, "We looks at what ya foun ta'morrow. Right now, ya needs ta get quiet."

The commotion near the cook's cabin subsided: the yelling stopped, dogs finished barking, and the plantation grounds returned to silence. Will wondered why the dogs hadn't been roped together to search the woods. Maybe Blackstone didn't realize there had been another person in the cabin. Or maybe he knew that the person who ran from the cabin still roamed the plantation.

2

A RAM HORN SOUNDED. ONE hundred fifty field hands lined up and formed gangs of twenty or more. Will, Tom, and the others stood with heads bowed, hoe and bag in hand, waiting for Blackstone to arrive. The morning sun outlined his large body as he inspected the slaves. The overseer always appeared sullen, but today he looked more out of sorts than usual. Below the brim of his hat, a dark purple bruise from his fall had ripened. Coal black eyes glared at the slaves. Pete, the driver for Will's gang, tipped his hat deferentially and said, "Mornin', sah."

Blackstone curled his lip and tossed a dirty sack in Pete's direction. The slaves watched it sail through the air and land. A partially opened bag revealed the tan and white fur of a lifeless animal. "Bury that damn thing before it starts to stink, then move yer Niggers out." Blackstone watched for a reaction. There was none. He mounted his charcoal mare and headed to the north field.

"It be Big Sam," said Tom.

Will stared solemnly at the lifeless cat that may have saved his life. Pete dug a hole next to the vegetable garden and quickly covered the animal with black soil. He gave a signal to the men and women in his group; they began a slow walk toward the cotton field.

At noon the ram's horn sounded again, calling the slaves to gather for their rations. Women too old to work the fields began wheeling out small wagons with wooden troughs on top. Pete's gang sat around one of the wagons waiting for permission to eat. Blackstone nodded. The slaves proceeded, using a small gourd to scoop out a mixture of cornmeal and buttermilk. On a good day, the cook threw in a few vegetables and a little meat, but today it was just mush.

Only ten minutes later, Siebert decided enough time had been wasted. "Everybody up! Get back to work!"

Joe Siebert was a wiry little man who went by the name of Jake. He went everywhere with his "Buddy," a long whip attached to his belt known as a "Black Snake." Both overseers carried rifles as they watched the pickers. Will looked at the field filled with over a hundred slaves and wondered how many thought about running. Or had they given up, believing that their fate was to die under Pritchard's rule?

Shadows grew long as evening fell and darkness approached. Pritchard emerged from the ornate doorway leading to the veranda. He plumped the pillows on his favorite chair and surveyed the land surrounding the big house. Spanish moss draped the huge oak trees, and beneath them, green grass led to fields of white cotton. The colonel settled into his chair, lit his cheroot, and watched stars appear in the darkening sky. After a sip of bourbon, he smiled and congratulated himself for obtaining such a grand estate.

Later that evening Blackstone joined Pritchard. While pouring himself a whiskey he informed the colonel that a slave ran from the cook shed the night before.

"I think the bastard was trying to steal food, but I'm not sure. Maybe he was looking for somethin' else."

Pritchard's tranquil mood changed; he was furious. He assumed the public punishment of "Runaway John" last month would have prevented this type of insubordination. He finished his bourbon and growled, "When this bastard is caught, I want him beaten to a pulp, and then I want him killed."

3

TOM OPENED THE DOOR TO the slave cabin, making sure not to wake anyone. Inside he hung blankets on the walls to prevent light from seeping between the boards. Will lit a grease candle, retrieved the apron, and placed it next to the dim light. He tugged at strings and his hands began to tremble as the contents tumbled to the floor.

"Whad is all dis?" Tom whispered.

"I think it might be money from another country. It's got English words, but doesn't look like Federal money." A packet of folded papers, once held together with a red wax seal, was lying next to the currency. Will carefully unfolded it, and within seconds said, "Oh, Lord! Listen to this!"

Their voices had interrupted the sleep of one of the older slaves, and now he roamed from room to room, trying to locate the source of the disruption. With the man shuffling around, Will couldn't take a chance. He stuffed the money and documents back in the apron and quickly tucked the bundle under his mattress.

Several minutes passed before he felt it was safe to whisper, "That was Master Douglas' last request. I read the part where it said, 'Last Will and Testament,' and right after that it said, 'No living heirs.' I think this is what Blackstone was looking for that night in the cook shed. Once everyone's asleep I'm gonna get these things out of here."

"Oh, Lawd! You know what dey gwonna do if dey finds we gots dis? Look wha dey do ta John."

Will and Tom stared into the darkness, watching the big house and remembering John's torture vividly…

John lived in a dilapidated cabin about a mile from the plantation. Mary Dale slaves didn't pay much attention to him, and Ben Douglas decided it

6

wasn't worth the trouble to bring him in and force him to work the fields. When Pritchard took over, he told other slave owners that Douglas should never have tolerated this insubordination. He would correct the old man's mistake.

Once captured, John's well-orchestrated punishment began. He was strapped to a large mill post. His shirt was ripped off, and Pritchard gave Siebert the signal to begin. After fifteen lashes criss-crossed the slave's back in an angry red pattern, the Colonel raised his right arm to temporarily halt the proceedings. A slave was ordered to wash the gashes with the "Devil's Brew"—a watery red pepper concoction so strong it would sting a man's hand on contact. When the fiery liquid touched the raw and bleeding wounds, it produced a searing pain that caused John to howl. His muscles trembled and wild convulsions caused his head to slam against the post. Blood streamed from his nose and mouth.

Pritchard ordered forty lashes before the man's restraints were removed. John pleaded as he wobbled from side-to-side, "Please, massah, no mo! Please stop, please stop! Doan beat me no mo!" Someone threw a thick blanket over his wretched form. He slumped to the ground in a bloody, pulpy heap. Slaves forced to watch looked to the sky and uttered desperate prayers.

Blackstone stood at the barn's entrance, a fifteen-pound blacksmith's hammer in his right hand. John lay trembling. He couldn't see. Silence enveloped the yard, until the sound of dry soil grinding under someone's boots disturbed it. Blackstone paused in front of the shrouded figure. His voice boomed across the grounds, "John, you worthless bastard, your running days are over!" In one smooth motion he raised the hammer, and in a burst of speed, brought it down on John's foot. A terrible scream erupted.

Witnesses covered their eyes. The crowd let out a collective moan. Even Pritchard felt stunned. A group of slaves carried John's twitching body to the barn and deposited him on a pile of raw unginned cotton. A red circle formed below his legs.

As slave owners and slaves who witnessed the gory event solemnly departed, a bent-over figure moved slowly down the hill toward the plantation.

Granda, the hoary conjure woman, had been summoned to tend to John. She manipulated an intricately carved walking stick in one hand and clutched a bag of amulets in the other. She looked at the errant slave's mangled foot and muttered, "Damballah, show yer mercy…let him die."

Will shuddered at the memory of John's torture. If caught, his fate would be even worse. He looked out the window. The mansion finally went dark. Will gathered up the old master's last request and the currency, stuffed them in a worn leather satchel, and sprinted to the north field.

He dug a short trench with a hoe blade and carefully deposited the satchel. Will tamped the soil and counted, "Seventh row, twenty paces in." He retreated through tall grasses that bordered the Mary Dale Cemetery. Soft moonlight illuminated the mausoleum that housed the tombs of Master and Misses Douglas and their two children. From the direction of the shrine, a reedy voice called to him, "Will, come over here."

He thought it was his imagination. The voice called again, "Come here be'fo people starts wakin' up." Granda gestured to Will. She had a cloth sack in one hand, and her walking stick in the other.

He pulled the heavy gate and proceeded warily. Granda tilted her head to one side, "I knows why ya be out here, Will, ya got plans ta run."

Will appeared dumbfounded. "How did you know?"

"I knows cauz ya work in da big house for da ole Massah. Ya kin read an' write, an' ya seen poss'bil'tees. Ya doan wanna die workin' in dem hot fields." Granda raised her arm and pointed toward the sky. "You gonna have a full moon in three days, an' den it fade. Use dat light while ya can."

She handed him a small sack. "Dis be pepper smut fer yer feet ta keep da hounds away." From her black shroud she pulled a jagged piece of fur. "Dis foot be frum a rabbit kilt by a one-eyed slave in a graveyard when da moon wuz full. Dat why it be lucky. Take it an' go now be'fo Blackstone an Siebert get dem selves outta bed. An' re'member, evil spirits creeps 'round at night, an' dem spirits is able to hex people, even smart ones like you." Will nodded as though he understood what she meant and softly said, "Thank you." He gave a slight wave, then turned and darted from the graveyard.

Sweat dripped from field workers the next day; they moved along rows of plants, and prayed for relief from the heat. When the day's work finally ended, Pete led his gang to the cook shed. Will waited until everyone had gone before returning to his cabin. He lifted the corner post of his bed and retrieved two small pieces of paper Reverend Abernathy had given him. Abernathy had been minister of the Bolivar County Colored Church and had served as a link to the Underground Railroad. Once local slave owners discovered his subversive activity, they burned the church and the Reverend disappeared.

Before this catastrophe, Abernathy had provided Will with directions and a crude map for the first part of the journey. Will read the instructions one more time.

> Stay close to the river until you see limestone bluffs. Between the bluffs is a stream. Follow that stream until you see four hills of the same size. Between the first two is a cabin. The conductor uses his lantern as a signal. If it is by the door, he is telling you it is safe. If it is on the front stoop, stay away: slave hunters are in the area.

The moon disappeared and thunder rumbled faintly in the distance. Will slid the papers back under the bedpost. He lay in his bunk silently repeating, "Seventh row, twenty paces in." In the distance flashes of jagged lightning seared the black sky like the lashes that had seared John's back.

A **SERIES OF VIOLENT THUNDERSTORMS** halted work in the fields. A few older slaves remained in the barn weaving baskets, but most slaves took refuge inside their cabins. Will stood behind the meat-curing shed, out of the rain, and out of sight. He stared at his reflection in a shallow pool of water and began to think about how life had placed him here.

Jeff and Priscilla Owens purchased Will at auction when he was three years old. He had lived on their small plantation for a year when his childhood companion Teeny was born. Her mother, Elsa, was an attractive quadroon who worked the loom and crafted clothes. Jeff's on-going sexual relations with Elsa led to the birth of a beautiful baby girl. Her mother named the girl with cream-colored skin, "Taniah."

Priscilla Owens finally had enough of her husband's philandering and issued an ultimatum: "You're gonna get that pale Nigger woman off our property. I want her sold as soon as that baby stops sucklin." Elsa was sold, but the baby girl remained. Priscilla disliked the child's birth name, so she registered her in the county records as, "Teeny, a female slave, owned by Jeff and Priscilla Owens."

The task of raising the two children fell to Momma Dee, an elderly slave. Over the years, as the small slaves thrived, their value grew. Hard times fell on the planters in the summer of 1840, when a weevil infestation decimated Tennessee farmers' crops. Landowners did whatever they could to survive. In the Owens' case, they staved off foreclosure by selling their most valuable assets—Will and Teeny.

On the day of the Memphis auction, Priscilla Owens had personally scrubbed both children clean and dressed them in their best clothes. Neither child understood what was about to transpire, but Momma Dee knew, and she begged Master Owens to let them stay.

He gave an angry retort, "I got no choice, woman. If you weren't so damn old, I'd sell you too!"

Will was ruggedly handsome and tall for his age. The auctioneer ordered the boy to stand on a box so the doctor could examine him. "Will is fit and ready to be sold," he said.

Teeny had reddish-brown hair, hazel eyes, and delicate features. She looked like a porcelain figurine standing next to other slaves whose complexions ranged from light brown to coal black. The doctor looked at her in disbelief. He said to Priscilla, "I need to see this child's papers." She handed him the birth record drawn up years ago. The doctor shook his head and the little girl was sent to auction.

The auctioneer ordered children who were being sold to stand on a wood platform. Off to one side, a well-dressed couple paused and looked them over. Teeny squeezed Will's hand; the two stared nervously at the couple. The man signaled for the auctioneer to bring Will forward. A large bony hand grabbed his arm and pulled him to the front of the platform; Teeny held tightly to Will's hand and refused to let go.

"It's all right, let them both come," said the gentleman. He tapped the platform with his black and gold walking cane indicating where he wanted the slaves to stand. He placed a pince-nez on the bridge of his nose and examined Will, then ordered him to open his mouth. After examining his teeth, he said, "Young man, what is your name?"

"Name's Will, sah."

"Will, eh? How old are you?"

"I's been told I's al mos four'teen, sah."

"Who's your friend here?"

"Teeny, sah."

"How old is she?"

"She be ten, sah."

He rubbed his chin and looked at the auctioneer, "What do you think, could the little one work in the big house?"

"She be strong enough, an if she be lazy, the whip will cure that."

"Very well, I think we are interested in a purchase. What say you, Mary?" Mary looked at the two children. "Will, Teeny, do you think you would like to come live with us?" Teeny remained too frightened to respond.

"Yes, Missus," said Will. He placed both hands on his chest and bowed. Teeny followed Will's lead and did the same.

Mary Douglas laughed. "Well, Ben, I think we have found two new house servants."

5

"NO NEED FOR YOU TO trouble yourselves about your belongings," Mary Douglas said as she steered the two children away from the auction pen. "We will have clothes made for you and make sure you have everything you need."

Teeny still clung to Will's hand as they approached the Douglas' white and gold carriage. A handsome slave named Steven—dressed in fancy gold, green, and white silk clothes—occupied the front seat. Will took a seat on one side of him and Teeny on the other.

In less than a day they were transported from a small plantation to a grand mansion in the Mississippi Delta surrounded by majestic oak trees. In this household, servants enjoyed plenty of food, which they ate from plates, not from a trough. The Douglas' allowed them to celebrate holidays and weddings, and any couple that "jumped the broom" was provided private space in the slave quarters.

One year after Will and Teeny arrived, the Douglas' established a plantation school for their two children, Catherine and Frederick. Peggy Lockwood, a young, white, missionary teacher from Kentucky, served as governess. Children from nearby plantations were invited to attend. In less than a month, fifteen children sat learning to read, write, and figure math equations in her school. After the white children departed, Lockwood was allowed to teach Will and Teeny.

It took Will less than a year to master the alphabet and to begin stringing words together to form sentences. Before long, he could read entire books. One of his favorites was a story about Margery Meanwell, a poor orphan whose life changed once she had shoes to wear.

Will was in the library late one afternoon and held up *The History of Little Miss Goody Two Shoes*. "Miss Lockwood, is this story really true?"

"Will, stories don't have to be true to make us think and ask questions."

"Thinking about some of the things in this book makes me sad. Especially if I can't do nothin' about it."

"Anything about it."

"Yes, ma'am, anything about it. But sometimes these books get me even more mixed up." He returned the book to its place on a shelf and looked at the governess. "How come Teeny and I have to learn our lessons after everybody leaves?"

She gave him a sad smile. "Will, I think you know the answer to that."

"Is it because white people don't want us colored kids to spend time learning to read and write if all we're gonna do is pick cotton and wait on them?"

"It's a little more complicated than that. A lot of money is being made from slaves working the fields. People don't want that to change. If slaves were taught to read and write, they would begin asking questions—just like you. They might even run away or refuse to obey."

"Do you think Master Douglas would let you teach some of the other slave children?"

Lockwood folded her arms and gave him a worried look. "Will, if the sheriff found out I was teaching you and Teeny, he would close the school and send me away. Mr. Douglas is already taking a risk."

"Is it ever gonna change, Miss Lockwood?" Will asked angrily.

"I wish I knew. A lot of people are writing about how important it is for slavery to end."

Will thought about that. "Are coloreds doing any of the writing?"

"A few, not many. Maybe you could be one of those writers some day."

Teeny giggled. "Will kin hardly write his name!"

"Yeah, but I know my math, and two tickle fingers are much worse than one." With this, the discussion ended, and the chase was on. Teeny took a familiar path through the dining room and darted toward the mansion's entryway.

She stopped abruptly. "Will, stop! Stop chasing me!"

Will noticed that something outside had captured her attention. They both looked out the window at Doctor Willis' buggy.

"Why is he here?" Will wondered. He decided to try to find out. So, he tiptoed around the first floor,

"Nobody's down here," he informed Teeny. Then the two house slaves stood by the stairway leading upstairs and listened. They could faintly hear the adults' voices. The discussion sounded serious; one word they heard clearly was "Malaria."

6

THE DOUGLAS' ASSIGNED WILL to watch over Frederick during the night. At midnight, chimes in the mansion's tall clock reverberated softly. Half an hour later Frederick's fever ran high. In his wild-eyed excitement, he spewed out rambling sentences. Frightened, Will hurried down the hallway to summon his master.

Ben Douglas appeared shaken when he saw his son thrashing about.

"Tell Steven to fetch Doc Willis, and get me laudanum from the parlor," he ordered. Will woke Steven and quickly returned to Frederick's room with the bottle. Ben combined the powder with water, and Mary held her son's head so he could drink the mixture. Several minutes passed before the convulsions subsided and Frederick drifted into sleep.

Dr. Willis arrived early the next morning. Even in the pale dawn light the yellow pallor on Frederick's face was undeniable. The Douglases thought he was sleeping deeply, but Dr. Willis told the distressed parents he had fallen into a coma. Will noticed a disturbing rattling sound as the boy fought to get air into his lungs.

Catherine survived the disease, but life at Mary Dale never returned to the level of contentment that existed before Frederick's death. Frantic to keep her only remaining child healthy, Mary Douglas started consulting with Granda about herbs and potions. The distraught mother wanted help from any source: Voodoo potions or Dr. Willis' medications; she didn't care, as long as Catherine remained well.

To everyone's dismay, Catherine relapsed a year later. Her symptoms were similar to Frederick's, but minus the stormy convulsions. She remained lucid, able to speak with her mother and father as they struggled to keep her alive. Catherine was strong, and it seemed for a brief time that her spirit and physical strength would win the battle. But within a month after the disease returned, Dr. Willis' medicine, and Granda's potions couldn't prevent the yellowing of her skin and eyes.

After Catherine's funeral, a major change came over Mary Douglas. She was no longer the lovely woman Will had met when he first arrived. Lines around her face and mouth grew deep. Her golden hair turned white. With both of her children gone, she became withdrawn, moody, and brooding. Some days she never left her bed. Other days she spent staring out a window at some distant object.

Dr. Willis diagnosed Mary's condition as melancholia, and he believed a change of scenery would do her good. He suggested a return to her ancestral home in New Orleans for a month or two.

"The connection to her past might provide a return to normalcy," he explained.

Barely two weeks later, Mary found herself aboard the riverboat Louisiana Belle, bound for New Orleans. Dr. Willis instructed the Mary Dale servant accompanying her to administer the laudanum sparingly.

After her first month in New Orleans, Mary sent an encouraging letter to Ben.

> Dear Ben,
>
> My old friends are taking good care of me. Last night the Brunel's held a party in my honor. Colonel Pritchard, an officer in the New Orleans military, escorted me to dinner. After hearing about the death of our children, he was very kind and extremely sympathetic. The colonel said he would provide a doctor from his regiment to accompany me on my return trip.
>
> I hope the sadness that has consumed me will wane. Please be patient and understand that my illness seems beyond my control. I will be home soon. You are always in my thoughts and prayers.
>
> With much love,
> Mary

After reading her words a second time, a smile crept across Ben Douglas' face. *Mary says she will be home soon, and things will be back to normal*, he mused happily.

But Ben had to wait almost two months for his wife to return. Richard Walther, a medical officer under Pritchard's command, escorted her back to Mary Dale. Will barely recognized the frail woman who stepped cautiously from the carriage. He sadly shook his head.

Once home, Mary tried for weeks to present a positive facade, but before long melancholy enveloped her once again. For relief, she relied on opium from the New Orleans garrison, prescribed by Dr. Walther. If the drug was in short supply, or unavailable, she grew agitated and nervous.

During one of these distressed moments, Mary told Peggy Lockwood, "Your service here is no longer needed. I am closing the school." Then she assembled the house servants. "Teeny and Will are going to remain in the main house. The rest of you will go back to working the fields."

Benjamin Douglas was reluctant to contradict his wife's orders for fear of causing her health to deteriorate even more.

Early one October morning Teeny entered Mary's bedroom to wake her, but there was no response. On the nightstand by her bed stood an empty opium bottle. The drug that provided relief from her suffering also caused her heart to stop.

Without his Mary, Benjamin Douglas lived a lonely life, rambling through the silent twenty-four-room mansion. He had once traveled extensively and was still considered the smartest, most successful plantation owner in Bolivar County. But during the last year of his life, he grew confused and desolate, quickly losing the faith and self-reliance he had once possessed. No longer able to make sound business decisions, he relied on brokers in Natchez and New Orleans to sell his cotton.

Ben Douglas had always enjoyed his bourbon, but now he began to drink heavily. Late one July evening he thought he heard someone call his name from the library. Ben turned awkwardly and fell from the veranda to the stone path below. It was an hour before Teeny found him. He was unable to move. Will carried him to the bedroom, and Steven rode to town to fetch the doctor.

Dr. Willis created a splint for Ben's broken hip. "Plan to be bed-ridden for several weeks," he informed his patient. More bad luck followed. While still recovering from his hip injury, pneumonia took hold of the forlorn planter's lungs. When Benjamin Douglas realized he was never going to leave his bed, he began planning for dissolution of his great estate.

He summoned Brent Marshall, a Memphis lawyer, to draw up his last will and testament. Marshall took notes while Ben Douglas dictated the terms: "Mary Dale is to be sold and all slaves living here are to be freed. My executor is to provide them with safe passage to a free state and each shall be given two hundred dollars. Since Mary and I have no heirs, any proceeds that remain are to be donated to the new state university."

Will had been waiting outside Master Douglas' bedroom, holding bourbon and medicine on a silver tray. He could not help overhearing his Master's last request. His ears burned with this amazing news.

Marshall returned the following afternoon carrying a document bound together with a red wax seal. "I have completed the final draft and my assistant penned an extra copy for you." He paused and tried to remain polite as he addressed his employer. "Mr. Douglas, the chances of this actually happening are not realistic. How will your slaves, who have never been anywhere other than Mary Dale, survive? They cannot read or write - people will take advantage of them, and steal the money you are leaving them."

"These men and women are much more resourceful than you think Brent. They deserve a chance." Ben didn't feel like arguing the point further. In a weak but determined voice he said, "When I am gone, submit and execute the document just as I have requested." He signed the document, then called Will and Teeny to his room. Ben clasped Will's hand, and gave Teeny a hug. As she leaned over the bed he whispered his last request; "Take this copy of my will, and the money in the library, and hide them."

A local constable sent word to Colonel James Pritchard in New Orleans that Ben Douglas had died. Two weeks after the funeral, a large envelope arrived in Brent Marshall's office. Brent and the Bolivar authorities were stunned; they had just been informed that Mary Douglas had a cousin, the honorable Colonel James Pritchard. A legal document certifying this fact had been signed by Mary Douglas and notarized by Judge Edward Shreve. The letter also informed them that Colonel Pritchard would be arriving in one week to take possession of the Mary Dale plantation, its contents, and all of the slaves.

7

A FLASH OF LIGHTNING AND a loud thunderclap brought an abrupt end to Will's reveries. Panic consumed him—rainwater seeping into the ground could destroy the buried paper. Will searched for Tom and found him talking with Pete and a few field workers. When they were alone he said, "We may not have much time left to think about this. That stuff can't stay out there in the field with all this rain. We need to get it after dark and head north."

Tom looked around guardedly. "You means you be thinkin' of runin' ta'night?"

"Tonight is as good a time as any. The storm will have passed; it will be clear, and there should be a full moon."

Pete came up from behind and inserted himself between the two. "You got sumpin' secret goin' on here, or can I join dis here de'scusson?"

Will figured Pete couldn't have heard much, if anything, with all the rain, wind, and thunder. He replied to him, "We were just wondering who bought John and where Teeny is."

"I knows," Pete said. "I's heard Blackstone an' Jake talkin' by da barn las' week, after dey bin drinkin' sum a Pritchard's bourbon. John done got bought by a pig farmer who live 'bout fifty mile frum here. Guess ya doan need two good legs to slop hogs."

"What about Teeny?"

"Dey say Pritchard give her to a doctor frend in Sain' Louis. Den dey all laugh when Jake say, "Dat be one lucky doctor. He gonna have a fine lookin' fancy girl fer a nurse." Pete put an arm around Will and Tom, and the three began a soggy walk back to their cabins. A flash of lightning sent them scurrying at a faster clip, then they separated. "See ya t' marrah," yelled Pete. He gave a little wave and hurried to his quarters.

Later that inclement, moonlit night, had Pritchard looked out his bedroom window, he would have seen two slaves making their way toward the north field. Will carried a hoe blade and Tom an old burlap sack. When the men reached their destination, Will counted as he moved through the plants, "Seventh row, twenty paces in." When he was within a few feet of his target, Will noticed a mound of wet dirt pushed to one side. He began frantically digging in the mud with his bare hands.

"It's gone! Somebody took it!" Will fell to his knees and shook his head in disbelief.

As he looked around in shock, his eye fell on a small bracelet made of twine and stones hanging on a cotton plant. "Granda! Granda has it! She'll be at the cemetery. Let's go!" Will called to Tom.

In the cemetary, the two snaked onwards among the headstones until Granda's stooped figure, silhouetted against the white limestone mausoleum like a question mark, rose into view. She gestured with her cane for the two men to meet her by the entrance. She looked at Will and Tom with a wry smile and pointed to the satchel lying at her feet. "You be smart, Will, but why ya leave dis stuff in da ground? You bury hard stuff an' dead people, not cowhide an' paper. Don't know what all dis be, but ya sure nuff needs ta take bedder care of it."

Will nodded weakly in agreement.

"You boys got lotsa trouble a'head. You gots to be smarter dan da people who be after you. How you plan on gettin' outa Miss'sippi?"

"I got some passes signed by the late master, and once we get near Memphis we meet up with a conductor. Reverend Abernathy gave me a map and directions to his cabin."

"Abernathy was burned up inside his church. Dat conductor could'a moved on or been hanged," Granda commented.

Will nodded and said, "We'll have to take that chance."

Granda reached inside her cloak and produced a small pouch filled with brightly colored beads. She handed them to Will. "Put dese in your pockets an' al'ways keep 'em wif ya. Ya put 'em in yer hands wen ya pray—sum day ya gonna give 'em to yer own chillin—if ya stays alive."

Will slipped the glossy stones in his pocket and looked appreciatively at the old woman. "Thanks Granda…for taking care of my satchel, and for the beads."

She looked up at him and in a kindly way said, "Ya needs ta go now. Birds got to fly free 'fore da moon go dark."

The old conjure woman watched the two young men depart. She wrapped a small white cloth around the serpent head carved in her walking stick. She beseeched her God, "Protect 'em, Damballah. Dey be smart an' strong, but dey not yet wise."

Pete stood on the stoop of his cabin and watched his friends climb the fence and disappear into the Mary Dale woods. He looked at the bundle of belongings wrapped in a ball, then dropped to his knees, clasped his hands together, and prayed.

THE TWO FUGITIVES SPRINTED THROUGH the Mary Dale woods to John's deserted cabin. They circled around to the back, stopping at the crumbling stone chimney.

"Gimmie your knife."

Tom reached behind him. "Careful wit dat. It doan look so good, but it be real sharp."

Will counted thirty rows of stones and inserted the knife. He pulled one stone out, and then removed stones from above and below. He reached into the narrow opening and pulled out an envelope. "Our passes." He reached in one more time to retrieve a burlap bag and a small leather pouch filled with coins. "Granda's smut, the rabbit's foot, and a little money."

"Why you hide all dis stuff out here? Ya coulda saved us a long run by hidin' it in our cabin."

Will shook his head. "Couldn't take that chance, Blackstone and Siebert have snitches go through the cabins when we're in the fields." Will looked up at the bright moon. "Let's get moving."

Will took the lead, the leather satchel strapped to his back. As moonlight waned, it became harder to spot the sharp rocks and thistles. Tree branches left scratches, and soon both were covered with mud and dried blood. They ignored everything around them, crashed through bushes, and charged across open fields. Some unknown force took over their bodies; they ran continuously, oblivious to the pain.

As the sun rose, the two fugitives paused to survey their surroundings. A ridge rose in the distance, fronted by a meandering rivulet. They climbed to the crest where rows of corn stood tall. They found no signs of life. They entered, dropped their belongings, and lay in the furrows. Before falling asleep,

Granda's words echoed in Will's head: "Evil spirits creeps around at night, and tricky spirits is able to hex people—even smart ones like you."

9

THE HUMID AIR WARMED WILL'S body as he awoke. He lay between the thick corn stalks with eyes shut, basking in the dappled sunlight slipping through the leaves. He opened his eyes to a river of puffy clouds rolling slowly across the blue sky. What a beautiful day to be free, he thought. His joy lasted only a second, however.

"Tom," he whispered, shaking his friend awake. Panicked, Will lifted his finger to his lips, indicating Tom should stay quiet. Voices murmured nearby, and the men struggled to make out their meaning. One voice was clear—Jake Siebert. Will cursed himself. How could he have been so stupid, stopping to rest near a well-worn trail.

Three men sat in a clearing rolling cigarettes. It was Siebert and two other men, most likely patrollers hired by Pritchard. As they lit their tobacco, two large hounds rose, sniffing the air. The dogs whimpered. The men watched the animals move in circles toward the cornfield. The patrollers pulled their guns and followed the dogs up the hill. The tall patroller called the dogs. Will and Tom could hear his voice moving away from them.

Siebert stayed behind, however, edging his way through the rows of vegetation. He was nearly on top of the runaways when his voice pierced the silence. "We need to catch those bastards during daylight. If they run through the night and make it to the river, we'll never find 'em."

Just then the hounds began yelping. "Jake, over here!"

"What's goin' on?" yelled Siebert.

Siebert and the two patrollers quickly mounted their horses and took off across an open field.

"Now's our chance," cried Will. "Rub this smut on your feet." Their eyes watered from the fumes of the putrefied material. They grabbed their bags and started to run. As they emerged from the corn field, they suddenly froze: they were stunned to see a black man running through the yellow grass, men and dogs in pursuit.

Shots rang out, but the slave kept running. It took only minutes for two snarling dogs and three men on horseback to surround him. Will and Tom heard another blast. They didn't wait to discover the outcome; they scrambled down the ridge, running as fast as their smut covered feet could carry them.

For their friend Pete it was too late.

10

ON THE SIXTH DAY OF their perilous journey, the weather changed abruptly. Clouds rolled in from the west, and a hard rain pelted the runners. Will and Tom scrambled up the bank of a swollen stream and continued to climb the hilly terrain. By the time they reached the top, sun sporadically broke through the clouds. As they stopped to catch their breath, both were awestruck by the sight before them.

A large serpentine body of water glinted in the sun, eventually flowing to a point miles away where water and land appeared to merge. On both sides of the river, trees of differing hues, flowering shrubs, and grasses of yellow and green painted a breathtaking portrait. From the runaways' vantage point, it was a magnificent sight.

Both were tired, scratched and dirty. They found a large clump of bushes to hide behind, shared a bit of food and water, and slept longer than they intended. It was dark when drops of rain ended their slumber. Clouds covered the moon making it difficult to see. The terrain gradually became steeper. They were no longer certain they were on a hill, but possibly a bluff that could drop off at any time.

The wet grass and mud made walking difficult. Eventually they crawled. Something that sounded like a twig snapped under Tom's right hand and his forearm sank into mushy goo. He let out a yelp. A mass of small writhing worms covered his arm. He grabbed a clump of grass and wiped them from his arm.

"What was dat on da groun'?" Moonlight broke through the clouds long enough for Will to see the outline of a body. Ragged clothes covered what remained, and larvae crawled in the foul soil next to the decomposed body. Will felt nauseous. He looked at Tom and reluctantly said, "It's what's left of a person."

"Oh, God," said Tom as he slumped to the ground. "Were he a slave?"

"Can't tell. Can't tell anything. Most of the skin and clothes are gone."

Just then a dim light appeared between the trees. As the men were deciding whether to run, more lights began to flicker. Music and laughter punctuated the silence, and a deep mellow sound resonated through the night air. A magnificent steamboat appeared, its tall stacks billowing plumes of gray smoke as the gigantic white structure glided along in the moonlight. The runaways could just barely make out people strolling along decks. The band on board played a peppy refrain, and flags flew from bow to stern. They stared until the boat rounded a bend and faded from sight. "Dat was sumpin'!" Tom whistled.

"Yeah. I heard about those big boats, but until you see one, you can't understand what all the fuss is about. Master Douglas said it was like a holiday when a big steamer arrived in a small town. Bands played and people paddled out to greet them."

The two men made their way along the sloping bank for another half mile until they reached a point where a stream flowed into the larger river. White rock protruded from hills on each side of the rivulet. Will's crude map showed two limestone bluffs with a stream in the middle. "This is it," he said. They followed the curves of the stream inland and slogged their way through mud, water and biting insects. Will looked to the horizon and said, "There, over there! Four hills…"

They sprinted toward the valley between the first two hills and crossed a shallow stream. Finally they spotted a cabin. Will wondered aloud what they would do if the conductor had been discovered or no longer lived there. As they approached the dwelling, both were relieved when they smelled burning wood and saw smoke rising from the chimney. They moved closer. A faint light from a candle in the window emitted an orange glow.

While they waited for a signal Tom took out his old knife and began to whittle a thin sapling "Dis knife be older'n me, Will. I thinks it gonna gimme my freedum sum day." Will gave him a questioning look.

If ever I gets in a real bad place, I gots my knife. An' if my luck go frum bad ta worse, my knife kin cut me good'nuff to send me on my way."

"What the hell are you talking about?"

"I means send me to da promise land. Jus' like da body we find back dere. Dat be da only way a slave get free."

A faint noise from a rusty door hinge interrupted the gloomy conversation. A thin elderly man appeared brandishing a latern, which he held aloft and then placed on the porch. Will reached in his pocket, gave Granda's beads a squeeze, and moved toward the cabin door. He hesitated a moment, glanced at Tom, ... then knocked.

11

THE ELDERLY MAN OPENED THE door part way, peering warily at the two bedraggled runners. Everyone was tense. He opened the door further. "Yes?"

In a shaky voice Will said, "Mr. Anderson…Reverend Abernathy sent us." Anderson gestured for them to come in, and in a somber tone said, "Son, we heard the Reverend was dead."

"Yes, sir. It was over a year ago when he told me how to find you. He was killed when they burned his church."

A thin gray-haired woman appeared, and in a soft voice said, "Oh my, so it's true, he's really gone."

John pointed to chairs next to a square table. "You boys come in and have a seat. You must be hungry and tired. This is my wife, Emma. She'll prepare a little food and you can rest. We can talk more when you're ready."

"I think we're ready, sir. My name is Will Douglas, and this is Tom Douglas. We've been running for almost a week. We're grateful for your help." John looked at Will in a friendly, but curious manner. "Son, where did you learn to speak like you do?" Will seemed embarrassed. "I was a house servant for many years. My old master allowed me to study with the plantation school teacher."

"Tom, did you study with her too?"

"No sah, I work da fields since I be five year old. Never got no chance fer book learnin."

John clasped his hands together and with a solemn expression remarked, "Well, you boys need to know the river route has become more dangerous. Patrollers have stepped up their watch, especially at the wharves and landings. We heard the last two runaways that left our cabin never made it up river."

Will thought of the body back on the bluff and wondered whether it was one of them. "We understand, sir. A few days ago patrollers shot one of the men following us. We're pretty sure they killed him…but we can't go back."

29

"Well, I want you to have hope, and for now you're safe. Neighbors east of here will ring the church bell if patrollers are in the area." He looked toward the hearth where Emma was cooking. "Momma, how's the food comin?"

"It's comin. Here, boys, let me start ya off with some soup."

Emma ladled a mix of potatoes, carrots, peas, and broth from a large cauldron suspended over the fire. She placed a bowl in front of each man. They were starving. Minutes later Tom finished and wiped his chin with his sleeve. "Dat be da best soup eber Missus Emma."

Emma smiled and moved lithely in front of the pots hanging over the fire, humming a tune as she worked. "Fresh bread and chicken comin' up shortly. Y'all go ahead an' keep talkin."

John took a seat across from Will and Tom. "Men, tomorrow you can rest, but on Sunday you've got to head for the river and find the Federal landing. It's a small wharf, about a mile down river from Memphis. There should be two or three boats anchored there. One of them's a government snag boat. It will have two hulls in the front that look kinda like a bird's beak. In the middle there's a big crane with a hook." John cocked his arm into an L shape and curled his finger to look like a hook. "She's a side-wheeler, and she's called the Missy T."

"Yes, sir, we'll remember that. What do these boats do?"

"They pull trees out of the river and chop 'em up so they don't poke holes in the bottom of steamboats. Some folks call 'em 'Uncle Sam's tooth pullers'. Allen McGee is her captain. He's tall and usually has a neatly trimmed beard. Tell him you're John Anderson's cargo being shipped north. If things work out, he'll get you to a safe house."

"Dinner's ready, boys." Emma set two places. A small loaf of bread and half a stewed chicken steamed on each plate. A short time later the bread was gone, and only a few polished bones remained. Tom smiled. "Missus Emma, dat be da finest bird an' bread I eber eat. But dere be nuthin lef, cuz dat piggy Will eats everythin' in sight." Will looked at the bones picked clean and piled on Tom's plate. He shook his head and smiled at his friend.

"You boys are gonna sleep in the storeroom tonight," said Emma. "Tom, you make sure piggy Will doesn't get into the food supplies."

"Yes, ma'am," said Tom laughing, "I keeps an eye on him."

12

THE EARLY MORNING SUN FAILED to wake the runaways, but the smell of coffee, fat back, and frying eggs caused Tom to stir. "Wake up, Will. I think we done die and gone ta heaven."

"Come on you two, breakfast is waitin," Emma called into the storeroom.

The men nearly ran toward the kitchen, where they quickly polished off their food and mopped up the last of the egg yolks with a slice of bread. John looked at the polished plates. "You boys make Momma proud the way you enjoy her cookin."

Tom smiled and said, "We's happy to make her proud."

John stood and looked out the cabin window. "Boys, it's a warm day. You might wanna head down to the stream and get cleaned up." Will and Tom looked at each other's mud stained clothes.

Tom said, "You right Mistah John, we a mess."

Emma chuckled and said, "Leave your clothes on a tree limb. John can bring 'em up, and I'll give em a good washing."

The cool green water contrasted with the bright blue sky. A few water bugs skittered along the surface. Tom shook his head as he looked at Will. "You be wearin' dat soap out…An' ya still gonna be brown when ya done."

Will shot a stream of water at Tom with his cupped hand. Tom retaliated, and then paused. He looked at activity going on around him: nuthatches flew low and landed in a nearby tree, a squirrel chattered nervously on a branch above. Will noticed Tom wiping his eyes. "You all right?"

"Got some soap in ma eyes." After a long pause he said, "Will…I wants ta live. I doan wanna git caught, an' I doan wanna die."

Will gazed at his reflection in the water. "No, neither do I," he said softly.

Wind blowing from the northwest began to chill the air; they put on the temporary clothes John left behind and began a slow walk up the hill. It had been a fine day, but it was quickly coming to an end. Tomorrow they would be running again.

After the evening meal John said, "It's time for a few last minute warnings." He clasped his hands together, a serious expression on his otherwise kind face. "Slave hunters are clever, and will try all sorts of tricks. They'll pretend to be abolitionists, part of the Underground Railroad, or they'll bribe other slaves to tell them where you are. Watch and listen. If something doesn't seem right, get away as fast as you can. Slave hunters don't care whether you're free or a run-away; they only want the money you bring."

Both men fidgeted; their chance of reaching a free state seemed daunting. John continued, "Be at McGee's boat before sundown. Don't forget, the first thing you tell him is John Anderson's got two packages he wants shipped north. Now you'd better get some rest. Your clothes are hanging on the line. Momma will pack a little food." He paused, "Will, that satchel you're carrying, do you need it?"

"Yes, sir. It's got our passes and other papers."

"Okay, but always travel as light as you can. Your beads are on the shelf in the storeroom. Are they supposed to bring good luck?"

"I hope so."

"Yeah. I hope so too."

13

LEAVES STIRRED IN THE EARLY morning breeze. Will and Tom dressed and gathered their belongings. Emma put buttered bread and slices of ham in Tom's sack. Will tied the satchel to his back and the group said final good byes. Then the two young men set out across the stream, enroute back to the river.

When they arrived at the inlet, everything looked different. Water that glowed in the moonlight and sparkled in the sun a few days ago now appeared an ominous grayish-brown. Dead foliage lay strewn all along the riverbank. On the far side the current swept an enormous tree down river. Ever-changing whirlpools on the surface loomed, daring an escaping slave to swim across. The runaways had no choice, they started up river.

Before long, a low bellowing sound made them stop. Both scrambled to the nearest tree and ducked out of sight. A large sternwheeler slid into view, every one of her decks covered with crates, barrels, livestock, and people. Laden with so much cargo, the water lapped only a foot below the main deck. Passengers bore no resemblance to the revelers on the big steamboat from a few nights ago.

"Dem folks doan look happy," Tom observed.

Will nodded and said, "You're right, they look as sad as the animals next to them—maybe worse. Wonder where they're headed."

"Dey probly jus' like us, dey wanna get to a bedder place."

Anderson had forgotten to mention the packets, big sternwheelers, barges, and rafts that travelled up and down the river. The men were startled every time something new came along, taking refuge behind a rocks, trees, or brush piles. As the shadows grew longer, the fugitives' anxiety about their rendezvous intensified.

Finally, they reached an inlet where four boats anchored. Will spotted the Missy T at the end of the boardwalk. Between the snag boat and the two men lay a wide strip of brown water. "It's almost dark. If we circle around this, we're gonna miss him," Will mused aloud.

"How deep dis be?" Tom looked apprehensive as they inched into the murky water. It was deeper than expected. The water came above their waists, almost to their chins. Will struggled to keep the satchel dry. Suddenly they heard a voice: "Poker game starts in half an hour, McGee, bring whatever you can afford to lose."

"I'll be there," came a voice from the wharf. "First I've got to find a big sack to carry all my winnings."

The rejoinder came quickly, "Don't need no sack, bring a thimble."

Following these taunts, the river grew quiet again. Will and Tom stood chest deep in water, waiting until it seemed safe. Slowly they waded through the muck to the base of the boardwalk and huddled beneath the wood structure. A tenor voice shouted, "You two under there! Step up and show yourselves!"

Will and Tom looked nervously around.

"Come to the end of the dock!" the gruff voice barked.

The runners did as they were commanded. When they reached the final section of wood planks, McGee approached. He was six feet tall, sported a well-groomed beard, and wore a white shirt, black pants and boots. "Gentlemen, I am Allen McGee, and I need to know why you're here."

"John Anderson asked that you ship two packages north."

"Do these packages have names?"

"Yes, sir. I'm Will Douglas, and this is Tom Douglas."

"Well, Will and Tom, I don't have much time. My card game is about to begin, and you need a safe place for the night. Follow me." They circled around the base of the large crane and up stairs that took them over the top of a paddle-wheel. They stopped in front of a wall filled with wood pegs that held ropes, tools, and men's coats. McGee reached up and released a lock. A portion of the wall, with pegs and paraphernalia still in place, opened. "In here, men."

Will and Tom peered into a small room that had a round porthole in the back. Cotton mattresses and blankets were stacked in one corner. On the opposite side were clothes, a small table, and a lantern.

"Make yourselves as comfortable as you can; there are dry clothes over there. Knowing Emma, she provided you with food. Keep this door closed unless you need to go to the privy—it's the small room above the paddlewheels. I'll let the crew know you're here, and we'll see you in the morning. Right now, the queen of hearts is calling," he winked.

"Thank you, Captain. Good luck in your card game," Will replied.

McGee paused and gave him a sly grin. "Luck's kind smile has to be earned. You should know that."

The Captain ducked through the door and closed the panel. Will pulled the beads from his wet pocket and checked the contents of the satchel. Tom, who was changing clothes, said, "Whad'ya think he mean by sayin' luck gotta be earned?"

"I think he means we can't rely on beads, a rabbit's foot, or anything else—just ourselves."

14

THAT NIGHT THEY LISTENED TO water lapping against the side of the boat, wood creaking, and ropes groaning. At dawn they heard a clanking noise, steam hissing, and a series of thuds that shook the entire ship. McGee yelled, "Untie the lines!" Under his instruction, the boat changed direction several times before the Missy T was finally underway. Once things settled down the panel slid open. "Gentlemen, come out and meet the crew."

Will and Tom squinted as their eyes adjusted to the bright light on deck. "This is my engineer, Zachary, and my first officer, Richard. Over there is the deck crew, Andrew and Bernard; and behind them, the wooders, Sam and Ben." Sam and Ben were black. They eyed the newcomers with curiosity and then left with the rest of the crew.

"You're the first runners we've had traveling north with us in a few months. We're heading up river to deal with a logjam. You need to know what we do in case we're stopped and you're questioned." Will was listening intently, but Tom was hunched over, miserable. "You okay, son?" McGee said.

"Feelin' like I needs sum re'leef, sah."

"Follow me." McGee led Tom past the boilers and up the starboard stairs to a small room above the paddlewheel. Inside was a shelf holding a pitcher of river water, a cake of soap, and a tin basin. There was a metal grate on the floor and a bench with a circle in the middle; both opened to the water below. A wooden box by the bench held scrap cotton. "Take care of your business. Come back and join us when you're done."

McGee made his way back to the stern. Will was watching the crew work when McGee said to him, "They're a good group. Andrew over there is my younger brother. His nickname is the Bee."

Will smiled. "You mean like a bumble bee?"

"Yeah. He's always buzzing around making sure everybody's got what's needed to do the job. He always tries to make things right. Got that from mom, I guess. After patrollers burned me and ran me off the river, he took it personally. He became a soldier for the cause, a real abolitionist. He'll do more to help you reach free soil than I ever could."

Will didn't know what "real abolitionist" or "burned me and ran me off the river" referred to, but decided this was not the best time to ask too many questions.

"What can Tom and I do to help? We would like to repay you any way we can." McGee ignored the question. "Where'd you learn to speak, Son? You talk like an educated white man."

"A teacher who ran a plantation school taught me to read and write. She even taught me a little math."

"Be careful, ya never know how somebody's going to react to a colored talking that way. You would be better off making your way like this river, strong and silent," McGee warned.

When Tom returned McGee continued his explanation. "You have to know what this boat does and how it works. Our job is to find snags and sawyers and get them out of the river."

"Whad do dem words mean?"

"A snag is a large tree in the river, heavy ends on the bottom and the top sticks out of the water. A sawyer is pretty much the same except the top is below the water, and harder to spot. Either one can poke a hole in a steamboat. Once that happens the boat will sink or be out of commission."

McGee escorted them toward the front and pointed to a space between the hulls. "We take a run at a tree and catch it in here. That large crane pulls the tree up and the crew saws it into smaller pieces – we load it on a barge or throw it overboard. You two can help with the sawing and chopping."

"I kin do dat. Ain't sure bout Will. He work in da big house fer so long he ain't got no mussels." McGee grinned. "Let's see how he does. He looks pretty strong. There are apples, biscuits, and coffee up front. When you're finished, the Bee will show you around." McGee started up the stairs to the pilothouse, but then yelled back, "If a boat approaches, head back to your room and close the panel. If we're boarded, stay silent, don't let any sounds betray you."

As soon as they finished their coffee, Andrew appeared. He was tall like McGee, with the same gray eyes, but his hair was dark, and his beard unruly.

Andrew used few words when he spoke. "Old shirts, gloves, put em on. Watch your heads. Chains everywhere."

Will and Tom followed Andrew around to learn what tools were needed for each task. He explained that river water could be used for drinking but advised against it. "Rain water over in that barrel is better." He pointed to a hand-pump that forced river water through a spigot. "Shower requires a little work. Worth it on a hot day."

A few hours later the boat pulled close to the logjam. Not far away several large boats were tied to trees, waiting for the snag boat to clear the main channel. McGee gave orders to Zachary through a speaking tube, telling him to proceed at three-quarter speed toward a large mass of trees and limbs. "Brace yourself!" Andrew yelled to Will and Tom.

The Missy T struck the jam with a hard jolt, then stopped abruptly. Moaning and screeching sounds erupted as trees separated. The crew used long poles to push several limbs away, but the core of the jam remained. McGee took aim, and the boat steamed forward again. Another jolt. A giant oak was securely trapped between the hulls. A chain dropped down from the crane. The crew wrapped it around the tree, and large wheels began turning. The chain tightened, and the massive trunk was pulled out of the water.

Mechanical saws and a variety of axes dissected the tree into smaller pieces. Some wood was hauled to the stern and stacked; the rest was thrown overboard. Will and Tom watched the debris being swept away by the strong current.

Tom stood by the rail and shook his head. "Dat was amazin'! Da whole thing wuz amazin'! Dis boat, da way it work, dat big hook. I can't ba'leev I never knowed bout any a dis."

"You don't hear about these things when you're working the fields."

"Yeah, you be right, I wonders what else dere be I doan know nuttin bout."

Will smiled and said to his friend, "We both got a lot to learn."

McGee came down from the pilothouse and said to his crew, "Excellent work, men, excellent. Tonight we go ashore for supper. Where's my mud clerk?" Ben came from behind one of the large wheels. "Ben, once we reach shore, set up a campsite. You and Andrew prepare the best food we have."

"Yes, sah," said Ben, with a wide smile. "Good food and good company shorten the miles," he pronounced to no one in particular. Then he told the crew, "Tomorrow's last stop will be Horseshoe Bend."

Tom and Will stretched out by the campfire after their meal. McGee appeared and gave the two a mischievous smile. "You men play cards?"

"No, sah. I doan know no card games."

"Me neither, but I watched Master Douglas play poker in Natchez."

"Well, tomorrow I'm gonna give you a lesson in gambling. It will help you understand how games are played in the city." Both were puzzled by the statement; Tom spoke up, "I doan know what ya means, sah."

"An honest card game should be played where everybody has a fair shot at winning." He was about to continue when Andrew yelled, "Need to store the landing plank!"

"We'll talk more tomorrow," McGee assured them. Then he added, "You men have a rough road ahead; but never forget, a poor freedom is better than a rich slavery."

Tom threw sand on the fire and said to Will, "I knows what he talkin bout dis time, an' he be right."

Back on board they weaved between hanging chains and machinery. Andrew emerged from their cabin. "You got important papers in there, get 'em to the captain in the morning." Will went into the cabin and opened the satchel. Tom looked over his shoulder. "Papers an' stuff still in dere?"

Will fumbled with the contents. "Yeah, everything's here."

Tom scratched the top of his head. "Hope dat Bee person like us. It be a prob'lum if he doan." Will nodded. They extinguished the lantern and bedded down. Will curled up on the thin mattress and began thinking about Mary Dale, Teeny, and Pete…and Pete's words before they ran.

"The doctor he gonna hav' a fine lookin' fancy girl fer a nurse."

15

EARLY NEXT MORNING WILL AND Tom moved gingerly around the mechanical equipment toward the forecastle. Zachary and Richard were finishing their coffee. Will was anxious to take his papers and currency to McGee. "Mister Richard, do you think I might go up and visit Captain McGee?" he asked.

Richard was surprised by the way Will spoke and eyed him in a quizzical manner. "You can try. If he's not busy, he'll talk."

"Thank you, sir," Will replied. Then he proceeded up the narrow stairs to the pilothouse. Tom was close behind. Just as they reached the top deck, Andrew appeared and saw the duo standing before the wheelhouse.

"You need to know who you're dealin' with. He was part of the gold-braid trade. He don't suffer fools. Ask your questions. Get his advice, an then leave," Andrew advised.

Will nodded as though he understood what Andrew was talking about. He knocked on a windowpane. McGee signaled for them to come inside.

"Andrew said you would be visiting," he acknowledged. "What can I do for you, men?"

"Captain, I have some papers and money that I was hoping you would look over. I believe you could tell us what we should do with them." McGee glanced over at the satchel. "Leave them on the desk, son. I'll take a look later."

"Thank you, Captain." Andrew's words rang in his head. "Sir, what's the gold braid trade?"

The question surprised the captain. He backed up a few steps and stood next to a portrait hanging on the wall. The man in the painting was wearing a double-breasted suit, small bow tie, and cap with gold braids across the brim.

"That's me, when I was younger," he reminisced. "On the big riverboats we all had fancy uniforms with gold braids. I had a nice run on the riverboat

Natchez for several years, but got caught trying to smuggle a few slaves out of an auction pen. Lost my license and my fancy uniform. Almost lost my life."

"Someone tried to kill you?"

"They thought about it, then the patrollers decided it was better to teach me the error of my ways." McGee rolled up the left sleeve of his shirt. Two ugly white scars had been burned into his arm between the wrist and elbow, forming the letters S S.

"These letters mean slave stealer." Will and Tom winced.

I guess the bastards thought burning me would get me off the river. Ugly aren't they? Not to worry though; misfortune is what makes us stronger." He rolled his sleeve down and said, "We'll talk more later."

Will and Tom started down the stairs. Andrew was waiting at the bottom. He pointed a finger at them. "Never lost a boat. Never stranded one on a sandbar. Government gave him his license back. Hired him to clean up snags and jams. Might be the only honest man on the river. Do what he tells ya." Before Will or Tom could say anything, Andrew had moved on.

"Let's go chop wood," said Will.

Tom chuckled and said, "Okay, I hope ya can chop wit dem tiny liddle arms a yers."

Will rolled his eyes upward. "Yeah, I hope so."

Three large snags were hoisted aboard the Missy T that day. Will and Tom did their fair share of chopping and sawing, gaining a measure of respect from the crew. Late in the afternoon McGee sent Andrew to tell them to report to the pilothouse. The captain was standing behind his desk when they arrived.

"Before we talk about the items in your satchel, we're going to have a lesson in how things work in the city." He fanned out a deck of cards in a neat arc on his desk.

"This is a deck of fifty-two cards. The object is to obtain two, three, or four of the same number cards or face cards, or five of the same suit, or five that are in numerical order. Understand?" Will and Tom said "No," simultaneously.

"Doesn't matter. The game can be rigged. Watch."

McGee shuffled the cards and fanned them out again. This time only the decorative backs were visible. "Do you gentlemen see any difference in the cards spread out before you?"

Tom looked carefully. "I doan see no diffrence."

Will leaned over for a closer look. "They all look the same to me."

McGee pointed to the back of a card and told them what it was before turning it over. "This is the ace of spades. This is the king of hearts. This is the two of diamonds." McGee continued and named seven more cards before turning them over.

"How you know whad dey be if dey all look da same," said Tom.

McGee pulled a small penknife from his coat pocket. He used the tip of the blade to point. "Here is a watermark. This card has a crease. This one has a small fingernail indentation in the corner." McGee pointed out seven more imperfections in the cards. "Once I memorize these marks and know what's on the other side, I have the advantage over my opponent."

Both men were confused; neither knew what being a sharp-eyed cheat had to do with them. "Sah, I not sure whad all dis mean fer us."

"Cheating goes on all the time, gentlemen, not just in cards. I read the Douglas' last request. There were no heirs, and money from the sale of the plantation was supposed to free the slaves; anything left over after that was for the State University. Somehow the new owner convinced authorities he was related to Ben Douglas or his wife. In other words he cheated to obtain ownership."

McGee walked over to the desk and pulled a handful of currency from the satchel. "This is English currency. You need to find someone who will exchange it for American money. It's a large sum. If anyone finds out you have it, they'll take it and most likely kill you."

He paused and pulled the wheel slowly to the left. "Now that you have money, you might be able to buy your freedom. But you will have to bribe a few people."

Will was surprised and said, "Isn't that the same as cheating?"

"That's right…you see the person appointed to hear your request is being paid ten dollars to rule you remain a slave, but paid only five dollars if he sets you free. Your hearing is rigged from the start, just like a crooked card game. Use some of your money to improve your chances; get someone to pass it under the table and hope you get a fair hearing."

Tom was bewildered. "Ain't dere no'body playin' fair?"

"Not likely when money is involved. Don't be ashamed to do this. Applaud the man who cheats a cheater." He returned to the large wheel and looked down river. The lesson was over.

That afternoon McGee piloted the Missy T to an area on the east bank known as Horseshoe Bend. The boat hugged the shore and glided past trees and sand bars. The crew used spars to guide it to a spot where the boat had moored several times before. Ben walked through the muddy water toward an old elm tree. A strip of white fabric hanging from a branch signaled a message was waiting. A small wooden box was nailed to the tree; Ben reached in, pulled out a slip of paper, tucked it in his trousers, and returned to the boat.

McGee read it and frowned. A few minutes later he called his crew together. "Men, Captain Kinney left a message. Patrollers are waiting for us at Cape Girardeau. Since we have been warned, we will take refuge at La Tour and get our supplies there. We'll be traveling through the night."

A collective groan went up among the crew. A bustling river town like Cape Girardeau meant music, gambling, liquor, and women. La Tour was a small town, not the destination they wanted. Will and Tom knew they were responsible for the change and looked apologetically at the crew.

It was two in the morning when McGee told Andrew to extinguish all torches, lanterns, and candles. A wide ribbon of twinkling lights on the opposite shore was visible as the Missy T glided quietly past the bustling town of Cape Girardeau. As lights from the city faded, the paddlewheels revolved faster as the boat steamed toward La Tour.

16

TOM AND WILL STOOD ON deck gaping at two tall mounds of dirt and rock jutting out of the river. "They're called the Twin Towers," said Andrew. "Be docking soon. Ya can go ashore if you want."

Shortly, the Missy T settled into Wood Yard Landing near the town of Grand Towers. Carriages hauled passengers to the town's restaurants and shops from a large packet that had docked nearby. Will and Tom watched the activity on shore, both looked forward to getting off the boat for a few hours.

McGee gave last minute instructions: "I'm sure you know where the saloons are located and where the women reside. Ben, Sam, even though you're free men and we're in Illinois, don't take any chances. I expect all of you back on board by midnight. Will, Tom, come with me. You, too, Sam."

From a small desk drawer McGee produced two rawhide necklaces with a rectangular metal tag attached. Each tag had an inscription indicating the person wearing it was a slave hired out as a temporary worker. "These will work better than those paper passes. Keep them around your neck at all times. If anyone asks, you are wooders on the snag boat. Sam, I want you to keep an eye on our cargo."

"Yas, sah," said Sam. Sam was anxious to leave; as soon as McGee finished he ran down the gangplank. Will and Tom felt wobbly but eventually gained their legs and caught up with him. "Where are we going?"

"We be headin' to a safer part a town, keep your head down, and doan look no white person in da eye. If you got coin, dere be a store where ya kin buy sumpin."

Ten minutes of brisk walking led them to a small village on the outskirts of Grand Towers. The first thing they noticed was a two-story building, with a general store on one side, and saloon on the other. It was flanked by long rows of crudely built cabins. Chickens, dogs, cats, and pigs roamed freely among the men and women in the street. Locals exchanged stories, bartered for supplies, and surveyed the newcomers.

A young woman in an indigo skirt and faded white blouse ran across the dirt road and grabbed Sam's hand. She gave him a quick peck on the cheek and nudged him toward the saloon. Sam gave Will and Tom a mischievous grin. "You boys look 'round. I be back shortly."

Will and Tom weren't sure what to do. They walked over to the old store, peeked in a window, and went inside. Barrels of seeds stood behind the counter, and wicker baskets filled with apples, peaches, tomatoes, and corn lined the sides of the room. On one wall the owner had fashioned a small display of used tools and knives, and handmade talismans. Tom found the store fascinating.

A large jovial woman behind the counter asked Will whether he would like "Sweet tea and cakes fer five cent." Will pulled the small leather pouch from his trousers and gave the woman a five-cent piece. "Dat be five cent each." Will handed over another coin.

"Thank ya, boys. Have a seat out front an enjoy yer selves."

They sat on the front stoop eating the crispy, buttery little cakes and drinking sugary tea when a tall man wearing a long black duster waved to them from the other side of the dirt road. His face was reddish brown, his long black hair was braided in back. He wore black leather pants, red shirt, and a wide brimmed hat adorned with colorful feathers.

The stranger took long strides toward the general store and stopped directly in front of them. "I'm glad you boys had the courage to run, ain't nothing like breathin' air as a free man, is there?" Will and Tom had no idea how to deal with this intruder. They sat motionless and stared at the ground.

"Come on boys, speak up."

Will held up the medallion around his neck. "We're wooders on the Missy T, working our way toward St. Louis."

"That's where I'm heading. I'd like for you two to join me. In fact, I insist you join me. With that the gangly stranger pulled back his long coat and revealed a revolver and knife with a curved blade. "Rise up men and head toward that buckboard over there."

They rose to their feet, looking around, hoping Sam would show up. Suddenly the woman who ran the general store came out and shouted, "Greef, get oud a dis town and let dem men alone."

"Go to hell, woman, and don't make any more noise or I'll take you along with me." The woman glared at him and went back inside. People milling about earlier had disappeared. Will mustered the courage to speak.

"Where are you taking us?"

"We're goin fer a little ride. Gimme them things around your neck and don't say nothin else."

Will handed over the metal tags and said, "But we're supposed to be back on the boat."

"Damn it, boy! Wha'd I just say?" Will felt a sharp pain on the side of his face. He was stunned by how quickly he had been cut. He held the palm of his hand against his cheek and slumped to his knees. Bright red blood seeped through his fingers. "Sass me again, boy, and I'll cut the other side a yer head."

Tom lunged at Greef. The lanky slave hunter sidestepped the charge. He flashed his knife. "Try that again, nigger, and I'll kill you."

Will's cheek throbbed and he tasted blood. He was staring down at two black boots with metal tips when, without warning, one of the boots was swiftly planted in his side.

"Get up," yelled Greef.

Will was curled up and struggling to breathe. His jaw clenched and he was overcome with rage; he blocked Greef's next kick and shoved him. Tom grabbed the slave hunter's wrist and bent it backward. The knife fell to the ground. Stunned and angry, Greef reached for his revolver.

"Stop!" came a booming voice from across the road. McGee, Andrew, and Ben stood menacingly. McGee pointed a rifle at Greef. "Those men are part of my crew, now put your gun on the ground."

Greef immediately recognized the man holding the rifle. He snarled, "I'll be damned, is that you McGee? After they scarred you, and ran you off the river, I figured you learned yer lesson. I guess I was wrong."

"Yeah, you were wrong. We old dogs can't change our bark. Now put your whip and knife next to the gun." Greef watched Andrew collect his weapons and yelled, "I want them all back McGee; I'm gonna bring patrollers with me to get em."

"I'll leave them on the dock. Now get aboard your wagon and get the hell outta my sight." Greef was furious; he climbed on the buckboard and sneered at McGee. McGee ordered everyone back to the boat.

Word spread quickly in Grand Tower that there was a fight in "Nigger Town" between a riverboat captain and a slave hunter. McGee knew he had to avoid a meeting with the local sheriff. Back on board he addressed his crew. "Knowing when to leave is as important as knowing when to stay and fight. Shore leave is over. Make the necessary preparations to get underway."

Before the Missy T departed McGee told Zachary, "Fix the barrel of that slave hunter's pistol." The engineer grinned and placed the barrel of the gun on a bed of hot coals in the firebox; once it glowed orange, he struck the barrel several times with a blacksmith's hammer so that the barrel of the gun now angled to the left. Richard grabbed an ax from the tool bin and chopped the handle from the Greef's whip

A few minutes before the sheriff arrived, McGee eased the snag boat into the main channel and headed up river. Greef's weapons were left on the dock as promised.

THE SNAG BOAT WAS SEVERAL miles from Grand Towers when McGee ordered Will and Tom to the pilothouse. He motioned for Will to take a seat and picked up a small barbless fishhook with a piece of black thread attached. "Will, we're gonna have to sew that cheek of yours back together. You better take a few swallows of this."

Will looked at the amber liquid inside. Two swallows produced an intense burning sensation in his mouth and throat. He coughed and sputtered. "Whiskey?" he gurgled in a hoarse voice.

"Yeah, mostly," said McGee.

Andrew entered carrying a kettle of warm water and towels. He looked at Will's cheek. "Nasty cut. Seen worse. Anything else Captain?"

"Yeah, grab that Red Salve from the storage bin, and bring up a few more towels. Will, I'm gonna have to clean that. Tom, hold Will's head steady once I start stitching."

"Yes, sah," said Tom. He looked apologetically at his friend. McGee poured water from the kettle on the wound. As the dirt washed away blood began streaming down the side of his face. Will was light headed and perspiring heavily. He was therefore thankful for the cool breeze wafting up from the river.

He flinched as McGee inserted the hook and tried his best to keep his head from jerking. Each time the hook was inserted the pain felt worse than the cut from Greef's knife. It took ten crude stitches to close the wound; Will's cheek was swollen and throbbing. McGee applied an oily red salve to the wound. "No sawing or chopping for a day or two until that stops bleeding."

Tom put his arm around his friend and helped him down the stairs. Will sank to his mattress in the tiny cabin, dazed and sick to his stomach. Tom offered him a drink of water and propped him gently against the wall.

Throbbing pain kept him awake that night. He listened to Tom's light snoring and the sounds of the river. He pressed a wet towel against his face and closed his eyes. Thoughts of Teeny entered his mind; he remembered the time he watched her bathe in a stream, and the first time he held her hand. He imagined how her body would feel next to his, and he wondered whether some day they could still have a life together. But Teeny's current life was far different than anything Will had ever dreamed.

03   03   03

Shortly after Colonel Pritchard took over Mary Dale, he composed a letter to his friend, Richard Walther, who was now living in St. Louis.

> *Dear Richard,*
>
> *I was sorry to hear about the great fire and outbreak of Cholera in your newly adopted city. Hopefully you and Louise are well, and things will soon be back to normal.*
>
> *You mentioned in your last letter you are thinking of purchasing another slave. I have a house servant I would like to offer you as payment for the information you provided me.*
>
> *She is an attractive quadroon and will fetch a fine price. She is a distraction to the men here, and I plan on sending her to the Memphis slave auction the last Friday in September. You, or your personal representative, will need to collect her before noon. Otherwise she will be sold.*
>
> *Your loyal friend,*
> *James*

St. Louis was in the midst of a deadly cholera epidemic. Over four thousand people died, mostly poor immigrants who lived in the north and south ends of the city. So many deaths occurred in such a short period that bodies were dumped into trenches that served as mass gravesites. The majority of doctors in St. Louis knew little about the disease, but Richard Walther observed many cholera deaths in the military. He knew unsanitary conditions and contaminated drinking water spread the sickness.

His prescription to his patients was simple: change bedding every two days, drink water from secure wells, and stay away from any area where the disease was known to exist. He also provided pills laced with laudanum to keep his wealthy clientele calm. None of Walther's patients died. Within a short time he was recognized as one of the finest doctors in the city. His medical practice grew, and by the end of the epidemic he hired a nurse and another doctor to assist him.

In early September, Pritchard's letter arrived. Walther remembered the attractive young house servant and was eager to accept the colonel's offer. He told his wife the Mary Dale slave would be the perfect person to care for their country estate. Louise Walther knew her husband wanted more than a young caretaker, but she acquiesced. She believed there was a more important job for the young woman.

18

IN LATE SEPTEMBER A CAGED wagon carrying Teeny and five other slaves rumbled into the Memphis auction house. Teeny was quickly ushered to a holding pen along with three other female slaves. The next day a burly patroller walked her to a small platform. It was almost noon. Everyone was surprised to see a fair skinned octoroon being bid on at auction. The auctioneer began his sales pitch.

"Look what we have here gentlemen! Is she a fancy girl, or a slave? This beautiful woman is a first-rate house servant who has cooking and sewing skills. She worked on the finest Plantation in Mississippi, Mary Dale, and as you can see she is ready for breeding." Teeny was humiliated. Her blouse had been opened so that her breasts were exposed. The auctioneer lifted her skirt with his cane, and ordered her to turn. The men gawked and whistled.

From the back of the crowd a bid-runner made his way to the platform. He handed a note to the auctioneer. Angry shouts rang out when the auctioneer ordered Teeny to step down. A cotton sheet was thrown over her shoulders, and a burly patroller escorted her to a waiting carriage.

A well-dressed man wearing round spectacles stepped down to greet her. His straw-colored hair, white shirt, and clean-shaven face, presented a stark contrast to the patroller's full beard, rumpled plaid shirt, and wide brimmed hat. Richard Walther held out a clean, manicured hand to assist his new slave mistress. He dismissed the patroller and said, "Do you remember me? My name is Richard Walther."

"Yes, sah, I knows who ya be. Ya vis'ted Mary Dale."

"We will be traveling to St. Louis by riverboat and are leaving in a few hours. Get in the carriage." Teeny stepped into the carriage and sat on the bench opposite Walther. She did not look up when he spoke; she was wary of making eye contact.

"Have you ever been to a large city?"

"Yes, sah, I been to Na Orlans wid Mastah an Missus Douglas."

"Did you enjoy your time in the city?"

"Doan know much 'bout en'joyin life in da city, we wuz only dere a few...."

Walther interrupted her in mid-sentence. "Enough! I know from my time at Mary Dale that you read and can speak proper English. This charade of yours is annoying me."

Teeny made eye contact. She examined his square face, protruding ears, and blue eyes. His demeanor was harsh and demanding. She responded, "My people feel uncomfortable when I speak the way you do."

Walther scoffed, "Your people? Who are your people?"

Teeny wasn't sure how to answer the question. She didn't know her mother; she knew Jeff Owens was her father but he had nothing to do with her. She fought back tears as she stared out the carriage window. Walther ended the discussion with a curt warning. "Speak proper English when you are with me."

Outside the carriage two large steamboats came into view. Walther pulled out a small package from under his seat. "Here is a towel and clean clothes; there's a traveling bag for you on the back of the carriage. After you change we will board the Silver Cloud. Carry yourself as if you belong in my company—walk erect, don't stare at the ground."

Teeny removed her torn top and tattered skirt, then slipped into the beige dress and brown leather shoes. The shoes were several sizes too large, and she wondered how she would maneuver in them. She ran her fingers through her tangled hair, and used the towel to wipe the dust from her face and arms. Teeny emerged from the carriage and stood in line with Walther to board the riverboat, then followed him across the gangplank, head up and shoulders back.

Walther handed one of the crew a few coins and instructed him to escort Teeny to her stateroom. She followed the young man up the circular stairs and looked down a long elaborate passageway. The grandeur spread out before her was unexpected—carved columns led to ceilings covered with Gothic decor and stained glass windows. The floor was covered with thick carpet, and the sparkling chandeliers above dangled copious amounts of cut glass.

"This way, ma'am. The ladies' cabins are toward the back," called the steward.

Teeny thought about the fact a total stranger was treating her as though she belonged in a "white only" environment. They came to a door with an engraved number on a brass plate. The young man placed her bag inside. "There you go, ma'am, pull that cord over in the corner if you need someone to assist you. The women's facility is located two doors down. I hope you enjoy your trip."

Teeny ran her hand on the bed surface, delighted to discover a cotton mattress covered with clean white sheets. A mahogany dresser stood next to the bed. Another door led to the promenade deck. Beneath a small window a washbowl, pitcher of water, soap, and several folded towels neatly adorned a small hutch. She shook her head in disbelief. Two hours earlier she had been locked in a filthy slave pen.

A noise outside drew her toward the window. Passengers waved, a calliope played, and a low moaning sound filled the air. Teeny walked to the promenade deck and surveyed the scene. Soot and sparks whirled upward from the tall stacks, and a band on shore played *Hail Columbia*. Down below, crewmembers scurried to arrange cargo and guide deck passengers to roped off areas where they could cook and sleep.

Amidst all this activity was a line of slaves, six men and four women, linked together by leg irons and chains. The soul-driver prodded them with a stick toward a small stockade near the stern. Scared and looking disoriented, each clutched a cloth bundle containing a few belongings. Teeny looked away and silently retreated to her cabin.

She lay on the bed thinking about her new owner. Judging by the lines around his eyes he was at least forty, maybe older. He was demanding and arrogant. A gentle tapping on the stateroom door interrupted these thoughts. She assumed it would be him, but it was the young steward who had escorted her to the cabin. A covered tray lay balanced on his upright arm.

"Doctor Walther thought you would prefer to eat in your room rather than deal with the commotion in the saloon. I'll put your dinner here on the dresser. There's also a carafe of water, but I can get something from the bar if you like."

"Water will be fine, thank you." Before he left she said, "How long does it take to get to St. Louis?"

"Usually three days, ma'am. Depends on the number of sand bars we got to dodge—river's a little low this time of year." Teeny thanked him. He nodded politely, and gently closed the stateroom door.

Beneath the tray cover was a china plate covered with slices of roast beef, boiled potatoes, green beans, and buttered bread. A piece of heavily frosted cake sat along side. Teeny felt famished—she hadn't eaten in two days. She quickly finished her meal and glanced at the traveling bag on the bed. Inside she found two dresses, shoes, a scarf, and something she had only seen Mary Douglas wear, silk undergarments. She wondered who packed the bag.

That evening she lay awake listening to the piano music drifting up from the saloon. The pianist was well into his second set when she heard a knock, and a note was slipped under the door. She turned up the kerosene lamp.

> My profession has enabled me to become a man of some means. In addition to my city home, I own another property in the country. Because of your experience at Mary Dale, I believe you are quite capable of being the caretaker of this property.
>
> There will also be responsibilities of a personal nature you will provide me. Tomorrow we will meet in the saloon for the evening meal. I will address questions you might have. Wear the light blue dress.

The following evening a waiter escorted Teeny to a table in the back of the saloon where she sat and waited. Richard emerged from the gentlemen's area at the front. He was dressed in a dark blue suit, highly polished black shoes, and a starched white shirt. Diners nodded and greeted him as he made his way toward her. Before taking a seat he looked at Teeny and grinned. "I see the dress Izzy selected was a good choice."

Teeny picked at her food and listened to Walther. He told her about his country property, a caretaker's responsibilities, and what he expected from his mistress. When it seemed they had nothing more to discuss, Teeny folded her napkin, and placed it on the table. "I understand my responsibilities, and I will do my best. I appreciate the food and the room you have provided. I have not slept for several days and hope you will allow me to return to my cabin."

Walther was startled by this mild rebuff and slowly rose to his feet. He looked around to see if anyone was listening. "You may go and rest. But you will be better served if you perform your duties willingly. If not, the alternative, as you well know, will be unpleasant."

The parting words left her feeling resentment, but at the same time she realized her life had taken a turn for the better. She crawled under the covers and listened to music and laughter coming from the saloon. Her anxiety subsided, and before falling asleep she experienced a long dormant feeling…hope. Hope that the future would be better.

19

THE AFTERNOON SUN ILLUMINATED A long line of riverboats cueing up to find their mooring places. By the time the Silver Cloud docked, it was early evening. Teeny paced and waited. A tap on the cabin door was followed by a young man's voice, "Can I assist you with your bag, Miss Douglas?" She followed the young attendant down the circular stairs to the landing stage where Walther waited.

Teeny walked behind him as they wended their way between workers, newly arriving immigrants, and settlers heading west. At the top of the levee a line of carriages waited to take passengers to various destinations in the city. Walther gave the driver directions to his country home. The cabby shook his head. "Nope, I'd lose ten customers and tips by makin' that trip. Talk to the old guy with the calico horse. He might take ya."

Walther moved further back and found a well-worn rig pulled by a sagging brown and white horse. The elderly cabby said, "Dollar fifty, plus another dollar for my lost time. Pay in advance."

Their bags were loaded and the old carriage began rolling down Market Street. Neither spoke as the cab crept through the business district into the residential area. Walther broke the silence. "My city home is over there." Teeny looked to the left at the elegant stone entryway with the name "Lucas Place" engraved. "We have another half hour before we reach my country home, don't you have questions?"

Teeny thought for a moment and said, "Do you have children?"

Walther looked out his window. "No, no, I don't. We lost two. It took its toll on my wife and our marriage."

"Oh, I'm sorry." She momentarily felt sympathy toward the man who now owned her. There was silence for several more minutes, then Walther spoke up, "When I introduce you to my housekeeper and others, you will be known

56

as Elizabeth Douglas. Your slave name sounds like a child's name and will no longer be used." She peered into the darkening landscape and remained silent. The road soon ended in front of six large homes, each separated by several acres of land.

"We're here," Walther announced. "I assume you are prepared to take on your new responsibilities." The response was a perfunctory, "Yes, sir."

The carriage crossed a small wooden bridge, and moved slowly toward a large stone home with a covered portico. A small slender woman wearing a checkered headscarf was waving. The cab stopped, Walther stepped down, and his diminutive slave housekeeper came forward to greet him.

"Welcome back, Docta Walther. I gonna get sum chicken fryin', an' coffee brewin'. Who dis lovely woman wif ya?"

The introduction was brief and devoid of emotion. "Izzy, this is Miss Elizabeth Douglas. She's from Memphis and will be our new caretaker."

"Welcome, Miz Douglas. I's sure you gonna like it here. Come in, Come on in." Richard entered ahead of Izzy and Teeny and left two large carpetbags for them to bring inside.

"Izzy, Miss Douglas will take the back bedroom on the second floor. Help her get settled." Richard took his bag, grabbed a bottle of bourbon, and headed up the stairs. Teeny received a quick tour before Izzy led her up a wide stairwell and proceeded down the hallway to the back bedroom. A tented four-poster bed adorned the center, and to the left she found a small room containing a washbasin, ornate chamber pot, and small tub for bathing.

When they returned to the main floor, Izzy guided Teeny through a brick hallway leading to the kitchen. The two women were alone. Izzy looked at Teeny with arched eyebrows and a knowing nod.

"Memphis? I doan think so. I thinks you frum a bit more south -- les say Mis'sippi? I'd also say you be a slave wit sum educashun. What's you say?"

Teeny nodded. "How did you know?"

"You lookin' down too much, an' Walther not treatin' ya like a lady he hire, he treatin' ya like a lady he own. Beside dat, I know he be frend wid dat Colonel who live in Mis'sippi—he probaly sent ya."

She looked at Teeny sympathetically. "Ya can't fool ole Izzy. If ya gonna pass as white, ya need ole Izzy ta help. Come wif me now an I get ya sumpin to eat." Teeny started to follow, slowed, and then stopped. She felt dazed and tears began to form. Izzy guided her to a chair next to the table.

"It gonna be okay. Docta Walther not be too bad. He doan hit da way sum men do." She picked a tumbler from the cupboard, grabbed the water pitcher and filled the glass.

Teeny took a few sips. "I'm not hungry right now. Could I just go to my room?"

"Sure ya can. Come dis way. Wif luck, Docta will a had plenty ta drink, an' he be a'sleep. Ya sure doan need him pawin' on ya right away." The two women proceeded up the stairs and paused. Light snoring sounds came from Richard's room. Izzy gave a silent wave and Teeny followed.

"Dis a nice room. Dere sum clothes in da dresser ya kin wear till we goes shoppin'. Now ya try an' get sum rest."

Walther was up at sunrise. Daniel, the groundskeeper, had his horse ready. With a flick of the reins he headed back to the city. When Teeny awoke, she met Izzy on the landing and looked puzzled. "He gone ta check on da business an' his wife. Dat doctor business been real good ta him, so he gotta make sure da mice doan play while da cat be away. He be back in a day or two. Mean time we got lots ta do."

Louise greeted Richard with a quick kiss when he arrived home. She was relieved that he returned safely and anxious to hear about the new slave girl. "Tell me everything. Can she manage the country home? Does she understand what we expect?"

Richard filled her in on all the details and then smiled. "Louise, things are going to work out just fine."

20

DANIEL HITCHED THE BUGGY AND drove Teeny and Izzy down a dirt road to the general store. Izzy introduced her to Jake Buckner, the postmaster. Jake not only handed out the mail he delivered the local gossip. "Mista Jake, dis be Miss Elizabeth Douglas. She be Doctah Walther's new care'taker, an' she gonna be pickin' up his mail."

"Pleased to meet you Miss Douglas. I'm sure I speak for every man in the county when I say we hope to see you often."

Teeny blushed. They left the post office and Izzy muttered, "By tomorrow Jake hav word spred all over San Louis dat Walther got a fine lookin new care'taka. Probaly doan madder if he spread da word ta'morrow or next week, but I shoulda waited. No need ta ask fer truble right away. Miz Louise gonna be awful upset when she hear how pretty you be."

Two days later Walther returned in good spirits. The medical practice was doing well. He had an amiable discussion with Louise about their new slave, and the trouble Izzy predicted never materialized.

When Walther had finished his evening meal, he dismissed Izzy and asked Teeny to join him in the parlor. Between sips of bourbon, Walther gave Teeny a brief history of his time in the army and his friendship with Pritchard. After he stopped talking, the room fell ominously quiet. Walther crossed the room to where Teeny was sitting. He placed his hand on her shoulder. Instantly she became rigid.

"I'm sure you understand your other responsibilities," he reminded her.

Teeny remained sitting and looked away. He pulled her from the chair and led her to his bedroom. Teeny tried to conceal her humiliation as he unbuttoned her blouse. She murmured, "No, no," as he stripped away the remaining clothes, but she knew what she had to do and coached herself to stop acting like a child.

His first touch below the waist was rough and caused her to cry out, "Stop!" He covered her mouth. "We'll have none of that." She tried to tell him it didn't have to happen this way, but the words and her voice became nothing more than shrill whimpering sounds. He quickly finished the first assault, then ordered her to roll over. He began again. Finally he made a loud moaning noise and collapsed on top of his new octoroon fancy girl.

"I can't breathe," she cried out.

Walther rolled to the side of the bed. While he put on his robe, he watched Teeny try to cover her body with a sheet. Before leaving the bedroom he smiled, and in a manner that lacked any heartfelt feeling said, "Things will get better. I'll see you again in the morning."

A few minutes later Izzy appeared, holding a plate of peach slices. "Take some bites. Ya needs some sweet'nes in yer life right now." She reached into her apron and pulled out a towel. "Put dis on yer pri'vets til da bleedin stop. Come down an' Izzy make ya some sassafras tea." Teeny felt dazed but mustered a nod. As she struggled to stand, she glanced back at the bed and silently vowed to remain strong.

ဢ   ဢ   ဢ

By the time the first snow fell in November, Teeny's life had settled into a familiar routine, but a few days after the Thanksgiving holiday Walther took relations with his slave to a new level.

"What's this?" Teeny asked when Izzy handed her a neatly wrapped package.

"It be a present from Docta Walther." Izzy watched Teeny open the box. She removed a green silk dress and held it close to her body. Izzy knew what the gift meant. "You be goin out."

"This is awfully fancy. Where does he plan on taking me?"

"To da Silk Ribbon. Docta Walther be a mem'ber."

Teeny eventually learned about the Silk Ribbon: It was a gentlemen's club similar to ones in Boston, New York, and New Orleans. Wealthy white men would rent or buy establishments where they could take their kept woman. Upper middle class rules of behavior were ignored, the men could drink, gamble, and have sex with their own, or someone else's, mistress. Fathers would frequently bring their sons, and the Silk Ribbon women were delighted to meet fresh, young, well-heeled sponsors.

Women at the club were usually attractive, conversant, and fairly well-educated quadroons or octoroons. Club members did not view their women as prostitutes, but as companions who lived quietly in the background of their lives. A woman in this arrangement could take a portion of her "maintenance money" and find a decent place to live, even buy her freedom if her owner agreed.

While attending her third Silk Ribbon event, the club's madam invited Teeny to observe activities taking place in a restricted area on the third floor. At first Teeny was startled and embarrassed. Once the initial shock wore off she realized the costumes and various sexual acts made the woman more desirable and more valuable. After subsequent viewings, she began to fantasize about what it might be like to indulge in this type of activity with someone she actually cared about.

Dreary winter months eased into spring. Walther began spending increasing amounts of time at his country home, and in the process, neglecting his wife. Louise Walther had agreed to this arrangement, but she was not going to be ignored.

೮೮   ೮೮   ೮೮

Louise was the first of five girls born to the wealthy Stiverson family of Louisiana. She was red-haired, green-eyed, and from an early age displayed a feisty disposition. She was almost twenty when introduced to Richard, an army doctor stationed in New Orleans. Louise's inner strength and energetic spirit was too much for many suitors, but not the handsome and confident young Army doctor.

They married, and two years later their first child was conceived. June Alice Walther was a healthy baby, doted on by Richard and Louise. Before her first birthday, however, she developed a raspy cough and ran a high fever. Her breathing became labored, and a week later she died from what was diagnosed as the croup.

After their child's burial, the normally high-spirited Louise became a quiet, listless army wife with few outside interests. In 1848 Richard left the military and began a medical practice in St. Louis. The change of cities seemed to provide the cure the couple needed—cultural activities, new friends, and a successful medical practice renewed the their hope. One year after they arrived, Louise was again pregnant.

She insisted her cousin, a well-respected doctor in New Orleans, consult with Richard and assist in the delivery. In the eighth month of her pregnancy, Jonathon Stiverson journeyed from New Orleans and took up residence in the Walther's home. During his first consultation with Louise, he spent several minutes placing his stethoscope—one of the new ones with a flexible listening tube—to Louise's swollen belly. He sounded reassuring. "Everything seems fine, this should be a healthy baby." After Louise left, he stared blankly out the window.

When Richard returned home Jonathon was waiting. He pulled Richard aside and said, "I don't know whether something's wrong with my new equipment, but at an opportune moment, please take your ear trumpet and listen for the baby's heartbeat."

When Richard and Louise settled into bed that night and began discussing names for the baby, he said, "I have an idea, let me listen to the heartbeat and we will know whether it's a girl or boy. That will help us winnow down the names."

Louise looked surprised. "You can tell by the heartbeat?"

"It's just a theory, but the heartbeat of a girl is supposedly faster."

Louise was skeptical, but thought it might be fun to see if Richard's prediction proved accurate. He finished listening and set the ear trumpet on the night table.

"It's a boy, now we can concentrate on a name for him." He forced a smile, kissed Louise good night, and turned down the lantern. In darkness the anguish on his face was not visible.

A few weeks later, the child arrived—stillborn. Blame was superfluous, but Louise was devastated and angry. "Two doctors should have been able to do something to prevent my baby's death. I would have been better off with a voodoo woman taking care of me."

Jonathon returned to his practice in New Orleans, leaving Richard to care for Louise's fragile emotional needs—a role that left him drained and out of sorts. To make matters worse, Louise fell while exiting her carriage. The resulting injuries required her to use a cane and the physical setback rendered her even more distraught.

A few weeks passed. Louise needed Richard to act like a loving husband. One day, while he was getting dressed for work, Louise smiled seductively and placed his hands on her breasts. "Let's try again to make a child," she urged.

Richard wasn't in the mood. "We just lost our baby, let's wait."

"Then make love to me because I want you to."

"Louise, it's getting late. I must get to my office, there are patients waiting."

Louise welled up with humiliation and held back tears until Richard left. She silently vowed to make herself more attractive, walk normally, and eventually...she and Richard would have their baby.

21

IT WAS A SUNNY NOVEMBER day when the Missy T glided into the slip reserved for federal boats. Tom and Will were on the second deck surveying the scene: steamboats were docking and departing, bales of cotton were stacked twenty feet high, bells were ringing, people were shouting. Tom was excited and scared. "Will, I doan know, I just doan know. What we gonna do when we get off dis boat?"

"Andrew's gonna lead, and we're gonna follow. That's all I know."

"Dere so many people out dere, I knows we gonna be caught."

Will tried to reassure him. "No we're not." He placed his hand on his friend's shoulder. "We'll be okay, we have to act like we know what we're doing, and where we're going." Will picked up his leather satchel and Tom his burlap bag. They found McGee waiting for them at the landing stage.

"Will, Tom, have hope that your best days are ahead; hope is the poor man's bread, it will sustain you."

Andrew stood on shore and signaled that it was time to move on. They said good-bye to the captain and made their way through the crowd. They followed Andrew's lead. Whenever he sighted a shore official or police officer, he took them in a new direction. They passed several large buildings and eventually reached Seventh Street. He pointed to a house on the corner, "Big house over there is Rutgers Mansion. She's colored. Owns several houses."

Tom was amazed. "A colored lady own dat big house?"

"Yeah, owns quite a few properties. Bought her freedom years ago. Important person around here."

They left the cobblestone street for a dirt road that led past rows of run down houses. A beggar, hobbling on wood crutches, approached with his hand out. "Keep moving. Look away. We're almost there. Two more blocks," their leader urged.

Except for Andrew, all the faces in the neighborhood were now black. Two men sitting on boarding house steps saw Andrew and tipped their caps. He was welcome as long as he didn't linger: a white man in the neighborhood was sure to attract patrollers. They stopped in front of a frame house surrounded on three sides by a narrow porch. "Wait here, I'll be right back." Andrew knocked on the rickety screen door and a large round woman wearing a white headscarf appeared. She and Andrew talked, then she waved to Will and Tom.

"Come on up boys, big Lucy need ta see who she gonna be keepin."

Will and Tom crossed the small dirt yard and smiled when the jovial woman greeted them. "My, my, Andrew, dese be two fine lookin men. Whad happen to dis man's face?"

"Met up with a nasty half-breed slave catcher. Should be fine in a few days."

"Welcome to Happy Hollow, men." Lucy gestured for Will and Tom to follow her. "I'm gonna put a poul'tice on dat cut after I gets you both a little sumpin to eat. Andrew, you best be getting on fore da paddyrollers get nosey."

"I'm leavin' Lucy. I'll check back in a couple weeks."

"Take care ya self Andrew. Hope da next packages ya bring be as good lookin' as dese."

Will and Tom took a seat in Lucy's kitchen. Half an hour later she served up fried chicken gizzards, greens, and rhubarb pie. Tom examined his plate for tiny remnants of pie. "Miss Lucy, dis sure be better food den what we eats on dat snag boat."

"Well thank ya, Tom. Now dat ya both be plumped up, I gots sum bad news. Until we knows ya ain't bein hunted, ya gonna have ta hole up down below. It ain't much, but it be safe." Lucy walked to the adjoining room, moved her rocking chair, and pulled back an old throw rug. A wood panel was exposed. Lucy picked it up and moved it to one side. Will and Tom could see steps descending into darkness. "Okay boys, take dis lantern down an' have a look see. I's too big ta make it down or I'd join ya."

Will took the lantern down the narrow steps. The room had a musty smell, no window, and no way out except for the stairs. In one corner was a crude bunk bed; above it a small opening let in air and a little light. "I's not sure how long I kin hole up like dis, Will. I gets squirmy when I's cooped up," Tom fussed.

They heard Lucy call their names and headed back up the stairs. Lucy had blankets, candles, and a bucket. She went back to the kitchen and poured three glasses of sweet tea. "Here's how dis work. Dat rug an' chair go back over dem stairs if a paddyroller come lookin'. I sits in da chair an' rocks and does my sewin' till he leave. I tells ya when it be safe to come up. Ya thinks ya gonna be okay?"

"Yes ma'am, we should be fine. Thanks for taking us in." Lucy took a hard look at Will. "Where ya learn ta talk like dat? Ya sound like a teacher, or a preacher."

"Miss Lockwood, a plantation teacher taught me." Lucy shook her head. "You jus be careful talking dat way. Sum body think ya be actin' uppity an' cut ya up agin."

Will and Tom went down the stairs and Lucy slid the panel back in place. They started to unpack when Tom paused. In a hushed tone he said, "Will, gimme my knife." Will pulled the old knife from the burlap bag. Tom grasped the blade with two fingers, cocked his arm and threw. A reedy squeal pierced the dank air.

Will was shocked. "What did you do?"

"Hope I kill dat thing, whad eber it be." The two men cautiously approached the dark corner. Will held the lantern over an animal with a pointed nose and beady eyes.

"That's a big rat," Will commented, staring in wonder at the creature. "How'd you learn to throw a knife like that?"

"I guess da same way you learn ta read—I practice."

Morning came and Lucy moved the rocker, rug, and wood panel to one side. "Mornin' boys." She looked down at the bucket Tom was carrying. "What da hell ya got in dere?"

Tom looked up sheepishly. "A big rat an' sum pee."

"God, rats be all over dis part a town. Dey ain't fraid a people neither. I'm gonna dump dat nasty thing out back an' dogs kin carry it away. Sorry, boys. Hope ya got sum sleep."

"We dun aw'right," Tom replied as they made their way to the small table in the kitchen. As they ate the grits and fatback, Will felt compelled to ask about an issue that was vexing him.

"Miss Lucy, do you know where we can get a City Directory? Captain McGee gave us names of people we're supposed to get in touch with— a lawyer named Bireman and a preacher by the name of Meachum."

"When I goes ta town dis afer'noon I be deliverin laundry to Miss Rutgers, she got one. While I be gone hav ya self sum coffee an' a bite to eat, but keep an eye on da street. Ya see any people nosey'in 'roun', ya lock da front door an' gets outa sight."

That afternoon the wind blew leaves along the street and large charcoal clouds filled the sky. Lucy clutched a small white book when she entered the kitchen. "Gettin cold out dere, men, but I gots yer di'recory. Miss Rutgers want it back when ya done." Will thanked her and flipped to the back. He looked for the letter "B." Halfway down he found the name Bireman, Attorney, page 19. Will went to page nineteen.

> Bireman,Abraham–
> Attorney Specializing in liabilities involving riverboat
> and stagecoach companies. Expert in commercial and
> financial paper and immigrant citizenship disputes.
> 108 Washington Street.

Will committed the address to memory and asked Lucy if she knew how to get to Washington Street.

"I draws ya a little map when ya go, but doan go fer a day or two. Ya gots to act like ya knows what ya doin an' knows where ya goin." Lucy paused and rubbed her chin. "Gots an idea boys. Since ta'morrow be Sunday, why doan y'all go wid me ta church? Ya gets out a bit an' learn yer way a'roun."

Tom locked his hands together and said, "I doan know bout dat, I jus doan know." Will arched one brow, and gave Tom a look.

"Yes, Miss Lucy, we would like to go with you," Will shot back.

22

A **COLD FRONT ROLLED IN** on Sunday. Street puddles were covered with a thin sheet of ice. Will and Tom walked with Lucy along the muddy streets to the First African Baptist Church. She found an empty bench where the three of them could sit. Soon it was so crowded people were standing in the aisles.

"Sumpin goin' on, I ain't ever seen so many folk who wanna hear da gospel. I guess you be here on a speshel day."

After traditional hymns and announcements, Reverend Thaddeus Brown stood before the congregation and asked for "Respectful silence.

"Brothers and Sisters, the Reverend Berry Meachum couldn't be with us today. In his stead I have the honor of introducing Mr. Moses Dixon. As you know, Mr. Dixon is an important member of our community. He wants to share his thoughts about the new Fugitive Slave Law, and the manner in which it is being enforced. He would like to tell you…"

From the back a voice boomed; "Then let him speak!"

The laughter quickly subsided when a square jawed man, dressed in a black suit and white shirt, stepped to the pulpit. His eyes gleamed, his demeanor was serious, and a hush fell over the congregation.

"Good morning!"

The crowd responded with a resounding, "Good Morning!"

Dixon wasted no time, in a strong voice he began; "Brothers and sisters, see that flag in the corner, the one police placed there. Many view it with pride, and some, like Ruffin's fire-eaters, view it with hatred." Dixon paused and looked to the back of the church for white police officers, then continued.

"For the Negro that flag means nothing. The stars in the flag are against us, and the stripes are against us. We are not allowed to be part of this country. The flag represents a government that says we are only three-fifths of a person." He took a lengthy pause to allow the crowd to stop murmuring. "Things will not change unless you help bring about that change."

Lucy nudged Will in the ribs and said, "I doin' my helpin' part right now."

While Dixon spoke, a few men wearing Knights of Liberty armbands went up and down the aisles with small baskets, collecting coins. Dixon took off his suit coat, laid it on the pulpit, and rolled up his sleeves.

"The laws that govern this country are finally being questioned. People have rightly come to believe that this country cannot have one set of laws for the white man, one set of laws for the black man, and another set of laws for the red or yellow man. Should you be angry because this country has laws that humiliate us, break us, do not allow us to learn to read or write? Yes! Yes you should!"

Applause, cheers, and shouts broke out, making the two white policemen stationed outside suddenly curious to know what kind of disturbance was taking place inside. Dixon spotted a signal from the back and quickly concluded his speech. He pointed a finger at the congregation and said, "Never be ashamed of who you are. You did not choose to be in this country, and you certainly didn't choose to be treated like this." It was time to go; Dixon grabbed his coat and disappeared.

Reverend Brown hastily stepped to the pulpit and eyed the police walking down the aisle with clubs in hand. Calmly he said, "Brothers and Sisters, today's service has come to an end. Before we go let me remind you to obey the nightly curfew for coloreds, and let the words spoken here today guide you."

Police heard the Reverend's concluding remarks and listened to the final hymn. Everything seemed normal. They wandered back outside and watched the crowd disperse. Will and Tom were speechless. The two men from Mississippi had never heard a black man speak like Dixon.

Lucy rose from the bench. "Men, we gots to go. Dat Moses be full a piss an' vina'ger, but he sure get people thinkin'."

Outside the church, Lucy talked with Will and Tom about areas of the city where they might safely travel. She also filled them in on the wealthy coloreds, mostly mulattos, who lived in the city.

"Dem folks be smart an' knows how ta greaze da palms of pol'ticians and po'leez. Dey be left alone to make more money."

"How dey gets so rich Miss Lucy?"

"Lotsa ways. Missus Lyon, she buy an' sell property. So do da Labadies and Charlevilles. Mordecai and White be chin scrapers who sell fancy soaps and run bath houses. Some sell supplies ta riverboats, an' ta people headin' out west. Every one a dem rich colored folk got a differ'n story. Maybe you men get rich one day and give ole Lucy a piece a da pie." Before they returned to the small house with the underground room, Lucy said, "First thing ta'marrah, I draws ya a map. Dress nice as ya can, Will, cuz ya be goin up town."

Lucy couldn't read or write, so the map she drew for Will the next morning consisted of lines that indicated streets and intersections. "Da big bank buildin wid lots a windows be where ya turn, dat be Washinton Street." Lucy drew a square with dots on it to let Will know that was the bank building. "Ya turns to face da river." She drew squiggly lines to represent the river. "Da buildin you be lookin for be b'tween da river and dat bank buildin."

Tom looked worried. "Will, does ya want me ta go wif ya?"

"I think it's better I go alone. Two of us walking the streets will draw more attention. I'll tell you everything he says as soon as I get back. Miss Lucy, can I take the directory?" Lucy nodded. "Sure, but doan let it get away frum ya."

Will took off down the street; he followed Seventh Street to Washington, but the bank building wasn't there. He headed in the direction of the river and was relieved to see the bank at the next intersection. A few blocks later he spotted a two-story brick building with 108 above the entrance.

He started across the street and then stopped abruptly. Slaves, joined together by chains around their necks and ankles, trudged past. Clanking, jangling chains reverberated on the cobblestones. The guards toted shotguns. Will stood off to the side with his head bowed until they passed, then he ducked inside the building. He saw "*Abraham Bireman, Attorney*" painted on a wooden finger pointing up the stairs. He knocked on the office door.

"Enter," came a confident voice from within.

Will eased into the room filled with books, landscape paintings, and a huge desk in front of a large window. Sitting behind the desk sat a clean-shaven curly haired man, wearing a dark blue pin striped suit. "Can I help you young man?"

"Are you Abraham Bireman?"

The lawyer came from behind the desk. "I am. And you are?"

"Will, Will Douglas, sir. Captain McGee said you might help us."

"McGee, eh?" Bireman gestured to a chair. "Have a seat and tell me why the captain sent you."

"My friend and I would like to become free men, sir. And, I have this money, and a last will and testament from my late master. The captain thought you should look at them and give us advice." Will opened the satchel, withdrew the contents, and carefully placed them on Bireman's desk.

The lawyer looked at the money and said, "My goodness."

Bireman cleaned his spectacles and began examining the bank notes. He wrote down the numbers and multiplied the total by another number. He startled Will by letting out a high-pitched whistle.

"Mister Douglas, even with the bank taking their share for exchanging this currency, you have almost three thousand dollars here." Will felt stunned; he had no idea he had been carrying around so much money. He sat in a solemn stupor. Bireman opened the last will and testament of Ben Douglas. His face changed from surprise, to disbelief, to consternation. He peered at Will over the top of the document. "Who owns Mary Dale now?"

"Colonel Pritchard. He used to be in the military. I think he was in charge of soldiers in New Orleans."

As a big city lawyer Abraham Bireman had encountered many unusual things—immigrants wanting to recover money taken by con men, widows whose rich husbands forgot to name them in their will but remembered their horse, and slaves without a penny to their name who wanted to buy their freedom—but he had never read anything quite like the last will and testament of Benjamin Douglas or had bundles of English currency dumped on his desk by a runaway slave.

Bireman pondered the problems. Manumission often required the consent of the slave's owner, and in this case the owner was most likely a charlatan who obtained the plantation illegally. He would never allow his slaves to be set free or risk having his own corruption exposed.

Will watched and waited until he thought it was a good time to ask another question. "Sir, my friend Tom is in the city with me. I would like him to become free, too."

"I'll do my best for you both," said Bireman. "But this is going to be a contentious process."

Will didn't understand. "Sir, I don't know what that word means?"

"Difficult, Will, difficult. Colonel Pritchard may decide to come to St. Louis and forcibly take you back. I'm sure he will avoid a hearing. Do you think you want to continue?"

Will nodded.

"Very well, then. Be back here next Friday at the same time. Meanwhile, be careful. No doubt there are people out there already looking for you."

23

THE SAME MONTH WILL AND Tom arrived in St. Louis, Teeny received a letter at the Walther's country residence. *Elizabeth Douglas* was elegantly spelled out in script on the envelope. Teeny anxiously opened the sealed flap, and pulled out a sheet of parchment with a large swirling *W* at the top. The letter informed her that she would be meeting with Mrs. Louise Walther at her Lucas Place residence.

She read the letter to Izzy and said, "Why do you suppose she invited me to her home?"

Izzy smirked, "Probaly wanna thank ya for keepin' da doctor outa her hair."

"You're right. She should thank me," Teeny replied bitterly.

"Do ya think she know you wid child?"

The next day Daniel pulled the buggy up to the portico and waited. Teeny was wearing a calico dress and black woolen shawl, both gifts from Richard. The carriage progressed east at a leisurely pace. Half an hour later, the Lucas Place gatekeeper greeted them; "Morning, Daniel, who's the pretty lady?"

"Guest of Missus Walther. Her name be Miz Eliz'beth Douglas."

The guard tipped his hat and the carriage proceeded down the private lane. Daniel rapped the elegant brass doorknocker and said to the housekeeper, "Miz Eliz'beth be here."

During the past year Louise's health and spirits improved. She even managed to walk without a cane now. The doctor's wife greeted Teeny and invited her to the parlor.

"Please sit down. My, you are every bit as attractive as Mr. Buckner said. Do you enjoying working in my country home?"

"Yes, Mrs. Walther, it's a beautiful home." Louise's appearance and demeanor surprised Teeny. She did not seem sickly and was far more attractive than Richard had described.

"I don't want to mince words, Elizabeth, so I will get right to the point."
She paused, and her bright blue eyes looked directly at Teeny's midriff. "How
far along are you?

Teeny was surprised and embarrassed. "Almost four months. How…how
did you know?"

Louise gave her a faint smile. "Richard and I discuss everything. Despite
what you might think, we are happily married."

Teeny tried not to appear surprised at anything else that was said and
sat quietly with hands folded. Louise stood and addressed her in a formal
manner. "Elizabeth, southern women know when they marry that their husband may be the father of a slave child or two. They hide their husband's
unsavory conduct by transferring the child to a slave-trader. The child, of
course, is property, as marketable as a pig or any other farm animal. I invited
you here to tell you that there are honorable exceptions." Teeny was curious,
but afraid to ask questions.

"Many women in my position would feel disgraced, but I am not like those
women." Teeny forced a smile and nodded; she was now wary.

Louise looked Teeny in the eyes. "I am not ashamed to do what is morally
right, and raise your child as my own."

Teeny hadn't thought through the details about her child's future. She
naively assumed the baby would live with her and Izzy. This pronouncement
was unexpected. Teeny stared blankly at Louise, her mind whirling.

Richard's wife continued. "The child will be given a good life, a good education, and will be loved." Teeny replied as respectfully as she could, "Mrs.
Walther, it is very kind of you to make the offer, but this is *my* child."

Louise gave Teeny a thin smile, and shook her head in a dismissive manner.
"It certainly is not, and I don't know where you got that idea."

Teeny felt shaken. "Has doctor Walther agreed to this?"

"Of course. This is a new beginning for both of us."

Teeny felt helpless. Her child was to be taken at birth, and there was
nothing she could do. She felt queasy and politely asked for permission to
leave.

Louise called the housekeeper, who escorted Teeny to the door. Louise
came up behind her as she waited for Daniel to bring the carriage.

"It was very nice to finally meet you Miss Douglas, I'm sure we will be
seeing more of each other."

Teeny didn't respond or look back. Daniel guided the rig back to the country home at a leisurely pace. She watched the red and gold maple leaves float slowly to the ground and wondered what life might have been like if Ben and Mary Douglas, and their children, had not died so soon. Then her thoughts turned to Will—how she missed him at this moment!

24

WILL RETURNED TO BIREMAN'S OFFICE the following week. He found Richard Walther's name in the city directory, and he was anxious to ask the lawyer how he might get in touch with Teeny. He knocked on the office door, but failed to hear Abe's assured voice. He opened the door slowly and saw the lawyer staring at a piece of paper on his desk. He remained oblivious to Will's presence. Will finally decided to ask, "Are you okay, sir?" The lawyer looked up and tugged at his vest.

"Sorry, Will, I just received a letter from my sister in Boston. She informed me that my brother is dead. Although she has no proof, she believes he was murdered. He was an abolitionist and a Jew...a bad combination. Died of a head injury from a fall, or so the authorities say." Bireman slowly picked up the letter and softly said, "They already buried him." He dropped the telegram to the desk, and put his head in his hands.

Will moved back, stepped outside, and closed the office door. He sat on the hallway floor, processing what he had just seen and heard.

A few minutes later the door opened. "Please come in, and please accept my apology for my unprofessional conduct."

"I'm sorry for your loss, sir."

"Thank you. I knew his days were numbered. He had been writing articles against slavery for years, a lot of people hated him." Bireman cleaned his glasses with a handkerchief and then removed a sheet of paper from a tall stack in front of him. "We have a lot to discuss."

Will took a seat and looked across the big desk and said, "Sir, what's a Jew?"

"It's my religion, Will. Our beliefs and traditions are different enough to cause distrust and sometimes hatred."

Will shifted uneasily in the chair. "Are you in danger, Mister Bireman?"

"No, I don't think so. I am not completely accepted by those who run the city, but as long as I contribute money to the right people, I'm tolerated, and pretty much left alone."

"That's the same thing Lucy says about the rich colored people in this town."

Bireman looked up and said, "Miss Lucy seems to know how things work, is she one of Andrew's contacts?"

"Yes, sir, she's the lady who's hiding us. She's an abolitionist and a Negro. I think that's another bad combination." Bireman smiled for the first time that day.

"Let's talk about your situation. The bank gave us a favorable exchange on the promissory notes, and you now have three thousand five hundred dollars in the bank."

Will shook his head in disbelief and finally said a barely audible, "Oh, my God."

Bireman let the news sink in, then continued. "The money has to be in my name, but I will withdraw it for you as needed."

Will recovered from his initial shock and said, "There's something else I need to ask you, sir. There's another person I would like to help. She lives somewhere in the city."

"Is this someone you are fond of, or related to?"

"Fond of, sir. We grew up together, but were separated when Colonel Pritchard took over the plantation. He gave her to a friend who is a doctor here in St. Louis. His name is Richard Walther."

"Will, when Teeny was given as a gift she legally became the doctor's property. He can do anything he wishes with her—make her a house servant, loan her out as a worker, or he could keep her for himself. She might even become his…"

Will completed the thought. "His fancy girl."

"Yes, Will, that is a strong possibility, especially if she is attractive."

Will assumed Walther was using Teeny for his personal pleasure; having it said aloud gave it a finality he had been avoiding. "I would still like to find her."

"Okay, I can help you with that. A private investigator works for me and can look into it. We'll find out where she is and how she is faring. When you come back next week, I'll have the information for you."

Will left the office. Bireman sat at his desk and smiled as he thought about the comment "Abolitionist and Negro, another bad combination."

He chuckled; he liked Will.

25

WILL MANAGED A WEAK SMILE when he spotted Lucy and Tom waiting for him at the front door, both eager to hear about his meeting with the lawyer. Lucy poured coffee and put a handful of biscuits on a plate. She waited patiently for only a moment, then gave him a stern look. "Is you gonna tell us what be goin on or is we su'pose to guess?"

"Yes, ma'am. I'm going to tell you, and it's mostly good. We got some money, and Mister Bireman is hiring someone to find Teeny. And, he is going to see a judge and ask if we can buy our freedom."

"And?" Lucy wanted to hear the rest of the story.

Will rotated his coffee cup slowly. "Mr. Bireman thinks Teeny is, uh, being kept. She is...she is most likely the doctor's fancy girl."

Lucy looked toward the ceiling and shook her head. Tom looked at his friend and sighed. Both knew how upset he was.

Lucy broke the silence. "Well, Mista Douglas, is ya pleased, or is ya sad? Which it gonna be?"

"Let's go with pleased and sad."

"No, we gonna go wif pleased. By da way, did ya say sumpin bout money?"

"Yes. Tom and I can give you a little money now. But we can give you a bigger piece of the pie when we know how much we have left."

She looked at Will with raised eyebrows. "Bigger piece? How much pie money you gots? An' where it come frum? She refilled the coffee cups and softened her tone. "Neva mine, ain't none a Lucy's bizness. Ya tell me what ya wants me ta know, an' dat be good e'nuf. You two gonna meet wif Rev'ren Meachum?"

"I looked him up in the directory, Lucy. He's not only a preacher, but he owns a barrel factory. Did you know he has been invited to speak in other parts of the country?"

Lucy didn't respond right away. She returned to the table and sat with her arms folded across her chest.

"Ya know dat church we went to? Well, da Rev'ren go to dat church durin' da week. He go on Friday ta tune da choir, an' his self, fer da Sunday service. You ought'a go dere an' try ta meets him."

"Do you think he would talk with us?"

"Why not? He be good at talkin. Pay him a visit."

Will thought about it, and then looked at Tom.

"You're right Lucy, we're gonna go and see him this Friday." Tom wasn't as confident. "I doan know bout dat Will, I can't talk good e'nuf ta meet a man like dat." Will looked at his friend and said, "Let's give it a try. If he's too busy, he'll tell us."

Lucy retrieved a deck of cards from a shelf above the stove. She smiled at the two men. "Now it be time ta have sum fun."

Will picked up the deck and looked at it. He relayed to Lucy McGee's story about cards being marked.

"Whad? Ya think I messed wid dese?" Lucy looked shocked.

"No, I'm just telling you what McGee said."

Lucy sat down at the table. "Dat McGee, he sumpin. Slave ketchers hates him and Andrew."

Will thought about the scars on McGee's arm, and his love of cards. "Lucy, why does he enjoy gambling so much?"

"He ain't a'lone. Evry'body love ta gamble. Look out dat window. See dem men sittin on dat stoop? Dey playin a dice game an' bettin match sticks. It be a way of helpin 'em deal wif life. Dey hope dey gonna win a little sumpin dat'll make 'em feel bedder."

"McGee says there is no such thing as luck. It's mathematics, and watching the other players."

Lucy started to shuffle the cards. "Dat cap'an be smart, but dere be part a da game no body kin con'trol, an' dat be God's plan fer who gonna win, an' who gonna lose."

Will shook his head. "McGee would bet you that's horse shit."

All three laughed as Lucy began dealing the cards.

Friday arrived as a mild December day. Will and Tom weaved in and out of street traffic enroute to the First African Baptist Church. They arrived just as the choir finished rehearsing.

"That was beautiful," said the Reverend. "Anyone not feeling the Christmas spirit after hearing your angelic voices should be sent down river."

Will cautiously approached Meachum. His voice quavered. "Sir, may we speak with you."

Meachum reminded departing choir members to arrive early on Sunday, then turned his attention to Will and Tom. "What would you two like to discuss?"

"We were told you might help us find a job, maybe help us become free men." Meachum seemed amused. "Who told you that?"

"Captain Allen McGee."

"McGee? I'm surprised that old salt's still alive. Andrew still with him?"

"Yes, sir." Will wasn't sure whether the Reverend had responded in a favorable manner. For a split second Meachum's intense eyes seemed to look right through him, and then he smiled.

"Will, you talk like you've had some education. Can you read and write?

Tom answered for his friend. "He sure can, an' he know math, an' now he teachin me."

"Men, let's talk again when I have a little more time. Meet me at my factory Monday morning."

Will was barely able to contain his excitement. He had no idea where the factory was but said, "Yes, sir. We'll be there!"

26

EARLY MONDAY MORNING, WILL AND Tom headed out with another of Lucy's maps; this one directed them to Meachum's barrel factory. They ran down Clamorgan's Alley and along a back street parallel to the levee. Before long, they arrived at an unimposing brick building and saw a hand painted sign above the door:

ST. LOUIS COOPERAGE

Inside everyone appeared to be in motion. Carpenters beveled staves and blacksmiths hammered out metal hoops. Meachum greeted them with a smile and led them to a small room in back. He set his coffee mug down and said, "Will, I asked you here for a specific reason. I run this factory but I also run a school. It's on a boat anchored in the middle of the river. Police closed my city schools, but state law doesn't apply to the river; that's federal territory. I figured the only way of educating young colored men without getting arrested was to put it out there."

Will wasn't too sure what Meachum was talking about and looked toward the river. "Is the school out there now?"

"Follow me."

They stood in front of the factory and Meachum pointed to an old steamboat anchored a few hundred yards away.

"That's her over there. The school is up and running and I've got a good teacher, a minister's son. But, what I don't have is a young black man who can read and write, and show these kids it can be done." He chuckled. "Know anybody like that Will?"

"And Tom, you're a rugged young man and I'll bet you're a hard worker. But take advantage of my school while you can. We can talk about a job later."

Meachum signaled to a drayman and said, "John, row these two out to the school and give Graham this note. Gentlemen I'll talk with you again in a few days."

A short wagon ride ended next to a couple of tattered skiffs. The small boat they boarded was aided by a strong breeze, and in a few minutes they tied up to a worn-looking paint-weary riverboat. Inside stood tables of different shapes and sizes, with paper and graphite sticks scattered about. A few dozen well-used books made up the library, and a slate board dominated the wall. Twenty young men gaped at them when they entered.

John introduced the newcomers to Bradley Graham, a tall friendly looking white man with a shock of wavy brown hair and bright blue eyes. He handed him Meachum's note.

Graham tapped his forefinger on his desk and said, "Well, let's get started and see how Mr. Meachum's plan plays out."

Graham walked over to the board and wrote Will and Tom Douglas in large block letters. He said to the students, "I would like you to write three sentences that describe our new friends. Raise your hand if you are having trouble, Mr. William Douglas here will help you."

The class looked at one another with raised eyebrows. Will found himself just as surprised. His nerves quavered as the first hand went up. He had scarcely answered the student's question before two more hands shot up. The more questions he answered, the more confident he became. Graham was impressed.

Tom sat down and wondered whether he could really learn to read and write. He picked up a lead stick and tried to form one of the letters he saw written on the slate board. "Damn, dis be hard," he said softly.

Late in the afternoon, four skiffs filled with young black men left the floating school for shore. Will and Tom found the day so exciting, they actually forgot they were still fugitives.

In building 108, a private investigator was relaying his findings to Abraham Bireman regarding Miss Elizabeth Douglas. The lawyer sat with arms folded and listened intently while the investigator read his report. When the report concluded, Abe shook his head and appeared dejected.

27

A MORNING ROCK TOSS DETERMINED who would row the skiff to the floating school. The stone closest to the water without touching was the winner, and the winner could pick someone to row the boat. On this blustery December day, Tom was picked. Wind gusts and heavy riverboat traffic in the main channel made it difficult. As a result, Tom's skiff reached the boat last. When they entered the classroom, everyone appeared unsettled.

"Good morning, Gentlemen," said Graham. "I was just explaining to the class that someone nailed a rather ugly note to my door last night. It seems the pro-slavery folks are not taking kindly to my teaching efforts here and have threatened my life. I am going ashore to meet with the authorities. In the meantime, Mister Douglas is going to help you with today's assignments, and tell you about a rather unusual event that takes place on this river."

With that, Graham nodded respectfully to Will and the students. He headed toward his skiff, locked the oars, and began rowing toward a small group of friends waiting on shore. The class watched as he then boarded a carriage bound for the city.

The students returned to their desks and looked dubiously at the new teacher. Will took a deep breath, put on his best teacher voice, and began the lesson.

"There is an island in the middle of this river, not far from our school, that's called Bloody Island." Will wrote "Bloody Island" on the board. The word bloody seemed to generate a spark of interest.

"Men would challenge each other to a duel on this island. Who knows what a duel is?" No one responded.

Will selected two students, asked them to stand back to back in the middle of the room, and then told each to take eight steps forward. They stopped. "Now turn and face each other. Hold your arm straight out and imagine you have a pistol in your hand. I will count to three, and you will fire one shot at the man opposite you." Looks of awe spread over the students' faces.

"Why would you wanna do sumpin like dat?" asked one of the young men. "Dey kill each other bein dat close!" added another.

Will explained; "If two men exchanged angry words and said something that implied the other person was dishonest or dishonorable, the dispute would often be settled like this. The first St. Louis citizens who fought a duel on bloody island were standing about thirty feet apart. They fired their guns. One man was hit in the throat, the other was hit in the knee." Now the class was enthralled. A hand shot up. "Do dey die?"

"No, they were wounded. But neither man was satisfied. Once their wounds healed they decided to duel again. This time each took four steps forward instead of eight." Will had two students reenact the duel a second time. "When they faced each other they were only fifteen feet apart."

"Dat be crazy! Ya could'n miss when ya be dat close!" one boy called out.

Will nodded. "It does sound strange, but these men were not crazy. They were well-respected lawyers who believed if you were accused of doing something illegal, you had to defend your honor."

The class mulled that over, and another question popped up. "Who dey be?"

"One man's name was Charles Lucas, the other was Thomas Hart Benton. In this duel Lucas said Benton hadn't paid his taxes and shouldn't be allowed to vote; Benton called Lucas a liar."

Another hand shot up. "Who won?"

"Benton fired and hit Lucas in the chest, Lucas missed when he returned fire. Lucas apologized to Benton after the duel, but Benton would not forgive Lucas. Lucas died a few minutes later."

One of the older boys said, "Wait? Is dis da same Benton who dey call 'Old Bullion', da one who now be a sen'ator?"

Will was surprised he made the connection. "Yes, it's the same man."

"He kill som'body an' now he be a sen'ator. How kin dat be? Why nobody go ta jail?"

"Men who fought here were never arrested because the island was in the middle of the river, and the laws of Missouri or Illinois didn't apply, just like they don't apply to our school. So many men fought on this strip of land that they called it Bloody Island."

"Tell us bout more duels."

Will smiled and shook his head. "I will share more stories about Bloody Island another day. I promised Mr. Graham we would go over your math homework and you would practice your writing. Let's start by copying the sentences on the board."

Will's first day turned out better than he hoped—students worked on their math problems, practiced writing, and began calling him Mist'ah Teacher.

At the end of the day they boarded the last skiff available and headed to shore. Tom looked at his friend and smiled. "Good job, Mistah Teacher."

On shore, a man dressed in a dark suit and bow tie stood waiting. Will waved an arm in greeting. Abe returned the gesture, but his solemn appearance indicated something wasn't quite right. Will's happiness ebbed quickly.

When the skiff was secured, the two friends hurried over to Bireman.

"Mr. Bireman, this is my friend, Tom, the one I was telling you about."

"Pleased to meet you, Tom." Abe pointed to the top of the levee, where a carriage awaited them. "Gentlemen, I have secured a cab. We can go over the report from the agent back at my office."

But as Will and Tom approached the vehicle, the carriage driver held his arm straight out with his palm facing them. "Stop right there. You two smelly cane hoppers go sit on the luggage rack."

Bireman looked apologetic, while Will and Tom grimaced knowingly. They jumped onto the luggage rack. At least the cabby let them ride. Bireman's office would have been an exhausting, sorry walk after their long day.

When they reached the law office, Bireman paid the driver and said, "A bit of civility might earn you a bigger tip."

The driver made a crude racial slur, cracked his whip, and the carriage rumbled away.

Inside the office at last, Bireman pulled the report from a desk drawer and began a summary of the investigator's findings. Tom listened intently. Will sat hunched over, hands locked together.

Abe was almost finished. He removed his glasses and directed his gaze upward.

"Is there more?"

"Yes, Will, there is. Your friend Teeny is expecting a child. Will felt as though someone had just punched him in the gut. He looked away.

Tom finally cut through the awkward silence. "Do we gets ta see her?"

"I believe I can arrange that. I'll have her in my office a week from today. Is that acceptable?"

Tom looked to Will.

"Yes," said Will, very softly.

"Very well," replied Abe, "then we shall meet here at noon."

Tom took his friend's hand and gently pulled him from the chair. "Thank ya sah. We be goin now. It be a hon'or ta meet ya."

Will walked in a daze as the two men made their way back to Lucy's. Whatever hopes and plans he had for a possible reunion with Teeny, now seemed like a dream, fabricated by a foolish young man.

28

LUCY SPOTTED WILL AND TOM as they made their way across Sixth Street. She waited for them in the doorway. "Hey Tom, what be da matter wit Will? He look like sum body shoot his pet dog."

"We hear news 'bout Teeny, Miss Lucy. Will gonna tell ya 'bout it when he feelin' better…I thinks he need ta sit a spell."

Later, when Lucy called the two men to supper, Will wasn't himself. He picked his way through the greens and potatoes she had prepared, trying his best to relay the information gathered by Bireman's investigator. Lucy got up from the table, wiped her hands, and gave Will a sympathetic look.

"Will, it seem ta me ya made yerself a romance outta sumpin' frum long ago. You can't be travelin' da streets lookin' like a sick pup, or ya git picked up by a paddyroller. Lucy like ya too much fer dat, so I be askin ya to be puttin' dis love sick'ness behind ya."

"I'll try Miss Lucy," Will responded, simply in hopes of changing the subject. "I'm going to look through this newspaper Mr. Bireman gave me and try to find news stories I can share with the class tomorrow."

With that, he wandered off with the paper into the back room. Time passed slowly; he tried to concentrate on creating a lesson, but couldn't stop thinking about Teeny carrying a white man's child. A white man who had served as an informant for Colonel Pritchard!

Two days later, a lean middle-aged man on horseback approached the portico of the Walther country home. He dismounted and knocked. The door opened slowly and stopped halfway. Izzy peered out at the stranger suspiciously.

"Who you be mister, and what you want?"

"My name is Andrew, ma'am, and I have a message for Miss Douglas from two of her old friends."

She nodded and said, "Waits here, an' I find Miz Douglas."

A few minutes later, Teeny cautiously approached the door, worried that Louise had sent someone for her.

"Miss Douglas, my name is Andrew. A lawyer by the name of Abraham Bireman sent me. He's representing Will and Tom Douglas."

Teeny couldn't conceal her surprise. In a halting manner she said, "Will and Tom are here, in St. Louis?"

"Yes, ma'am. Here is the message from Mr. Bireman. He wants me to wait for your answer."

"I can't believe it! I can't believe they got away! Please come in."

"Miz Douglas, should I gets you an' Mista Andrew some sweet tea, or coffee?"

"No need, ma'am. Not enough time," Andrew responded.

He watched as Teeny opened the note.

> Miss Douglas,
>
> Will Douglas and Tom Douglas have requested a meeting with you next Wednesday. They are aware of your present circumstances, and would like to help you in any way possible. Andrew will arrive with a carriage at eleven and will transport you to and from my office.
>
> Please provide him with your response.
>
> Abraham Bireman

"Yes! Yes. I'll be ready. Thank you Andrew! Thank you!" Teeny cried.

But the young woman had little time to reflect on this exciting news, because Richard would be arriving shortly. She tucked the note back in its envelope and handed it to Izzy. "Do you mind getting rid of this?"

"It be a good thing to start a little fire wif."

Teeny started to walk away, but changed her mind. In a pleading voice she asked, "Izzy, what should I do? What if he starts hitting me again?"

"You gonna hav ta make plans Miss Elizabeth, but keep da Doctor happy. He be actin' crazy when ya doan wanna get in bed wif him."

Teeny sighed, clenched her jaw, and silently vowed again to do whatever was necessary.

When Walther arrived that night in time for the evening meal, he found Teeny overtly polite and friendly. She poured his bourbon, and they discussed the plans Louise was making for the baby. Teeny asked him whether they had picked out a name. Richard quickly became bored with the conversation and poured himself another bourbon. After a few sips he told her to stop talking. "Go upstairs and get ready, I'll be up in a minute."

Teeny knew he would be right behind her, and he was. He pushed her to his bed and pressed his lips to hers, forcing his tongue into her mouth. His whiskey breath and crude fumbling with her clothes disgusted her.

"Let me do it." She removed her blouse, and asked him to lie back. "I want to make things right. You don't have to be rough."

Teeny did an excellent job of disguising her feelings. From his perspective, Walther saw a beautiful, sensuous young woman who wanted to please him. Lessons from the Silk Ribbon served her well. With a leg on each side she lowered her body on top of him. She quickly settled into a position that allowed her to create a rhythmic motion. Walther moaned loudly. When he finished she said, "See how good it can be when we don't fight?"

Relieved to have the business over with, she rolled to her side and started to leave. But Walther reached up, grabbed Teeny's hair, and pulled her back down on him. She recoiled but feigned a smile.

"Later, right now you need to get some rest. We have all day tomorrow." Normally Walther would not have allowed her to refuse him, but tonight he was exhausted, and had too much to drink. Within seconds he was asleep.

He slept late. When he awoke, Teeny and Izzy were gone. A note on the kitchen table informed him that Daniel had taken them to the farmer's market.

When she returned, Teeny suggested to him that they picnic by the pond since the weather was unseasonably warm.

"No, I'm delivering a baby this afternoon, I'll be leaving shortly." Resentment in his voice made it clear her shopping trip had already spoiled his plans. He told Izzy to get his breakfast, and informed Teeny he would be back next Friday, "For the entire weekend." He pointed at her with a fork. "Remember where we left off," then flashed an insolent smile.

With a forced expression of anticipation she nodded. "I'll remember."

She watched Walther ride down the country lane. When he was out of sight she went to the bookcase and pulled down a leather-bound volume. It was filled with maps and illustrations of different states and the western territories. There was a foldout map that showed a large expanse to the north, with Canada spelled out in large letters.

Izzy, who stood watching curiously, asked, "Watcha got dere?"

"A book of maps." Teeny stared at the large foldout.

"Izzy, do you know anything about Canada?"

Izzy looked at the geographic area Teeny was pointing to and said, "It be cold, an' full'a bears."

"It's also a place that doesn't allow slavery."

Izzy sounded cynical, "Dey probly gots it, dey jus call it sumpin' else."

Teeny sat down on the stairwell and looked at the map. She read the words Quebec, Ontario, Rupert's Land, and the colony of British Columbia. The unfamiliar names and size of the territory seemed intimidating. She ran a finger along the Mississippi river north until it ended. Teeny bowed her head, and a tear fell to the map. She had no idea where to go or how to get away.

29

WILL AND TOM DARTED THROUGH Friday morning traffic to the skiffs that took them to the floating school. In another part of the city, Abraham Bireman walked down Fourth Street toward the Courthouse. Sellers and buyers of slaves had assembled in front of the courthouse, getting ready for the weekly auction. Slave families huddled together, held hands, and prayed that a buyer would allow them to remain together.

Across the street, a handful of abolitionists passed out handbills and carried placards calling for an end to the slave trade. Bireman paused momentarily and thought about his brother's abolitionist writings, and then entered the courthouse.

He sat outside of Judge Dashner's chambers and waited for his name to be called. Once summoned, Bireman grabbed his briefcase and walked briskly toward the judge's desk. The judge peered over the top of his glasses and smiled. "Abe, I can always count on you to provide me with something unusual, what do you have this time?"

"I have outdone myself, Your Honor. I am here to request manumission for two slaves who have no legal owner."

Dashner looked dumbfounded. "Abe, do you have proof they have no legal owner."

"Please take a look at this last will and testament judge. The two men I represent presented me with this. I don't believe it was ever filed, or recorded with the authorities in Mississippi."

Dashner looked at the document with mild interest, but became intrigued when he read the section detailing how Mary Dale slaves should be freed and provided with two hundred dollars. "So these men you represent stole this document and ran away?"

Abe looked astonished. "Judge...they are two men hoping to obtain their freedom."

Dashner gave a wry smile and continued. "What happened to the plantation, Mary Dale?"

"It is now occupied by a retired military officer. I am quite certain he obtained it under false pretenses, claiming to be a relative."

"Well, Abe, the first thing I will have to do is find out if this document, which was drafted and signed by a lawyer, was ever filed. I am going to request that the Memphis law firm send me an affidavit verifying that it was."

"You and I both know there will be no response, your honor."

"The request still has to be made. I will also send an official letter to the authorities in Bolivar County inquiring whether they received any notice of a last will and testament. I am postponing any ruling until I receive an answer."

"Postponing? For how long?"

"I will give them two months. If I don't receive a response you may proceed with your manumission request."

Bireman shot back, "How about one month?"

"Sorry, Abe, you know these things move slowly. Two months. I will put you on the docket for February eleventh. See you next year."

Bireman thanked the judge, made his way to Fourth Street, and entered the Bonton restaurant. Andrew was waiting at a table in the back.

Before Abe could take his seat, Andrew said, "She'll be at your office on Wednesday. She's anxious to see her friends."

Abe sat down and seemed to be thoughtfully examining the contents of his coffee cup when he said, "You know, Andrew, these young people would have little chance of getting away without your help. I hope everyone appreciates what you do."

Andrew nodded. "You, too, Abe. You, too."

Across town Will and Tom had just returned to Lucy's after spending the day on the floating school. Will had a book that he borrowed from the school titled, *The History of St. Louis*. An appendix in the back listed the Missouri Slave Laws and the punishment for each violation.

He read the law that closed Meachum's schools.

Anyone operating a school or teaching reading and writing to any Negro or mulatto in Missouri will be punished by a fine of not less than $500 and up to six months in jail.

30

WEDNESDAY WAS COLD AND CLOUDY, with occasional bursts of sunlight dotting the city buildings. Andrew guided the carriage from Walther's country home toward Bireman's office. Will and Tom had left Lucy's and were headed to the same location.

The two friends arrived first and sat anxiously waiting to see Teeny. Finally, Andrew knocked, and then slowly opened the door.

Will's eyes lit up when he saw his old friend and love interest. He never imagined Teeny looking like this: A Lapis blue dress flowed softly around her breasts and hips and tapered downward to her ankles. She had draped a simple white cape over her shoulders that emphasized her hazel eyes and soft reddish brown hair. Gone was the girl in pigtails who climbed fences and played uninhibitedly in the swimming hole. Will's childhood friend and companion stood before him, now a beautiful young woman.

"Oh, Will, I can't believe you're here. I can't believe you made it." Tears formed as she kissed him softly on the cheek. "What happened here?" She touched the purple scar on his face.

Will could barely talk much less explain his altercation with Greef. "It's a long story." He held Teeny at arms length, gazed at her and said, "Teeny, you're all grown up! You're so beautiful!"

Teeny moved back, gave a slight bow, and thanked him for the compliment. Simultaneously the two realized that events had changed them, the close relationship they once experienced—now relegated to fond memory.

Teeny walked over and hugged Tom. "It's so good to see you Tom...I'm so glad you're both here!"

Abe approached. "Another introduction is necessary, Miss Douglas. I am Abraham Bireman. Will has told me a great deal about you, and I'm pleased to finally make your acquaintance." With that, Bireman pulled a stack of papers from his desk and politely added, "Numerous things must be discussed, so please, let's all be seated."

The lawyer asked Teeny to take a few moments to read his investigator's report and verify whether the information was correct.

She did not look at Will as she responded, "Yes, it is correct." Teeny paused for a moment. "There is one other thing; the Walthers plan to raise my baby as their own."

"Well, that's interesting. Have they discussed this with you?"

"They told me it's what they intend to do; there was no discussion."

Abe turned and retrieved a document and two envelopes from his desk. "Miss Douglas, my investigator believes Walther's angry outbursts make your current situation precarious. We both believe you need to leave the city as soon as possible. Would you say that is accurate?"

"Yes, but I don't know where to go, and I have very little money. I've read that many slaves go to Canada, but that seems impossible, it's so far away."

"Please excuse my presumptiveness, but I have devised a plan that I hope you will find acceptable."

Will and Tom looked at Abe; he sensed their surprise.

"Will, Tom, I hope you also find the plan acceptable." Bireman moved his chair closer to Teeny and held up two envelopes. He began speaking in a matter-of-fact monotone.

"This envelope contains a birth record for a child named Elizabeth Douglas, born twenty-one years ago. According to the document you were born in St. Louis and your parents were Edward and Diane. The other envelope contains riverboat tickets. One is a ticket for the riverboat Durock, the other for the riverboat Adele. You will board the Durock around noon. It is important that crewmembers, the dock master, and any officials on shore see you on board that boat."

Confusion registered on the young woman's face. "Why am I doing this?"

"With a bit of luck, the people who see you will tell Walther and the bounty hunters you are on board that boat—it travels the Missouri River to St. Joseph."

"Bounty Hunters!" she replied, alarmed.

"Yes. Walther will most certainly post a reward and possibly hire someone to find you. You have monetary value, and he and his wife want your child."

Will and Tom grew concerned and were anxious to hear the rest of the plan.

"You will leave the Durock later in the day and board the Adele," Bireman explained. "If all goes well you will be in St. Paul in two weeks. Friends of my late brother will assist you in finding a place to live. You may decide to remain there until the baby is born, or you may continue farther north to Canada."

Will was listening, but remained silent.

Tom finally spoke up. "Seem like ya done sumpin' like dis b'fore, Mistah Beerman."

"I have, and I believe this is the best way to get Teeny away from Walther."

"What does we gots ta do ta help?" Tom queried, his voice anxious.

"Teeny is going to need money for herself and the baby. You can help by giving her a portion of the money you have in the bank."

Will and Tom nodded. "Tell me how much you want her to have, and I will make arrangements to withdraw it."

Tom looked to Will, who seemed lost in thought, then he said, "Dere be three a us, so it should all be da same."

"You want Teeny to have a third of the money?" Tom looked to Will for help.

Will finally stepped in, "Yes, that would be fair. If she needs more we would agree to that as well."

Teeny grew curious. "How much money are we talking about?"

"Your portion would be almost twelve hundred dollars," Bireman told her.

"Mercy! I had no idea!" Teeny exclaimed in shock.

"Andrew, can you meet Miss Douglas on Friday and give her the money?" Andrew responded confidently, "I can handle that, Abe."

Teeny appeared wide-eyed and apprehensive. "You mean I leave this Friday?"

"Yes. This time of year there aren't many big boats going that far north, so we have to act now or wait at least another two weeks, maybe longer."

Teeny couldn't believe she would have to commit to this plan so soon, just when she had been reunited with her old friends; but then she thought about Richard's violent outbursts…and Louise raising her baby. She knew she had no choice and acting quickly served hers—and the baby's—best interests.

"I will be there on Friday, Daniel will bring me to the levee."

Abe handed her the envelope containing riverboat tickets. "Very well. God willing in a couple of weeks you will be in St. Paul."

Teeny's eyes traveled the room and settled on Will. "I guess I won't see you or Tom again."

Will felt a pulse beating in his ears and realized there was nothing more to do but wish her well. "I guess not. Maybe you could write me once you're settled."

"If I can, I'll do that. I have a lot to do before Friday, so I had better be leaving." Then she spoke softly to Andrew. "Do you mind if I say good-bye to Will alone before we go?"

Andrew nodded. "We'll wait downstairs."

When the door closed, the two longtime companions stood facing one another. Will gently took her hand and gazed at the upturned freckled nose he used to tease her about. He exhaled softly, and put his arms around her. She was a thing of softness and beauty and the embodiment of a woman he never anticipated. Will dropped the tender hold and gazed at her.

"Goodbye, Teeny. I'm glad we were able to see each other again. Be careful, and take care of that baby." He thought his heart would rupture.

Teeny gently touched the scar on Will's cheek, "You take care, and don't look sad. I want to remember you with that big smile," she offered bravely.

Will grinned.

"That's better," she said.

Moments later Teeny boarded the carriage and looked up at the second floor window. Will stood watching and tossed her a heartfelt wave. Teeny motioned back. Neither smiled.

31

TEENY GREW PENSIVE AS SHE searched her room for items she felt were absolutely necessary to take with her. Izzy watched as she laid out coats, dresses, shoes, shawls, hats, and gloves. She followed Teeny around and finally said, "Is you gonna take da wash tub?"

"You're right," Teeny laughed nervously, "I can't take all this stuff."

"Gonna tell me where ya goin'?"

"It's better I don't," Teeny replied hesitantly. "Then you won't be lying when Richard asks you where I've gone."

"I's gonna be sad afta ya be gone."

Teeny stopped sorting her belongings and placed her hands gently on Izzy's shoulders. "I'm going to miss you more than anyone, Izzy. But I have to leave, and soon."

"I knows." Izzy took Teeny's hand. "Miz Elizabeth, when ya does hav ya baby, an' settle in, I hope ya finds someone ta marry. But doan go back. Go furder white, marry no one darker, an' neva look back. It be best fer you and yer baby."

Teeny hadn't expected that advice, but knew Izzy meant well. She hugged her sweet friend.

"Thank you Izzy. Thank you for everything."

Friday morning Daniel guided the buggy past the portico where Izzy waved to Teeny and said, "Ya takes care a ya self an' dat baby girl."

Teeny shouted back, "How do you know it's a girl?"

Izzy laughed and retorted, "Izzy know!"

Daniel steered the carriage through throngs of people when suddenly a police officer directing traffic barked, "Get that damn buggy outta here."

Frightened, Teeny grabbed her bags and told Daniel, "Do what Izzy tells you to do when you see Doctor Walther."

Teeny found herself immersed in a sea of strangers. She spotted a sign-board with an arrow pointing to the Durock's mooring site. As she walked up the landing stage, a nattily dressed officer with black hair and light green eyes greeted her.

"May I show you to your cabin?"

Bireman's instructions were to be seen by as many people as possible, so she replied, "If you don't mind, I'll leave my bags and dine first. I can go to my cabin later."

"Certainly, miss, please allow me to escort you."

Teeny followed the officer's lead up the stairs to the saloon. In the dining area, he politely pulled back Teeny's chair.

"May I join you, Miss . . ?"

"Elizabeth Douglas. Thank you, Captain, I would appreciate the company."

"Thank you for the promotion, Miss Douglas, but I'm Roger Morris, the striker pilot. The captain will be on board shortly." They began polite conversation that continued throughout the meal. After the tables were cleared, a trio of musicians began playing. Morris smiled. "Would you consider a dance, even though I'm not the captain?"

"Thank you, Mr. Morris, but for now could you just show me around?" They moved past crowds gathering at the gaming tables and climbed the stairs to the Hurricane Deck. They were over thirty feet above the water. Teeny smiled and waved to several people on shore.

Late that afternoon, Teeny handed the steward her claim check and retrieved her bags. She found a quiet section near the forecastle and waited. It was almost four when a small group of immigrants began arguing with a police officer on shore. Andrew took advantage of the distraction and waved to Teeny with a red cloth. She grabbed her bags and moved swiftly down the gangplank.

When she reached him, Andrew slipped her a tan leather purse and guided her toward the Adele. His instructions were typically brusque, "Con men are on board even the best boats. No one can know how much money you have. Don't lose sight of that purse."

Smoke was rising from the Adele's stacks and deck hands prepared for departure. Andrew escorted Teeny up the landing stage, and a cabin boy took her bags. "Please follow me, ma'am."

Teeny thanked Andrew one last time and followed the young man up the stairs. Roustabouts stacked wood near the boilers, deck hands untied the lines, and bells called everyone to attention. A shrill whistle came from the top deck, and Teeny felt the machinery shudder.

Andrew watched the big stern-wheeler move slowly forward, begining its long journey up river. With his head down, he walked briskly toward Clamorgan Alley.

32

LANTERNS AND STREET LAMPS GLOWED throughout the city. Andrew stayed in the shadows, surveying the pedestrians, looking for his contact. Someone called from a darkened doorway, "Andrew, over here."

He moved toward a dimly lit alley and recognized one of Dixon's men from a previous encounter. "Need some protection for Abe Bireman," Andrew said in a hushed tone.

The man shook his head. "Dixon an' his men ain't doin' that strong-arm stuff no more. The Knights is only workin' with tha undergroun' railroaders. He told me ta find ya sum body. It's gonna cost ya ten dollars a week."

Andrew let out a small whistle, informing his contact what he thought of the price. Nevertheless, he agreed to the deal. "Here's the address and first week's pay. I want someone over there right away."

"I'll get him there soon as I finds da right person. Can't have just anybody hangin' 'round on Washinton Street. I'll get it done. Nice doin business with ya, Andrew," the voice assured him.

The two men parted, and Andrew walked toward his boardinghouse. He wondered whether Walther had been notified that Teeny was gone.

Izzy gave Daniel last minute instructions; "Ya goes to da docta's house firs thing in da mornin. Ya gotta look real upset when ya meets him; den say, Miz Douglas is no where ta be foun', an' some a her things be missin'. An' re'member, he gots to be'leev you be as su'prised as anyone."

Daniel arrived at Lucas Place shortly after sunrise; he did his best to look agitated. When Nelly opened the door a crack and peeked out, Daniel blurted out, "Needs ta talk ta docta Walther right away!"

"Hold on ta yer britches, I gets him."

Walther was dressed and ready to leave; he had planned on spending the day at his country home. He trudged down the stairs and shot Daniel an annoyed look. "What is it?"

"Docta Waltha, Miz Liz'abeth be gone! Izzy an' I looks ebry where an' doan find her! Sum a her clothes be gone too!"

Walther couldn't contain his fury.

"Louise! She's running! She left with our baby!" he yelled up the stairs.

Walther wasted no time scrambling aboard his buggy. He cracked the whip and urged the horse forward as fast as she could move, proceeding rapidly toward the courthouse.

Once there, he filled out paperwork advertising a reward for his runaway:

RAN AWAY
$1,000 REWARD

Attractive Mulatto slave woman, No scars, reddish brown hair, five foot seven inches tall, one hundred and twenty five pounds, passing as white. The reward of $1,000.00 will be paid if delivered in good condition. Respond to: Bolton, Dickens and Company.

Next, Walther had the information printed and delivered to ship captains and officers all along the levee. Bolton's office sent the information by telegraph to any town that had a wire along the Missouri and Mississippi Rivers.

The following day Walther received a hand delivered message from Charles Bolton; several people saw a young woman matching Teeny's description aboard the Durock. Walther sent a return note telling him to investigate further and to summon the best available slave hunter. Bolton sent telegrams and letters to authorities in Cape Girardeau, Memphis, and Natchez, asking them to locate Jackson Alvarez, a slave hunter known to locals as...Greef.

Cß Cß Cß

A deputy from the Bolivar County courthouse, Jeb Thornton, rode down the winding dirt road toward the Mary Dale plantation. His mission was to deliver a message to Colonel Pritchard and return with the man's response. As Thornton passed through the gates, his horse began to whinny and prance nervously. Just beyond the wrought iron entry a post had been planted in the ground. Atop the post was what remained of a severed head. Birds and other animals had removed most of the flesh and eyes from Pete's skull. The macabre exhibit served as a warning to any slave contemplating escape.

Attempting to rid his mind of the ghastly image and keep down his breakfast, Thornton continued on to the front of the plantation. A servant greeted him politely and asked him to wait on the veranda.

"Colonel Pritchard will be with you shortly," the young man said with a bow.

Jeb surveyed the grounds and was struck by the serene beauty of the plantation; everything seemed a perfect representation of southern wealth and privilege. Pritchard emerged from a side door, instructed a servant to fetch two sweet teas, and invited Jeb to take a seat. Pritchard's demeanor was friendly, but he knew any unplanned visit from a county representative might be problematical.

"Well, son, why did the judge send you out to the country on a fine day like this?"

"Colonel, I have a letter for ya. Y'all need ta provide me with an answer so I kin tell the legal folks in town how ya wish to proceed."

Thornton handed him the letter from St. Louis. Pritchard read the request for verification that the Douglas Will had been recorded. He turned in his chair and yelled, "Jack, come here!"

Blackstone sensed the urgency. "What is it Colonel?"

"Those two bastards that escaped are in St. Louis! Get whatever you need, we're leaving. Tell Jake he's in charge while we're gone."

Thornton watched this frenetic scene unfold. "Sir, what should I tell the sheriff an' the lawyers?"

"Tell them there is no need to respond. And tell Randy Sikes at the post office I want two tickets on any packet going from Rosedale to St. Louis."

Thornton wasn't sure he heard the request correctly. "Rosedale? Are you sure, Colonel?"

"There are a couple of boats that stop there every day for wood. Get us on any one ya can. Tell Sikes I'll be there tomorrow. I'm going to give you a letter. I want it mailed as soon as you get back to the courthouse."

Pritchard moved swiftly through the doorway and headed to the roll top. He wrote a few lines and stuffed the paper into an envelope. He returned to the veranda and handed Thornton a small coin. "Here's a gold piece for your trouble son. Now, get moving."

Three days later Pritchard's letter arrived at the Walther residence in St. Louis. Richard sliced through the seal and read, while Louise listened carefully to the news.

> *Dear Richard,*
>
> *I am writing this in great haste so that it will be delivered before my arrival in the city. Two of my slaves escaped a few months ago. I now know they are hiding in St. Louis. They may try to contact the slave girl I gave you. I hope you will assist me in retrieving my property. I look forward to seeing you and Louise.*
>
> *Your loyal friend,*
> *James*

Richard handed the letter to Louise and said, "Well, it seems Elizabeth may have had assistance. It's possible the two slaves who escaped from Mary Dale contacted her before she ran."

Louise's face revealed her distress. "Richard, we have to find her. How long before the colonel gets here?"

"A day or two, and a slave hunter's on his way. We'll find her."

Pritchard and Blackstone waited at Rosedale, Mississippi, for the River Angel to dock and take on wood. Once Pritchard was on board, he immediately regretted his hasty booking. He handed the tickets to a deck hand and received a curt, "Up the stairs."

Pritchard and Blackstone looked disgruntled as they carried their bags past immigrants huddled around small stoves. They entered a constricted passageway with three doors on each side. Pritchard looked at his ticket, then at the number on the door. "This is it." Inside they discovered two bunks covered with faded blankets, a washstand, and a pitcher filled with river water. Pritchard rolled his eyes and said, "Thank God this is only temporary."

Two days later, Pritchard was situated first in line to get off the boat. He stood next to the gangplank, anxiously waiting for the boat to be secured. On shore horses, oxen, drays, and bales of cotton stood squeezed together so tightly any movement would have impressed him.

Pritchard aired his frustrations to Blackstone; "How does anyone get through this menagerie once they get off this filthy goddamn boat?"

They were about to find out, shortly. Blackstone laboriously elbowed his way through the crowd and managed to secure a carriage.

When evening arrived, the Colonel had settled into a comfortable room at the Planters Hotel. He also found the meals and gambling to be quite satisfactory.

Blackstone, however, felt more comfortable with the drink and brothel prices at Molly's Tavern. Both men displayed lively spirits when they met in the Hotel bar the next morning.

Pritchard ordered a coffee and a shot of bourbon before remarking, "We need to talk to Walther. I'm going to his office, and I want you to go to the courthouse to see if the handbills advertising a reward for my two missing jackals is being circulated."

Bireman was in his apartment sipping his morning coffee, and thumbing through the *Missouri Republican*. He was about to toss the paper aside when the section where hotels informed readers of distinguished visitors staying at their facility caught his eye. A name on the Planter's hotel list looked familiar.

```
Planters' Hotel...Lt Blakely, Capt Hill, Lt Lecust,
Lt E.C. Lewis, H.B. Weibling, G.W. Allen, Mexico;
J. Reiley, Philadelphia; R. McMarriatt, Maryland;
J.L. Woolsey, F. Papponeau, New Orleans; G.W.
Horton, Col J. Pritchard, Mississippi.
```

Bireman sent a courier to Andrew's boardinghouse with a message requesting that he come to his office. The lawyer paced the floor and anxiously looked out his office window. If Andrew bought protection, where was the person hiding?

33

THE FOLLOWING EVENING, PRITCHARD, BLACKSTONE, and Walther met in the hotel bar. Walther told Pritchard the story of Teeny's disappearance. The colonel shook his head and mumbled a string of obscenities. He was certain all three Mary Dale slaves had made contact with one another. Pritchard asked Walther what steps he was taking to track the girl.

"I've recruited a professional slave hunter and posted a thousand dollar reward," Walther assured him.

"A thousand dollars and a slave hunter seem excessive."

"Louise and I want her back. She's pregnant. Since Louise and I haven't been able to have a child we're going to raise the baby as our own," he explained.

"You the father?"

Walther nodded. Blackstone flashed an oily grin.

Pritchard lit a cheroot and said, "Do you know anything about the lawyer who filled the preliminary petition to have them manumitted?"

"Yes, he's a Jew. His name is Abraham Bireman. He's well respected, and well connected."

Pritchard's expression turned menacing. "I don't give a damn. He has a document, a Last Will and Testament that I want back. And he's probably being paid with money the niggers stole from me. I want Jack to pay the bastard a visit."

"Very well," said Richard, "But don't forget I hired a professional, Jackson Alvarez, who will be here shortly. You might wait and see how he wants to handle this."

Pritchard shook his head. "There's no reason to wait. Jack will get him to talk. We'll have the information waiting for Alvarez when he gets here."

They finished their bourbon and prepared to leave. Blackstone turned to Walther; "I need an address for the Jew."

Walther pulled a card from his pocket, "Here's the address, and Jack, try to be discreet."

Blackstone grunted dismissively.

Andrew was in a good mood when he visited Abe the next day. He received a letter from McGee informing him that the Missy T was leaving dry-dock and heading up river. "He's working his way toward St. Louis. Should arrive shortly."

"That is indeed good news, considering everything that's occurred in the past few days."

Andrew looked at him. "What do ya mean?"

"Pritchard's in the city. He arrived yesterday, and I'm sure he's not alone. Walther put out a huge reward for Teeny. He's also hired Greef to find her."

Bireman clasped his hands behind his back and began to pace. He continued to tell Andrew his concern; "Once Greef gets here, Pritchard will send him after Will and Tom. If they're captured, that ornery bastard will force one of them to tell Walther where the girl is. We need to get them away from the city as soon as possible."

He paused and stared out the window, then turned and gave Andrew a worried look. "By now they know who filed the request for manumission. Do I have protection?"

Andrew nodded, "Yeah, we're payin' plenty for it. Should already be here."

Abe paused for a moment. "One other thing, you need to warn Lucy. Greef knows she helps runners. I'm sure he'll pay her a visit."

Will and Tom looked forward to Lucy's Tuesday dinner of greens, potatoes, and ham hocks. They found Lucy waiting for them at the door, but her usual welcoming smile was missing. She waved them into the kitchen with a dishtowel. Andrew was waiting.

"Hello, men. Sorry to be here with bad news. Pritchard and his overseer are in the city. Greef will most likely be joining them soon. He was hired by Walther to find Teeny."

Tom placed his hands together on the top of his head and looked down. "Da Colnel, Blackstone, an' Greef, oh my Lord."

"Yeah, they'll come lookin for ya. The first thing we have to do is get you away from Lucy's. Greef knows she hides runners."

Lucy looked on, anxiously wringing her dishtowel. She could see disappointment in the two men's faces. "Ya gots no choice, boys. Ya knows I gonna miss ya."

Andrew rose and moved toward the door. "I'll be back here first thing in the morning."

"What about the riverboat school?" Will asked.

Andrew shrugged. "It's gonna have to go on without you."

That evening the two runaways gathered their belongings. Will pulled the leather satchel from under his bunk and dumped the contents. There was the small sack filled with coins, Granda's beads, some clothes, and Teeny's torn letter.

"We need to settle up with Lucy," Will reminded Tom, picking up the beads and the small sack of coins.

They found Lucy putting dishes in a tin washbasin.

"If ya boys comin' back ta say more goodbyes, I doan wanna hear 'em. I aw'ready feels bad ya be leavin'."

Will handed Lucy the bag of coins. "We want you to have this Lucy."

She emptied the contents on the kitchen table. Will placed Granda's brightly colored beads next to the money.

Lucy picked up a few of the coins. "Will, dis be a lot a money."

"We want you to have it, Miss Lucy. Maybe you can use it to help others the way you've helped us."

Lucy wasn't sure of the amount, but said, "Ya can't gimme all dis, an' what dem beads fer?"

"Granda, the old Voodoo lady at Mary Dale said they would bring good luck, but I'm not so sure anymore. Maybe they'll work better for you."

"Whad'a ya talkin bout? Ya be alive an' ya gots money. Dat be as lucky as it gets fer black folk. Dem beads be workin; keep 'em wif ya."

Will thought about that for a moment. "Yeah, I guess you're right."

Tom put his hand on Will's shoulder and gently said, "Waits a min'it." Then he turned to Lucy and said, "We did'n say dis be'fo Miss Lucy, but Will an' I wants ya to know we both loves ya. Ya been better ta us dan most anyone. Thank ya. Thank ya kindly." Will nodded in agreement.

Lucy wiped her eyes with the dishtowel. "Ya gots ta stop now cuz ya makin' Lucy weepy. Go on now an' get sum sleep, an' re'member, I be prayin fer ya."

The next morning they gave Lucy a hug and the three said their final good-byes. With Andrew leading, they maneuvered through seemingly endless alleyways and back streets. Finally they arrived at a large church. They followed the stone path in the churchyard until they reached the heavy oak door. Andrew knocked three times, listening for a response.

"Who's it?" a wary voice called from within.

"A friend of a friend," Andrew replied.

The door opened slowly. A stern looking man wearing a long black robe gestured for them to come inside. Will and Tom looked around. They were surprised to find themselves in a room filled with young black children. Groups of four or five were huddled around tables with a candle in the center.

They children gazed inquisitively at the newcomers.

"Father, this is Will and Tom Douglas. They'll be staying with you for a few days."

The priest's severe expression softened. "I'm Father Hoffmann. Welcome, welcome to the Church and to our little school."

Tom studied the dimly lit room. "Dis be a school?"

"Yes, we work by candlelight, away from windows and prying eyes." The priest turned to his students and said, "Young men, practice writing while I make our guests more comfortable." Then he plucked a candle from one of the desks and led the visitors down a hallway to a small austere room. Two beds, a lantern, and a chair served as the only furnishings.

"Gentlemen, the privy is out back, through the small door. Father Thomas and I have our supper at six. Please break bread with us, and if you like, visit us in the classroom."

Will and Tom nodded and looked around.

"Andrew, what kinda church dis be?"

"Catholic. Father Hoffmann and Father Thomas run a school here for coloreds."

All three walked back to the large oak door; Andrew turned and said, "No one can see you men enter or leave. I'll be back in a day or two." He looked both ways and quickly departed.

Standing in the back of the classroom, Will and Tom watched students point to words in the book as Father Thomas read aloud. The initial apprehension they felt had dissipated; both felt safe inside the church.

Back in their room, Tom examined the iron bars on the window. "Hard to tell if dese bars be keepin' somebody frum gettin' in, or us frum gettin' out."

Will laughed. "I think those bars were here before they knew about us."

"Yeah, you be right. Maybe dey here to keep da rats out. I gonna tell Lucy she need some a dese bars."

Will rolled to his side and turned down the wick of the lantern. "I doubt we're ever going to see her again, but if we do, you can tell her."

Soft mellow sounds wafted down from the pipe organ in the chapel. Will drifted into sleep, his head filled with thoughts of Teeny. Tom remained wide-awake, thinking about all that happened and how uncertain tomorrow seemed. He reached into his burlap bag. Eventually he fell asleep, clutching his knife.

A few blocks away the post office had just posted new handbills offering a reward for two particular runaway slaves:

RAN AWAY
$1,500 REWARD

Ran away from James Pritchard, residing in Bolivar County, Mississippi, on Monday the 5th of October. A Negro man slave named Will. Full 6 feet high, camel complexion, speaks well; weighs about 180 pounds; 23 years old, had with him at least one change of clothes, a leather bag, and possibly a substantial amount of money. Also, a Negro man slave named Tom. 5 feet 10 inches high, charcoal color, weighs about 200 pounds, is very strong. $750 will be paid for the return of each Negro if caught in a free state, or a reasonable compensation if caught in a slave state. Contact Bolton, Dickens and company in St. Louis when captured

34

BIREMAN WEAVED THROUGH CROWDS OF Christmas shoppers and returned to his office early in the evening. He placed a map of the Missouri River on his desk and began to circle the location of safe houses where conductors for the Underground Railroad resided. A creaking sound made him pause. He glanced over his shoulder at the doorway. He sighed, walked to the door, and slowly opened it. Nothing there.

Cautiously, he leaned forward to look into the hallway. He never saw the large hand that grabbed his arm and threw him down the stairs. He lay on the stone entryway barely conscious. Panic swept through him. He tried to yell for help. A creaking sound emerged from his bloody mouth.

A guttural voice growled at him, "Where are they?"

Just then the front door flew open. Vile cursing, grunting, and the sickening sound of knuckles striking flesh and bone rang out. A man with a burlap scarf covering his face dragged Blackstone toward the street. Blackstone struggled to free himself. A fist struck him flush in the face. Blackstone stumbled backward and reached for his revolver. His gun had just cleared the holster when a heavy club struck his hand, sending the gun careening down the cobblestone street. Someone yelled for the police, and within seconds a shrill whistle pierced the air. The men glared at one another, then disappeared in opposite directions.

Police officers helped Bireman climb the stairs and eased him into a chair. He thought it best not to make too much of this event and declined when asked whether he wanted a doctor. He did, however, agree to file a police report.

The next edition of the *Missouri Republican* led with the headline,

ATTEMPTED ROBBERY OF PROMINENT LAWYER—

Assailant's Pistol Recovered.

When Pritchard entered the hotel lobby, he saw Blackstone's purple fingers and swollen, misshapen nose.

"What the hell happened?"

"Son of a bitch had somebody protectin' him," Blackstone groused.

"Did you get anything out of him?"

"No...Lost my gun, too!" He replied angrily.

Pritchard opened the hotel lobby door. "Come on, we need to get you to Richard's office so he can patch you up."

Walther told Blackstone to hold his head still. Blackstone flinched as Walther reshaped the bone and cartilage.

"Ya bout done?" he asked coldly.

"Yes, keep your hands and everybody else's away from your nose. When you see the colonel, tell him Alvarez is in town. We're going to meet at the hotel tonight."

It was half past eight that evening when Greef, Pritchard, Blackstone, and Walther sat around a table in the bar. The four were an eclectic looking group: Pritchard had donned a cream colored suit and pale blue shirt; Walther sported a red cravat and long charcoal dress coat; Blackstone had on black wool pants, a plaid shirt, and a wide brimmed hat; and Greef dressed as usual in leather clothes and a black hat adorned with bright colored feathers, from which his long black braid protruded down his back.

They talked for several minutes, and then Walther stood up. "I have to take my leave, gentlemen. Let's convene tomorrow and hopefully by then we'll have more information." The others agreed.

On the street, Richard clasped the reins of his horse and prepared to depart. Greef signaled for him to wait.

"Tell me how to get to your country place," the half-breed said.

Walther looked west and gave him directions.

The temperature dropped below freezing during the night. At daybreak, light snow drifted lazily through the leaden sky. Greef rode to the entrance of Walther's country home. He formed an imposing presence with his large black cape draped around his body. He dismounted and tapped the butt end of his whip on the door.

Izzy peeked out and barely got the words, "Who you be?" out of her mouth, when the door flew open. The thin little housekeeper screamed. A fist to the stomach silenced her. Lying on the floor, she struggled to breathe.

"Where did she go? Where did the slave girl who lived here go?"

"She doan tell me. She doan tell no one," Izzy moaned.

Greef placed the heel of his boot on the back of her outstretched hand. "I want answers or bones are gonna break."

"Doa'n matter cauz I doan know nuttin!"

Greef pressed the heel of his boot on her outstretched hand.

"I doan know," she screamed, "I tell ya I doan know!"

"Who else works here?" he demanded.

Izzy clutched her fiery bruised hand. "Daniel, but he doan know nuttin. She doan tell us where she go!"

Greef shot her a nasty look that assured her he didn't believe her, then walked out the door toward the small barn. He looked at the buggy, the two horses, and the small potbelly stove, where a pot of coffee steamed away on top. He removed a tin cup from a hook and poured. Steam rose from the cup through the cold morning air.

"Care to join me Daniel?" he announced.

Daniel had tried to hide; but now he emerged from behind the buggy, confused and scared. He walked guardedly toward the black draped figure.

"Just wanna talk, Daniel. I just wanna know where she went."

"She doan say were she go."

Greef looked over at the buggy and back at Daniel. "Did ya take her in that?"

"I doan know whatcha mean."

Greef's arm shot forward, the steaming coffee immediately covered Daniel's surprised face. He ran blindly for the door. Greef's whip hissed, and a leather band coiled around Daniel's ankles. He was on the ground, unable to free his legs. Greef pulled a pitchfork from a barrel and strode toward him. One swift jab to the thigh caused six tiny holes to ooze blood. Greef smiled derisively at the doubled-up body screaming in pain. He raised the pitchfork with both hands and calmly said, "This next one's goin' in real deep Daniel."

"I takes her to da city! She doan say were she goin'! I swears she doan wan' us ta know!

Greef knew he wasn't going to get more information. He angrily threw the pitchfork to the ground and uncoiled his whip. He grabbed the gardener by his shirt and snarled, "If you lied to me, I'll come back and kill you!" Then Greef wrapped the cape around his shoulders and headed back to the city.

Late that afternoon Greef rode up Sixth Street to Lucy's. He sprinted up the front steps, looked left and right, and opened the door.

"Where are you woman?"

Lucy was sitting at the kitchen table. Three large men from the neighborhood stood next to her. "Been ex'pectin ya, Greef."

Greef didn't react or reach for his gun. He coolly said, "Hello Lucy. Long time between visits. The two men ya been hiding here, care ta tell me where they are?"

"Doan know whatcha talking 'bout Greef. Now ya needs ta go bout yer business be'fo da boys here gets angry an' hasta see ya off."

Greef gave her a devilish smile. "I'll be seein ya again, Lucy."

He left in a nonchalant manner that belied his anger. The day was over, and he hadn't learned anything about the whereabouts of the girl or the two male slaves. Greef mounted his horse, but then paused. Who had told Lucy he was coming?

Greef was still pondering when he reached Planters Hotel. He waited at the bar and watched card games in the lounge.

"Two bourbons," said Pritchard as he edged up next to the slave hunter. Greef downed the amber liquid in one swig and faced the Colonel.

"Need a little money. Got ta grease the wheels to get some motion. There are people who have seen things, and they need something to help them remember."

Pritchard reached into his pocket and removed a leather fold. "How much?"

"It won't take much. Lotsa Niggers in the Hollow are starving."

Pritchard handed him two ten-dollar bank notes.

The same day Greef visited Lucy, Bireman paid a visit to the courthouse, where Judge Dashner invited him into his private chambers.

"Nasty bump on your head, Abe. I heard you were beaten and robbed," the judge commented.

"I wasn't robbed, your honor. I was attacked. I'm sure it was one of our friends from Mississippi. Seems your request for verification of the Douglas Will riled a few folks."

"I'm sorry, Abe, how can I help?"

"I would like to see the weapon that was recovered and taken to the police station."

Dashner peered down through his reading glasses, scribbled a note, and put his signature on the paper. "Don't let it go off in your hand."

It was almost time for the officer on duty to leave when Bireman arrived. He handed him the judge's order. Annoyed, the officer brought out a wooden box and dropped it on the counter. He pointed to the clock behind him. "I'm leaving in five minutes."

"I'll only be a minute, officer."

Bireman set the box on a table and inspected the contents. Inside he found the gun, a cloth bag containing gunpowder, and another bag filled with firing pins and lead balls. An official looking slip of paper recorded the date and location where the gun was recovered. Bireman deftly picked up the bag of powder, slipped it into his coat pocket, and replaced it with a new one. Then he returned the box to the desk and thanked the officer.

ॐ ॐ ॐ

At St. Joseph's, Will asked Father Hoffmann whether they could leave the church to say goodbye to Reverend Meachum.

The priest looked concerned. "You'll have to leave early and return after dark. None of the parishioners can see you."

Will grew curious. "Father Hoffmann, do the people who go to church here believe slavery is a good thing?"

Hoffmann rubbed the back of his neck and appeared reticent. "Most of them don't think about it too much because they've got their own problems. People who come here just want their lives to be better, if not now, then in the hereafter."

"So most of them don't care one way or the other?"

Father Hoffmann nodded solemnly. "I'm afraid that's right, Will."

They left before dawn and arrived at the river just as the rising sun silhouetted the clouds. Will and Tom lingered a few minutes and listened to a calliope from a distant boat. Meachum was taking inventory when they arrived. "You boys are up early. Come on back and tell me what's going on."

Will brought Meachum up to date, then said, "We have to leave the city, Reverend. I'm gonna miss your school."

"What about you, Tom, are you doing okay?"

"Yas, sah, I be okay. I was learnin' da alpha bed—I was gonna su'prise ya wid a letter askin' fer a job."

"If you come back, write me that letter, and I'll hire you. And Will, I hear you're a pretty good storyteller and teacher. Keep telling those stories and keep teaching. Our people need you."

Just then one of Meachum's employees entered with a question about supplies. "I'm going to have to get back to work. What are you men going do until you leave?"

"We gonna be good Cath'lics," said Tom.

Meachum laughed and walked with them to the factory entrance. He pointed toward his floating school. "Education, that's the black man's path to respect. Never forget that."

Will extended his hand. "It's been an honor to meet you Reverend."

Meachum shook their hands. "Will, Tom, be careful…this country is coming apart. The closer it gets to splitting in half, the crazier people are going to act."

35

GORDON STRICKLAND WAS A HANDSOME man in his late fifties, with twenty years' experience piloting riverboats on the Mississippi. He and his first officer were dining with a beautiful young woman from St. Louis when the cub pilot informed the captain they were approaching Louisiana, Missouri. The captain and officer excused themselves. The crew lowered the landing stage, while roustabouts began loading wood, and dockworkers brought more cargo aboard.

Amidst this flurry of activity, a post office employee handed a telegram to the Adele's first mate. "Give this to Captain Strickland."

The message was delivered to the pilothouse shortly after the Adele resumed her journey up river.

```
ATTRACTIVE MULATTO SLAVE WOMAN
ESCAPED STOP

PASSING AS WHITE STOP

RED BROWN HAIR STOP

NO SCARS STOP

5 FEET 7INCHES STOP

$1,000.00 REWARD FOR RETURN STOP

CONTACT BOLTON AND CO. IN ST. LOUIS
STOP
```

The Adele docked that evening in Davenport. On Christmas morning, a steward knocked on Teeny's stateroom door and handed her a note. "Message from the captain, ma'am."

Miss Douglas,

I received a telegram we need to discuss. A member of my crew will escort you to my cabin at noon.

Teeny clutched the note; had she already been discovered? The tall clock in the saloon struck twelve, and a steward arrived to escort her to the captain's quarters. She had a sinking feeling as she knocked on the captain's door.

"Miss Douglas, come in. Please have a seat." Strickland retrieved the telegram from his desk and handed it to her. After reading it, Teeny held the note in her lap. Her face registered a defeated expression.

"Our options are somewhat limited," he said. "It would be risky for you to remain on board. I would recommend you take a stage to Peoria, from there continue on to Chicago."

Teeny felt relieved the captain wasn't going to arrest her, but concerned about his recommendation. "I'm sorry Captain, I don't think I could take a stagecoach."

"I know they are unpleasant and not always reliable, but I'm afraid we have no other choice."

Teeny bowed her head and said softly, "I am with child, Captain."

Strickland hadn't anticipated the complication and was momentarily at a loss. He folded his arms and said, "Well then, the stage isn't a good choice, but there may be another option. We will alter your appearance. Bessie, a Negro woman on board, is quite gifted in the art of applying wigs, powder and paint. I'll have her pay you a visit. And, I would suggest you adopt an affliction, or appear that you have suffered an injury. Wear a brace, walk with a limp, put your arm in a sling, anything like that."

Strickland circled to the front of his desk. "I'm afraid we don't have much choice. My boat will be boarded and inspected by patrollers at every stop from now on." He paused and gently took the telegram from Teeny. He put it in his breast pocket and said, "Bessie will be visiting you shortly. I'll check back with you later this evening."

An hour later, a tall thin woman wearing a bright red bandana appeared at Teeny's door and introduced herself.

"Miz Douglas, I's Bessie. Da cap'an send me down ta work ya over."

Bessie walked past her toting two large cloth bags. She dipped into one of them and deftly pulled out two grey wigs. "Sits, Miz Douglas, an' lem'me try dis on ya."

Bessie snuggled the wig on Teeny's head and then pulled out a small tin of grey make-up. She massaged the cream into Teeny's eyebrows. Bessie penciled in dark lines and the applied light brown age spots to her forehead. She pulled a matronly dress and shawl from the same bag. "Puts dese on later." Finally, Bessie placed a round mirror on the small table next to Teeny. "Wha'cha think?"

Teeny was speechless; her image appeared at least twenty years older.

An hour later, one of the stewards presented Teeny with a wooden splint and cane, both tied together with a bright red ribbon. A note accompanied it:

Merry Christmas!
Gordon Strickland.

Teeny strapped the wooden brace to her leg and practiced walking. She put on the dress, wrapped the shawl around her shoulders, and limped into the saloon. Passengers moved aside as the apparently elderly woman shuffled toward a chair in the lounge.

That evening Strickland joined her and commented on the new look, "Very convincing Miss Douglas."

When no one was close by he added, "For the remainder of the journey you will be known as the widow Elsie Graham. Anyone who asks about Miss Douglas will be told she disembarked in Davenport, and you are now occupying her stateroom. Enjoy the remainder of your trip Mrs. Graham."

Teeny sat looking at the drab fabric in her dress, felt the wooden brace, and thought about Will's surprise when he saw her in Bireman's office. She smiled and wondered what his reaction would be to the elderly and lame Teeny Douglas.

36

MUSIC FILLED THE SANCTUARY AT St. Joseph's, where the choir was rehearsing "Good King Wenceslas," "Adeste Fidelis," "The Holly and the Ivy," and other Christmas favorites. Will and Tom loved the music and visiting students in the "candle classroom." They were grateful for the security and kindness but knew it was temporary. Andrew would arrive in a day or two, and once again they would be on the move.

Several blocks away Andrew entered Abe's office building and noticed freshly painted wood on the repaired entryway door. A "NO SOLICITORS" sign was prominently displayed in the hallway. Abe greeted Andrew and asked him to take a look at the map on his desk. He began pointing out possible destinations for the slaves when there was a knock on the door. McGee let himself in and greeted both men with a broad smile.

"Greetings, gentlemen. Arrived a few days early and thought I'd stop by to see what type of mischief you're up to." The reunion turned serious as Andrew told McGee about the attack on Abe. Then he said, "There's more bad news. Walther hired Greef to find the girl. He's also searching for Will and Tom."

McGee frowned, "That piss-ant is back?" Andrew nodded. "He's already been to Walther's country home and paid Lucy a visit."

"Well, men, a cloudy morning can still end in a fine day."

Bireman shook his head. "I'm not as optimistic, Allen. They're closing in and they're ruthless. You have to consider transporting them on the Missouri instead of the Mississippi."

"The Missouri? McGee's surprise showed on his face. "Where are you thinking I could drop them...Kansas Village?"

"Maybe, but that town is being watched closely." Abe continued to examine the map. "Maybe you could go further north, into Iowa, or South Dakota."

"Where in Iowa? And what the hell's in South Dakota?"

Andrew spoke up. "There's a fort in South Dakota, and Indians."

"A fort and Indians!" exclaimed McGee.

All three looked at one another and began laughing.

"Well maybe that's not so good," said Abe. "Let's think about the alternatives in Kansas and Iowa."

"Can't we consider alternatives on the Mississippi? If I'm gone too long the government is going to want to know where I've been."

Abe shook his head. "The Mississippi is too risky. Patrollers and slave hunters are everywhere."

McGee shrugged and acquiesced. "Okay, how soon can we get them on board?"

"Will and Tom are at St. Joseph's. Others are scattered about the Hollow. Be ready to go in a couple of days," Andrew replied.

Abe's face bore a mischievous look. "There's one other thing. The gun that belonged to my attacker was military issue and has a carved white handle. It belongs to Pritchard's overseer. It now has a serious flaw."

Andrew cocked his head in a questioning manner, "What kind of flaw?"

"There is new powder for the chambers, a very potent powder. The gun should explode when fired. I like to think of it as Abe's revenge." He grinned deviously.

"How the hell did you manage that?" asked McGee.

"A former client, experienced in the art of explosives, concocted the powder for me. Judge Dashner gave me permission to examine the weapon, and I substituted the powder."

Andrew and McGee shook their heads and smiled.

On December 24, Pritchard journeyed to police headquarters and politely spoke to the officer on duty.

"There is a gun being held here as evidence. It was stolen from me aboard the River Angel. I would like to have it on my person for protection when I make the journey home."

The officer refused. When Pritchard presented him with a ten dollar gold piece, however, the box containing the gun, lead balls, and powder suddenly appeared in his hands, readily handed over.

That same day a street peddler saw Andrew leave Lucy's with two men. For ten of Pritchard's twenty dollars he relayed that information to Greef. For the remaining ten he told him, "I hears a rumor dey be hole up in St. Joseph's." Greef conveyed the news to the group that night.

"They're in St. Joseph's Church, not far from here. We can get our weapons and be there in less than an hour."

Pritchard stroked his conical beard and looked at Greef. "I'm not sure that's a good idea. We can't just barge into a large church on Christmas Eve."

Greef remained adamant. "Damn it! We should grab em right now!"

Walther intervened. "Gentlemen, let's develop a reasonable plan. It would be foolish to conduct a search of St. Joseph's without the help of local authorities. And, they are not about to invade a church tonight or on Christmas Day."

"I agree," said Pritchard. Blackstone nodded.

"It's settled, then. I will enlist the help of the police the day after Christmas. The colonel can go with me and identify his runaways. Jack and Mr. Alvarez can cover the streets behind the church if they try to escape."

They all agreed, except for Greef. He sat and shook his head in disbelief. Pritchard ignored Greef's solemnity and ordered brandy for everyone. He retrieved a box from beneath the table and presented it to Blackstone. "Merry Christmas, Jack."

Blackstone opened the lid to the box and smiled. His revolver, lead balls and powder were inside. "Thanks, Colonel, you know I'll put this to good use."

Walther rose from his chair. "Gentlemen, I promised Louise I would be home for Christmas Eve, so I will take my leave. I propose we raise our glasses and vow to retrieve our property. A year from now I hope you will all join me, my new baby, and Louise for a real Christmas celebration."

Three of the four hoisted their glasses; Greef scowled and sat with his arms tightly crossed.

37

WALTHER WAS UP AT DAWN the day after Christmas and headed toward the Planter's Hotel. Andrew sat sipping coffee across the street, monitoring the group's activities. He saw Walther enter, and a few minutes later Greef and Blackstone arrived. He was certain they had gathered because they had discovered where Will and Tom were hiding. He gave a coin to a young man and told him to rouse McGee.

Andrew walked briskly down First Street, then to Sixth and on to St. Joseph's. He warned Father Hoffmann that the authorities were on their way, probably within the hour. The priest hustled his students out the back way and on home. Then he hastily rearranged the classroom so it appeared set up for social gatherings.

With a pained expression, Father Hoffmann said to Will and Tom, "Gentlemen, please come with me."

He led them down a long hallway and pointed to a narrow stairwell. "Lots of steps, it's a long way." When they reached the top of the steeple the priest opened a small trap door that led to a wooden platform; two large wheels and a bell were anchored in the middle. Father Hoffmann took a moment to catch his breath and said, "Hopefully you will only be here a short time. Don't look over the wall to see what's going on, if you're spotted Father Thomas and I will be in terrible trouble."

Will and Tom sat cross-legged, staring at the bell in front of them. They waited, breathlessly, while horse's hooves clacked, voices murmured, and a large wagon rumbled as it pulled up to the front of the church. They heard a stern voice barking out orders.

"You three go around back, the rest of you come with me."

A loud knock sounded at the door. Four or five police entered, and muffled shouts came from inside the sanctuary. Ten minutes passed as men talked below the steeple.

"They're not here. Next time you ask for our assistance make sure you get your facts right. Sorry, Father Hoffmann, to have caused you and Father Thomas this aggravation."

The two fugitives heard the wagon pull away, but one man remained. He drawled a bitter "Sons-of-bitches." They recognized it as Pritchard's voice. Thankfully they heard him mount up and ride away a moment later. Will and Tom heaved a deep sigh of relief.

When everyone reconvened, Father Hoffmann said, "Close call men. A well-dressed man insisted there were two runaways inside the church. Police asked how to get to the top of the steeple, but I told them it was sealed off and we rang the bell with a pulley from the first floor." Father Thomas made the sign of the cross; Father Hoffmann shook his head and gave Thomas a weary smile.

Four angry and frustrated men gathered in the bar at the Planter's Hotel. Greef was admonishing the others.

"Goddamn it, I'm the professional here, you should have listened."

Agitated, Walther replied, "If they were at the church, they can't be far away."

"What do we do now?" asked the colonel.

Greef responded quickly. "I think they might still be at that church, or close by. But they're gonna run. I want Blackstone to keep an eye on the church, and I'll watch the levee. You and Pritchard get some money together in case we need a boat."

"You mean a steamboat?" Pritchard asked.

Greef looked at him and in a firm voice said, "Yeah, a snag boat captain is helping them. They got here on his boat and that's likely the way their gonna try to get away."

Four men and two women, linked together by iron anklets and chains, trudged down Chestnut Street toward the river. The Missy T's first officer led them along the levee and eventually to the deck of the snag boat. They gawked at the sight of the large crane and heavy equipment; frightened and bewildered they huddled, and began to hug one another.

McGee tried to reassure them. "Follow me, we'll get those chains off and get you something to eat." Once the chains were removed the group was hustled up the stairs to a large cabin in the forecastle.

"There's six of em hiding up there," Richard said apprehensively to McGee. "If Andrew brings the other two we'll have more slaves than crew. Are you sure about this?"

"No one gets into trouble without his own help. Andrew should be here soon, after that we'll get underway. In a few days we'll know if we have promised more than we can deliver."

38

FATHER THOMAS GREETED ANDREW AND quickly led him to the back room. Will and Tom were sitting on the edges of their beds, looking extremely worried.

Andrew called out, "Get your stuff. We're leaving."

Will and Tom collected their belongings and said goodbye to Father Thomas and Father Hoffmann. They left through the small door that led them to the steeple earlier that day. They ran to a side street and down an alley. Just then an imposing figure emerged from a dark stairwell. Will instantly recognized the broad shoulders and wide brimmed hat. "It's him! It's Blackstone!"

Andrew gestured toward the alley and told them to keep moving toward the river. Blackstone yelled for them to stop. He pulled his pistol. Andrew spotted the white handle. Blackstone took aim and cried out, "Tell them to come back or you're dead!"

A flash of white light exploded with a loud crack. Blackstone rolled on the ground in agony. The blast had removed two fingers and burned his hand; the right side of his face was badly singed. Like a wounded bull, he stumbled into a nearby wall and struggled to stand. He cursed and screamed. People on the street gathered and peered down the alley to see what was causing the fracas.

The instant the gun exploded, Andrew felt a sharp pain above his right knee. Blood now seeped through his dungarees. He located a bandana in one of his pockets, wound it around his thigh, and pulled it tight.

Will and Tom had heard the commotion and had doubled back. In the middle of the alley, they discovered Andrew hunched over, laboring to take steps.

They had to act quickly. They each took an arm and moved Andrew carefully along the back streets with them toward the boat. By the time they reached the Missy T, Andrew could no longer walk. McGee saw Will and Tom carry him aboard and sprinted down the stairs to the main deck. They laid him gently on the mess table. McGee cut the cloth sticking to Andrew's skin and pressed his fingers gently around the wound.

"We need to find a doctor."

"No time," said Andrew. He was resting on his elbows and looking at his leg. "They're gonna be coming. Blackstone's hurt but he survived. Gun blew up just like Abe said it would. Wish you coulda seen that damn thing explode."

"Yeah, but the ball from that damn thing is in your leg. Richard, see if you can find a doctor on any of the boats near us. If there is, bring him. Will, you and Tom keep a look out for Greef. Use my spyglass."

The sun was starting to set as Tom scanned the levee from the top deck. Will pointed to a crowd gathered fifty yards away. "See what's going on over there by those street lanterns."

Tom focused the telescope on a portly man entertaining the crowd; he played a squeezebox while a small dog wearing a nautical cap did a variety of tricks. The scene fascinated Tom, and he momentarily forgot to keep watch.

Will tapped him on the shoulder. "Look to the left of the big guy and his dog."

Tom trained the spyglass on a tall thin figure surveying the line of boats. "Oh, God! It be him!" Tom said in a panic.

"Stay here, don't let him out of your sight. I'm gonna tell McGee." Will scrambled down the steps. "Captain, he's here! He's on the levee and coming this way."

Just as Will delivered the news Richard escorted a ruddy-faced man across the bridge. "Captain, this man's a doctor."

"Thank you for coming. I'm Captain McGee. I'm hoping you can help a member of my crew. He caught a gambler using a marked deck and there was a scuffle. My man was shot."

The doctor looked skeptical, but said, "Let me have a look. By the way captain my name is Reed, Michael Reed." The doctor called for more light, water, and towels. He moved his fingers quickly around the wound. "The ball is in there." He looked at McGee in a detached professional manner and said, "It has to come out."

Reed asked whether the captain kept whiskey on board. McGee signaled to Ben, and he brought a jug to the table. "Give him as much of that as he can stand." Ben poured the liquid into a tin cup and handed it to Andrew.

Greef crept along the line of boats, scrutinizing each one and asking questions along the way. McGee called Zachary and pointed to shore where Greef was about fifty yards away and talking to an officer. "Rabid dogs don't always travel on four feet, Zach. That one is going to sniff us out in short order. Get a little heat going in those boilers."

McGee went back to the table where Reed was working. "Doctor, we are going to pull away from shore and head up river. Please continue your work, I will compensate you for this inconvenience."

The doctor seemed perplexed. "It sounds like a kidnapping to me!"

"Please don't be alarmed. I'm trying to avoid any other confrontations. I'll make sure you are safe."

Reed gave a dubious nod and went back to work. He took scissors from his bag and removed the remainder of the pant leg. There was a jolt as the paddlewheels turned and the boat moved forward. "I need a warning if you are going to make moves like that Captain. What the hell is this contraption anyway?"

"It's a snag boat, doctor. I'll make sure there are no more sudden moves."

Reed called for more light. Will and Tom each held a lantern above Andrew's leg. The doctor retrieved a pointed tool from his bag. "You two hold him. Put something in his mouth to bite down on." Richard removed his leather belt. "Hang on to him gentlemen."

Reed inserted his finger into the wound, searching for a pathway to the bullet. Andrew bit down hard on the leather strap, breathing heavily.

"I found it," said Reed. With a finger deep in the wound he guided the point of his pliers toward the piece of lead. Andrew's face was bright red; tears streamed down his cheeks. It seemed a very long two minutes of agony before Reed dropped the ball into a tin cup.

Just as Reed fiished, Greef spotted the Missy T moving slowly up river. He immediately recognized the two black men holding the lanterns. "Bastards are gettin' away!" he grumbled. He hailed a buggy. "Planter's hotel. As fast as you can."

Reed wiped the blood from his instruments and placed them carefully in his bag. He turned to the captain and said, "I'll stitch him up, and you can take me back to my boat."

McGee looked to shore and saw a large sternwheeler. "We'll tie up alongside the riverboat Jefferson, doctor. Richard will go with you and make sure you get a carriage." He handed Reed a twenty dollar gold piece.

The doctor nodded his approval and said, "Your brother won't be able to do much for awhile; keep him off that leg, change the bandages, and make sure you have plenty of whiskey on board."

At City Hospital Walther and Pritchard stood inside a small room looking at Blackstone. His hand was heavily wrapped and gauze bandages covered the right side of his face.

"You're lucky to be alive," said Walther, "but I'm afraid that right hand's not going to be of much use. What the hell happened?"

"The goddamn gun exploded!" Blackstone informed them angrily through the gauze.

Pritchard shook his head and mumbled, "Somebody must'a messed with it." Blackstone pulled the gauze away from his mouth. "Who could'a messed with it?"

Pritchard threw up his hands up. "How the hell should I know? This city is filled with abolitionists, immigrants, and crazy people."

Blackstone swung his feet to the side of the bed and stood up. He pulled away what remained of the bandages. Pritchard and Walther were shocked when they saw Blackstone's peeling flesh and misshapen eye. Half of his burned mouth didn't move when he said, "Did Greef catch 'em?"

Walther said, "No, but he knows they're aboard that snag boat and headed up river. Now lie back down before you fall down. We'll be back for you in a few days."

Pritchard grabbed his hat and started for the door. He looked back to Blackstone and said, "Greef got us a boat. We're going after them."

Blackstone wobbled toward the end of the bed. "I'm comin with ya!"

Pritchard and Walther knew they couldn't stop him.

On the levee, Greef lounged beside a collection of signboards smoking a cheroot. He flicked the remains of the cigar toward the ground when the three approached.

"Hear you had a bad accident," he said to Blackstone. He looked at the heavily bandaged hand and facial burns. "Jesus, you look like shit. Ya gonna be able to do anything?"

"I can snap your neck with my left hand, the same one I'll use to fire a gun that works."

Greef shot Blackstone a sinister smile, "Save it Jack. I'll point out the necks to snap and people to shoot." He gestured toward a sternwheeler about fifty yards away. There's our boat, the Dahlia."

The Dahlia was an excursion packet that took people on tours and delivered light cargo, but seldom made runs over two hundred miles. During the cold winter months not many people wanted to look at a brown landscape, so when Pritchard offered two hundred dollars to track down a slow moving snag boat, the Dahlia's captain, Pierre LaFarge, was eager to oblige.

He hastily assembled a crew and confidently predicted, "We'll be alongside that snagger in two hours or less."

Greef spit on the ground and said, "We'll see."

Greef, Pritchard, and Blackstone positioned themselves on the bow and looked to shore as the Dahlia eased away from the dock. Walther watched the packet move backward into the darkness and yelled, "Good Luck! If you have to kill them make sure they tell you where the girl is first."

39

ABOARD THE ADELE, TEENY LOOKED dowdy in the "old lady" clothes Bessie gave her. She dined alone at a small table and waited for Captain Strickland, who was currently enjoying himself telling stories, proposing toasts, and entertaining first class passengers. Half an hour later he joined Teeny and told her about the abolitionist family she would be meeting. She listened intently, and looked around to see whether anyone could hear. "Captain, do you believe I should continue on to Canada?"

"I don't believe it's necessary. Once you're off the river and further inland, slave hunters won't be able to track you. You might consider Canada, but places like Chatham and Buxton have their problems and not much social life."

"What do you mean, not much social life?"

"By the way you were dressed when you came aboard I can't imagine you living on a farm, or in a small village. Something tells me you belong in a city, a big city, Detroit, maybe Chicago. St. Paul may be a big city some day, but right now it's a cow town. My advice would be for you to have your baby, then move east. Use your last few days on board my boat to make plans."

"I should have plenty of time to do that. This disguise makes people shy away. I've been left alone the entire trip."

An officer signaled that the captain was needed on deck; Strickland rose to leave. He smiled and said, "I'm sure your being left alone is only temporary, Miss Douglas."

The boat was taking on wood when Teeny ventured below. She stood at the bow and watched loud commotion on a nearby dock. One of the Adele's roustabouts was being harassed by a group of white men. A female passenger next to her said, "The Nigger smiled at that white woman over there, and now he's in real trouble."

132

Teeny thought a member of the crew would step in, but no one seemed to be paying attention. A few minues later the first mate came to escort Teeny and the other woman back to their stateroom. "Ladies, I suggest you come with me, this situation could become ugly."

Teeny refused to leave. "Why are they doing this? He hasn't done anything! Please get Captain Strickland!"

The officer nodded and said, "Yes, ma'am, but first allow me to escort you to your cabin."

Teeny grew louder and more insistent. "Please, get Captain Strickland!"

In the short time it took for Teeny to have that conversation, the roustabout was tied to a post. A large man with a bushy red beard began lashing him with a bullwhip. Before Strickland made it to the main deck, the wooder's back bore five deep cuts and chunks of flesh dangled from the wounds.

"Stop!" yelled Strickland. The striker pilot and first officer accompanied him; all carried rifles. The bearded man turned to look and took a few steps back. Men that had gathered to watch now retreated into alleys and nearby buildings. "He's part of my crew, now stand back!"

"Hell, no! He was oglin' a white woman! Nobody puts up with that round here!"

"Back away or I'll shoot your sorry ass."

"You Nigger lovin' son of a bitch! Jus caus' you wear that fancy uniform don't make you better'n me or give ya that right to tell me what to do!"

McGree refused to back down. "The uniform's got nothing to do with it. Now get the hell out of here!"

The bearded man hooked his whip to his belt, and then spat on the wooder's bleeding back. He made an obscene gesture to the captain and sauntered away.

Strickland approached Teeny on the Promenade deck a short time later. He was about to speak when she turned abruptly. "I thought Iowa was a free state; how could something like that happen here?"

The captain shook his head and sounded discouraged. "There are slave hunters and pro-slavery people everywhere. Half the time ya never know whether the stranger next to you is friend or foe."

"Well, Captain, you told me to use this time to make plans. Seeing what just happened made me realize you are right. Some day my past could be revealed, and my fate could be similar."

Strickland shook his head. "No, patrollers would never beat a beautiful woman like you."

Teeny looked him in the eye. "They would, and they would do other unspeakable things."

Strickland looked away, embarrassed by Teeny's retort to his naïve statement. Before departing he said, "We will dock in five days; after that I can no longer be of help."

"I know, Captain." She nodded. "And thank you for everything."

"By the way, Miss Douglas, it's a very good disguise. I'm sorry you have to wear it."

Teeny rapped her cane against the wooden leg brace. "If you don't mind, I would like to keep it."

"It's my parting gift. Good luck in your new life, wherever you and your baby decide to settle."

40

TWO HOURS AFTER LEAVING ST. LOUIS, the snag boat reached the confluence of the Missouri and Mississippi Rivers. Will and Tom seemed transfixed by the wide expanse of water.

Richard joined them and said, "We're goin' on the most contrary river imaginable. She's as deceitful as a two-bit whore. Traveling at night on this water is just plain crazy."

"Cap'n McGee be da best, ain't he?" asked Tom.

Richard pointed to the swirling water and somberly replied, "The Missouri is dangerous, even for the best."

McGee paused on the top deck, focusing his spyglass on a faint light from another boat. He hoped it would stay on a northern course, but the light moved west. McGee called Richard to the pilothouse. "There's a boat coming up behind us. Seems like no day goes by without trouble of some kind. Hold her steady, Richard, I'll be back shortly."

"What's the current pressure?"

"65 pounds to the inch Captain."

"Take her to 75," commanded McGee.

McGee then sought out Ben and Sam, who were on the second deck, trying to calm the six new slaves. The slaves realized they were being smuggled out of the city; but the ship's noisy engines frightened them, none could swim, and they had no idea where they were going. Eyes widened as McGee stuck his head inside the cabin.

"Ben, Sam, we've got a problem. I need you below," he announced.

The wooders followed the captain to the table where Andrew was lying. "Take Andrew to my cabin. After that, start stacking wood three or four feet high around the boilers and the pilothouse."

Andrew was barely conscious when they placed him on the bed. In a hoarse voice he asked Sam to send Will and Tom up.

A few minutes later they entered; a pale and weary Andrew gestured for them to come closer.

"Listen to me. The satchel in your cabin has two money belts. Keep those belts on you at all times. The papers saying you're free men are in there, too, along with the money. Only a lawyer or judge will know they're forged."

The conversation seemed to exhaust him; within minutes he slipped into a comatose sleep.

Will and Tom found the brown satchel lying on the floor. Will uncoiled two money belts and separated the leather folds. Tom looked over his shoulder and shook his head in amazement. "Whooee! Did ya eva think we have dis much money Will?"

"No, and Andrew's right, someone would kill us in a minute if they knew we had it. We're going to have to wear these belts all the time."

Tom laughed, "My old belt be a rope. Dis one be lots bedder."

Zachary was keeping watch on the pressure gauges and paying little attention to the wood barricade being built around him. He tapped his finger on the gauges and spoke into a small tube. "75 to the inch, Captain." A small bell tinkled above Zachary indicating McGee heard the message.

The snag boat cut through the water much faster now, but the boat behind was still gaining. Will and Tom helped Ben stack wood in layers around the boilers.

"We gettin ready for da game ta be'gin," said Ben.

Will and Tom looked to him for an explanation. "Boat be on our tail. We can't outrun it, so we gonna play hide an seek."

Just then McGee appeared on the deck and yelled, "Ben, get a reading!"

Ben pulled out a multicolored rope with a lead weight on it. He dropped it in the river. Seconds later he retrieved it and checked the marks on the line. "Mark One, Cap'an."

"Let me know when we're at four and a half."

McGee pulled twice on the bell pulley signaling Zachary to cut the pressure and move to half speed. The Captain looked to an inlet fifty yards ahead and steered toward it. Ben tossed the weighted line in the water a second time. "Qua'ter Less, Cap'an."

McGee hit the bell pulley one more time. Zachary cut the pressure. The boat slowed and veered from the main channel into a narrow inlet. McGee ordered all candles and lanterns extinguished. Sam waded through the muck and wrapped the cordelle around a large elm. They cleated the vessel and brought her to a halt.

Every few minutes the wooders stoked the Dahlia's boilers, causing flashes of bright light to pierce the darkness. McGee trained his spyglass on the riverboat as it passed; it was some type of excursion packet decked out with lots of gingerbread to impress the passengers.

Zachary spoke into the tube leading to the pilothouse. "Captain, they're poking a ton into her. She can't run at that speed for long without burning up all their wood."

McGee strode onto to the main deck and informed Richard, "We're going to remain here for the night, then go ashore in the morning for wood. Tell everyone to keep the boat dark—no candles, lanterns, matches, anything…

Ben woke first. He looked up and down river but saw only tree limbs and swirling water. There was no sign of the Dahlia. He tossed a few logs into the stove to heat water for coffee. Once everyone roused, McGee gave the order, "All hands are going ashore, I want as much dry wood as you can find. We're going to make a run for Jefferson City during the night."

Two young black girls stood on the second deck listening to the captain below. The younger of the two began to fidget.

"I gots to pee," she said to her friend.

The older girl took her hand and led her down the narrow walkway to the small room above the paddlewheel. "Go on. I waits fer ya here. Den you keep a look out while I goes."

While waiting for her friend, the older girl watched the crew gather saws, axes and ropes. Tom looked up at her and smiled. She smiled back. Tom tugged on Will's sleeve. "Dat be a preddy young lady up dere. Suppose we gonna meet dem folks soon?"

Will grinned and said, "Her name is Rosie."

Tom looked surprised. "How you know dat?"

"She told me."

Tom looked at his friend wide-eyed. "You lie."

Will chuckled and said, "Yeah, Ben told me, and her friend's name is Darla."

Tom grinned sheepishly. "I wants to meet Rosie."

 **41**

CAPTAIN LAFARGE DOCKED THE Dahlia at St. Charles and tried to explain how the snag boat eluded them,

"They tied up in the shallows and let us pass. They didn't turn back and go to St. Louis. It's too risky, there's too big a bounty on them slaves."

Pritchard's frustration showed. "What if they have, and what if we've lost em?"

"Then you've had a free boat ride," replied LaFarge. "But I'm willing to bet they're gonna make a run for Jeff City during the night. If they do, we'll catch 'em before they reach Boonville."

Blackstone glanced toward Pritchard. Then they both looked at Greef, who questioned LaFarge. "How are you gonna catch 'em if they're traveling and we're sitting?"

"We'll get our wood supply and leave at dawn. This crew ain't qualified to travel the Missouri at night—too many sandbars, shallows, and snags. We'll catch 'em by tomorrow evening."

Greef glared menacingly at LaFarge. "You'd better be right this time."

Doggedly the snag boat plowed through the fast-moving current, dodging ridges of sand and submerged trees. It was midnight when Will went to check on Andrew. He eased into the cabin and peered through the dim candlelight. Andrew stirred. "Whatcha want?"

"Want to know if I can get ya anything."

"Whiskey. How's the new group doing?"

"We only met the two girls, Rosie and Darla. Tried to talk to the men, but they didn't say much. They're scared." Then he smiled, "Tom's love-struck."

"With Rosie?"

Will laughed. "Yeah, how'd you know?"

"Thought so. She's a good-looking gal. Did ya find the bourbon?"

Will brought Andrew the bottle. He heard the order for a dark boat and pinched the wick of the candle.

Two chimes from the key-wound clock signaled the time; moonlight was gone and fog enveloped the river. The snag boat slipped silently past St. Charles and by dawn had a six-hour lead on the Dahlia.

An hour before sunset McGee's boat approached the inlet of the Osage River, ten miles from Jefferson City. It was the last day in December, and the weather was unseasonably warm. McGee tried to get a read on the clouds and changing wind direction, which seemed to indicate a looming storm. He gave the order to tie up for the night. Richard volunteered to take the first watch. He sat on a tall stool in the pilothouse, nursing his bourbon and watching for the Dahlia.

The temperature dropped rapidly. A fierce rain pelted the boat. Rain turned to hail, and bursts of lightning shot through the thick rolling clouds. In the midst of the ghostly lightning flashes, Richard spotted the Dahlia. Strong winds pushed on her elevated superstructure, and the boat's flat bottom prevented LaFarge from maintaining a straight course. Richard rang the bell in the captain's cabin. McGee threw on a Mackinaw and joined Richard. "The Dahlia's fightin it, Captain. I doubt they're gonna make it to Jeff City."

By morning the storm passed, leaving the river finally calm. The snag boat took on wood and glided away from the inlet. An hour after leaving the Osage Landing, McGee spotted the Dahlia mired on a sand bar. He proceeded past at a safe distance and grinned. "We should be halfway to Kansas Village by the time they're off that ridge." He pulled the cord above his head. A sharp piercing whistle echoed through the river valley.

Aboard the Dahlia, LaFarge was furious. He knew the snag boat's loud whistle was sending a shameful comment about his piloting skills. He pulled a rifle from the wall and fired at the Missy T. The lead balls fell short, adding another insult to his damaged pride.

Pritchard and Blackstone watched the other vessel disappear around a bend. "Sons a bitches!" drawled Pritchard.

Greef walked to the bow where LaFarge barked orders to his crew.

"What's the plan to get this damned thing moving?"

LaFarge turned and faced the half-breed slave hunter. "We'll be off this sooner than you think. We're not that far from the water. That capstan up front is gonna pull, and we're gonna use the paddlewheel to push."

A risky maneuver for sure, but LaFarge remained determined to get the boat back in the water as quickly as possible. A roustabout took the yawl to shore and wrapped a heavy chain around a large oak. Crewmembers secured the other end to the capstan and inserted wooden staves into the large metal cylinder. When the boilers hit a pressure the engineer felt sufficient, the bell rang in the pilothouse. "Let's go men," said LaFarge, "Start reeling her in."

The crew strained to turn the capstan; the chain tightened. Paddles of the sternwheeler pushed against the sandy surface. The Dahlia groaned when the wood wheel lifted the stern a few inches above the sand bar. The boat lurched forward and moved closer to deep water.

"I'll be damned," Pritchard remaked, as he watched in amazement. The Dahlia's crew seemed just as surprised this maneuver was working. LaFarge was ecstatic—the paddlewheel remained intact and within minutes the Dahlia was floating.

"Fire up them goddamn boilers and prepare to get underway!" He ordered.

Then LaFarge yelled to Pritchard and Blackstone, "Those bastards are gonna be surprised to see us so soon!"

He spun around and sprinted back to the pilothouse to find Greef waiting for him. The slave hunter made a show of checking the chambers of his revolver and simultaneously pointing it at LaFarge. "We're gonna catch 'em this time, ain't we, Captain?" he said menacingly.

"There's no need for threats. I'll make sure you have them in your sights before dark."

Greef turned the revolver backward and placed it in his holster. "You damned well better be right."

LaFarge's hands shook as he turned the large wheel and steered his boat to the main channel.

By late afternoon the Dahlia had the Missy T in view, and Pritchard, Blackstone, and Greef began checking their firearms.

McGee guided his boat toward the shallows and tried to create more distance between the two boats.

LaFarge issued orders to raise the steam pressure. The engineer yelled to the Captain, "Pressure is 78 pounds to the inch." The boilers limit was 85.

"Take her to 83!" Lafarge responded.

The Dahlia continued to close the gap, and within the hour she steamed forward from fewer than a hundred yards away.

McGee called Richard to the pilothouse. "Richard, we're going to the narrowest part of the channel. I'm going to take a chance. I'm going to ram them!"

The first officer couldn't believe his ears. "Captain, are you sure?"

McGee nodded. "I'm afraid it's our only hope. Tell everyone to take cover behind stacks of wood and other sturdy objects."

McGee went to his engineer and explained what he wanted. Bullets from the Dahlia now pelted the stern of the snag boat. When McGee signalled Zachary, the paddlewheel on the port side stopped, while the wheel on the starboard side continued to turn. The Missy T suddenly faced the oncoming Dahlia.

"Goddamn it!" shouted LaFarge. He knew the oak and steel hulls of the snag boat could destroy his boat. LaFarge wasn't sure there was enough deep water to get his boat past. He was red faced and bellowing orders. "Tell everyone to fan out. We got to distribute the weight. Mr. Herschel, what's the pressure?"

"83, Captain."

"Take her to 85 and fill the fireboxes. I want as much steam as you can muster. Throw rosin in the box and lock down the safety valve. We're gonna get through these shallows even if we have to take the goddamn river bottom with us." The Dahlia steamed at top speed past the Missy T.

McGee and Richard watched this scene unfolding from the pilothouse. "What she doin' now Captain?"

"She's gonna try to get past us and move to deeper waters. We'll keep the bow facing her when they start shooting."

Louie Herschel, the engineer aboard the Dahlia, noticed a seam leaking in one of the boilers and shouted into the tube. LaFarge ignored the warning and yelled, "Boil the hell outa that water." Blackstone, Pritchard, and Greef busily loaded their weapons.

The Dahlia's paddlewheel continued to rotate as the hull dragged along the muddy bottom. Seconds later she made it to deep water. LaFarge sported a huge grin as he pulled the wheel and piloted the boat to the widest part of the channel.

Now only thirty yards away, everybody aboard the Dahlia was firing weapons. Lead balls splintered the starboard side of the snag boat. Pritchard and Blackstone took aim at the pilothouse.

Without warning there was a sudden flash of light and a deafening roar. Portions of the Dahlia's hull disintegrated. A large section of the hurricane deck hurled skyward. Bodies tumbled out of the air. A grey and white plume of steam rose from the iron boilers as the boat sank into the river.

"My, God!" McGee cried out as the Missy T's passengers and crew observed the horrific scene. The snag boat slowed as it approached the debris. The remains of the Dahlia were being pulled apart by the strong current. A large black hat floated past, followed by Blackstone's outstretched body. Pritchard's corpse bobbed up and down before rotating slowly and then disappearing into the murky brown water.

The Missy T's crew and passengers gathered on the starboard side to look for signs of life. They were unaware that one person aboard the Dahlia had jumped the minute he heard the explosion. The survivor swam silently to the port side of the snag boat, grabbed a rope, and pulled himself up. McGee and the others were distracted, still searching the water, when the intruder slipped into the small cargo hold. By the time the Missy T's crew resumed their work, the watery footprints had dried, and no one was aware Greef was aboard.

42

MCGEE DOCKED AT A WOOD yard near Boonville to provide a safe berth for the night. Twelve chimes from the captain's clock signaled the end of a harrowing day. The boat fell quiet. Will managed to drift into sleep, but Tom kept reliving the explosion and the carnage he had witnessed. He walked to the panel, slid it open a crack, and looked at the cabin where Rosie was staying. He went back to his bunk and lay there, unable to sleep.

In the cramped cargo hold, Greef began a last minute check of his weapons. The knife and whip, he secured to his belt. A small derringer inside an oilskin bag lay secreted inside his jacket. He removed the gun carefully and made sure no moisture had seeped in. Greef crawled along the inner deck on his hands and knees. He slid the hatch aside. With uncanny silence, he moved from the small opening to the wood stacked in front of the firebox. Sensing no movement and hearing no sounds, Greef approached the stairs above the paddlewheel.

His plan was simple; kill McGee, then force the crew to take the snag boat back to St. Louis. The reward for returning Will, Tom, and a government boat being used to transport escaped slaves would be generous.

He entered McGee's cabin and saw the outline of a body. Removing the whip from his belt he crept toward the bed, paused, and in a matter of seconds slipped a coil of leather around his victim's neck. The struggle ended quickly. Greef uncoiled his whip and looked down at the body. He struck a match and saw the distorted face and bandaged leg.

Greef cursed silently and crossed the room. He opened the cabin door a few inches; a lantern flickered outside the pilothouse. He went to the next set of stairs and started to climb.

Tom was lying in his bunk, looking up at Rosie's cabin through the narrow opening. Will was fast asleep, snoring softly. Tom thought he saw movement. He blinked, rubbed his eyes, and went to cabin door. Someone was climbing through the darkness up to the pilothouse. He slipped on his jacket.

Greef was standing outside the pilothouse, peering through the window. McGee was asleep on a cot in front of his desk. Greef removed the small two-bullet pistol and pushed the door open. It bumped the end of the make-shift bed. McGee awoke with a start. "What the?" He instantly recognized the intruder's face. Greef placed the barrel of the derringer on McGee's forehead. With an evil grin he said, "Goodbye, you slave stealing son of a bitch!"

Before he could pull the trigger, a glint of sharp metal passed swiftly by the lantern on the wheelhouse entry and buried itself deep in Greef's neck. The slave hunter didn't move for a few seconds, then staggered and fell against the door. Blood began to form around the corners of his mouth. He slid down the doorframe twitching, struggling to remove the knife lodged below his ear. McGee grabbed the small pistol from Greef's hand. Seconds later the convulsing stopped.

Tom was trembling as he looked at the blood pooling by the pilothouse entry. McGee walked over. Looking grateful and bewildered, he placed his hand on Tom's shoulder. Suddenly he called out, "Andrew!"

McGee ran to the cabin below and held a lantern over his brother's life-less body. Richard stood in the doorway behind him, trying to piece together what had just happened. He went back to the top deck and found Tom sitting cross-legged, nervously rubbing his hands together. Richard helped Tom to his feet. McGee looked at the trembling slave and said, "Richard, take him down and give him a shot of whiskey, and wake the crew."

The crew was groggy, but came alert when they saw the captain. He looked pale and haggard. "Men, we had a stowaway on board. It was that goddamn slave hunter. Somehow he survived the explosion and hid on board. I'm sure he thought if he killed me he could take command of the boat. He killed Andrew, then came looking for me."

The crew shook their heads, moaned, and cursed.

"Tom, over there, killed him. He saved my life."

They looked at Tom in an appreciative manner, but he was too upset to notice. Slaves on the second deck watched and listened, trying to compre-hend what had just happened.

McGee gave a few last minute instructions. "Ben, Sam, get Greef's body away from the pilothouse. Take it to the stern. I'll dispose of him when we get underway. Richard, assist Zachary in making a coffin for Andrew. The rest of you, try to get some rest. We'll leave for Kansas Village tomorrow."

None of the crew or slaves got much sleep. By dawn everyone was awake and talking about the previous day, still trying to figure out how the slave hunter boarded and went unnoticed. They began preparing the boat for departure and Andrew for burial.

Richard told Will and Tom to help him retrieve Andrew's body. When they pulled back the sheet, Andrew's eyes were still open and a grotesque expression of shock remained. Will and Tom winced as Richard pushed the dead man's eyelids down and reshaped his face. They wrapped a sheet around him, gently placed his body in the wooden box, and carried him to shore.

McGee stood next to a barren opening in the ground. He looked down at the pine box and mustered a few last words. "My brother Andrew did right by most people. His family consisted mostly of friends he made and people he helped along the way. If there is a higher ground, Andrew is making his way there now. If you were his friend, or one of the people he helped, please thank him, and say goodbye."

McGee gave the order to untie the lines and steered the Missy T toward the main channel. He told Richard to take over, left the pilothouse, and walked slowly to the stern. Greef's body lay wrapped in a tattered blanket on the edge of the deck. McGee stared at the rigid bundle. He unceremoniously shoved the body overboard with his foot, turned his back, and walked away. The blanket unfurled, Greef's face was visible for a few seconds before the current sucked him under.

43

IT WAS THE FIRST WEEK of the New Year when the Adele steamed into St. Paul. Strickland was making the rounds and saying good-bye to first class passengers. He spotted Teeny on the hurricane deck looking toward shore. "Good Morning, Miss Douglas."

"Good morning, Captain. Captain, what is that area on the bluff with all the tents?"

Strickland looked to where Teeny was pointing. "It's a Sioux Indian village. There are lots of them around here. The cabin in the middle belongs to a missionary priest who's trying to teach them to read and write."

"So it's legal to teach Indians to read and write?"

Strickland nodded. "Yes, it's also legal for them to own slaves. I hear tell they're every bit as mean to their slaves as the whites, maybe even meaner."

Teeny shook her head. "Sometimes I feel like a stranger in this country, so many things don't make sense."

A low rumbling sound emerged from the steam whistle to announce the boat's arrival. Teeny walked with her cane to the steps, slowly lowered one foot, rested, then lowered her foot again. She reenacted this charade several times until she reached the main deck. Passengers stood aside to let the elderly woman with the gimpy leg make her way to the bow. Strickland took her arm and escorted her toward shore. A patroller standing at the landing showed no interest in the elderly woman.

"Very convincing, Miss Douglas. Now look to my left. Do you see the post office three streets over? It has a federal flag above it."

Teeny scanned the rooftops. "Yes, I see it."

"Next to it is a barber shop run by a man named William Taylor. He's well known in the underground. Should you experience difficulties, or need advice, go to him. He can arrange transportation and provide you with contacts in other parts of the country."

Two distinguished looking men approached. The older man extended his hand and said, "Captain Strickland, I am Robert Granemann, and this is my son Charles." Locals referred to Robert as the Grand Granemann because of his aristocratic appearance. His son was a few inches taller and considered every bit as handsome. Both men were surprised to see Captain Strickland escorting a limping elderly woman.

"Robert, Charles, this is Miss Douglas." Both men were gracious as they welcomed Teeny, but found it hard to believe this was the person Bireman described in his letters. Strickland sensed the confusion. "Miss Douglas is wearing a particularly effective disguise—so effective that the patroller ignored us when we passed."

When the carriage pulled to the front of the Granemann's large two-story home, Charles's mother, Helen, came out to greet them. Charles introduced Teeny and picked up her bags. Robert walked with Helen and said, "Wait until you hear how this lady escaped the patrollers."

"We're going to let her rest and get cleaned up first. Frieda, please take Miss Douglas's bags to the guest bedroom."

Frieda took the bags and looked sympathetically at the woman limping through the entryway. Helen led Teeny up the stairs to a sunny yellow bedroom on the second floor. She scurried about explaining where everything was, trying to make Teeny feel welcome.

"Miss Douglas, I'm going to have Frieda heat some water so you can take a bath. You've had quite a journey, so take your time and join us downstairs when you're ready."

"Thank you, Mrs. Granemann. You and your family are very kind to be helping me. "

After everyone was gone Teeny removed the wig, make-up, and leg brace. For the first time in weeks, she took a bath. She removed the encrusted make up, washed and dried her hair, and applied a little powder and rouge. She selected the blue dress and white shawl that she had worn to Bireman's office.

Helen was the first to see her when she came down the stairs.

"Oh my!" Helen said, startled. Then she said, "Come in, join us in to the parlor. My, you certainly look lovely."

Robert and Charles both looked up, speechless.

"Do you think one of you can stop gawking and offer Miss Douglas a comfortable place to sit?" Helen said.

Charles jumped to his feet to escort Teeny to the chair he had occupied.

"I'm sorry, Miss Douglas. I was just so surprised. The disguise you wore when we met was a very good disguise, but...there was no way of knowing."

"He means to say how beautiful you are," Helen added as she signaled for the two servants to meet the new guest.

Gabe and Frieda had been with the Granemann's for several years. Frieda's parents died of cholera during one of many outbreaks that hit poor immigrant families. Gabe was a young slave girl who had planned to go to Canada with her brother before a rogue bounty hunter captured him. Both girls were taken in by the Granemann's and ended up working there permanently.

"I's pleased ta meet ya," said Gabe.

"Likewise," Frieda chimed in.

Frieda was not pleased with Teeny's transformation, nor was she happy with how attentive to the new guest Charles had suddenly become. Frieda was an attractive young woman who believed Charles would eventually realize that she was the person who would make him an ideal companion and wife.

As Gabe and Frieda served dinner, Teeny provided details about her past and her escape from Walther. She explained the telegram that was sent to cities along the Mississippi and the necessity for the disguise. "I believe they will hire someone to track me down. His wife lost two children. She desperately wants to raise my child as her own."

Then Teeny asked where she might find a place to rent.

"Nonsense, you will stay on our property until the child is born," Robert insisted. "We have a small cottage not far from here where you will be safe. Gabe and Frieda can help with the chores as you get further along."

"Are you sure, Mr. Granemann? I can't put your family in danger."

"We have a loyal group of abolitionists working in St. Paul, Miss Douglas. I'm not concerned."

Then Charles spoke up confidently. "You'll be safe, I'll make sure of that."

Frieda, who was serving their coffee, seethed when she heard the enthusiasm and bravado in Charles' voice.

44

TELEGRAMS STARTED ARRIVING IN ST. Louis and Kansas Village. Authorities quickly identified the destroyed boat as the Dahlia. Walther sat at the Planter's hotel bar waiting for additional news. He sent a courier to the *Missouri Republican* to retrieve the latest wires. When the young messenger returned, he found Walther carefully nursing his third bourbon.

"They're all dead, Doctor Walther. There were no survivors." The boy reported.

Walther gave the courier a coin and swallowed his bourbon. He mumbled, "Goddamn it," and ordered another. Pritchard had been a friend for years and now he was dead. All his allies in the hunt for Teeny were dead. He returned home feeling morose.

Once inside the house, Richard hugged his wife and shared the bad news. With a grimace he sat down next to her by the fireplace. The couple contemplated the flickering flames, wondering what to do. Finally, Louise said, "Can't we hire another slave hunter?"

"I don't know. It's hard for anyone to track a slave who looks white. For all we know she's already in Canada."

"Let's not give up," pleaded Louise.

Richard thought for a moment. "Let me see what I can do. I've heard about a detective who is supposedly the finest in the city. I'll talk with him. We'll see whether he thinks we have a chance of finding her." The following day Walther scheduled an interview with Martin Lunt.

Martin Lunt was methodical and planned his moves carefully, even the interview with Richard Walther. It would take ten minutes to travel from his office to the doctor's. He would wear a proper dark suit, white shirt and unpretentious cravat.

He arrived as planned at the scheduled time, but the nurse told him Walther was still making a splint for a broken bone and the meeting would be delayed.

Lunt had anticipated this possibility. He produced a copy of Melville's *White Jacket* from his topcoat and began reading. One his favorite characters in the book, Jack Chase, was a man to whom Lunt could relate. Chase represented the epitome of a good sailor—a professional among incompetents.

A half-hour later Walther invited Lunt into his office. Lunt appeared cool and detached, sitting with his arms folded and legs crossed. He waited for Walther to begin.

"Mr. Lunt, you were recommended by a patient of mine as a detective of rare talent. Are you part of an agency?"

"I have associates, but I usually do the preliminary investigating on my own. Life has taught me the importance of doing things in a precise way, and that usually means doing them myself."

"And what makes you more successful than other detectives?"

Lunt didn't sound like he was boasting when he responded, "I am well organized, pay attention to details, and have an excellent record."

"How would you feel about hunting for an escaped slave, one who is expecting a baby?"

"I am paid for the job," Lunt replied nonchalantly. "My feelings do not enter into it. I assume if she is an escaped slave, she is a fugitive, and in violation of the law. Are you the father of the child?"

"I am, and my wife and I want to raise the child. I think we both should meet with you and provide all the details."

Richard and Louise met Lunt at the Missouri Hotel the next day. Lunt listened, but said little. He assured them Greef's plan to torture the escaped slaves in order to find the girl was simplistic. And, there was no backup plan if they escaped. Lunt lit a cigar. Louise and Richard found it difficult to tell whether he was interested in pursuing the case or not.

"Did anyone interview the striker pilots, or look at the passenger manifests the day she left?" Lunt asked.

Walther looked puzzled. "I have no idea what you're talking about."

"The clues are often in the more obscure details, Doctor. Records kept by clerks and lackeys reveal facts bounty hunters ignore. If you hire me I will begin the search for your slave as soon as I conclude my current investigations. From what you have told me, the child will be born in May. I should have the baby returned to you by the end of July or early August. You will have to decide whether you want the mother returned as well."

Richard and Louise looked at one another. They couldn't believe the matter-of-fact manner in which Lunt said he would find Elizabeth and the baby.

"Can't you begin your investigation sooner?" Louise asked, perplexed and concerned.

"I cannot abandon my other clients, and this case cannot be given to an associate. A bounty hunter may track her down and claim the reward, but I doubt it. She is most likely residing with someone in the underground."

Louise felt confident in Lunt's manner and matter-of-factness. She also believed they had no other options. She stood wringing her hands, and in a pleading manner said to her husband, "Please Richard, we have wanted a child for so long! This may be our last chance!"

Richard nodded in agreement. "Very well Mr. Lunt. We will give you the opportunity to prove yourself."

"A search like this is expensive," Lunt responded. "I will need a two hundred dollar retainer, and when the child is returned, I want all of the reward money, plus a five hundred dollar bonus."

Without hesitating Louise wrote a check for two hundred dollars and asked for a receipt. Lunt produced one from his vest pocket along with a contract that had already been filled in with the financial conditions he stipulated. Lunt picked up his topcoat and prepared to leave. Before he reached the door Louise asked, "Who will take care of the baby during the trip back?"

"I will make arrangements. Is there anything else?"

"Yes," said Richard, "How did you know we would hire you?"

"I made the assumption based on our initial discussion; you told me then how much you and your wife wanted this child. Very nice meeting you Mrs. Walther, I'll keep you apprised of my investigation."

45

TWO DAYS AFTER THE DAHLIA exploded, the snag boat reached Independence, Missouri, one of the busiest of the bourgeoning western towns, and floated peacefully, securely tied to a pier. The riverfront looked like a smaller version of St. Louis, with boxes, barrels, and all types of merchandise piled on shore. McGee and Richard hired a driver to take them inland to the post office. They watched the telegraph operator as he posted the latest news. McGee surveyed the reports until he found the headline he sought:

BOILER EXPLOSION SINKS DAHLIA

He read on,

REMAINS OF AN EXCURSION BOAT, THE
DAHLIA, HAVE BEEN FOUND SCATTERED
ALONG THE RIVERBANKS NEAR
BOONVILLE. EIGHT CREWMEMBERS AND
THREE PASSENGERS ARE MISSING AND
PRESUMED DEAD.

The writer had offered no explanation why the excursion boat had steamed so far up the Missouri River or why it had so few passengers.

On his way out, he scanned the rest of the wall; over fifty handbills offering a reward for escaped slaves filled the space. Richard searched until he found one with information about Will and Tom and stuffed it in his pocket.

Then Richard returned to the snag boat. McGee remained behind, rented a buggy, and guided it down a well-worn trail used by settlers and trappers heading west. Half an hour later, he pulled up to a whitewashed brick farmhouse and knocked on the front door. "Schmiddy, Sis, you in there? It's McGee."

The door opened a crack and a thin muscular man wearing bib overalls and a red wool shirt peered out.

"McGee! Damn it's good to see you!" Schmiddy exclaimed as he threw the door open wide. The men shook hands and made their way over to a round kitchen table.

A voice called up from the fruit cellar. "Who is it, Pa?"

"Come up Marie; you won't believe who's here!"

Marie hurried up the stairs and saw her brother for the first time in two years.

"Allen!" Marie hugged him and looked outside. "Where's Andrew? How come he's not with you?"

McGee glanced down, and in a somber manner replied, "That's what I came to tell ya, Sis; please, have a seat."

Marie knew the news had to be bad. McGee placed a hand on her shoulder and said, "Andrew's dead, sis. He was killed by a slave hunter."

"Oh, no! No!" Marie held her head and cried. McGee sat down next to his sister and put his arm around her.

He told her about events leading up to Andrew's death and said, "The slave hunter was after me. Andrew was weak from the bullet wound and didn't have enough strength to put up a fight. The slave hunter would have killed me if one of the slaves on board hadn't killed him first."

McGee paused and turned to face Schmiddy. "Now I've got eight slaves on my boat. Andrew's gone, and it's up to me to get them to a safe place."

Schmiddy stared at him wide-eyed. "My God, you've got eight runners on your boat? What the hell were you and Andrew thinking? Where were you gonna take em?"

"They were supposed to be dropped off near Kansas Village. Problem is Andrew was the one who knew the conductor and how to contact him. I could send a telegram to St. Louis to get the information, but patrollers will be all over my boat before I get a response."

Schmiddy looked somber. "Kansas Village ain't no good, it's a tinderbox. Fights breakin' out there and in Westport, folks arguing whether Kansas is gonna be slave or free."

McGee appeared discouraged. "Got any suggestions?"

Schmiddy thought for a moment, "Do they have papers?"

"Yeah. And two of them have money to buy supplies. They might make it if they can get further north."

"Can't you take 'em any further north?"

McGee shook his head. "Not this time of year. And if I don't get my boat back on the Mississippi soon, the government will be calling for my license."

Schmiddy paced, rubbing his chin anxiously. "You said they got some money?"

McGee nodded. "Suppose we take some a that money and buy a wagon. I could ferry 'em into Kansas. The Williams family can steer 'em north from there."

"Schmiddy, are you volunteering? And what are you gonna do after ya get 'em into Kansas?"

Schmiddy massaged his forehead with the tips of his fingers. "Can't do much but turn around and come back. I'll leave the wagon. The Niggras are gonna need that an' whatever animals are pullin' it."

McGee regarded his sister and shook his head. "I don't know, Schmiddy; it sounds risky."

"Ya got a better idea?"

McGee was at a loss. Marie paced nervously at the thought of her husband getting involved in transporting escaped slaves. She straightened the tablecloth and in a quavering voice said, "Schmiddy, if ya do this, when ya think ya might leave?"

"Gotta go right away. It's dangerous for them coloreds to just sit around on that boat. Marie, we both know Andrew would have wanted us to help. I'll go with McGee an' find a wagon. Bundle up some clothes, extra blankets, and provisions. I'll gather 'em up on my way out of town."

Marie couldn't believe what was happening. Prior to this moment, she could always count on her husband to act cautiously, and now here he was calmly making plans to haul eight slaves out of the state. She circled her arms around him, bewildered, hoping he knew what he was doing. She looked at McGee. "Ya need to write an' let us know where ya are. Now that Andrew's gone, there ain't hardly none of our family left."

McGee kissed Marie's cheek and promised he would write.

Then Schmiddy and McGee climbed aboard the rented buggy and headed back to Independence. McGee began thinking about his experience after he was caught smuggling slaves. "Ya ever done anything like this before?" He asked his brother-in-law.

"Nope. Just hope by doin' this I ain't makin' Marie a widow."

McGee nodden solemnly.

When they reached the livery, they asked the crusty old stable owner, Luke, about purchasing a covered wagon. He spat a wad of tobacco on the ground and gave the captain a questioning look.

"What ya want it fer? Those things don't float ya know." Luke snorted at his little joke and was still chuckling as he led the two men outside. There were covered wagons of varying size spread out in a field along with holding pens for horses, mules, and oxen.

"Tell me where yer goin' an' I'll tell ya what kind a wagon ya need."

McGee tried to give a plausible answer. "I'm buying it for Schmiddy here. He and my sister are going to visit relatives in Iowa."

"Well ya don't need a heavy duty rig for that. Ya want mules, horses or oxen to pull it?"

"Which is cheaper?" Schmiddy asked.

"Oxen. They're slow but the Indians won't likely steal em—or eat em."

Luke showed them a farm wagon that was smaller than the large Conestogas. Schmiddy walked around and checked the axle, wheels, canvas covering, and brake lever. "These brake blocks are worn down to nothing."

Luke fiddled with the straps on his overalls before responding. "Ya ain't goin in the mountains, so don't worry about it! Oxen don't pull fast enough that ya need good brakes." Luke snorted and chuckled again.

"How much?" asked McGee.

"Well, two oxen, the wagon, grease bucket, double yoke, toolbox, and harness is gonna come to three hundred fifty dollars."

"Three hundred," said McGee.

"Three twenty-five, an' you can take it or leave it."

McGee thought about calling his bluff, but since their mission was urgent, he said, "We'll take it. Can you have it ready before dark?"

"You bring the money; it'll be ready." Luke spat, signifying the deal was finalized.

McGee and Schmiddy returned to the snag boat and called the slaves together. The group huddled behind the boilers. McGee introduced Schmiddy and revealed the plan to take them by wagon into Kansas. There was a long silence and Will finally spoke up. "Captain, when do we leave?"

"Tonight. Gather up whatever belongings you have. When the lanterns on shore go out, we'll get you loaded in the wagon. Take all those blankets in your cabin with you. "

After the group dispersed, McGee pulled Will and Tom aside. "Men, I'm gonna need three hundred and twenty-five dollars for the wagon and oxen. After Schmiddy gets you to Kansas, they're yours and will come in handy if you make it to Iowa."

"If?" said Will. McGee regretted the slip. "When you make it, but it's not going to be easy. You and Tom are going to have to lead this group and keep a sharp lookout for patrollers and Indians. And don't forget your own people will turn you in for easy money."

McGee and Schmiddy returned to the livery. Luke led them to two oxen yoked together and hitched them to the wagon. Schmiddy examined the animals and said, "These sure are two dumb lookin' bovines."

"Names are Sarah and Clyde, an' you're lucky to be gettin' 'em."

McGee smiled after hearing the names. He handed Luke a roll of currency. Luke didn't bother counting; he stuffed the money in his pocket. "Snow's comin. You be sure them animals gets enough to eat so they don't starve or freeze ta death." Schmiddy patted the backs of the oxen and climbed aboard. Luke spat and gave a slight backhand wave as the wagon pulled away.

Townspeople and traders bustled around, getting ready for the rush of business that the big packet from St. Louis would bring. No one paid any attention to the farm wagon that came to a halt a short distance from the snag boat.

McGee signaled to Will and Tom to follow him to the pilothouse. He rolled out a map of the territory and went over the route they would take. "One last thing: hang on to those manumission papers Abe gave you. They're not of any use right now but could come in handy when you get to Iowa."

"Is that it, Captain? Are we ever gonna see you again?" Will remarked.

"I don't know, Will. Maybe when you get settled you can write and let Abe know where you are. He'll know how to reach me. But if we don't meet again, well…" McGee extended his hand as his voice trailed off.

Several hours later, lanterns along the shoreline were being extinguished and dockworkers started their trek home. Aboard the Missy T final preparations were being made for the slave group's departure. Ben gave each person a sack of food, Sam passed out blankets, and Zachary handed Will one of his well-used hammers and a tin can filled with nails. "Never know when yer gonna need a hammer ta nail that rickety wagon back together, or start building a new one."

One by one slaves ran from the boat to the back of the wagon. They lay on the bottom and covered themselves with blankets. Richard placed straw, empty crates, and empty barrels on top. Will climbed aboard and sat on the bench next to Schmiddy. McGee and the snag boat's crew stood at the Missy T's bow and watched them leave. By the time the wagon reached the trail leading to St. Joe, a light snow had begun to fall.

46

SNOW HAD BEEN FALLING FOR several days in St. Paul when Charles arrived at Teeny's cottage carrying an armload of firewood. His hat and shoulders were covered in white when he knocked. Teeny invited him in.

"I've got bread, butter, and other supplies in the wagon. I'll get those and be back in a minute." Charles informed her.

Teeny looked at her reflection in a mirror, adjusted the collar of her blouse, and ran her fingers through her hair.

She hung a kettle above the logs and invited Charles to join her for a cup of hot cider. He reached into his jacket and produced a small flask. "Do you mind if we make that cider a little more flavorful? I carry this with me for special occasions."

They sipped the warm bourbon-laced cider and talked about the city, the weather, and the Granemann's real estate business. Then Charles asked Teeny a personal question. "What was the baby's father like? I know he was a doctor, but did you like him, or love him?"

Teeny's answer was not what Charles expected.

"Doctor Walther owned me. After several months he seemed to become somewhat fond of me. I'm sure that had to do with the fact he found me interesting…in the bedroom."

Charles's cheeks reddened and he lost his grip on the mug of cider. "Damn," he said, as the cup hit the floor, splashing liquid on his pant leg.

Teeny laughed. Charles gave a flustered smile and retrieved a handkerchief from his coat pocket. He dabbed at the liquid, but Teeny said, "Here, let me do that." She took the handkerchief, knelt down in front of him, and brushed the liquid from the fabric.

The two were so engrossed that the loud knock at the door took them completely by surprise. Through the window they could see Frieda holding a broom and bucket. Teeny brushed snow from the doorstep and invited her in. "Mrs. Granemann asked me to help ya tidy up."

"How thoughtful," said Teeny, trying to sound pleased. Frieda noticed the cup on the floor and saw Charles dabbing his pant leg.

"Did you have an accident?" Frieda asked playfully.

Charles feigned a laugh. "Yes, Miss Douglas was trying to be a gracious host, but I was a bungling guest. I hope she will forgive me."

"Of course she will."

Charles wasn't sure whether the remark was sincere or snippy, but Teeny knew.

Charles sensed Frieda was going to be working in the cottage for quite awhile. He retrieved his hat and coat and prepared to leave. Teeny touched his shoulder. "Thank you Charles, and thank your mother and father for the food."

"May I visit again, tomorrow?" He asked gently.

Teeny nodded.

Charles arrived at Teeny's cottage the following afternoon. Lessons from his parents and the church about gentlemanly behavior quickly evaporated. Gentle kisses gave way to touching and groping, and they began undressing each other before they made it to the bedroom. Even though Teeny was younger, the lessons learned at the Silk Ribbon made her a far more experienced lover. Once the newness and variety of their liaison concluded, the two lay breathless, looking up at the ceiling. Charles rolled over and placed his hand on Teeny's stomach.

"We should be careful, we could hurt the baby."

Teeny sighed.

Charles tried to backpedal. "I'm sorry, that's not a very romantic thing to say. It's just that I've never experienced anything quite like this, and don't know exactly what to say. This was so much more…"

"Hush, you've said enough." Charles laughed, and looked affectionately at her. "When can I see you again?"

Teeny grew evasive. "I'm not sure, but you had better get dressed and go, it's almost dark."

He was about to leave when he saw that it was snowing harder. "Do you have enough wood? Enough food?"

"I'm fine. Go, before your mother and Frieda get worried." Charles gave her a questioning look. "Frieda?"

"Yes…surely you must know how much she cares about you."

Charles stammered out a response. "But she is our housekeeper."

Teeny arched her eyebrows and benignly said, "She is in love with you. And I am sure she resents you showing so much interest in a slave."

Charles ignored Teeny's comments about Frieda. "You're not a slave. I can't even imagine someone calling you that."

Befuddled, Charles struggled to find the right words while he collected his hat, gloves, and coat. He never wanted Teeny to feel awkward with him. At the door he finally blurted out, "I will never think of you as someone's property."

"Please, Charles, you need to go now. Say hello to your mother and father for me." Teeny closed the door half way and watched him pull away. For a brief moment she entertained the notion of romance, then returned to the reality of her situation.

As Charles wheeled his buggy into the barn next to the Granemann home, Frieda watched from the window of her room. She knew Charles had spent most of the afternoon at the cottage. Though she bit her lip in frustration, she consoled herself in knowing the light-skinned woman remained a slave and would be moving on once the baby was born.

The following day Frieda passed through the small room where Robert kept papers and correspondence. Two letters in a cubbyhole above the desk protruded. One had an address that she looked at with interest: 108 Washington Street, St. Louis. She started to remove it but heard footsteps in the hallway. She quickly pushed the envelope back.

"Are you okay, Frieda? You look a little flushed."

"Thank you for asking Charles, but I'm fine." Frieda took a deep breath, resumed her chores, and attempted to conceal her irritation and concern.

When Frieda dusted the roll top desk two days later, she found a new letter from St. Louis stored there. Helen was in town shopping, Robert and Charles were at the real estate office, and Gabe was busy preparing the evening meal. Frieda held the letter and looked at the cracked wax seal; her hands trembled as she pulled the letter from the envelope.

Dear Robert,

I was pleased to read in your last letter that Miss Douglas arrived safely and that your family is assisting her during this difficult time. I mentioned in our earlier correspondence that Dr. Walther and his wife have offered a sizeable reward for her return. Now they have hired a detective.

His name is Martin Lunt. He is a relentless and successful investigator. My sources tell me he plans to begin a search for Elizabeth in another month. I will write as soon as I have additional information.

Sincerely,
Abraham Bireman

Frieda carefully put the letter back in the envelope and returned it to the cubbyhole. She thought about what she had just read, then continued her chores. For a few moments, she experienced pangs of guilt over betraying the Grannemann's; but more ominous thoughts quickly returned.

47

SCHMIDDY GUIDED THE OXEN DOWN the worn dirt path toward the St. Joseph ferry. He nudged Will and said, "Hop down and take hold of them reins. Don't say nothin' except 'yes, sir' and 'no, sir', and don't look up."

Will led the oxen slowly toward the barge under the watchful eye of the ferryboat operator and a patroller on horseback. The patroller dismounted and waited for the wagon to arrive.

"Need to see yer papers."

"Here ya go." Schmiddy handed over the bill of sale for the wagon and a receipt for the purchase of Will. The patroller wasn't tall, but the long duster, wide brimmed hat, and shotgun gave him added stature. He examined the papers, then pulled from his pocket handbills offering rewards for slaves. He looked carefully at Will. None of the leaflets mentioned a facial scar. "Where ya headed?" he asked.

"Nebraska, gonna bring my sister and her husband back to Missouri. They can't make it farmin out there. Maybe they'll have better luck livin with me an' my family."

"Yeah, it's rough startin out. One bad year and yer pretty much finished." He walked around the wagon, looked at the boxes, crates, and barrels covered with snow and returned to the front. "Get on with ya then, an' watch for Indians when crossin into Nebraska. They're starvin' an' gettin desperate."

Schmiddy tipped his cap, and Will led the oxen up the platform. Will stood silently by Sarah and Clyde and waited for the chain to tighten. The flat boat moved slowly to the Kansas side. A cold north wind cut through Will's cloth coat. His hands felt numb; ice formed around the nostrils of the oxen.

"Get back on the wagon before ya freeze ta death," said Schmiddy. Will climbed aboard and blew warm air into his cupped hands. The ferryboat ground to a stop, and Schmiddy guided the oxen down the wooden platform.

He handed the fare to a clerk wearing an odd looking nautical cap with something resembling a pinecone sewn on the front.

"How far to the Atchison trail?"

The clerk grinned at Sarah and Clyde. "'Bout half an hour by horse; 'bout three hours with these cows pullin' ya."

"Thank ya, officer." Schmiddy urged the oxen forward; they moved slowly down the dirt road toward the Williams' farm. When the ferry was out of sight, he yelled to his cargo, "Gonna be a while fore we can stop an' stretch. Everybody okay back there?"

"Purdy much okay," replied Tom. "But we be cold."

An hour later Schmiddy pulled off the trail and stopped the wagon in front of the Williams farm. He climbed down and introduced himself to Joel and his wife, Beth Ann. He pointed toward the wagon. "I got a full load—eight altogether."

Joel grimaced. He guided Schmiddy away from the wagon for privacy.

"How the hell did you get involved in transporting eight runners at one time?" Schmiddy explained the circumstances. Joel stared at him incredulously.

"Ain't no way all of them gonna make it to Iowa. The first patroller who spots a group this size will corral 'em all an' sell 'em. An' what were they gonna do if they did make it to Iowa?"

Schmiddy glanced back at the wagon. "Two of 'em got a little money. One of 'em can even read an' write. All I know is they're either gonna make it or they ain't. They ain't safe in Missouri, an' Kansas has free soilers and slavers fightin' each other. Their best chance is ta get to Iowa."

That afternoon Joel led the slaves to the back of his barn. He swept away a layer of hay and opened a hinged door on the barn floor. "Follow me," he said. The farmer led them down a stairwell and into a narrow underground room. He lit lanterns on the wall and then addressed the group.

"If we get unwanted visitors, this is where ya hide. If I tell ya ta skee'daddle, go to that opening back there—it's a tunnel. Crawl through till you reach the cornfield. From there ya high tail it back into the woods."

Joel led the slaves back up the stairs and started a fire in the stove. He looked at the bedraggled group and tried to sound reassuring. "Beth Ann will be bringin' food out shortly. When I get back from town tomorrow, I'm gonna bring someone who'll help y'all sort things out. After that, ya can be on yer way."

Joel returned from St. Joseph early the next morning accompanied by a large burly man wearing a beaver pelt hat, a red wool vest, and knee-high leather boots. Joel introduced the slaves to Steven Dobbs, a trail boss. Dobbs walked slowly toward them. He withdrew a machete from beneath his coat and used the blade to draw lines in the dirt.

"Here is where ya are right now," he made an X on the ground as he explained. "I'm looking to take 'bout fifty people here." Dobbs dragged his blade behind him and stopped about ten feet from where he started. "It's a long way from that first X to here—'bout a thousand miles. It's called the Santa Fe Trail, an' from there we go here." He made a diagonal line that joined the long one and then made another X. Dobbs positioned himself on the final X.

"This is where we end up—the Sierra Nevada Mountains and the Feather River. Gold's comin' outa tha ground there, an' that's where I'm takin' a bunch of prospectors. I need help scoutin', cookin', buildin' fires, an' doin' hard work. Y'all get twenty cents a day, an' yer free ta go yer own way once we get there. If ya wanna go with me, step forward."

The slaves gazed at each other quizzically. Four men took a few steps forward; Will and Tom remained behind. Darla hesitated at first, but then stepped forward. Rosie looked at Tom. He looked back at her and shook his head.

"What about you three?"

Will tried to sound confident. "Going north, into Iowa."

"Well good luck to ya. The rest of ya, get yer belongins an' follow me."

Tom, Will, and Rosie remained at the entrance to the barn and watched the fugitives climb aboard Dobbs' wagon.

Will barely knew the names of the slaves who were leaving for California. He never learned where they were from or how they escaped. He knew they couldn't read, and he doubted they understood what they had just committed to. Thankfully, fate had provided him with options; otherwise, he would be in that wagon with them, heading to California.

48

MARTIN LUNT CHECKED THE BILLS of lading and passenger records for riverboats that went north the day Teeny escaped. The Durock sold one hundred twenty-five tickets, but one female passenger remained missing from the roster. The Adele sold two hundred and six tickets, with all passengers accounted for. Lunt noticed there were forty-eight stateroom passengers. There was one woman traveling alone.

Lunt decided to seek more information about the Adele's current itinerary. He strode over to the dispatcher's office, where a clerk informed him the boat had left for New Orleans weeks ago and would not be returning to St. Louis until early June.

Lunt returned to his office and drafted a letter to the captain of the Adele in New Orleans asking whether there had been a young woman aboard his riverboat last December.

After receiving the letter, Strickland responded by telegram.

```
RECORDS INDICATE A YOUNG WOMAN
DISEMBARKED IN DAVENPORT
DECEMBER 25 STOP

NO ADDITIONAL INFORMATION STOP
```

Lunt's next step involved sending a telegram to the Davenport post office asking for the name of the young woman who disembarked from the Adele on December twenty-fifth.

He only had to wait a day for a response.

WE HAVE NO RECORD OF ANY
PASSENGER DISEMBARKING FROM
THE ADELE STOP

From this reply, Lunt concluded that the young woman he was looking for must have stayed on board. Most likely she would have continued on to a city with a strong abolitionist contingent that would hide her—St. Paul.

Two weeks later he gave a brief summary of his investigation to Richard and Louise. As he prepared to leave the Walthers' home, he remarked, "I will be leaving shortly, and I must ask you again, do you want the child's mother returned, or just the baby?"

Richard looked at Louise. "Both," he replied. "She has value and will fetch a good price at auction."

49

WILL AND TOM WERE MAKING final preparations for the journey into Iowa. Schmiddy led Will around the small covered wagon. He explained how to grease the axles, operate the brake, and hitch the oxen. Determined, Will practiced by guiding Clyde and Sarah in a large circle, then down the trail.

As Schmiddy watched, he commented to Joel, "I think he's gonna do okay—drives the wagon pretty good."

Joel shook his head. "Three coloreds, drivin' their own wagon? They'll kill 'em and take the wagon."

Schmiddy looked at Joel. "Who are *they*?"

Joel gazed at the horizon. "Damn near anybody. Indians, border raiders … anybody."

Schmiddy handed Will a map. The trio's destination was marked with an X—the town of Kanesville. A wiggly line next to the X had been labeled 'MO RIVER.'

Beth Ann loaded whatever provisions she could spare. Joel explained what the oxen should eat and told Tom how to secure them at night. Will climbed onto the bench, and in as confidant a voice as he could muster said, "It's time to go."

The wagon moved slowly down the path toward the trail leading north. Joel, Schmiddy, and Beth Ann waved good-bye, wished them luck, and walked back to the farmhouse with heads bowed. "Be a miracle if they make it," said Joel solemnly.

After the slaves' departure, Schmiddy struck a bargain with Joel for one of his mules. He made preparations for his return journey and asked the Williams to write if they received any news. At dawn, Schmiddy began his trip back to the St. Joseph ferry, and home to Marie.

Late in the afternoon of the fourth day a cold wind started to blow. Will decided to make camp before snow started to fall. They rationed the provisions Beth Ann had provided and ate while sitting around the campfire.

"Sure be dark out here," Rosie observed.

Will poked the fire. "Dark and damn cold."

"Lucky we gots our fire," said Tom. He grabbed two more logs to place on top of those already burning.

After dinner, the fugitive party prepared to bed down. Rosie slept inside the wagon; Will and Tom bunked underneath. After a few hours sleep, Tom awoke and shuffled away to relieve himself. On his way back to the wagon, he thought he heard a cat mewing. Cautiously he made his way through the darkness toward the forlorn sound.

Will lay partially awake. He rolled over and noticed the empty bedroll. "Tom, where are you? You okay?"

"Will, bring dat lan'tern over here." Light from the lantern revealed a tattered blanket covered with leaves and snow. A human voice whimpered softly, and then a skinny crooked hand emerged and pulled back the blanket. An old Indian woman rose on her elbows and peered into the light. Her wispy silver hair hung down over her face and shoulders. Her mouth was open, paralyzed with fear. She attempted to stand but fell backward on the frozen ground. A sad groan emerged. She rolled to her side and raised her hand to protect her face.

"It be okay. We ain't gonna hurt ya." She lay trembling and unable to speak. Will and Tom gently helped the old woman to her feet. She steadied herself and started to walk away into the darkness.

"No, no, this way," said Will. He wrapped his coat around the frail old woman and guided her back to the campfire. They eased her to the ground and let her rest against a wagon wheel.

Rosie climbed down and regarded the spindly, grey-haired woman. "My God, who you be? Why you be out here alone?"

The old woman tried to speak, then began waving her hands. Rosie gave her a tin cup with a little water in it. They wrapped her in blankets and handed her a biscuit and slice of dried beef. She ate slowly and methodically. The old woman returned the cup to Rosie, closed her eyes, and began breathing in a slow, labored manner.

"Is she dyin'?" asked Rosie.

"I think she's going to sleep," said Will. They sat around the fire, occasionally glancing back at the scrawny body curled up in the blankets. The woman had already fallen asleep, her loud snores like staccato notes filled the air.

"Won'er what we gonna do wif her." Tom pondered aloud. He threw a few more logs on the fire before turning in for the night.

Will was up at dawn. The Indian woman had already risen and sat stolidly in the back of the wagon watching him. He waved in a friendly manner, and she slowly lifted the tin cup indicating she wanted more water. Tom was now awake and poking the fire.

"Wha's goin on Will?"

Will pointed toward the wagon. "Looks like we got a new passenger."

Rosie crawled up next to the old woman and tried to communicate using both words and gestures. A few minutes later she joined Will and Tom by the fire.

"She kin speak a few words. I think she done been put out ta pasture. She no longer be any use to her people cauz she too old, so dey lets her go some place ta die."

Will reached into his back pocket and pulled out the hand drawn map. He approached the woman, held up the map, and pointed to a spot on the wrinkled paper.

"Kanesville?"

The old woman shifted her eyes from the paper to Will and nodded. She raised her arm and pointed a bony finger straight ahead, then mumbled something that sounded like, "Five moons."

"I'm hoping you can get us there," Will said.

When Sarah and Clyde were hitched and the wagon loaded, the travelers began following two thin ribbons of dirt etched in the prairie grass. Four days later they came to a new trail. Without hesitating the old woman raised her arm and pointed to the right. On the fifth day they reached a clearing filled with carts, wagons, and canvas tents. Smoke rose from cooking fires. Sheep and cows grazed on grassy slopes nearby.

"Damn, why ya supose dem folks put up all dem tents?" Tom observed.

"I don't know, I guess they didn't plan on staying too long, or they would have built something sturdier. I'm pretty sure those houses and buildings on the other side of the river are what we're looking for."

Will pulled out Schmiddy's map. On the back he had written the name of a man who would help them obtain supplies and find a place to stay.

"Let's keep moving. Rosie, would you see what grandma is doing and whether she needs to walk around a bit?"

Rosie looked inside the wagon, and then ran outside. She yelled to the men, "Gran'ma be gone!"

Tom quickly came to where she was standing. With one look, he understood the situation. He gently took Rosie's hand. "She ready for it ta end."

Rosie shook her head. "No, we needs ta find her. She gonna die all alone, an' dat ain't right."

Tom slowly pulled her toward him and held her. "I knows ya feel sorry fer her," he said tenderly, "but she doan wan' to go no furder. She wants it ta end dis way, an' we gots ta respec' dat."

Will guided the wagon along the fringes of the tent enclave toward the cluster of buildings across the river. They came to a small ferry painted barn red. The owner was a short man, bundled up in a black coat and wearing a red wool cap. Will handed him four coins. He gave one back. "Only fifteen cents, not twenty. Ya comin to farm or work in town?"

Will forgot to rehearse some explanation and said, "Not sure."

"Well, be careful, most people here are friendly, but there's always a few..." He walked to the middle of the barge and began turning a large wheel. The chain became taut and the ferry moved methodically toward the opposite bank. It was almost dark when Will stopped the wagon in front of a warehouse. The name Thomas & Company was spelled out in gold lettering above the door.

50

AT THE GRANEMANN ESTATE, GABE ran through the kitchen searching for Frieda and Helen. She darted out the back door to the garden where the two women were planting tomatoes. "Missus Granemann, it be time, it be time! The baby comin." Helen dropped the trowel and wiped her hands. "Frieda, take the buggy and get Dr. Becker. Gabe, come with me."

Helen and Gabe entered the cottage and heard Teeny moan. They hurried to the back room where she was drenched in sweat, looking scared. Helen pulled the dress up above her waist and elevated her pelvis with pillows. She placed a sheet over the mother-to-be's trembling body.

"Dr. Becker's on his way. He'll be here shortly." Gabe said, hoping to comfort her. She gently put a damp cloth on her forehead and held her hand. By the time Becker arrived, Teeny writhed with intense pain. Her belly undulated with the now-frequent contractions. Teeny squeezed Gabe's hand while tears streamed down her cheeks.

In a firm voice Doctor Becker said, "Miss Douglas, your child is coming out feet first. This will be painful, but I need you to push as hard as you can."

Helen grasped the frightened young woman's arm and shouted encouragement. Teeny screamed and shuddered. The left shoulder emerged, then the right, and finally the face and crown. Becker exhaled with relief when he saw the cord wasn't wrapped around the baby's neck. He coached Teeny to give one final push.

Finally a tiny wail signaled the ordeal was over.

"It's a girl, my dear," Becker announced in his kindest bedside manner. "One of the most beautiful babies I've ever seen." He tied the cord, wrapped the baby in a towel, and presented her to Teeny. She gazed at the baby's soft pale skin, large blue eyes, and delicate reddish blond hair. In a barely audible voice she declared, "Mary, I'm going to name you Mary."

Charles and his father passed the time by restlessly pacing about in the adjoining room. They listened to Teeny's screams, studying the ceiling as though it would provide clues as to what was happening. When the house became quiet, they grew worried that something had gone wrong.

At last Doctor Becker and Helen emerged from the back room, and their mood lightened. Helen smiled and proclaimed, "It's a girl, a beautiful baby girl!"

Charles had located a bottle of brandy and collected a few glasses in anticipation of a toast, but now his face portrayed a vacant expression. He set the brandy and glasses down. "Come along, Charles, come see that precious little baby. Mary is her name."

"I will, mom, just not right now."

Robert walked over and put his hand on his son's shoulder. "What do you mean? Surely you want to see Elizabeth and the baby."

"Yes, of course, dad. I just need a few minutes."

Robert turned away and gave Helen a puzzled look. Dr. Becker, Helen, and Robert moved to the back room and gathered around Teeny and her baby. Frieda stood by the door, listening to the bedside chatter. She watched Charles carefully. She knew he felt alone and confused, and she was determined to provide him with the legitimate comfort and companionship he deserved.

Frieda wasted no time implementing her plan. A few minutes later, she announced to the others her return to the main house to prepare dinner.

When she arrived, Frieda entered the living room, then quickly made her way to the library. Very carefully she removed a group of letters from the cubbyhole and opened the most recent.

> Dear Robert,
>
> I am afraid I have discouraging news. Two trusted colleagues have informed me Martin Lunt has booked passage on the riverboat Anthony. He seems certain that Elizabeth is living in St. Paul. Lunt is scheduled to arrive in late July. I would suggest you make arrangements for Elizabeth and her baby to leave as soon as she is able to travel. Please tell Miss Douglas that I wish her the best. I will write again when I know more.
>
> Abe

Frieda studied the calendar on the wall. Lunt could be in St. Paul in four weeks, maybe less. She slipped the letter back into the cubby and went to the kitchen. When Helen, Robert, and Dr. Becker returned, Frieda said sweetly, "Will Charles be joining us for dinner, Mrs. Granemann?"

"I don't think so, Frieda, he'll be home later. Save a plate of food for him. Oh, and Gabe will be staying with Miss Douglas for the next few days. Please deliver enough supplies for both."

"Yes, ma'am." Frieda politely excused herself and returned to the kitchen. Out the back window she could see smoke from the cottage chimney. "Please come home, Charles," she said softly.

CB   CB   CB

Martin Lunt was making final preparations for departure. His bags were neatly packed; the pistol and derringer were cleaned, oiled, and loaded. Two riverboat tickets and a legal order from Judge Lacey were tucked securely in his vest pocket. The legal document affirmed that Teeny and her baby were "Chattel Personal" and both must be returned to their owner. Lunt locked his apartment, placed two traveling bags inside the cab, and handed the driver a slip of paper.

The driver guided the carriage west and paused in front of an imposing three-story townhome. Lunt walked up the brick path and gave a firm knock on the door. The housekeeper invited him in and asked him to wait in the parlor while she summoned Terrence LaCroix. Moments later a slender figure emerged wearing a black robe and red silk scarf. LaCroix escorted Lunt to the marble entryway, where a stout black woman was waiting.

"Martin, I would like you to meet Shanara. She will accompany you on your trip. I believe she is exactly the type of servant you requested." The slave woman stood with head bowed while the two men talked. When the brief visit concluded, Lunt and Shanara exited and approached the waiting cab. The carriage moved smartly down city streets toward the levee, with Shanara perched stiffly on the outside bench in back. She clutched her bag, and fretted about her two-month old baby boy remaining behind, left in the care of another servant while she was away.

51

LEADERS OF THE MORMON CHURCH put out a call to Saints living in Pottawattamie to pack their belongings and bring their families to Utah. Mormons living in Kansas and Iowa soon began dismantling their tents, and made final preparations for the long journey West. Dave Thomas knew this migration represented a once-in-a-lifetime opportunity to make a small fortune. He would need help unloading supplies and stocking shelves in his warehouse. He urged Will, Tom, and Rosie to work for him before making any decision about their future.

The town of Kanesville had several hundred houses, a dozen or so trading and commercial establishments, five churches, a hotel, and 1500 inhabitants. A smaller community had developed on the outskirts of Kanesville, where draymen, stevedores and servants lived. Locals called it Shantytown. A makeshift general store, several rough-hewn cabins, and a church made up the little village. Shantytown also had a boarding house, run by Annie Jackson, where the three newcomers took up residence.

For several months they lived at Annie's and worked at Thomas's warehouse. As the weather began to warm, Will decided to approach Dave Thomas and ask him about buying a small plot of land to farm.

"That's a bad idea Will. Iowa may be a free state, but they ain't gonna sell you any white folks' land," Thomas replied.

"People in Shantytown say it was the Indians' land, stolen from them by the white people," Will argued.

"Yeah, and those Indians stole it from another bunch of Indians. This goes all the way back to Cain knockin' Abel's brains out. It's a matter of who's in control, an' right now the white man controls the land.

With that comment, Will's dream of owning a farm evaporated. He sighed deeply, then asked another question.

"Tom and I have some money; can we deposit part of it in the Kanesville bank for safe keeping?"

Thomas chuckled. "Sure, banks will take anybody's money."

"Would you go with us and make sure we do everything properly?"

Thomas pulled his suspender straps forward with his thumbs and thought about how valuable his three workers were. He agreed to go to the First Bank of Kanesville.

Dave Thomas led Will and Tom through the bank corridor the following afternoon. Customers and tellers stared as the trio made their way toward the bank president's office. As they entered, a man with long white hair combed straight back rose from behind the large, imposing desk. He shook hands with Thomas, then looked nonplussed at Will and Tom. "What did you bring with you, Dave, new colored customers?"

"That's right, Sam, they work for me, and they wanna deposit some money."

"Is that right? Well, I'll have to see their papers before we talk about that."

Will removed the documents that Bireman had drawn up months ago from his coat pocket and handed them over.

Bowers remained silent. He found it hard to believe two coloreds, free or not, would have any money. Not wanting to offend Thomas, he had no choice but to proceed.

The first thing he needed to do was respectfully add a third chair in front of his desk. In a loud voice he called out, "Sunny Lee, get me another chair."

Sunny Ruth Lee was the daughter of a Miniconjou Sioux tribal chief. She entered the office carrying a small cane chair. In spite of her drab calico dress and tattered shawl, she was a beautiful young woman. Will looked at her long legs, finely chiseled features, and coal black hair. He followed her every move as she placed the third chair beside the others. She did not make eye contact, however, departing as silently as she had arrived.

"All right, boys," said Bowers, "take a seat, and we'll get your accounts open. I need you to print your names and sign this document. If you can't write your name, let Dave do it, and then put an X next to it." He pulled a form from the desk drawer. Thomas looked at it and passed it across the desk. Will picked it up and began to read.

"What are ya doin?" The banker asked.

"Reading what it says, sir."

The man looked over at Thomas. "You didn't tell me he could read!"

"Didn't know I had to."

Will signed his name to his account. Tom, however, was having trouble. He closed his eyes and thought about how he strung letters together when he practiced writing his name. He opened his eyes, dipped the pen in the jar, tapped off excess ink, and slowly printed. He applied the letters with a shaky hand, but his name was legible. He smiled and gave the paper back to Bowers.

Bowers grunted. "How much are they gonna deposit?"

"Three hundred in each account," said Thomas.

Bowers could scarcely believe his ears. "Now, right now? Where the hell did they get that kind of money?"

"They earned it. Now let's get on with this."

Thomas handed Bowers a roll of federal currency. "They might deposit more if you treat 'em right."

Bowers counted the money and instructed Thomas to put his name on each man's account as well. The banker grudgingly thanked them for their business and escorted them back to the bank entrance. Will and Tom glowed with pleasure as they left. Each had a bank account with their names attached! They had achieved their own identities!

On the way back to Shantytown, Tom remarked, "Will, I be real proud a da way ya handle things. By readin' dat piece a paper ya let 'em know, by God, ya jus' let 'em know."

"Thanks. Next time you'll be able to read it too." He smiled at his friend. Then he added, "Tom, did you notice that girl, Sunny Lee?"

"Yeah, she sure were purdy."

Will smiled. "Yeah, she sure were."

52

CHARLES TENTATIVELY ENTERED THE BEDROOM where Teeny reclined, propped up on pillows, nursing the baby. He pulled a chair close to the bed, lifted Teeny's hand and cradled it gently. "Are you and little Mary okay?"

Teeny smiled. "We're good. Isn't she a pretty baby Charles? Old Izzy was right; she predicted a baby girl."

Charles smiled but seemed preoccupied; he slowly released her hand, got to his feet, and began pacing. "Elizabeth, what am I going to do? I want you in my life but you and my father seem certain that we shouldn't remain together."

"Charles, I'm too tired to discuss this now." He appeared to agree, but continued. "I'm sorry, I'm being inconsiderate. I just don't..." He didn't finish the thought and went to the other side of the bed; he looked down at the baby. "I wish she was ours, I wish the law wasn't against us." Charles leaned over the bed and gave Teeny a soft kiss on the lips. "I'll see you tomorrow."

"Charles, thank your mom and dad for everything." Charles nodded and left the room. He mounted his horse and rode away, but did not intend to return to the main house. Instead, he headed to town, stopping off at Harry's Bar, where he ordered a bottle of bourbon.

"You're becomin a regular here Charles, anything wrong?" Harry asked.

"Just trying to sort things out. Say, Harry, do you know anything about Chicago?"

"A little. It's an up an' comin' city, got a railroad, gonna be a helluva lot bigger than St. Paul. Why, you gonna visit?"

Charles looked up. "No, I'm thinking about living there."

"Then you ain't thinkin' right. Your old man owns half the property on the bluffs; it's gonna be worth a fortune in a few years. You need to stick around and help him cash in."

Charles spun the glass tumbler in his left hand, picking up the whiskey bottle with the right. He poured his first drink.

A week later Charles was at the ticket office checking the schedule of boats arriving and departing. He said to the clerk, "Is there any boat taking passengers ro Galena other than the Excelsior?" The clerk lowered the spectacles to the bridge of his nose and scanned the most recent schedule.

"Nope, not this time of year."

Charles paused before handing over the money. "Which stage goes to Chicago from Galena?"

"Frinks or Western Stage. I'd go with Frinks."

"Can you sell me the stage tickets?"

"No, but you don't need to buy those in advance. They're running through Galena every couple of hours. You shouldn't have any trouble getting a seat or two."

Charles had one more question. "When is the Anthony due to arrive?"

The clerk checked his schedule. "The Anthony should get here on the twenty fourth. It all depends on the weather and river conditions. Ya still want the tickets?"

Without any hesitation Charles replied, "Yes."

Teeny lounged before the fireplace, holding Mary and talking to Gabe. They heard a horse ride up to the cottage and Gabe looked out the window.

"Guess I needs ta make ma'self busy. Mr. Charles be lookin' like he got lots ta talk about," Gabe declared.

"I'm sure he does. Please don't go too far, I'm not sure what I would do without you."

Then Teeny began laughing, leaving Gabe looking puzzled.

"I was laughing because this slave really likes having a slave around."

Gabe and Teeny were both giggling when Charles entered the room. "Did I miss something?" He asked.

"No, we were just being silly." Teeny assured him.

Charles pulled up a chair across from Teeny and announced he needed to talk to Teeny alone.

Gabe dutifully picked up the baby. "Mary an' I be goin' for a little walk."

As soon as she left, Charles put two riverboat tickets on the table.

"What have you done, Charles?" Teeny asked.

"Bought two tickets to Galena and inquired about taking a stage to Chicago. I'm not sure what I could do to earn a living, or whether you're even interested."

Teeny looked at him and tears welled up as she looked into his eyes. Here was this handsome man, willing to ignore her past, leave a fortune behind, and build a new life with a woman who was a fugitive. Haltingly she said, "Charles, you are a wonderful person, but you shouldn't be doing this."

"Don't decide right now. I'll leave the tickets. You can think about it, but you will have to decide in two weeks."

Teeny didn't question the deadline; she was caught up in the moment, ambivalent about this latest proposal.

Charles returned to the main house for the evening meal, where the conversation quickly shifted to Teeny and the recent letter from Abe Bireman. Frieda served the food and listened carefully.

"Lunt is going to be here soon. Shouldn't we ask the sheriff to help?" Helen asked apprehensively.

Robert shrugged, "We can ask, but the sheriff can't do anything. The law is on Lunt's side, not ours."

Charles interrupted and said, "I bought riverboat tickets to Galena." Charles set his coffee cup down and regarded his distraught parents. Both waited for an explanation.

"I asked Elizabeth to go with me to Chicago, but I don't know if she will."

Robert made an effort to respect Charles's feelings, but believed his son's infatuation would end badly.

"We know you care for her a great deal, Charles, but your mother and I hope you will let reason, not emotion, dictate your decision. I'm meeting with the sheriff at the office tomorrow morning. You need to be there."

Robert dropped the napkin on his plate in frustration and stalked out of the room.

Helen glanced affectionately at her son. "She's a lovely girl Charles. It's easy to see why you care so much and why you want to be with her, but please, don't leave St. Paul. Leaving won't solve anything."

Charles sat quietly contemplating the discussion, and then abruptly left the room. Helen sat alone and began to cry; her son was in love, but it was a star-crossed relationship, and it would be only a couple of weeks before the detective arrived.

53

DAVE THOMAS WAS HAVING HIS morning coffee when Will approached.

"Tom and Rosie are getting married, Mr. Thomas," he said with a big smile. "Good, they belong together."

Will always found himself surprised by Thomas' observations; he delivered them with such certainty. Will thought about asking the older man how he knew they belonged together, but at the moment a more pressing question concerned him. "Mr. Thomas, do you know anything about Sunny Lee, the girl who works for Mr. Bowers?"

"A little. Her mother was a slave and her father a Sioux Indian; Sunny is considered a half-breed. When the old chief died, Sunny and her mother weren't allowed to live with the tribe. They traveled south, and her mother started working for those two old maids. When her mom passed away, they took Sunny in. She cleans and cooks for them, and they give her a place to stay."

"I was wondering whether you could ask Mr. Bowers to introduce me to her."

"That's not necessary. Go over to the bank and introduce yourself."

"I just thought maybe it would help if Bowers let her know who I am."

"She was there when you made the deposit; she knows who you are," Thomas chuckled.

Will opened his hands and raised them in frustration. "She didn't even look at me."

"She's an Indian; they don't give anything away." Will smiled. It was another one of those Dave Thomas observations.

Two days later Will lingered outside the bank at closing time, hoping to find Sunny. The girl was quick: she left the bank, walking at a rapid pace, weaving skillfully between horses and wagons until she had crossed Main Street. Will had to sprint to catch up, but stopped when he saw the two elderly women waiting for her. The taller woman extended her hand, into which Sunny dutifully dropped a few coins. Will noticed that Sunny followed several steps behind the women as they walked toward the Elliot home.

Will approached Dave Thomas in his office the next day and relayed what happened. Thomas leaned back in his chair.

"Those Elliot women are kinda strange, but I don't think they mistreat her. Let me find out what old man Bowers has to say."

That afternoon Thomas sat across from Bowers in the back office of The Kanesville Bank. Bowers placed his elbows on the desk and leaned forward. He gave Thomas a knowing grin and in a gravelly voice said, "Come on, Dave, you know how these things work. They take Sunny in so she isn't dumped on the streets. The Indians don't want her, an' most likely she ain't gonna make it on her own. The old ladies get a housekeeper and some extra money on the side."

"Seems to me they got themselves a slave who has to pay for the privilege of being a slave," Thomas shot back.

Bowers sat back and folded his arms across his chest. "Yeah, maybe, but I ain't gonna get involved. Sunny's a good worker and she's smart. Those old biddies taught her to read and to talk like a white person."

"Would ya mind if I send Will over tomorrow? He would like to meet her. He tried to talk to her yesterday, but the old ladies were waiting for her."

Bowers was not about to offend his best customer. "Sure, tell him to come at noon. She has her lunch in the shed behind the bank."

Bowers was talking to a grain broker at the bank entrance when Will arrived the next day.

"Sunny's out back having lunch. She's not due back for another twenty minutes," Bowers told him.

Will's nerves jangled, and he felt uncertain about what to say to this girl he was infatuated with. He paced back and forth, staring at the ground. Bowers watched him walk in circles. Finally he called out, "Get a move on boy, twenty minutes will be gone before you make it around the corner."

Will tentatively approached the small frame building. He saw Sunny through the window sitting at a picnic table. An apple, bread, and a slice of cheese were on a cloth napkin in front of her. Will tapped on the door, opened it part way, and leaned in.

"Miss Lee, I'm Will, Will Douglas. I don't mean to interrupt, but would it be okay if I talked with you for a few minutes?"

Will's educated dialect and the respectful manner in which he addressed her caught Sunny Lee completely off guard. Most men who approached her behaved crudely and made lewd sexual remarks. Intrigued, she motioned for Will to take a seat.

"I work for Mr. Thomas at his store," Will began.

Sunny remained unresponsive, but didn't look annoyed. She broke off a piece of bread and offered it. Will was pleasantly surprised by the gesture and accepted. Sunny took a small knife, sliced a piece of apple and handed it to him. He thanked her, but was concerned she hadn't spoken. He decided to be a little more direct.

"I tried to meet you the other day, but two ladies were waiting for you. Do you mind that I asked Mr. Bowers to let me join you?"

Sunny picked up a slice of apple with her knife, pretending to examine it. "Why did you want to join me, and what do you have in mind, Mr. Douglas?"

Will felt jarred by the first words he heard. The formal response didn't seem to coincide with her appearance. He smiled.

"Well Miss Lee, I can assure you my intentions are truly honorable."

The absurdity of a slave and half-breed Indian talking like educated white people caused Sunny to smile. Will found this encouraging, so he continued.

"Miss Lee, would those two old ladies allow me to call on you?"

"They might, but what makes you think I want you to?" She said coyly.

"I can tell by your smile. Would Sunday after church be okay?"

"Yes," said Sunny very softly, and she seemed embarrassed by her tentative response. Then in a louder, more assertive manner, she looked at him and said, "Yes, Mr. Douglas, Sunday would be fine."

Will laughed, and quickly composed himself. "I'll see you at noon. Thank you for the bread and apple, Miss Lee."

54

MARTIN LUNT STRODE CONFIDENTLY UP the landing stage of the riverboat Anthony with Shanara in tow. A member of the crew escorted her to the slave quarters while another took Lunt to his stateroom, where he made a thorough inspection of the bed, dresser, washbasin, and furniture. He handed a coin to the clerk and dismissed him. He opened the bag that contained his pistol and derringer and slipped the small gun into his coat pocket. Lunt situated himself at the entrance to the grand saloon, inhaled a pinch of snuff, and surveyed the scene with cool objectivity.

The boat wouldn't be leaving for several hours and the gaming tables, complete with professional gamblers and their shills, buzzed with a brisk business. Everyone, it seemed, wanted to make a fast buck before the boat departed. Lunt eased through the crowd toward a skinny man with a wide brimmed hat perched atop his head. To most he appeared honest and amusing. His hands moved with lightning-like speed around the small table in front of him. He enticed bets from onlookers with his lively patter.

"Keep your eye on the lady, the money card. Here it is—now I'll turn it over—follow it closely as I move it around and around, over and under and in-between. When I'm finished, point to the queen. I'll turn her over and you win. Nothing could be easier."

A clean-shaven rotund man stood and watched; he was positive he could pick the queen. He took a gold coin from his pocket and showed it to the dealer.

"Ah, I can tell you are a sharp-eyed card player, sir," the dealer hustled, "I should never play against someone as skilled as you." He moved the cards from side to side, up and down, and then paused. "But if you insist, place your coin on the lady." The man placed his bet.

"Well, sir, you placed the coin on the middle card, let me turn that card over. Oh, I'm sorry, Colonel, that's the six of clubs so I will have to take your gold piece." The dealer pocketed the coin. The man gaped in disbelief. He had been absolutely certain the middle card was the queen.

"Thank you sir, thank you. Care to play again?"

In the blink of an eye, the novice gambler found himself relieved of twenty dollars; he walked away shaking his head. Lunt filled the vacated space and said, "I'd like to place a bet Henry." The dealer recognized the voice and didn't look up.

"Shit. What the hell do you want?"

"I want to play, and I want it to be an honest game."

"It is honest," he hissed, "I'm just too fast for these rubes."

"I have a derringer in my pocket. You play it straight, and it stays there. Now, let's play."

Angrily, Henry showed Lunt the queen, placed two other cards next to it, and moved them around the table with incredible speed. Lunt put a ten-dollar gold piece on the center card. The dealer flipped it over. He gave Lunt a nasty grin. "Sorry, Lunt, you lose. I'm too fast even for you."

"Deal again," Lunt said dryly.

Henry let out a long disgusted sigh, and then threw the queen and two other cards down. Everything moved so quickly it all appeared a blur. Lunt took a hundred dollar gold piece from his vest pocket and placed it on the card left of center. The crowd gasped at the amount bet on such a simple game. The scrawny dealer looked disgusted as he flipped the card over.

"I'll have to take your money sir, thank you very much," said Lunt. His gold-capped tooth appeared to glow as he grinned deliciously. Henry folded his table in disgust and glared at the detective. The con artist had been conned; now he knew Lunt had lost the first game on purpose.

Lunt had mastered the art of three-card Monte, Casino, and poker. He had studied the ways professionals cheated, analyzed the way shills set up the unsuspecting, and learned when to walk away from a game. He favored Faro because the odds tipped slightly in favor of a skilled gambler, it made counting cards or marking the deck difficult, and the game allowed a man to test his intelligence and skill. In Lunt's mind gambling bore a strong resemblance to detective work. If you observed and eliminated known possibilities, then you had a good chance of solving the case.

As Lunt basked in the glow of his easy win, a low bellowing sound indicated the ship's imminent departure. From the front of the saloon, Lunt watched the tumultuous activity on the levee. He signaled the first mate to bring Shanara to his stateroom. When she arrived, she unpacked his bags and put a fresh coat of polish on his shoes. Lunt lit a cheroot and asked whether her accommodations were acceptable.

"Dey be okay."

"Okay is not good enough. You are going to be traveling on this boat for more than a week and you must eat properly and get enough rest. The return trip will be even more difficult. I will make sure you are taken care of."

"Dat be kind of ya, Mr. Lunt."

"It's business, Shanara, nothing can be left to chance."

That night Lunt circulated through the saloon observing various entertainments and parlor games. He knew at least two of the men in the saloon were professional gamblers, but the person he watched most closely was a con artist dealing poker at the high stakes table. By midnight, the game had attracted a rather sizable audience.

Leo DuVall—captain of the Anthony—and Bill Watson—physically notable because part of his right ear was missing—occupied seats around one side of the table. Bill's partner, Seth, who wore a traditional southern gentleman's white suit sat next to the captain. A businessman from St. Louis wearing a finely tailored pin striped suit, and a cowboy with boots, spurs, and ten gallon hat made up the third and fourth players at their table.

Lunt knew Bill by reputation. The hustler had been caught with a cold deck in New Orleans. Rumor held that one of the men he cheated bit off part of his ear during the ensuing brawl.

The businessman, the cowboy, and the captain had all been allowed to win small amounts of money. The competition had remained easygoing and friendly. When it came down to the last game of the night, the players agreed to a high stakes game. Bill wiped his brow with a handkerchief and called for a fifty-dollar ante. This steep figure surprised the players, but each of them pushed their money to the center of the table. Bill dealt the cards. By the time each man bet and called, nearly a thousand dollars lay piled on the table.

Lunt stood back and observed, and then stealthily moved behind Bill. He reached into his shoulder holster and nonchalantly withdrew his pistol. In a calm monotone Lunt said, "Care to tell these gentleman how you're cheating them, Bill?"

Bill spun around in his chair. "Who the hell are you?"

"Name's Martin Lunt. I want you to tell the captain how your con works."

Bill reached for his gun. Lunt instantly placed the barrel next to the side of the con's head and cocked the pistol. The crowd quickly scattered throughout the saloon, seeking cover.

"Put the gun down, or you'll have two missing ears."

Bill slowly laid his gun on the table; simultaneously, his partner reached for the revolver inside his coat.

"Leave the gun holstered and put both hands on the table," Lunt commanded, taking aim at the shill.

Captain DuVall stood up. "What's going on here, Mr. Lunt?"

"Well, Captain, when Bill here wiped his brow, he brought out the cooler. He dealt you all good hands from his new deck, and the betting increased. Captain, if you will turn your cards over you can show everyone that you have an excellent hand."

At first DuVall was reluctant, but then turned his cards over and revealed five spades.

"A flush," Lunt explained, "A very good hand. The gentleman next to you most likely has two pair. And the man seated next to him has three of a kind. You have all been dealt excellent hands and could all be winners. So, you continued to call and bet, but Bill's partner over there has been dealt a full house."

Beads of sweat formed on the shill's forehead. Captain DuVall ordered the man to show his cards. Lunt had identified the winning hand correctly. The players and onlookers mumbled and cursed.

With some difficulty, the captain restored order. Then he called for the first officer and two burly crewmembers to back him up while he dealt with the thieves.

"I'm turning you both over to the sheriff at Dubuque. You're lucky I don't throw you cheating bastards overboard." With that, the two crewmembers escorted Bill and his partner to a holding pen next to the boilers.

Later, the captain invited Lunt to the bar for a drink to express his gratitude.

"Mr. Lunt I appreciate what you have done, and for protecting the integrity of the games aboard my ship. What can I do to repay you?"

Lunt downed his bourbon, then quickly replied, "Captain DuVall, I would appreciate a favor. I would like to arrive in St. Paul ahead of schedule."

"Very well, Mr. Lunt, consider it done."

"One other thing, Captain, the slave woman traveling with me needs better accommodations and decent food." The captain nodded.

"Thank you, Captain. It's been a pleasure doing business with you."

55

EARL DUNCAN, THE SHERIFF OF St. Paul, and his son Harold were sitting in the back room of the Granemann real estate office. The sheriff clutched a piece of paper in his left hand. Charles brought another chair into the room and asked whether anyone wanted whiskey or coffee. "Naw, let's get on with it. I got a feelin I know what this is about."

The elder Granemann entered, extended his hand to Earl and his son, and took a seat behind his desk.

"Earl, thank you and Harold for coming. I have an unusual predicament and need your advice. We have a young lady staying with us who just gave birth to a beautiful baby girl. This should be a joyous occasion, but the young lady is a slave in the eyes of the law, and she is in danger. A detective from St. Louis is on his way to forcibly retrieve her and the baby."

Without looking up Duncan said, "His name is Martin Lunt." Duncan unfolded the paper he had been holding and handed it to Robert.

"Take a look. I received this yesterday."

```
ARRIVING IN TWO WEEKS STOP
RETURNING A FUGITIVE SLAVE AND
CHILD TO OWNERS STOP
WOULD LIKE YOUR HELP STOP
MARTIN LUNT
```

The elder Granemann handed the telegram to Charles and closed his office door. "This discussion must remain private. I don't want to put you or your son in a position where you're accused of not doing your job. My family and I are very fond of this girl and would like to assist her."

"Talk to Taylor or somebody in the underground. They can tell you how to get her out of St. Paul."

Charles had been listening intently and intervened. "She can't travel alone with a baby…I plan on going with her."

Harold looked startled. "You're gonna leave town with a Nigger woman?"

Robert put his hand on Charles' shoulder to calm him. He responded in a kind but stern manner.

"This young woman is a slave in the eyes of the law, but she is as white as you, Harold. This predicament is not of her own making—she had no choice."

Harold's face revealed a high level of confusion. He was trying to respond when his father intervened.

"Robert, Charles, let's not be angry with my boy. He was just expressing, in a crude sort of way, something that others in this town will be saying, or thinking. St. Paul has lots of anti-slavery folks, but it's still a divided town. Don't get too far ahead or they'll turn on you. An' ya can't afford that when you're running a business."

Robert knew the sheriff was right. "Earl, what do you suggest?"

"Hide her. Don't tell me or anyone else where she is, and send her packing."

"That's the same advice we received from the gentleman who sent her. I guess we'll have to figure this out pretty quickly. Do me a favor, will you? Don't go out of your way to help that detective."

The elder Granemann walked the sheriff and his son to the front office. After they departed, he retrieved a file filled with information about properties in the area. He flipped through the pages, selected one, and handed it to Charles.

"What do you think?"

Charles examined the page.

"The old Lutheran Church? Aren't they going to tear it down and put up a new one?"

"Not for several months. It's always had a few rooms where immigrants stayed until they found work or a place to live. Elizabeth could stay there and board a stage when the time is right."

"I notice you didn't mention travelling by boat, or going to Galena, or Chicago."

Robert looked frustrated and didn't respond. He picked up his hat and walking stick.

"I'm going over to look at the old church, why don't you join me?"

Two days later, Teeny joined the Granemann's for the evening dinner. Mary napped in a wicker basket next to her. Frieda poured coffee just as the polite dinner conversation turned serious. Robert revealed the written correspondence he received from Abe Bireman.

"Walther has hired a detective, and we think he'll be here before the end of the month."

Teeny cringed, visibly shaken by this news.

"You were in the last weeks of pregnancy and about to give birth. We didn't feel you needed something like this to worry about," said Charles.

"He won't be here for some time dear," Helen added. "Charles and Robert will take the necessary precautions before then."

Teeny picked up Mary and began rocking her. Charles could see the worry in her face and said, "Dad, Elizabeth needs assurance that we have a plan to help her."

"I'm getting to that, Charles. Elizabeth, we're pretty certain the detective will arrive here on the twenty-fourth. The sheriff can't protect you, since they passed that damned Fugitive Slave Act. Your best chance is to get away from here before the detective arrives."

Teeny responded quickly, "I agree. Do you have any suggestions?"

Charles remained silent as his father answered.

"There is an old Lutheran church near the levee. Gabe will stay with you, and we'll make sure you have everything you need. We will try to make arrangements for you to travel north by wagon or stagecoach. I would also suggest you talk to Mr. Taylor or Mr. Farr and see if either of them can offer any help."

Frieda had been eavesdropping from the hallway. Gabe came up from the cellar with a bottle of port.

"Ya gonna serve dis wine, or is ya jus gonna stand dere an' lis'en?" Gabe chided.

Gabe's comment triggered feelings of guilt. The Granemanns had always been kind. Now she was skulking around, reading their mail and eavesdropping on their conversations. She poured the wine into four glasses and carried them on a tray into the dining room.

"Thank you, Frieda. You always seem to know just what we need."

Frieda smiled at Robert, then at Charles. Charles failed to notice.

After the meal, Teeny returned to the cottage, tucked Mary into her crib, and joined Gabe by the fire.

"Are you scared, Miss Elizabeth?" The girl asked.

Teeny nodded and lowered her eyes. "Yes, yes I am. I'm afraid of being out there alone with a baby."

"Ain't Mr. Charles goin' wit ya?"

Teeny looked at the riverboat tickets lying on the table. "I don't know. I hope he soon realizes it's a bad idea."

"Miss Elizabeth, there be sumpin ya need ta know. Frieda not be thinkin' right. She think Charles gonna love her once you be gone, an' he ain't. She be actin' stupid, an' I doan trust her."

56

IT SEEMED THE SUNDAY CHURCH service in Shantytown would never end. When it finally did, Will began a brisk walk into town. He reached Main Street and quickly located the Elliot sisters' home. The house appeared grand from the street, but it's elegance faded the closer he got to the entryway. The home needed many repairs, and he wondered why two elderly women needed such a large residence. He lifted the heavy brass knocker and let it drop.

A tall elderly woman with her hair pulled back in a tight little bun opened the door. She peered through small round eyeglasses and eyed Will skeptically.

"I am Emma Elliot, and you must be the Nigger here to see Sunny."

Despite her rudeness, Will responded politely.

"Yes, ma'am. I'm Will Douglas."

Emma studied him for a moment. "Wait here, I'll get her," she said curtly.

Sunny had chosen a light blue dress and braided her hair for the occasion. She made a lovely vision as she glided into the foyer. Will was delighted: he had never seen her in anything other than dingy work clothes. When he regained his composure, he said to Emma, "We are going to the park for a little while. Nice meeting you, Miss Elliot."

Emma didn't respond and abruptly closed the door.

People on the street cast furtive glances at the couple as they strolled together through City Park. They found a secluded spot beneath a large oak and engaged in polite small talk. Suddenly, Sunny asked a question Will hadn't anticipated.

"Will, how did you manage to get the money you deposited last week?"

Will was uneasy, but knew he needed to respond.

"Well, my friend Tom and I had the money when we left St. Louis. We thought we should put it in the bank where it would be safe."

Sunny gazed blankly at the small lake in the distance. "Be careful Will. No colored man around here has ever had that much money. People are gonna want to know where you got it, and if you have more," She said.

Will went from lighthearted to apprehensive in a matter of seconds, which didn't go unnoticed by Sunny.

"I'm sorry Will. I didn't mean to upset you or spoil our time together."

"It's okay. I'm glad you warned me." He paused for a few seconds, "Do you mind telling me how you ended up with those two old ladies? Do they own you?"

Now it was Sunny's turn for reticence. She fiddled with the hem of her dress and looked around.

"My father was a Sioux chief. My mother was a slave he purchased from a fur trader. After dad died, mom and I were forced to leave the Indian village. Mom died a short time later. Those ladies don't own me, but I work for them and pay them for giving me a safe place to stay."

"It seems to me they're taking advantage of you," Will remarked.

She clasped her hands and placed them in her lap. "It's hard to explain, Will. I'm not really accepted by whites, coloreds, or Indians."

Will hadn't thought about that. He looked kindly into her eyes.

"You don't think I feel that way, do you?"

She paused a moment and shook her head. "No," she said softly.

Will smiled and did his best imitation of a southern gentleman.

"Well, Miss Lee, ya'all should nevah, evah think the honorable Colonel Will Douglas is a scalawag who judges others prematurely. My intentions, as I mentioned to y'all be'fo, are most proper," he drawled.

Sunny laughed.

"Well thank you, Colonel Douglas. But a lady just can't be too careful when approached by strange men in this wicked town."

Her reply struck something deep inside him. Will hadn't talked or laughed with a woman since he spent time with Teeny years ago. For a moment his mind wandered.

Sunny gently touched his hand. "Will, are you okay?"

He jolted back to the moment. "I am," he said. "It's just been so long since, since I was with anyone like you."

"Well, Colonel Douglas, I do believe you just paid me, and someone else, a compliment."

Will flashed a grin. His mind was now firmly in the present.

Time sped by much too quickly. The late afternoon sun began to wane and the couple reluctantly left the park. As they strolled back to the Elliot home, their steps slowed, both seemed to be searching for words that would make the day last a little longer. They paused at the front door. Will felt her warm hand on his arm. Sunny looked up and spoke delicately.

"I like you, Will. You make me laugh, and I think you're a good man."

Before he had a chance to respond or say good-bye, a doleful Emma stood at the door and gestured for Sunny to come inside. She glared at Will with scorn and hastily closed the door. Preoccupied with his thoughts about his happy day with Sunny, Will didn't seem to notice.

Will arrived at the warehouse Monday morning humming a tune he had heard a calliope play on the St. Louis levee. Thomas sat reading a newspaper and heard him coming. Without looking up from his paper, the boss said, "Indian women are very loyal, and Sunny is very pretty. You're a lucky man…if she's interested in you."

Will stood in front of Thomas' desk, embarrassed.

"Have a seat, Will. We need to talk." He faced Will directly and asked, "Ya still thinking about starting a school?"

"Yes, sir, with books, a slate board, desks, chairs, and everything."

"Can I give you some advice?"

Will grew uncomfortable.

"You got to find a way to start the school without paying for it. If people know you got money in the bank, and enough to start a school…" he looked out the window before continuing, "…well, when times are tough, somebody's gonna take that money. And if you got any more squirreled away, they'll take that too."

"Tom and I can prevent that. And, wouldn't the sheriff help?"

"No, and no! You and Tom couldn't protect your money from professional gunmen. And them papers sayin you're free don't say nothing about you having the same rights to protection as white people. The sheriff wouldn't lift a finger."

Thomas drummed his fingers on the desk for a minute. He saw Will's growing concern and decided to change the subject.

"Let me read you something. It's a review of a new book."

Will was still distracted by thoughts of gunmen taking his and Tom's money. Thomas knew Will wasn't completely on board and repeated his comment.

"Will, you think you want to hear the review?"

Will took his time responding. "I'm not exactly sure what a review is, Mr. Thomas."

"Well, it's an opinion someone has about a book, or music, or a play. The guy writing the review is supposed to know what's good and what's not. Anyway, listen to this. 'Possibly the finest work issued by an American publisher. In thrilling delineation of character…,' whatever that means, '…and power of description, it is without a rival, and will be read and re-read by every intelligent family in America.'"

Thomas paused, "It goes on and on like this. And, he's referring to a book that was written by a woman. You know what it's about? It's about slavery, and how bad slaves are treated, and how a few escape to Canada. And you know what else?"

Perplexed, Will had no idea how to respond.

"Right now it's the most popular book in America. It's called *Uncle Tom's Cabin*. I ordered a couple copies from Willard's Store, but they won't be here for a month or two. You know what I think?"

"No, sir, your questions are kinda sneaking up on me and I don't know the answers."

Thomas chuckled at the remark. "I think you should read it to those kids in Shanty, and tell them you're a teacher and you can teach them to read. Let's get started. I found a place for your school." He grinned and added, "You'll recognize it. We'll take my buggy."

Thomas walked Will around the outside of the old boardinghouse. "Look at this place, Will, it's perfect for your school."

Will had a puzzled expression. "It's Annie's boarding house!"

"That's right, and I bought it. I talked it over with her and she's grateful. She doesn't have to worry about keeping the old place up, and she's got a little money to boot. Annie wants you folks to still live here, and that big room in back is perfect for your school."

Will wondered why Thomas had done all this without talking to him.

"Think it over Will. If you don't like the idea just let me know. We don't have to do this."

Will still felt bewildered. "I think I need to talk to Sunny and see how she feels about your ideas."

Thomas pulled his suspenders forward with his thumbs, let them snap back, and said, "I'll bet she likes 'em."

57

TEENY LOOKED IN HER PURSE one more time to make sure she had the riverboat tickets. She held Mary tight and climbed into the buggy with Charles and Gabe. When they arrived at the old church, they found it deserted. Items of value had been removed weeks ago in preparation for dismantling the building. Teeny, Gabe, and the baby would stay in two sparsely furnished rooms in back. While they were unpacking, Charles looked out the window at the iron chimneys of the riverboats moored on the levee. It seemed a simple matter to leave the church, walk a short distance, and escape unnoticed on the Excelsior.

The next day Teeny stitched a wide hem in her "Old Lady Dress" to hold her share of the money. She applied the make-up, wig, and leg brace, and entered the adjoining room. She turned in a tiny circle to model the outfit for Gabe. "How do I look?"

Gabe playfully put her hand over Mary's eyes so she couldn't see and said, "Good Lord, Miss Lizabeth, I fergets how ugly dat outfit make you look."

"Thank you. I hope I haven't frightened Mary. Can you give me directions to Mr. Taylor's?"

"Mista Taylor be in da barba'shop on Third Street; dat's five blocks down an he be right next to da post office. If he not in his shop, he likely be in da little house in da alley cross da street."

Teeny kept her head down while hobbling past pedestrians, wagons, and men on horseback. She spotted the post office and crossed the street. Hanging on the barbershop door was a note, "Back in one hour." So, Teeny limped across the street to Taylor's home.

She approached a modest wooden structure on a side street, knocked, and was greeted by a black woman wearing a long black dress and red scarf around her shoulders. She looked at the elderly white woman and said, "I believe you have the wrong home dear."

"I am a slave," Teeny said haltingly. She looked about to see if anyone was near. "And I have a baby. I am wearing a wig and make-up. I was hoping to speak to Mr. Taylor."

The woman studied the figure in front of her for another moment and then opened the door. "Adeline is my name. Please come inside."

William Taylor was a stout black man in his early 40's with mutton chop sideburns and graying hair. He looked surprised when his wife escorted a white woman into the tiny parlor. Teeny removed her wig, introduced herself, and proceeded to tell Taylor about the birth of her baby and the detective hired to find her.

Taylor listened intently. The conductor heard many stories from slaves wanting his help, but this one was most unusual. He set his pipe aside and stroked his chin. "Riverboats are tha first place he's gonna look, stagecoaches second, and third are tha safe houses a'roun town. An', most likely, he aw'ready sent messages to patrollers tell'n them ta keep an' eye on them locations."

Taylor picked up a small sheet of paper. "Can ya read?"

Teeny nodded. "Here's the name of a Mormon family leavin' town with a wagon train next week. They'll let ya travel with 'em, an' that other name is a farmer who hauls supplies from tha levee to outposts. He'd be willing to take ya to one of tha nearby villages. When ya get a good ways from St. Paul, ya can start usin' tha stagecoach, but first ya need to get outa this town."

He looked at her sympathetically. "Travelin' in a wagon with a baby is gonna be hard, but it may be yer only way." He got up and started toward the door. "I'm gonna have to get back to my shop now, Miss. I hope you an' yer baby leave soon and ya stay safe."

Teeny put the wig back on. Taylor shook his head. "My, my, that's some de'sguise."

Teeny hobbled back toward the church. Charles waited at the entrance, watching her limp down the street.

"Excuse me sad little old lady, have you seen Miss Elizabeth Douglas?"

Teeny laughed. It was the first time in days either of them found something to smile about.

In the back room Charles and Gabe listened to Teeny relay her conversation with Taylor. Charles looked at the names on Taylor's list.

"You're not seriously thinking we could travel on a Conestoga or some other type of wagon with little Mary are you? She's only a few weeks old."

"I'm just telling you what Mr. Taylor said. I haven't made up my mind about anything."

Gabe began to feel uneasy with the tone of the conversation and worried the baby would become upset. She picked up Mary and carried her through the hallway to the empty chapel. She looked at what was left of the pulpit, altar, and then pointed to the mural depicting the manger scene.

"Look'a dere liddle Mary, dat lady be holdin' a baby dat look jus like you. An' her mama look jus like yer mama. An' look, look at dat big star in da sky—dat mus be da North Star."

Teeny entered the chapel and smiled when she heard Gabe's interpretation. She picked up her baby and said, "I hope she never has to think about running toward the North Star."

"How far north ya goin Miss Lizabeth?"

"I don't know, first I have to get out of St. Paul. Charles insists we can leave on the riverboat before the detective arrives. If he's right, that would be best for Mary."

Every day Robert walked from his office to the church to give Teeny and Charles updates on river conditions and news of any schedule changes. Robert grew increasingly worried that the couple was waiting too long.

"You should leave now with one of the wagon trains and catch a boat or stage after that detective leaves."

"Dad, there's no telling how long we would have to travel by wagon. And don't forget what happened last April," Charles said in an agitated tone. He intended the remark to remind his father of the Indian attack on a small wagon train west of St. Paul. The natives had killed the men, and rumors spread that they had then raped and mutilated the women.

Teeny faced a quandary: she agreed with Robert, but had concerns about a rough, possibly dangerous journey by wagon. Charles remained adamant; he wanted no part of travelling on land. He was certain the riverboat offered the best chance to escape. He asked for Teeny's patience. The Excelsior was sche-dued to arrive in two days, a day ahead of the Anthony.

That same day Frieda approached Helen and said, "Do you mind if I take the carriage and deliver a few sandwiches and milk to Elizabeth and the baby?"

Helen was pleasantly surprised by her request. "That's very thoughtful. I'm sure they would appreciate that."

After she arrived, Frieda exchanged pleasantries and made small talk. When she finally got Charles alone, she asked if he was still planning to leave. His answer was a simple, "Yes." Frieda struggled to conceal her disappointment.

"I will miss you Charles." She leaned forward to give him a kiss on the cheek.

Charles hadn't anticipated the gesture and awkwardly backed away. "I'll miss you too Frieda. Please take good care of mom and dad."

Frieda was teary-eyed and angry as she climbed aboard the carriage. Charles waved good-bye and watched her depart. He thought it strange she was heading toward the center of town rather than taking the more direct route home. Frieda pulled the Granemann carriage to a halt in front of the new St. Paul Hotel and said to the doorman, "Please watch this carriage, I'll only be a moment."

Frieda approached the front desk and smiled at the clerk. After a bit of flirty conversation she jotted down a note and made the clerk promise to give it to Martin Lunt as soon as he arrived. "Yes ma'am, I'll be sure he gets this. Pardon my forwardness Miss, but are you available, I mean do you have a steady boyfriend?"

"I'm involved with someone at the moment."

"Well, maybe you'll remember me if things don't work out, my name's Randall Simms."

Frieda gave him a sweet smile. "Maybe I will. Good-bye Randall."

Teeny was restless and barely slept that night. Before dawn she picked up her purse and removed the riverboat tickets. She sat alone in an old chapel pew, held the tickets tightly, and prayed the Excelsior would arrive on time.

Early the next morning Gabe made coffee and distributed Frieda's ham, cheese, and biscuits. Charles was pacing about with a mug of coffee when he stopped and stared out the window. Two new tall stacks were visible. It was a large boat. He set his coffee down and hastily retrieved his jacket. He turned to Teeny, "I have to see if that's the Excelsior that just docked."

Charles gave Teeny a quick peck on the cheek. "I'll meet you back here in half an hour."

One his way out, he noticed something. "Elizabeth, there's an envelope on the table. Would you take it to dad's office?"

Teeny hated putting the disguise on every time she went out but realized it was a necessity; anyone working for Lunt would most likely be looking for a young woman, not a gimpy old lady. She picked up the envelope. Written on the front was, "Mom and Dad."

Several blocks away, Martin Lunt was standing at the hotel's front desk reading the note Randall Simms handed him.

> *Mr. Lunt,*
>
> *The girl and child you are looking for are at the old St. Paul Lutheran Church.*

58

LUNT HANDED THE CLERK A gold coin and his business card. "The sheriff is expecting me. Tell your doorman to fetch him and meet me at the old Lutheran church, and tell him to hurry." He paused to check his pistol and derringer.

Lunt left the hotel with Shanara trailing behind, struggling to keep up. The doorman sprinted down Third Street toward the Sherriff's office.

Teeny was moving slowly, still a block away from the Granemann real estate office.

Charles surveyed the levee and saw a large boat tied to several iron ringbolts. Passengers had already departed and wooders were stacking logs. Panic set in after he saw the name on the side—the Anthony! Lunt had already arrived in St. Paul! Charles circled cargo and people in a frenzy and sprinted toward the hotel.

Breathing heavily when he stepped into the hotel, he asked the clerk, "Has that detective, Martin Lunt, checked in?"

"Not yet, Mr. Granemann, he came to the desk and then left with his slave woman. They were going to the old Lutheran church."

Charles ran as fast as he could down the street and through back alleyways. He was gasping for air when he arrived. His worst fears were now a reality. Lunt was in front of the church with the sheriff, the sheriff's son, and a slave woman. They formed a small circle around Gabe who clutched the baby and cried out, "Ya can't take her, she not yours, she be Miss Lizabeth's."

"Please, Gabe, This man has legal papers saying that Miss Douglas and the baby have to go back to St. Louis."

Charles tried to appear calm as he approached, "What's going on Earl?"

"You know what's goin' on, Charles. Stay out of this."

"Earl, this isn't right." He looked at the tall mustached man with the insolent expression. "Tell this mercenary to go back to St. Louis."

Lunt had presented the sheriff with the judge's order. He assumed local authorities would assist him. Now he was becoming annoyed.

Lunt pulled his pistol from beneath his long overcoat. He casually let it rest on his hip, "Let's all obey the law and no one will be harmed. Miss Gabe, hand the child over to Shanara. Charles, I don't know why you're here, but stand back. And Sheriff, kindly encourage everyone to obey the law."

Charles walked menacingly toward Lunt. Lunt fired a shot into the ground directly in front of him. Charles stared at Lunt in disbelief. Everyone else froze in shock.

"If you continue to move toward me, the next shot will be in your leg. The one after that will be in your head."

Charles boiled with rage. He lunged toward the detective. A shot rang out. Charles rolled on the ground and clutched his thigh.

Several blocks away Teeny slipped Charles' letter under the office door. She turned to leave, but heard gunfire. The shots came from the direction of the church. She tore off the leg brace, tucked it under her arm, and began running. A block from the church she ducked into the livery stable. She opened the back door a few inches. Teeny gasped when she saw the scene in the churchyard below. Charles lay on the ground, Gabe knelt on the ground cradling Mary, and the sheriff stood yelling at the man who fired the gun.

"Goddamn it, Lunt! Fire that weapon again and I'll arrest you!"

Lunt sneered, "You will do no such thing."

Undaunted, the sheriff yelled back, "I'm telling you to holster that gun! We don't want any more bloodshed! Harold, run and get Doc Williams."

Lunt retorted angrily, "If people obey the law there won't be any more bloodshed. I have the legal right to take this child and her mother. Now do your goddamn job! Get that sniveling bitch off the ground and make her tell us where the mother is!"

The sheriff knelt down and put his arm around Gabe. "Listen to me Gabe. I don't like this, but you have to tell him where Elizabeth is." Earl helped the slave girl to her feet. "Look at me. We got no choice."

The sheriff waited for a response.

"She be gone to da Granemann office. Oh, Lawd, please doan hurt her."

Lunt holstered his pistol. "Lead the way sheriff."

Teeny opened the door a few more inches and saw the doctor arrive. He wrapped a wide strip of cloth around Charles's leg. He was bleeding badly and barely conscious. A black woman standing next to Gabe held the baby. The group started up the hill. The woman holding Mary paused, opened her blouse, and began nursing the infant. Teeny stifled a scream for her to "Stop," and stumbled backwards in a daze. She sat cross-legged on the hard ground, hands pressed against the sides of her head.

She wiped away tears, adjusted her wig, grabbed the brace, and ran out the front of the stable. Teeny saw the union flag flying above the post office and ran toward it.

59

A DRAYMAN WAS RELAYING THE news to Taylor about a shooting at the old church just as Teeny burst in. Tearfully she pleaded with Taylor to do something. He quickly ushered her across the street and into his home. "Adie," he called out, "I need yer help!"

William Taylor had seen his share of escapes and captures and knew there was no chance of getting the baby back. Now he had to convince Teeny to get out of St. Paul.

"Miss Elizabeth, you'll have ta save yerself, an' then, maybe someday, ya can get yer baby back. That boat's leavin' at four a clock, and we have to do whatever we can ta get ya on it."

Taylor sent Adeline to find Henry Claibourne, a white abolitionist who had worked with the Taylors before.

"Tell him to wear some fancy duds an' bring a travelin bag. I'm gonna see who's snoopin' around and make sure the boats leavin' on time. Miss Elizabeth, you'll have ta wait here. Doan answer tha door unless ya know it's me or Adie."

The Granemann office stood empty when Lunt and the sheriff arrived. This setback fueled Lunt's anger. He returned to the hotel, where the clerk that handed him Frieda's note was still on duty.

"I need three patrollers. There will be a nice tip for you if you get them to the sheriff's office by noon."

An hour later the patrollers met Lunt outside the sheriff's office. The detective described the woman they were looking for and gave each man an assignment. One was to keep an eye on passengers boarding the riverboats, another would watch the livery where coaches stopped for fresh horses, and the third would monitor Taylor's barbershop.

Teeny sat transfixed in Taylor's home watching the clock on the mantle. The door creaked and floor moaned near the back door, announcing the arrival of a tall white man. He had entered the house and made his way into the kitchen. Teeny crept toward the fireplace and picked up an iron poker. Adeline quickly circled ahead of the man to protect him.

"It's okay, Elizabeth, it's okay. He's a friend." Adeline gently took the iron rod from Teeny's shaking hand.

"I'm sorry if we frightened you. We had to come through the back alley. This is Henry Claibourne. He's gonna help you get aboard that boat."

"I'm pleased to meet you, Miss Douglas. Adeline told me about the detective and what happened. I'm very sorry about your baby and your friend," the man said sympathetically.

Teeny stammered a barely audible "Thank you."

She stood wringing her hands, and spoke in a whisper. "Charles was the only one who tried to stop him."

She paused to catch her breath, then realized Claibourne could be another of Lunt's victims. "You're in danger by helping me…I'm very grateful."

Taylor came in the back door, entered the parlor, and looked through a small opening in the window curtains. "That detective's got people scattered all around town searchin' for ya Miss. One of 'em is at the levee and another's across the street. Word on the street is the Granemann boy was hurt pretty bad."

Images of Charles and Mary at the church filled her head and she tried to hold back tears. Taylor pulled the watch from his pocket. "Miss Elizabeth, you're gonna have to summon up yer strong self, 'cause ya needs to be leavin'. We got ta get ya to dat boat at least a half hour b'fore it heads down river."

Taylor told Henry, "Elizabeth will meet you at the hotel in fifteen minutes." Then he said to Teeny, "Your boat's first stop for wood is Galena. Get off in that town an' board a stage. I'm goin' out tha front way. I'm pretty sure the patroller outside my shop is gonna follow me. I'm hoping the other one hangin' 'round tha levee will too."

Teeny sat and stared at her small travelling bag. Taylor took her hand.

"Miss Elizabeth, it's up to you now. Five minutes after I'm gone, ya take that bag an' head out tha back way. We want everyone ta think you an' Henry be man and wife. After ya get on that boat, Henry's gonna leave ya."

Teeny shifted her gaze and looked up. "Mr. Taylor, will I ever see my baby again?"

"Hard to say. Once slave families get torn apart it's hard to get 'em ta'gether agin. Maybe you'll be one a tha lucky ones." Taylor unlatched the front door and was prepared to leave.

"Mr. Taylor, thank you." Taylor glanced over his shoulder at the sad face looking back at him.

"You're welcome ma'am. I'm sorry yer baby ain't with ya. Five minutes, then ya gotta leave." Taylor closed the door and crossed the alley toward his shop.

Adeline peeked through the curtain at the man keeping close watch on her husband. Taylor passed his shop and rounded the corner. The patroller flicked his cigarette to the ground and followed. Adeline handed Teeny her bag, put her arm around her, and led her to the back door. "I'll be sayin prayers for ya."

She closed the door and watched Teeny limp away. She wondered how much fight the young woman had left. Halfway to the hotel Teeny turned and looked in the direction of the church. She recalled the morning's events, clenched her fists, and moved faster.

Claibourne anxiously checked his watch as he waited outside the hotel. To his relief, he spotted Teeny making her way up the hill. He extended his hand and helped her inside a waiting cab. A whip cracked and the driver eased his rig into the line of traffic. Henry shouted to the cabby, "We would appreciate getting as close to the Excelsior as possible. My wife has trouble walking."

"I'll do my best, governor."

The buggy weaved through levee traffic until an officer held up his hand and ordered them to stop. Teeny felt as through everyone around her could hear her heart pounding.

"That's far enough. Step down. Are you two boarding this boat?"

"Yes, officer. We're running a little late."

The policeman took a quick look at the middle-aged couple and saw no connection between them and the slave woman being hunted. He turned and pointed to a landing stage.

"The Excelsior's clerk is over there. He'll check you in."

Teeny and Henry looked around for anyone who might detain them. The patroller who would have stopped and questioned them had joined his partner. Both were following Taylor.

Taylor doubled back to Fourth Street and led Lunt's men to the church where Charles was shot. They watched him enter the old building. Taylor paced back and forth in front of a window and appeared to be talking to someone. Lunt's men drew their pistols. Taylor moved swiftly out the back door. The patrollers burst through the entrance and ran to the back. They found suitcases and a baby crib.

The Excelsior's clerk looked at Henry's tickets and then checked the passenger manifest. "Your names aren't on my list." Henry explained that he purchased the tickets a few days ago from Mr. Charles Granemann, "I'm sure his name is there." The clerk found Charles' name and scratched a neat black line through it.

"Your name and your wife's name?"

"Henry and Lucy Ann Claibourne." The clerk substituted names and called for a cabin boy. Henry and Teeny followed him to the stateroom. Henry handed the young man a coin and asked, "How long before we depart?"

"We're scheduled to leave at four, but could be delayed. There's been some kinda trouble in town. A detective from St. Louis is lookin' for an escaped slave woman. He's offered a big reward for her capture." Henry nodded and tried not to seem too concerned. "Thank you, son. Should anything new happen in town, or if there is a change in departure time, please let us know."

Martin Lunt was on the levee looking for anything out of the ordinary: a woman traveling alone, a person trying to buy passage, or someone trying to board at the last minute. It was almost four when his men returned. "Where the hell have you two been?"

"We followed that Taylor guy to the church. We went inside to see what the son of a bitch was up to and he ducked out the back way." Lunt's irritation flared. He paced and surveyed the riverboats. The detective seemed certain the slave woman was still in St. Paul. He ordered his men to distribute more handbills offering a reward.

The Excelsior continued to make preparations to depart. Henry gave Teeny a hug and encouraged her to "Stay strong." He hastily exited the cabin and went to the starboard side of the main deck. Claibourne climbed over the rail, threw his bag ahead of him, and jumped. From a small building on the dock he watched to see if anyone was going to prevent the Excelsior from leaving.

Most riverboat steam whistles emitted a low moaning sound, but the Excelsior's was high-pitched and screeching. It startled Lunt and everyone else in the vicinity. The detective ran to the bow and called to the clerk doing a last minute check of passengers and cargo. "Sir, do you have a woman on board traveling by herself?"

"No, sir."

"Any last minute boardings?"

"No, sir."

The Excelsior drifted steadily backward and away from the dock. He yelled again. "Is there anyone on board using someone else's tickets?" The clerk struggled to hear him over the engine noise and ruckus made by passengers yelling good-byes. He cupped his hand to his ear. Lunt shouted out the question once more, but the clerk couldn't hear. He turned and walked away with the passenger list.

Lunt's patrollers found him standing at water's edge. His arms were crossed and he held a crumpled riverboat schedule. He was angry and said, "For the rest of the evening don't leave your posts." He walked back to the hotel in a foul mood. Everything was in the details. Lunt wasn't positive the girl was aboard the Excelsior, but the possibility she was gnawed at him.

Teeny reclined on the bed massaging marks left by the leg brace. A knock on the cabin door sent a jolt of fear through her. A voice outside the door asked, "Mr. Claibourne, are you there?"

She hobbled to the door and opened it part way.

"Good evening, Mrs. Claibourne. I brought you and Mr. Claibourne up to your cabin earlier."

Teeny nodded. "Yes I remember, is there a problem?"

"Mr. Claibourne asked me to let him know whether there was any news from town. Well, there is. The man who was shot by the detective was hurt real bad, and well, he died."

Teeny felt ill. She told the clerk she would tell Mr. Claibourne and slowly closed the door. The Excelsior's steam engines came to life and the pistons began a fore and aft thumping sound. As the large paddlewheel churned Teeny took a few cautious steps to the stateroom window. She watched the town fade. She wrapped herself in a blanket and sat on the edge of the bed.

"Stay strong," she murmured, "Stay strong."

60

SUNNY'S RELATIONSHIP WITH WILL HAD begun to generate ill feelings with the Elliott sisters. They referred to him as "The Nigger with money."

One morning, before leaving for work, Sunny asked Emma whether she could keep a little of her pay. "I'd like to get a new dress, and maybe some personal items. Perfume, powder, maybe a new hair brush."

"You get gussied up Missy and folks will start to talk."

"Start to talk! About me?"

"Yes, you. You start looking like you're getting above your place and it won't sit well with people."

Sunny looked confused. "My place?"

"You know what I mean. You're half Nigger and half Indian. Start acting like you're better than you're supposed to and people will talk. That goes for that uppity Nigger boyfriend of yours too. Where did he get that money? There are lots of white folks around here just scraping by. Then out of nowhere he and his nigger friend show up with six hundred dollars. Something's not right."

Sunny wanted no part of a confrontation with the sisters. She picked up her lunch sack and quickly headed out the door. Will joined her at noon behind the bank. Sunny was shaking as she filled Will in on her morning conflict.

"I beg your pardon, Miss Lee, but did y'all say the lovely plantation blossom Miss Emma referred to the honorable Colonel Douglas as an uppity Nigger?"

Sunny laughed, but still felt upset. "It's not that funny, Will."

"I know, I know. But maybe you'll like what Mr. Thomas had to say." Will gave her the details of his conversation about the boardinghouse. He paused for a few seconds. "He said he thought we could all live there."

Sunny wasn't sure whether she was amused or angry.

"Will, is Dave Thomas proposing to me?"

"I, er, uh, no, no...I guess I am."

Sunny stared at him. "You guess you are?"

"Yes, I mean no. I mean yes I am. I want us to be together." He slowed things down and looked into her eyes. "Sunny, I love you. Will you marry me?"

"You seem terribly confused, Colonel Douglas. She smiled sweetly and locked on his dark eyes. "I love you too, Will. My answer is yes." Then she wrapped her arms around him and kissed him sweetly on the lips. "Please tell Mr. Thomas I like his idea."

Sunny didn't feel she could share the plans she and Will were making with others at the bank, and certainly not the Elliot sisters. But Will was eager to share the news. He wanted to thank the people who helped make his new life possible. That evening he composed a letter to Abe Bireman.

Dave Thomas was having his coffee when Will approached him the next morning with a neatly folded sheet of paper. "Mr. Thomas you've been awfully good to us and I don't mean to be a bother, but can I ask another favor?"

"You know you can, Will. What do you need?"

"I wrote a letter to Mr. Bireman, to thank him and Captain McGee for helping us and to let them know where we are. I'm pretty sure the folks at the post office wouldn't take a colored person's letter seriously."

"I'm ordering supplies today. Soon as I get the paperwork finished, I'll mail your letter with mine. Say, have you shared my idea with Sunny?"

"You were right. She likes your idea." After a short pause he said, "There's something else … we're gonna get married."

Thomas smiled, "Congratulations, Will. Sunny's a fine young woman." He clasped his hands behind his head, leaned back, and started chuckling. "I wish I could be there to see Emma and Gertrude when Sunny tells 'em she's leaving. My, my, they're gonna have a hissy fit."

Thomas stood up and congratulated Will one more time. Then he said, "Hang on a minute Will, I've got a couple things I want you to have." He walked over to a large safe. Thomas adjusted his glasses, dialed the combination, and pulled open the heavy iron door. He removed a small cloth bag and a set of keys. He put them on his desk and said, "Wedding presents."

Thomas opened the bag and pulled out a silver necklace with a translucent blue stone attached. He held it up to the sunlight so that it could reflect tiny bits of light around the room. "This was mom's. Guess I never told you about her. She was a mulatto slave, owned by a cotton broker in Greenville."

Will was stunned by this revelation. "A mulatto slave…your mother?"

Thomas nodded. Will didn't know what to say. Finally, he stammered, "Where's Greenville?"

"It's in Mississippi, not too far from your old Mary Dale Plantation. Dad owned a dry goods store there, saw mom on the street one-day, and fell in love with her. He purchased her from a cotton broker, but knew they couldn't live together in Mississippi, so they headed up river. Dad thought they should go west and open a store in one of the new gold mining towns. They never made it past Kanesville. Dad started selling supplies to prospectors and anyone else going west. One of his first customers paid for supplies with this necklace. It was mom's favorite. I want Sunny to have it." Thomas put the stone and chain back in the bag and handed it to Will.

"Thank you, thank you Mr. Thomas. Sunny will love this."

Thomas picked up the keys lying on the desk and said, "Follow me." They walked along the warehouse corridor, past bins of merchandise, and arrived at a tall narrow door. Thomas used the keys to open a lock above and below the doorknob. He led Will inside. There were no windows and the room gave off a strong musty odor. The room's furnishings included a bed, chairs, sofa, and a small stove.

"Kanesville was a wild place when mom and dad moved here," Thomas explained. "Gangs of armed men on horseback would come to town, Border Raiders, they called 'em. They'd scare the hell out of the locals and steal whatever they could. There were also raids by Indians angry with the white man for taking their land. Dad wanted a safe place for him and mom. From the outside you can't tell there's a room back here. Anyway, I want you to have keys to this room."

"I'm grateful, sir, but are you thinking there's going to be trouble?"

"I've been reading the newspapers, Will. Since that Fugitive Slave Law was passed, bounty hunters have been going into northern territories and taking coloreds right and left. Men who can work the fields and women young enough to have children are the ones they want. Don't matter to them if they got free papers. I hope nothing happens, but if you see trouble coming, get to this room and stay out of sight."

Will thanked Thomas again and took off toward the bank to surprise Sunny with the necklace. He rounded the corner and saw Emma and Gertrude having a heated conversation with Bowers. Will was pretty sure the conversation had something to do with him, or Sunny, or both.

After they left Will and Sunny retreated to the shed behind the bank. "I saw the sisters out front talking to Bowers, any idea what they wanted?" Sunny nodded.

"They were in his office earlier. I was scrubbing the floor and heard them. They were trying to find out where you and Tom got all that money. He said it was none of their business and he wouldn't discuss other people's finances. They got mad and told him they were going to take their money out of his bank. It was getting a little loud. That's when Bowers closed his office door."

Sunny knew Will was upset by this news and thought it best to discuss something else. She reached over and touched his hand. "Did Mr. Thomas agree to mail your letter?"

"He did. And he gave me something to give to you—a wedding present." He retrieved the cloth bag and keys from his pocket and placed them on the table.

Sunny pulled the necklace from the bag and looked to Will for an explanation.

"That was his mother's, and he wanted you to have it."

Sunny looked at the necklace and began to cry. "Oh Will, I've never had a necklace, never had any jewelry. I can't wait to thank him."

Will decided to wait and tell her about Thomas' family history and the keys to the room some other time. He took the keys from the table and slipped them back in his pocket. Sunny noticed. "What are those keys for?"

"It's another present, another surprise. But you'll have to wait."

"It's not a good idea to tease me, Colonel Douglas. Please tell me what the keys are for."

"Let's wait until I can show you. It will make more sense. Speaking of surprises, when are you going to show the Elliot sisters your wedding present?"

61

"MY HUSBAND ISN'T FEELING WELL. As a courtesy to him and the other passengers may we take the meals in our room?" The first officer looked at the elderly woman who had limped aboard the Excelsior and obliged. For three days Teeny remained secluded, seldom leaving her stateroom. When the riverboat approached Galena she cautiously emerged, and sat quietly in the back of the saloon listening to the captain address first class passengers.

"Many cities are named after saints, kings, and famous people. Our next stop is a town prospering because it has lead mines. In honor of that fact, the town fathers named their fair city after the lead-bearing mineral, Galena. A local gentleman who disliked the town because of its lack of culture and low brow ways suggested the town be named after another mineral…Arsenic."

Passengers chuckled in amusement at the captain's river lore, but Teeny could focus only on thoughts of getting away from the town as quickly as possible. The mooring lines were cast. She waited while officers gave directions to first class passengers planning to visit the town's restaurants and shops. After they departed she adjusted her wig and touched up her make-up. She picked up her traveling bag and started to exit by way of the promenade deck. She heard a gentle rapping on the door.

"Mr. Claibourne, Mrs. Claibourne, will you be going ashore? It's a very pleasant little town." Teeny opened the door a few inches and said, "Thank you, but Mr. Claibourne is in the gentleman's facility. He's not feeling well. Maybe you would be kind enough to escort me ashore."

"I'll be glad to, Mrs. Claibourne. I'm sorry your husband has been feeling so poorly. I haven't seen him since we left St. Paul."

The young man politely escorted Teeny to shore, where she handed him a gold coin.

"This is very generous, Mrs. Claibourne. Thank you."

Teeny smiled and replied, "You're welcome. Oh, one other thing, if Mr. Claibourne doesn't answer the door please let him sleep."

Teeny remained as innocuous as possible as she limped toward the post office. She waited until the ticket seller was alone and inquired about passage to Chicago. "Frink and Walker or Western Stage?"

Teeny had no idea which to choose. "Which is leaving first?"

"That would be Western Stage, but it's all booked. Frink and Walker is comin' thru at six. There's one space available on that." The man raised his cap brim and looked at the elderly woman with a cane. "Traveling by stage can be pretty rough ma'am. We're not responsible for any health problems along the way."

"I understand. I would still like to purchase a ticket." She handed him the money. Without showing any further interest in the old woman he said, "Have a good trip."

She entered a busy restaurant, found a dimly lit booth, and lingered over a bowl of soup as long as possible. Teeny left a few coins, picked up her bag, and waited in the shadows of two narrow buildings for the six o'clock stage.

When the coach arrived, she crossed the street and held up her ticket. A tall man perched on the driver's seat stepped down. He smiled and said, "Welcome, Ma'am, I'll take your ticket, but we got to get fresh horses, grease the axles, and pick up the mail. And, these nice folks on board need ta move about a little. We'll be leavin' in half an hour." Teeny asked whether she might wait inside since she had difficulty walking. "Sure you can, your seat's in the far corner facing forward."

After the passengers went to the rest stop, Teeny took her seat and lowered the leather curtain to avoid being seen. Suddenly a round-faced man with a large bushy gray beard opened the carriage door.

"What you doin' in there?"

His interruption startled her. "I, I'm waiting for the stage to leave. Who are you?"

"I'm the stock tender from the livery, bringin' fresh horses. Does the jehu know you're in there?"

Teeny never heard that word before. "The jehu, who is that?"

"The jehu, the driver, he know you're in there?"

"A tall fellow took my ticket."

"That's him, that's Luke. I didn't mean no harm, Miss, its jus that most folks get some food and get cleaned up. They don't stay in the coach."

Teeny sighed, closed her eyes and said, "I'll be fine; I'm just tired."

A short time later, the other passengers returned and introduced themselves: the women were wives of army officers, two of the men were land agents for the federal government, and the last was a handsome businessman from Chicago.

Luke readied the group and the stage for the next leg of the journey.

"Next stop is in three hours. All aboard! Awaaay!" He called.

The stage lurched forward. An hour outside of Galena, the women and land agents partnered up for a game of Whist and invited Teeny to participate. She politely declined. She tried to sleep, but the images of her baby being nursed by another woman and of Charles lying on the ground struggling to stay alive kept her awake.

Around midnight the stage slowed and then braked.

Luke yelled, "Freeport, one hour stop!"

The stage made eight more stops before arriving in the tiny village of Sarah's Grove. It had been twenty-four hours since Teeny boarded the stage; every hour brought increasing confidence she wouldn't be found. The last trail stop was brief.

"We'll be in Chicago before midnight folks. All aboard! Awaaay!" Luke called.

The passengers, exhausted and queasy from being jostled about for so long, rallied at the prospect of finally reaching the end of the line. The two women said they looked forward to reuniting with their husbands, who were stationed at Fort Dearborn. The land agents had been invited to stay in the home of an aspiring politician by the name of Stephen Douglas. Arthur Irving said he looked forward to the hot bath and soft bed waiting for him at the Tremont Hotel. When Teeny's turn came, she made a vague reference to "visiting friends."

The stage rolled down State Street to the livery next to the post office—its final stop. Two soldiers in a military wagon waited for their wives. A private enclosed carriage stood parked there for the government agents. Next to the carriage was Arthur's cab sent from the Tremont Hotel. Teeny looked around, then asked the stage driver where she might find a hotel room for the night.

"Tremont's the nicest. Why don't ya ride with Mr. Irving an' see if they got a room?"

Arthur overheard the conversation and said, "I'd be happy to escort you to the hotel, Miss Douglas. Considering the miles we've traveled together, we're no longer strangers, and you'll be safe."

"I appreciate that Mr. Irving. I'm new to the city and failed to make a reservation," Teeny responded gratefully.

When they arrived, the hotel clerk at the front desk greeted Arthur. "Welcome back, Mr. Irving. We have your room ready."

"Thank you, Lester. Lester, this is Miss Douglas. She would like a room."

"I'm pleased to meet you, Miss Douglas, and I wish we could accommodate you, but we are completely booked."

Arthur jutted his chin, raised his eyebrows and spoke in a polite firm manner. "Lester, I know Mr. Paulsen keeps a room in reserve for emergencies. Please consider this an emergency."

"Yes, Mr. Irving, give me a moment."

Lester walked down a short hallway, knocked on the manager's door, and conveyed a brief message.

"Yes sir!" he said to his boss and hastily returned to the front desk.

"Mr. Paulsen welcomes you to the Tremont, Miss Douglas. He also invites you both to join him for a drink in the bar," the clerk relayed hospitably.

"Please tell him we have been aboard that stagecoach for two days and are very tired. But we appreciate the offer and would like to join him tomorrow evening. Lester looked over at the bellhop and said, "James, take Miss Douglas' bag and escort her to room twenty-four. Mr. Irving, allow me to take your bags. May I bring you a libation?"

"Not tonight, thank you, I just need some rest."

Arthur followed Lester down the hallway and spotted the other bellhop returning from room twenty-four. Arthur signaled, and asked him to deliver a message to Miss Douglas. On the back of a card he wrote:

> *Please join me for dinner at seven tomorrow.*
> *Come without your disguise.*
> *Arthur Irving*

The trip had left Teeny physically and emotionally drained. Arthur's note seemed overwhelming at the moment. She placed it next to her pillow. Exhaustion trumped worry and she was soon asleep.

CR   CR   CR

In St. Paul, Robert Granemann sat alone at Harry's bar sitting, nursing his third bourbon. He had been a regular every night since Charles' funeral. His dream of growing old, watching his son take over the family business, and spoiling a passel of grandchildren was over. He stared morosely at the bottle in front of him. Harry came from the back of the bar and slipped into the seat next to him.

"Robert, I got some information ya need ta know. It may be a bad time. If it is I'm sorry, but it's about Charles."

Robert looked up. "What is it, Harry?"

"My wife's cousin works at that new hotel in town, the one where that detective was stayin'. And she says, somebody tipped that detective off as to where Charles and the girl were hiding. She said there was a note waiting for the detective. He read it and went straight to the church."

Robert's face took on a new level of seriousness. "Excuse me, will you?" He grabbed his hat and stood to leave.

"Of course," Harry nodded, he knew immediately where Robert was headed.

Questions raced through Robert's mind as he drove his carriage to the hotel. Once inside he inquired at the front desk, "Who was on duty last week when the detective from St. Louis arrived?"

"I was, Mr. Granemann. My name's Simms, Randall Simms."

"Randall, did you give that detective a note?"

Randall hesitated, and in a shaky voice said, "Yes, sir."

"Who requested that you give it to him?"

"A very pretty young lady with blonde hair and blue eyes. I asked her name but she wasn't interested in telling me."

Robert had a sinking feeling. "Does she live in St. Paul?"

"I think so, she drove up in a carriage. Quite a nice one."

A pained expression overtook Robert's face. "Randall, please come with me for a moment."

The older man led the young clerk to the front of the hotel where the Granemann carriage stood waiting.

"Is this the carriage?" Robert asked.

Randall nodded. "Yes, sir, that's the carriage."

"Thank you," Robert responded and handed the young man a small tip.

Robert returned home immediately and woke Helen. He told her what had just transpired. Both were bewildered. They had taken Freida in, grown to trust her, and now considered her a member of the family.

"Why? Why would she do that, Helen? I thought she liked us—all of us."

"She does. But she loved Charles. She probably thought with Elizabeth gone, he would pay more attention to her."

"I want to speak to her. I'm not going to wait until morning." Robert's voice betrayed his pain. Helen nodded her agreement.

The couple strode to the back of the house. Robert knocked on Frieda's door several times, but there was no answer. Across the hall Gabe came out in her nightgown and robe.

"She be gone, Mistah Granemann. She leave early dis mornin, an' she had her bag wif her."

This news rendered Helen and Robert even more confused and upset.

"I don't think she ever thought Charles would be hurt, Robert. I'm sure she didn't," Helen reasoned.

Robert sat on the edge of the bed and stared at the floor. He looked at his wife through weary blood shot eyes and said, "I'm not going to have it end like this, Helen."

62

IT HAD BEEN TWO WEEKS since Sunny left the Elliot sisters' home. Emma now referred to her as "The Indian whore." The Elliot sisters marched to the bank the day she left and insisted that Sam Bowers "Fire that ungrateful tramp! If you don't, we're taking our money out of your bank."

That afternoon Bowers relayed the story to Thomas.

"Whose money would you miss the most, Sam, theirs or mine?" Dave retorted like rapid fire.

In Shantytown Will and Tom started fixing up the room in the back of the old boardinghouse. Newspapers and books stood neatly stacked on shelves. The Reverend Nate donated a few tables and chairs. Dave Thomas gave them a slate board from the warehouse. Tom helped Will create the classroom, but was worried. "Will, how ya gonna get dem kids to come here?"

"Well, I'm hoping they'll come 'cause they want to learn to read and write. And I'm hoping their parents will encourage them."

"I doan know Will, I hopes ya be right."

On Sunday, Reverend Nate announced, "Will Douglas, who was a teacher in St. Louis for the honorable Reverend John Berry Meachum, and who is now a member of our little community, is gonna start a school for our children. I want all of you to join Will and me after church to find out more about this wonderful opportunity."

After the service Will and the Reverend talked to members of the congregation. There were plenty of handshakes and lots of "God bless" wishes, but not one of the parents said they would send their children to attend his school.

Will looked dejectedly at the minister and said, "What's going on Reverend?"

"I'm not sure, Will. They don't know you all that well, and maybe they don't want to get excited about this unless they know you're going to be here for the long haul. Give it a little time and let's see what happens."

Will had planned lessons, even bought graphite sticks and paper. His discouragement showed when he reported the story to Dave Thomas.

"I hope you didn't make a mistake when you bought Annie's place Mr. Thomas."

Thomas smiled. "I got a plan. Look what I've got here. This is a copy of *Uncle Tom's Cabin*, the book I was telling you about. It's more popular than the *Bible*. People want to hear the story, and you're gonna read it to them. That way you can sell them on the idea of reading, an' writing, an' maybe a little arithmetic."

Dave Thomas was used to having the things he wanted accomplished quickly, especially if he intended to use these things to help a friend. He walked into Trimble's Print and Signs and said, "Sam, I need fifty hand bills printed up. Here's the copy. Make 'em look good."

Sam read the copy, then looked at Thomas skeptically. "Have you thought this through, Dave?"

Thomas locked his thumbs around his suspenders and said, "What do you mean?"

"Are you gonna hand 'em out, an' then read it to them?"

Thomas realized his mistake, but wasn't discouraged.

"Print 'em anyway. We can use 'em to make a point." Thomas went back to the warehouse and found Will.

"Come on, Will, let's pay Reverend Nate a visit."

When they arrived at the boardinghouse Annie told them the Reverend was most likely sleeping in one of the pews. "He likes to take a little time off from the Missus an' rest up."

They woke Nate from his nap and Thomas explained how they would use the handbills and *Uncle Tom's Cabin* to recruit students.

"What kin I do to help?" The reverend responded, intrigued.

"Cut your sermon short next Sunday. Let Will read a few passages from the most popular book in America to your flock."

Nate laughed. "Sure, this may be the first time everyone stays awake for the Sunday service."

Will began reading *Uncle Tom's Cabin* that evening, and every evening for the next week. He found the book challenging. He struggled with the language and had difficulty relating to some of the characters. Will also worried the congregation would have trouble following the story. It took him until the wee hours of Friday morning to finish. He looked over at Sunny, who had fallen asleep hours ago.

The next day Will rehearsed what he was going to say after the sermon. Then he carefully picked out a passage to read. Sunny listened to the excerpt, and in a playful manner said, "Why don't you mosey over and invite the Elliott sisters for the Sunday service? They would be flattered to have an invitation from the honorable Colonel Douglas."

"We can laugh about them, Sunny, but they're mean. They tried to get you fired, and Thomas says they've been talking to the sheriff. They told him Tom and I stole our money. Those old ladies thought you'd be taking care of them the rest of their lives. They consider you valuable. "

Sunny smiled. "So, I'm valuable? How much would you pay for me Colonel Douglas?"

Will tried to look sincere when he deadpanned, "Tha Colonel would happily part with at least two or three dollars for y'all."

Sunny giggled. Delighted by his humor, she reached up and caressed the back of his neck. She whispered, "Colonel, I believe I need to show you how valuable I am."

On Sunday, Reverend Nate gave a short Eulogy, then he introduced Will as a special guest who would inform them about the most popular book in the country, *Uncle Tom's Cabin*. Nate held up the book so everyone could see it.

Will came forward and explained that he would summarize the first part of the story and then read a few passages. Will noticed the congregants' puzzled looks, but he proceeded.

"The story takes place in Kentucky, where Uncle Tom and his family work for a kindly owner named Shelby. Tom is such a good slave that Shelby can send him anywhere and Tom will always come back. He believes it is dishonorable to run away from his kind master."

Many parishioners appeared startled. Will continued.

"Mrs. Shelby's young maid, Eliza Harris, is also a happy slave, who adores her young baby boy, Harry. Her husband George ran away, but promised to return with enough money to buy Eliza and baby Harry's freedom." Men in the congregation rolled their eyes and began snickering. Will began to panic. He looked at Reverend Nate, who signaled for him to pick up the pace.

"The kind owner owes money to a ruthless slave trader named Simon Legree. Shelby plans to sell Uncle Tom and baby Harry to pay his debt to Legree. Eliza overhears this and decides she will escape with baby Harry rather than wait for George to return."

The eye rolling and snickering had stopped, but the incredulous looks remained. Will was perspiring. He cleared his throat. "The slave catchers are on Eliza's heels as she carries her little boy across ice flows on the Ohio River. Here's a description of her escape."

> The huge green fragment of ice…pitched and
> creaked as her weight came on it, but she stayed
> there not a moment. With wild cries and desperate
> energy she leaped to another and still another cake,
> stumbling—leaping—slipping—springing upwards
> again! Her shoes are gone—her stockings cut from
> her feet—while blood marked every step…; but she
> saw nothing, felt nothing till dimly, as in a dream,
> she saw the Ohio side, and a man helping her up the
> bank.

Will looked up and noticed a few interested faces, but most looked at him in disbelief. The Reverend knew it was time to intervene. He came to the pulpit and in a stern voice said, "Brothers and sisters I'm sure we all appreciate what Will Douglas is trying to do. You would be proud if your son or daughter could read from a book the way he just did. Now Will lives here and has volunteered to teach your children. Please visit his school in the boardinghouse next Saturday and find out more about this opportunity."

After the service Will sat with Sunny in their small bedroom. Sunny took his hand. "Will, I'm proud of you. You tried, but that book was a mistake." Sunny looked down at the copy of *Uncle Tom's Cabin* resting in his lap. "That book's not for us. It's for white folks who read and want to debate slavery."

He got up and placed the book on a table next to the bed. "I guess I got caught up in Mr. Thomas's enthusiasm. I thought it was a good idea at the time."

Saturday night Will and Sunny placed lanterns around the classroom. On the slate board they had written in large block letters, "WELCOME TO

THE COUNCIL BLUFFS SCHOOL FOR COLOREDS." Annie placed a plate of biscuits and jam on a table surrounded by an assortment of tin cups filled with sweet tea. Will waited at the door and looked down the dirt road, hoping someone would stop by.

Tom was on his third biscuit and second cup of tea when a tapping on the door broke the tension. A small group of parents were standing there with children of different ages in tow. "Mista Douglas, we hopes ya doan mind we come as a group," one of the fathers said.

Will was thrilled. He talked with the parents about times when the school would meet and what he hoped the children would learn. The children ranged in age from seven to fifteen.

Fifteen-year-old Zeke said to Will. "I think I be too old fer dis."

Tom put his hand on Zeke's shoulder.

"I hear what ya say, Zeke, but I be older den you, an' I gonna be here. We two old guys gonna stick ta'gedder."

"I give it a try, but I gots chores, so I not be here too off'en."

"Dat be okay. All a teacher kin ask is dat you come when ya can, an' ya try," Tom replied encouragingly. Zeke grinned at his new mentor.

The group stayed and had been talking with Will for almost an hour when a parent asked, "Ya gonna read from dat Uncle Tom book like ya said?"

Surprised, Will replied, "Sure, if you want me to."

"No, no, we wuz just wonderin'. That book ain't fer us, but we knows ya mean well."

Will smiled at the group, then at Sunny. "Thank you. Thank you all for coming. We'll begin our lessons next Saturday morning."

He saw Zeke and Tom by the plate of biscuits. "Zeke, make sure you get Tom to school on time," and winked as he spoke.

63

ABE PICKED UP TWO LETTERS from the St. Louis post office the same morning McGee moored his snag boat on the levee. One letter was from Will Douglas, the other from Robert Granemann. Will's letter thanked Abe and McGee for everything they had done to help him. Robert's letter informed Bireman he was coming to St. Louis to avenge his son's death.

When McGee arrived at Abe's office that afternoon he sat down and read both letters. The captain was pleased things were going well for Will and Tom, but he looked dumbfounded after reading Robert's letter.

Abe shook his head and commented, "Can you believe it, Allen? He's coming to St. Louis, and he wants me to help him even the score."

McGee folded the letter and handed it back. "I never had kids, but I can tell that man's hurting. Robert knows there will be no justice for his son. The best he can hope for is revenge."

Abe pondered that for a moment and then said, "Robert Granemann will be killed if he confronts Lunt."

"Then he should have someone do it for him. Put him in touch with Andre."

"Andre?" Abe circled from behind his desk and said, "Well now, that's an interesting thought."

McGee rose and headed for the door. "Abe, I'm treating you to dinner tonight, we can discuss it more then. But right now, I'm off to the poker games at the hotel before the tables get crowded. As you know, the first one in the boat has his choice of oars."

Bireman arched his eyebrows, baffled. "I have no idea how that relates to poker. I'll see you at the restaurant."

Before dinner with McGee, Abe stopped at a seedy little bar a few blocks from the levee. He made his way past regulars to the end of the bar in search of the owner. A balding man with a handle bar mustache sat alone. When Abe approached he said, "What's a high-priced lawyer like you doin' in this place? You must need a drink pretty bad."

"How are you, Rusty? No, I don't need a drink at the moment, just thought I'd stop by and see if you're willing to help people get together and discuss business. Do you still see Andre?"

Rusty nodded, "Yeah, why?"

"I know someone who might like to hire him." Abe conveyed the story about what happened in St. Paul and the details surrounding Charles' death. "That is what lead me here. The father believes the killing was unjustified, and unnecessary. He would like justice."

"I don't know, Abe, he might want a lot a money to go after someone like Lunt."

"The two of them will have to work out the details. The gentleman who wants to meet him should arrive here in two weeks."

Rusty wanted to make sure the lawyer comprehended his role in these plans.

"Ya know, Abe, I get paid for settin' up the meeting, whether they do business or not."

"Understood. The client's name is Robert Granemann. I'll be in touch with you when he arrives."

Rusty reiterated, "Don't forget ta tell yer man, I get mine up front."

Abe nodded as he slid out of his seat, exited the saloon, and hurried uptown.

When Abe reached the restaurant, he located McGee already sitting at a table, looking at his watch.

"Sorry I'm late. I stopped off at Rusty's."

"How's he doing?"

"The same, always ready to help if the price is right. He's going to arrange a meeting with Andre."

"Be careful, Abe, you never know how these things are going to play out. You're dealing with rough customers. Sometimes it costs more to avenge injuries than to bear them."

Abe looked thoughtfully at McGee. "I'm going to pass that bit of wisdom on to Robert."

꿍 꿍 꿍

Helen begged Robert not to leave, but despite her pleas he boarded the riverboat Hamilton for St. Louis. Robert couldn't stop thinking about his son's death and the man who killed him. He spent much of the journey pacing the riverboat's deck obsessing about Martin Lunt.

Two weeks after leaving St. Paul, the grieving father stood on the bow of the Hamilton, suitcase in hand, ready to disembark. He thought about how he would confront the arrogant detective. But doubts began to surface: could he really attack Lunt and shoot him? What would happen to Helen if he were killed in the confrontation?

He secured a room in the Missouri Hotel. *The Republic* listed him in the newspaper's first-class passenger arrivals as "Richard Markell, real estate developer." After depositing his bags in his room, Robert returned to the lobby and picked up a city directory. He scanned the pages until he found Lunt's address. He wrote the information on a card, left the hotel, and hailed a carriage.

Lunt's office was on the first floor of a three-story office building. Robert waited outside for an hour, but there was no sign of the detective. He clutched the revolver tucked in his belt and crossed the street. A notice tacked to the doorframe of Lunt's office read: "Martin Lunt is in transit and will return at the end of the month."

Robert was more relieved than discouraged. He returned to the street and found a cab. He told the driver, "108 Washington Street."

When Robert arrived, he hesitated in front of the door for a few seconds, then gave a firm knock.

"Coming," he heard a man's voice call out.

Abe tentatively opened the door.

"Mr. Bireman, I'm Robert Granemann."

Abe shook hands with the tired and disturbed looking man.

"Very good to finally meet you, Robert. Please come in."

Abe pulled up a chair for him.

"I'm very sorry about your son. I had no idea the young lady we sent to St. Paul would cause such heartache for you and your family."

"It wasn't her fault. We were very willing to have her stay with us, she was a lovely young woman."

Robert explained in detail his son's infatuation with Teeny, and the betrayal by one of his trusted house staff. Robert's speech became labored as he described his son's final hours. Tears formed in his bloodshot eyes.

"There was no reason for Lunt to shoot Charles." Robert pulled a hand-kerchief from his pocket. "Charles was unarmed and certainly no threat to a professional gunman. I just returned from Lunt's office. I was going to confront him, but he's out of town."

"What were you going to do if he had been there?"

"I wanted to tell him how much I miss my son and tell him he is a murderer. I thought I could shoot him, but now I'm not so sure…

"It would have been a mistake, Robert. You are not a killer, and you probably would have failed and been sent to prison."

"I know, Mr. Bireman, but he killed my son, the person who meant more…" his voice trailed off again.

Abe sat behind his desk rubbing his forehead.

"Robert, Martin Lunt was hired to find the girl and the baby. He was doing what the law allowed him to do."

"You and I know that law is wrong and that my son was unarmed. He wasn't capable of defending himself."

Abe got up and stood next to Robert. "I am not unsympathetic, but you should really end this now and return to St. Paul."

"You're saying I should do nothing?"

"That would be best, for you and your wife."

Abe hoped a reasonable response would be forthcoming. Robert sat with slumped shoulders and said in a soft but firm voice, "No, I have to do something."

"Well, if you insist on going through with this, let a person who has experience operate in your stead. If you want, I can arrange for you to meet someone."

"Please do so as soon as you can, Mr. Bireman," Robert responded eagerly.

"Give me a day or two. In the meantime, do not go near Lunt. It would be best if you leave town once your meeting is over. And Robert, if you tell anyone I arranged this, I will lose my standing as a lawyer, and most likely be thrown in jail."

Abe looked even more serious when he said, "You need to be aware you will be dealing with some unsavory characters. They are as dangerous as the man you are pursuing. Are you certain this is worth it?"

Robert remained undeterred. "I believe it is, Mr. Bireman. Who am I meeting?"

"The person arranging the meeting is Rusty Greenwood. He owns a rather sparsely furnished tavern on Chestnut Street. He will want to be paid in advance for arranging a meeting with Andre Garvens. Garvens is known in the underworld as 'Gar'. He's a big man, capable of doing a great deal of damage once he attacks."

"Thank you, Mr. Bireman, thank you. I appreciate your help." Robert picked up his hat and reached out to shake Bireman's hand one more time. "I am at the Missouri Hotel under the name Richard Markell. Please contact me there."

Two days later, a courier handed Robert a note providing directions to Rusty's tavern. That evening, Robert tentatively entered Rusty's and told the bartender he was there to meet the owner. The bartender gestured for Robert to follow and seated him in a small room. Rusty pulled back the curtain and introduced himself. He explained matter-of-factly that his fee for arranging the meeting was twenty-five dollars.

"That's pretty steep. What if this man doesn't show?"

"He's here. I'll bring him back as soon as I get my money."

Robert retrieved a leather fold from his pocket and counted out the money. Rusty did another quick count, then tucked the money into his pocket. Rusty placed two glasses on the table along with a bottle of whiskey. "Thank you Mr. Grandyman. Have yerself a drink. I'll be back in a few minutes."

Robert was going to correct Rusty's mispronunciation of his name, but then considered his location and the pointlessness of such a self-important act. He surveyed the room and wondered what he would do if he had been set up. He sat alone, vulnerable. His gun hadn't been fired in months, and there was no way out except the way he came in.

He listened to the chatter coming from the regulars on the other side of the curtain until the room suddenly became quiet. The sound of someone's heavy boots plodding across the floor increased his tension. Suddenly, Rusty pulled the curtain back and stuck his head inside, "Mr. Grandyman, He's here."

In his sixty-five years, Robert Granemann had never seen a man as big as Gar. The giant had to bend to enter the room. Robert rose and extended his hand, but the huge man didn't reciprocate. Instead, Gar nonchalantly pulled up a chair and sat across from him. Robert had difficulty determining the man's lineage. His reddish brown face bore a variety of scars, he wore his long black hair pulled back and tied with a leather band, and he had adorned his two massive arms with numerous tattoos of women and serpents.

Robert trembled, fumbling with the glass in front of him as he attempted to pour the whiskey. A hand three times larger than his quickly reached across the table and took the glass.

Robert's voice wavered. "I believe Rusty told you why I am in St. Louis."

Gar nodded, but didn't say anything. He poured himself another drink, finished it, and poured another.

"A detective by the name of Martin Lunt killed my son. I want him to pay for his criminal act."

The big man looked directly at Robert. He smirked and finished what was left of the whiskey. Then Gar responded in a deep calm voice that belied his image.

"What he did wasn't illegal. It just wasn't necessary. My fee fer payin' him a visit is four hundred—half now and half later. I'll make him pay for what he done ta yer boy. Leave two hundred with Beermun. I'll pick it up when the job's finished. I'll also leave a little sumthin' to prove I did my job," he explained ominously.

Gar stood up, which signaled that the meeting was over. Robert counted out two hundred dollars. Gar rolled the notes tightly and placed them in a small pouch attached to his belt. Next to the pouch was a decorative holster containing a small tomahawk. He ducked through the curtain and ambled past gawking patrons.

64

IT WAS LATE IN THE evening when Martin Lunt arrived back in St. Louis. He climbed the stairs of his townhome, unlocked the front door, and lit a lantern. Within seconds of entering the library, Lunt realized someone else occupied the room. He calmly reached for the pistol in the middle drawer of his desk and raised the wick on the lantern. In the yellow glow, he saw an enormous figure standing not more than ten feet away.

"What the hell do you want?" Lunt accused.

"You killed a man's son, and he asked me to pay you a visit."

Lunt cocked his pistol, but before he could squeeze the trigger, a small ax sailed through the air, hitting the side of his hand. Lunt's trigger finger dangled for a moment, now attached only by a thin shred of skin. Then it fell to the floor.

Lunt shouted the foulest curses he could muster, and pulled a derringer from his pocket. Lunt fired at Gar's head. The bullet hit Gar's shoulder.

Gar moved swiftly toward the detective and grabbed his arm. He twisted it violently before the fingerless man could even consider getting off a second shot. A bone snapped. Then Gar hurled Lunt against the wall. He reached inside the now unconscious detective's mouth and pulled the gold cap from his tooth.

People in the street who had heard shots fired began yelling for the police. Gar retrieved Lunt's severed finger. He made his way to the back door, which he had left propped open with a brick. He kicked the brick aside, then moved silently down the dark alley.

The next day the *Missouri Republic* reported the attack:

> An armed thug attacked and severely injured Martin Lunt, a prominent St. Louis detective.
>
> He is recuperating at City Hospital. Lunt said his associates would continue his agency's work until he is fully recovered.

When Bireman read the newspaper story to Gar, the giant wondered whether Lunt's associates were searching for him. He took the money lying on the desk and dropped a bloody rag in its place.

"Send this to Grandyman, along with that newspaper story. I want him to know he got his money's worth."

Abe looked at the crumpled cloth, and then at the dried blood on Gar's shirt. "Have you seen a doctor about that wound?"

"I'll be okay. Gotta lay low for awhile." With that, Andre stuffed the money in his pouch and said, "See ya Beermun."

From his office window, Abe watched Gar climb into the back of a covered wagon. He went to his desk and carefully unraveled the cloth. Abe grimaced at the sight of the gold cap and severed finger. He cut out the newspaper article, folded a handkerchief around the grisly items, and jotted a note. He placed everything in a small box and sent it to Robert Granemann.

Three weeks later, Robert carried the small package bearing a St. Louis post-mark to his desk. After Helen went to bed, he cut the twine and unwrapped the paper. He looked at the cigar box for a few seconds, and then opened the lid. He read the note.

> Robert,
>
> Enclosed is a newspaper story about Lunt and items Andre wanted you to have. He said it's proof that he did a good job.

Robert read the news clipping and unraveled the foul-smelling handker-chief. For a few seconds he wasn't sure what lay in front of him. He recoiled slightly once he realized he was looking at a blackening finger. Then he picked up the tiny gold sleeve. It took him a few moments to realize this was the gold cap from Lunt's tooth.

He leaned back, clasped his hands behind his head, and contemplated the injuries and how they might have occurred. Everything his religion taught him about "Turning the other cheek" and "Forgiveness" had vanished after Lunt killed his son. He stared at the objects for several minutes. With a satisfied grin he put them back in the box and turned down the kerosene lamp. He joined Helen in the bedroom and fell fast asleep for the first time in months.

65

TEENY KNEW THAT THE MONEY Will and Tom had shared with her would eventually run out. The only financially independent women she had ever met were those who inherited money or worked at the Silk Ribbon. After being kept by Walther for his personal use, and then having her baby taken away, she grew cynical about society's notions of right and wrong. Out of these considerations, Teeny had developed a plan. She had decided to start her own business—as a madam for a clientele of wealthy men.

When morning came, she felt a renewed sense of purpose. Teeny left her room without the leg brace, cane, and wig. She asked the doorman the location of the nearest women's clothing store.

"Two blocks down on the right ma'am," he replied.

Teeny reached the store easily, and once there, she purchased a conservative ensemble—a white lace blouse, black jacket, and matching black skirt with embroidering along the sleeves and hem.

"Dignified and elegant," the woman assisting the newcomer assured her.

"Yes, this will be fine. I'll need appropriate shoes, and a little jewelry," Teeny replied. Over the next hour, Teeny assembled a fashionable new wardrobe.

Pleased with this accomplishment, she took a buggy back to the Tremont and approached the front desk.

"I am in room twenty-four. Please have someone provide warm water for a bath," she requested in a confident voice.

That evening Teeny applied a small amount of rouge, brushed her hair, and draped a blue silk scarf around her neck and shoulders to compliment her new outfit. Lester was at the front desk and noticed a beautiful woman standing in the lobby. He hurried over to ask whether he could be of assistance.

"I'm dining with Mr. Irving," Teeny told him.

"Yes, ma'am, allow me to escort you to his table."

Arthur and the hotel manager sat enjoying finely aged bourbon at the house's best table when she approached. Arthur recognized the delicate hands as those of the woman who sat across from him in the stagecoach. Everything else had morphed into a delightful surprise.

"Good evening, Miss Douglas. My, my, you certainly look lovely. This is Mr. Paulsen, the manager of the Tremont." Paulsen stood to greet her. "Pleased to meet you Miss Douglas. I hope you're finding your stay here enjoyable."

Lester stood awkwardly, a befuddled look spread across his face after hearing the introductions.

"Are you going to help Miss Douglas with her chair, Lester?" said Paulsen.

Lester sprang back to life, pulling out Teeny's chair and indicating she should sit with a gentle sweep of his arm.

With the group now seated, Arthur and Teeny began to relive the highlights of their stagecoach journey. Paulsen kept Arthur and Teeny company for one more drink and a bit of polite conversation, but then he excused himself.

Arthur and Teeny took their time becoming reacquainted. Finally Arthur could no longer deny his curiosity.

"Why did you wear that disguise?"

Teeny had anticipated this question and had prepared a response.

"A lady can't be too careful when traveling alone, Mr. Irving. I recently separated from my fiancé and needed a change of scenery. A friend suggested I visit Chicago."

Arthur sensed his beautiful new friend might be telling only partial truths, but didn't want to press for more details at the moment. He so enjoyed her company that he simply responded by saying, "Well, it's an up and coming city. You should definitely consider living here."

"And, what do you do, Mr. Irving, besides reside at this lovely hotel?"

"I am a diplomat for the government and a businessman. It's my job to represent America's best interests while keeping our friends in Canada happy. Things get a little prickly when it comes to shipping and transporting large quantities of cargo and people across the Lakes. I reside in Chicago, but I also spend time in Detroit and parts of Canada. I was returning from a meeting with the Hudson Bay Company when we met."

"I can't imagine being away from home for so long. How do you stay in touch with your family?" Arthur shook his head. "No family, Miss Douglas.

My life doesn't lend itself to a family." Before the evening ended Arthur insisted they spend more time together. "Let me show you around the city tomorrow."

Teeny agreed, and the two spent the next day in a flurry of activity: sightseeing, a luncheon, more shopping, and finally a late dinner. After their meal, Arthur invited Teeny to his room for a nightcap. She initially hesitated, then accepted.

Arthur crossed the room carrying two snifters of brandy and placed one on a table next to her. He eased down next to her on the sofa, and in a kind manner said, "Would you consider spending the night, Elizabeth?"

"Arthur, I find you very attractive, but so many things have happened recently, I don't think…"

Before she could finish Arthur touched a finger to her lips. "We'll take it slow. If you want me to stop I will behave like a gentleman."

Teeny studied his well-chiseled, handsome face, but made no reply. So, Arthur began to trace the features of her face with his fingers, softly, barely touching her skin. He stroked her hair and massaged her temples and forehead. His hands felt warm and soothing, not harsh and demanding like Walther's. Teeny closed her eyes, lost in the moment. She realized she now felt aroused in a way she had never previously experienced. Arthur's hands moved gently around her ear, down the nape of her neck, and then to the buttons on her blouse. He opened the blouse slowly.

Arthur leaned in to initiate a kiss. The kiss started gently and lingered for several seconds. Arthur brought her hands to his lips and kissed each palm. Tension and pain that had been part of her life for months began to disappear. Teeny quickly began to reciprocate. She rolled to her side, climbed on top of him, and kissed him fully on the mouth. She helped him enter. Once he was inside Teeny thrust with such intensity that Arthur couldn't believe what was happening. He watched as her body shook and she erupted in a scream of pleasure. Arthur arched his back and hips and succumbed to his own pleasureable sounds.

When both lovers were satisfied, they lay together, exhausted but ecstatic. Arthur pulled her close and gently stroked her auburn hair. "This was quite a day, Elizabeth. I'm not sure we could do anything tomorrow that would top it."

Teeny faced him and smiled coyly. "We could discuss a business partnership."

Her response took Arthur by surprise. He began to laugh, then realized she was serious.

"Well, I suppose we could."

The next morning they had breakfast in Arthur's room. Teeny briefly explained her thoughts of opening a club modeled after the Silk Ribbon.

"Men who frequented that establishment were lawyers, doctors, politicians, and military officers. They complained they were married to women who had no interest in sex; their wives were too dignified, or too refined, or just didn't care. I'm sure there are men in Chicago who are willing to pay a great deal for the privilege of spending time with a woman who specializes in pleasing a man."

Arthur never would have dreamed that the beautiful, charming woman he made love to last night had this type of business proposal in mind, yet he found himself intrigued. He was less interested in why she wanted to open a brothel and more interested in the idea's financial possibilities.

"And, what is my role in this business venture?"

"I need help finding a location that is safe, and I need someone to invite the right clientele. You receive fifty percent of the profits, and I am available to you when you need companionship."

Elizabeth had piqued Arthur's interest enough that he spent the entire day with her discussing and refining the plan. Late in the afternoon they visited a large home in a restricted neighborhood. Teeny admired the manicured greenery and elegant stone path leading to the entryway.

"Are you sure this home is for sale?"

Arthur chuckled. "Everything's for sale if you are willing to pay the price." Arthur pointed to the house with his gold walking cane. "Oliver Robinson owns this place. He's getting old and might consider an offer. A lot of people wouldn't buy it because he's chopped it up. He put up walls and created extra rooms so he could rent out suites to select boarders. That may work to our advantage."

Fortunately for Teeny, Arthur Irving was part of a real estate investment group that specialized in developing Chicago properties. Shortly after inspecting the Robinson home he purchased it along with his partners. Arthur gave Teeny free reign to decorate and make whatever changes she thought necessary. Soon, the old Robinson estate hummed with busy carpenters, stonemasons, and painters.

The would-be madam's days now filled up with challenges and constant spur-of-the-moment decisions. It was in the evening, when she was alone, that Teeny thought wistfully about her baby and wondered how Robert and Helen fared, dealing with the death of their son. Every twist and turn in her life during the past year seemed to have been orchestrated by some evil sorcerer. Teeny wondered whether the future would be any different.

One day, before leaving for a conference with Canadian diplomats, Arthur made a final inspection of the Robinson estate. He looked around the property and said, "I love the way the place is shaping up, can't wait to see how it has changed when I get back."

Teeny wanted to tell him how much she cared for him and how much she would miss him, but hesitated. She watched as he crossed the street, boarded the stagecoach, and tossed her a final wave.

No matter how she felt about Arthur's departure, she knew she had no time to be distracted. The business still needed her attention. So after returning to the hotel, she discreetly asked the Tremont's doorman where "Night ladies" plied their trade.

That evening she visited a small park near the river. The sun lingered low on the horizon, filling the sky with hues of pink and blue. Seemingly out of nowhere young women in brightly colored dresses, small capes or scarves draped around their bare shoulders, started to inhabit the night scene.

Most men arrived alone, quietly prowling the park in search of a companion for an hour or two. At the opposite extreme, a group of rowdy sailors from one of the Lake ships, openly made lewd proposals to every woman in sight.

Teeny singled out a few of the women who appeared attractive and smart. She politely explained why she was there. Initially the women viewed her suspiciously, but Teeny eventually convinced them this was an opportunity to make a great deal of money.

When the evening grew late, Teeny hired a carriage to take her back to the Tremont. After retrieving her key at the front desk, she requested a cognac be brought to her room. The brandy arrived on a silver tray along with an envelope. The address was printed in block letters:

ELIZABETH DOUGLAS/TREMONT HOTEL/CHICAGO

Teeny thought it might be from Arthur, but the envelope bore no return address or post-mark. She opened the envelope and a sheet of paper dropped to the floor. She retrieved it; a few seconds passed before she realized what she was holding.

WANTED:

A young slave woman who is a fugitive in the St. Paul area. She has light colored skin, reddish brown hair, five foot six or seven inches in height, no scars, and likely wearing a disguise. Anyone with information should contact Martin Lunt at the St. Paul hotel.

$200 REWARD

On the side of the handbill she discovered a message printed in the same block letters as those on the front of the envelope:

THIS IS YOU!

Teeny's knees buckled. She eased onto the couch. Her new life was already unraveling. She tried to determine who sent it.

Someone rapped sharply at Teeny's door. As Teeny had no weapon, she dreaded answering. The knocking continued. Hesitantly she walked to the door, "Who is it?"

"The person who sent you the message," came a woman's voice that sounded familiar. Teeny unbolted the lock, slowly opened the door, and immediately recognized the blonde hair and blue eyes.

"Frieda! Why are you here? Why aren't you in St. Paul?"

Frieda looked distraught. "May I come in?" she queried.

Wearing a dress and shawl similar to those worn by the night women in the park, she entered. Though wary, Teeny invited her guest to sit down. After an awkward silence, Frieda revealed her role in Charles' death.

"I'm responsible for what happened to Charles…I loved him, and I thought if you were gone, he would pay attention to me."

She paused, pulled a handkerchief from a small handbag and wiped the tears away.

"I left a note at the hotel for that detective telling him where you were hiding. I thought he would just take you and your baby back to St. Louis."

Teeny glowered at Frieda.

"So, you didn't care if my baby and I were captured?" she said, icily.

"I just wanted you to go away. I didn't think they would hurt you, and I was angry that Charles was so fond of you."

Teeny clenched her fists into small balls of fury. At that moment she believed she could kill Frieda.

"And now…what do you want now?"

"I, I was going to ask for money. If you didn't give it to me I was going to send a telegram to that detective telling him you were in Chicago."

Teeny circled around Frieda, ready to strike.

"You were going to blackmail me?"

"I have no job, no money…I'm a whore. Tonight I saw you at the park. You were dressed so fine, I knew you had money, a lot of money."

Teeny had difficulty believing what she was hearing.

"Do the Granemanns know?"

"I knew they would eventually find out what I had done, so I left. I heard Charles talk about Chicago. I took what money I had and came here."

Teeny looked at the crumpled reward notice lying on the floor. "Are you still planning to contact Lunt?"

"No, I've hurt enough people. I don't want to hurt anyone again, ever." She began to cry. "I came to apologize, and I hope you will forgive me."

Teeny sneered out a response. "And my baby, do you want her to forgive you for taking her away from her mother?"

Face to face with the reality of what she had done caused Frieda to moan, "Oh please…I'm sorry. I'm so sorry. Please forgive me." She got up from the chair very slowly. "Before I go, please say you will forgive me."

Teeny did not respond. Frieda backed away from her toward the door.

Teeny looked at her with disdain. Then she had an idea. Frieda was red-eyed, disheveled, destitute, but still pretty. Maybe she could use her. If Frieda were in her employ, she wasn't likely to expose her to Lunt or anyone else. She would be under her control.

"Wait a minute."

Frieda stopped.

"Are you any good at what you're doing? On the streets?"

Frieda's face flushed. "I'm learning."

"How do I get in touch with you?"

"At the park or the women's shelter."

Teeny nodded and slowly closed the door. She picked up the handbill and read it one more time. She touched the paper to the flame of her lamp and placed it in the fireplace. As it shriveled into ashes she relived the confrontation with Frieda. Then she thought about her baby and wondered whether Mary was asleep in a safe, warm bed...and whether she had any memory of her mother.

66

DAVE THOMAS HAD THE *FRONTIER* *Guardian* lying on his desk with two announcements circled. He asked Will whether he would like to take a look at them. Will cradled the newspaper in his lap and began to read.

> July 27, – City officials formally approve name change of Kanesville to Council Bluffs. No opposition from respectable citizens, and the change is effective immediately.
>
> Meeting at the Council Bluffs Lyceum:
>
> Once again the question proposed to be discussed before this institution on Saturday evening next, we learn to be the following:
>
> "Will the admission of Slavery into our new territories contribute to the good of the general cause of humanity, to the honor of the nation, or only serve to advantage the Southern States?"

"Why are they discussing this, Mr. Thomas? Iowa is a free state!"

"This isn't just about Iowa, Will. It's about all the new territories, like Kansas and Nebraska, that people are fighting over. Seems groups of proslavery advocates have poured into these areas arguing for popular sovereignty."

"What does that mean?"

"They want people living in those places to decide the issue, not the government. Fights are breakin' out between those that want the territories to be slave, and those that want 'em to be free. They're talking about this all over the country. Problem is, once these debates get heated, some folks get out of hand. A couple years ago coloreds were attacked in Shantytown."

Will stared, wide-eyed with disbelief. "Attacked? In Shantytown?"

"Yeah. A group of pro-slavers, maybe they were patrollers, or border raiders, tore the place up and hauled some people away."

Will rubbed his hands together nervously, "Mr. Thomas, that meeting's happening the day after Sunny and I are getting married."

"Don't let it interfere with your plans, Will. Just be careful." Will thanked Thomas for the warning and for sharing the news. The newspaper lying on Thomas' desk contained another announcement both men failed to notice:

```
New Riverboat scheduled for St. Louis, St. Joseph,
Council Bluffs, and Sioux City. The newest, finest,
and fastest Passenger Steamer, POLAR STAR,
Allen McGee, Master, will ply to the above and all
intermediate ports on a regular schedule. Leaving
St. Louis on or about the 1st of September. Making
10 trips throughout the year.
```

In the back room of Annie's boardinghouse, Tom devoted an hour or two each night to conquering the alphabet. A month later he was beginning to write a few words. Putting his new skills to work, he carved "WILL AND SUNNY" into a wooden plank. Tom presented it to them the afternoon of the wedding.

"Ya kin put the sign on yer door so visters knows where ya stay."

Will gave an appreciative smile. "Thank you. I'll put it up first thing tomorrow, we might not want visitors tonight."

Reverend Nate let out an abrupt laugh and said, "Amen."

The celebration continued, but Dave Thomas wasn't his usual gregarious self. As the party began to wind down, he pulled Will and Tom aside. "Boys, we need to talk for a minute. I don't mean to spoil the celebration but ya need to know the Elliott sisters seem determined to punish you for taking Sunny away."

"Nobody took her away, she left on her own," Will replied defensively.

"I know, I know, but they thought they were going to have Sunny around for a long time. They don't like the way she left, and they especially don't like coloreds. Now they're talkin' to some people in St. Louis."

Will's voice cracked as he responded, "Who, who are they talking to?"

"Old man Timmers down at the post office told me they've been sending letters to slave buyers and sellers. I'm not sure what they're cookin' up, but make sure ya keep an eye out for anyone who approaches that ya don't recognize."

Lynch and Thompson specialized in the sale of slaves and had no qualms about having their agents capture free coloreds and bring them to auction. They were aided by the Fugitive Slave Act that imposed a $1,000 fine and six months in prison for anyone helping slaves escape or preventing them from being returned to their owners. Slave hunters poached free men and women and seldom met with any resistance.

The Samuelson twins had earned a reputation as notorious slave hunters. For years they delivered "Sturdy and sellable coloreds" to Lynch's slave pen. In the spring of 1853, they captured twenty-two Negroes in the Kansas territory. Their captives were chained together, taken back to St. Louis, and sold for over eighteen thousand dollars.

But in the summer of 1853, the twins were unable to locate "quality merchandise" in the town of Leavenworth. A month later, Methodist abolitionists ran them out of Lawrence. Cranky as hungry bears, the brothers arrived in St. Joseph to receive instructions from Peter Lynch. His letter informed them that slaves who fled Missouri were likely residing in Iowa border towns. Lynch instructed them to travel north to Council Bluffs.

Mark Samuelson was a large man with a black beard that circled his face. He had bright blue eyes and sported an odd floppy hat tied up on one side—a snug fit on his large round head. His brother Todd had high cheekbones, a flat forehead and large brown eyes. Above his lip he sported an elaborate mustache that curled on both ends. He wore a wide brimmed Stetson that appeared several sizes too large for his narrow face. No one was sure why people called the two men twins, but they were definitely bound together by a shared hatred of any one who wasn't white and by making a living capturing slaves.

Stories about border raiders started to circulate once again in Council Bluffs; they were described as men who traveled on horseback toting whips, chains, and guns. Rumor held that these men attacked without warning. But the Samuelson twins operated differently; they relied on bribery and cooperation from local officials to secure their victims.

The twins arrived in Council Bluffs a week after Will and Sunny's wedding. They had invited the sheriff to have drinks with them in the back room of

Jimmy's bar, where they discussed the best place to find "sellable coloreds." Abigail, a young girl from Shantytown who swept and cleaned at the tavern, listened wide-eyed to their words.

"Twenty dollars goes to you, sheriff, for every one we capture."

The sheriff smiled broadly. "I can sure use the money, and I'll help ya get started. Ya need to visit the old boarding house in Shantytown. There are young niggers living there that would fetch a fine price."

"Nobody would object?" asked the tall brother.

"Nope, in fact, two old sisters in town thinks them niggers are uppity an' stole a bunch of money. The sisters would be grateful for any help ya kin provide ta make Council Bluffs a safer place for respectable ladies like themselves."

The three smiled, hoisted their glasses, and ordered another bottle of whiskey. Abigail eased her broom quietly to the floor, and slipped out the side door. She trembled as she sat on the porch outside Thomas's retail store with her arms circled tightly around her knees. Will was returning from the warehouse, carrying a load of merchandise when he saw her. "Abi, what's wrong?"

"They're comin for ya, Mr. Will." Abigail relayed what she had heard at the tavern.

Will had to act quickly. He sent Abigail home and ran back to the warehouse where Dave Thomas was locking up for the night.

"They're here! They're coming for us Mr. Thomas!"

Dave faced Will with a worried look.

"Abigail was working at Jimmy's and heard two men talking to the sheriff. He told them about niggers living in a boarding house in Shantytown, and how they'd fetch a good price."

"Damn! Take my horse. Tell Tom and Rosie to get out of there. I'll go to the bank and tell Sunny. You've got those keys; you know where to hide."

Will rode back to Shantytown and told Tom and Rosie to leave right away. "Meet me at Thomas's warehouse as soon as you can," he instructed.

"Should we take da wagon?"

"No, leave it. Put Clyde and Sarah in the Reverend's barn. Go the back way, through Snyder's farm. Hurry!"

Tom and Rosie gathered a few items, circled to the back of the boarding-house and took off running through Henry Snyder's fields. It was almost dark when they reached the outskirts of Council Bluffs. They heard hoof beats. Both crouched down in the tall prairie grass. Two men on horseback galloped past.

Rosie shivered and watched them disappear over the hill. Their "Wunnerful summer," as Tom referred to the past two months, was coming to a frightening end.

It was dark when all four gathered together at the warehouse. Will pulled the keys from his pocket and unlocked the tall door. Tom surveyed the contents. "Who be livin here?"

"No one. It used to be a hiding place for Dave's parents when there was trouble in town. I don't think it's been used for years."

Tom touched a few stuffed chairs and picked up a blanket. "How long we gonna be stayin' here?"

"Until it's safe to come out," was all Will could think of to say.

Tom walked over to Rosie and gave her a hug, tears were rolling down her cheeks. "We tryin so hard to do right, why can't dey let us be?"

Will looked around the darkened room and said to his friends, "At least we're safe…for now."

The Samuelson twins returned to the sheriff's office, angry that they found no one at the boarding house. The sheriff wondered who had warned the slaves. He picked up his rifle.

"Come with me. If we can't find them, we'll find others."

67

THE OLD ROBINSON MANSION HAD a handsome reception area, a well stocked bar, and several luxurious private rooms. Teeny was pleased with the appearance of the "Gentlemen's Club," even through she was well aware patrons wouldn't be coming to view the decor or architecture. She discreetly asked one of the Tremont's doormen, "Besides the park, where might working women be found?"

"Theatre events, ma'am," he informed her.

So, Teeny paid a visit to one of the more popular venues that operated in a combination boarding house and saloon. Inside the saloon, patrons could also enjoy readings from Shakespeare and popular songs by Stephen Foster. Teeny sat at a dimly lit table and watched the women enter in groups of two or three. Alcohol flowed freely, and the men stomped, yelled, and threw money on stage to hear performers ad-lib obscene jokes. Some, of course, looked for a woman to spend time with after the show.

Teeny pulled three of the most attractive girls aside and asked them to join her.

"Let's discuss more profitable opportunities for you ladies."

One of the girls, outfitted in a blue cotton dress with a bright red scarf around her neck responded in a feisty manner.

"Whatcha got in mind, Miss fancy pants?"

Teeny told them about the Gentlemen's Club that would open in a few weeks and how much they could earn servicing a wealthier clientele.

"When do we start?" feisty girl replied.

"You don't start. You meet with me, and I will determine whether you are qualified to work in this type of establishment."

The girl snorted. "Qualified? How qualified do you have to be to spread your legs?"

Teeny responded tersely. "These men are wealthy and expect more, like conversation and other forms of intimacy."

The girl rolled her eyes. "What the hell are you talking about?"

"Meet with me. I'll explain and show you around the club. If you work for me, you'll receive a small sum for clothes and accessories. You will work exclusively for me," she explained, emphasizing the last part.

The three women looked at one another. The oldest, not more than nineteen, spoke up. "We'll meet with you. Tell us where and when."

While they were talking, a hawk-faced man with jet-black hair, dressed in a black suit and starched white shirt, eavesdropped on the conversation. After the group dispersed, he followed Teeny to the street where she waited to board a carriage.

"Do you mind if I join you? I'm also going to the Tremont."

Teeny had reservations about the uninvited gentleman, but felt she had little choice. If he was staying at the hotel, their paths would likely cross, and she didn't want to appear rude.

"Yes, please do, Mr. ..."

"Talbot, Reverend Jeremiah Talbot."

In the carriage Teeny felt uneasy; the Reverend stared at her with dark eyes, framed by bushy black eyebrows. Teeny thought initiating a conversation might jar him into a friendlier demeanor.

"Are you visiting Chicago, Reverend?"

"No, I live here. My church is not too far away." He continued to stare. "And you, Miss, why are you in Chicago?"

"I'm living here now. I'm staying at the hotel until my home is available."

"By home you mean that mansion where men and women will revel in debauchery?" Now he looked and sounded menacing. Teeny was taken aback by the remark and abrupt change in his demeanor. The carriage rolled to a halt at the hotel entrance. Teeny paid the driver and walked quickly away. The Reverend followed close behind and questioned her.

"Tell me, Miss, who is behind that vile project?"

Teeny turned and confronted him. "Please leave me alone, Reverend. I am not interested in your opinions of right and wrong."

He pointed a long thin finger at her. "You soon will be. I intend to find out who's behind your sordid endeavor, and I am going to shut it down."

Arthur returned earlier than expected and was waiting to surprise Teeny. He spotted her being hounded by the long-limbed man dressed in black. After hearing the last part of the conversation he approached.

"Hello, dear, who's your new friend?"

Talbot paused mid-rant and studied the well-dressed and imposing man. He directed his next outburst at Arthur.

"Are you aware this woman is recruiting prostitutes? She is violating the laws of God, and our city. I plan to take action against her and all the other whores."

Arthur shot back, undaunted: "Reverend, these women you are so angry with are just trying to survive. There are few options in this city for women who have to support themselves and possibly a child or two. Their choices are taking charity, or working like a dog for pennies."

Talbot hadn't anticipated a debate. It took him a moment to regain his composure.

"Sir, a person's good name is far more valuable than ill-begotten gain. Apparently you, and these women, plan on getting rich over a sinful enterprise. Well, my congregation and I will fight you, and try to save you, in spite of your wanton desires. I would like to know your name."

"Arthur Irving, and yours?"

"Reverend Jeremiah Talbot."

Arthur drummed his fingers on his chin for a moment and narrowed his eyes.

"Reverend Talbot, I believe your congregation is being allowed to use the old Mormon Church near the canal for your religious services. My partners and I own that building, and we have allowed you to use it for several months. If you act against me, you will have to hold your services elsewhere. I suggest you excuse yourself and rethink your position on this matter."

Talbot was at a loss for another retort. He glared at Arthur and Teeny as they walked away. He bowed his head and mumbled, "Reprobates, they are nothing more than reprobates."

The next morning Teeny and Arthur lay in a drowsy stupor, and planned to linger in bed a while longer. Teeny ran a finger over Arthur's bare chest and slowly moved her hand downward. Just as Arthur pulled Teeny toward him there was a jarring knock on the door.

"Message for Mr. Irving," called a young man's voice.

"Damn it," Arthur grumbled. He slipped on his robe and walked with as much dignity as possible to the door. A nattily dressed young man, holding an envelope in one hand and cradling his cap in the other, greeted him. He handed Arthur the envelope.

"I'm to wait for a reply, sir."

Arthur read the brief note.

> *Arthur, arrived a few days earlier than planned.*
>
> *Could we meet this afternoon for a drink?*
>
> *Looking forward to being one of the first customers in*
>
> *your new business venture.*
>
> *Harlan*

"Tell him to join me in the lounge at four."

The young man nodded and waited.

"I'll be glad to do that, Mr. Irving."

Arthur returned to the nightstand, retrieved a few coins, and handed them to the young man.

"Paying to be interrupted at a moment like this is ridiculous," he mumbled. Arthur sat back down on the bed, muttering a string of laments about lost opportunities.

"There will be other times, Arthur." Teeny slid from beneath the covers and began to freshen at the washbasin. "Let's visit the Gentlemen's Club. You can see how attractive the old place has become."

After inspecting the property, Arthur and Teeny climbed inside an expensive shiny black carriage pulled by two well-groomed black horses. A driver in a black suit, crisp white shirt, and silk top hat cracked the whip. The carriage passed through the old mansion's ornate gates and onto the main road.

Deep mud forced them to detour through an older part of Chicago, an area Teeny had never seen. Here, the scenery transitioned from mansions and manicured gardens to unpleasant looking tenement houses. People in the streets appeared different, too. Their worn and faded clothes and broken down demeanor seemed to match the buildings they were living in. Many seemed in poor health.

With sunken eyes they watched the elegant carriage pass. A few raised their arms and made obscene gestures. Teeny grew uneasy. She viewed this foray into the city's underside as a harsh reminder that a misstep or two could end the fine life she was living. The carriage rumbled on.

That afternoon Teeny and Arthur waited in the lounge for Harlan Chambers. Many people knew of the state senator. His name was often associated with controversial political issues confronting the new republic. Frequently quoted in the newspapers, he was sought after by reporters to comment on a variety of topics, but always sidestepped the highly charged issue of slavery. The senator preferred to speak in favor of westward expansion, forcing a confrontation with Mexico and acquiring more land for the United States.

Arthur sipped his bourbon and said, "Harlan is one of the respectable men of political power and influence who will likely be one of our best customers."

After hearing about the senator, Teeny expected to see a commanding presence. But the gentleman who arrived was slender, with a pointed chin and nose, and spoke with an affected French accent. "Ah, mon ami," he said as he clasped Arthur's hand. His eyes grew wide as he looked at Teeny.

"Harlan, this is my good friend and business partner, Elizabeth Douglas."

"Enchante," he said, with a tinge of disappointment.

After ordering drinks, discussion between the two men quickly took on political overtones. While they were talking, Teeny happened to look up and recognized a familiar face in the lobby. A flattering dress and a small amount of make-up enhanced Frieda's blonde hair, blue eyes, and attractive form. Teeny excused herself.

"Hello, Frieda. You certainly look better than the last time I saw you. Have you had a run of good luck?"

Frieda avoided eye contact and looked down. "No. One of the women at the boardinghouse told me the type of girl you are looking for. I spent what little I had to make myself presentable. I'm still hoping you will forgive me and possibly allow me to work for you."

Harlan spotted Frieda talking with Teeny. The discussion with Arthur no longer interested him. The fresh young girl standing in the lobby had him mesmerized. He circled the table, pointed to Frieda, and said to Arthur, "How much?"

68

THE SAMUELSON BROTHERS AND THE sheriff were in Shantytown, going door-to-door and forcing people into the street. They demanded residents of the tiny village show documentation proving they were manumitted. Even when they produced the proper papers, the slave hunters wanted to know whether they had paid a fee to have them renewed. From among those who had no papers or hadn't renewed them, they picked four young men and two women to take back to auction. A scuffle, tearful screams, and shouts of anger ensued as the unlucky were led away. The sheriff stood armed with a shotgun and made it clear he would use it to subdue any further resistance.

Inside the warehouse, the four slaves who escaped from Shantytown waited for daybreak. Although the room held beds and stuffed furniture, the four found it impossible to sleep. Occasionally they heard someone shouting or a horse neighing, but for the most part the town remained quiet.

They waited for Thomas to give the "all clear" signal, but it was noon before they heard a knock on the door.

"Will, it's me, come on out."

Will and Tom emerged; Rosie and Sunny stood beside them, watching and listening.

"Sorry to keep ya waitin' so long, but there's been all sorts a trouble. Last night those slave hunters hauled away some young folks from Shantytown."

Will and Tom anxiously waited for Thomas to fill in the details.

"Those two brothers had some phony documents from a judge in St. Joseph saying a bunch of families in Shantytown owed manumission money. To pay off the debt, the sheriff told the Samuelsons to haul away six coloreds. I think one of 'em, a fella named Zeke, was going to your school."

"Didn't nobody try ta stop 'em?" Tom asked angrily.

"Yeah, Reverend Nate tried to keep 'em from puttin' chains on the young folks. The twins busted him up pretty good. And, they hurt Annie when she tried to stop em from tearing up the boardinghouse."

Will turned irate. "Are Nate and Annie going to be okay?"

"Reverend Nate's got some cuts on his head, an' Annie's got a broken arm."

Will paced nervously. Finally he calmed himself.

"Mr. Thomas, those bounty hunters will come back, especially if those old ladies and the sheriff are in on this."

Tom turned to Thomas and asked, "Is dat true, Mr. Thomas? Would dey come lookin' fer us agin?"

Thomas sighed and shook his head. "I don't know Tom, but you both still got a job with me and a place to live. We'll get through this."

That afternoon Thomas sent a young doctor to the boardinghouse to treat Annie. He placed a splint on her arm, bandaged it, and gave her a tin of laudanum to ease the pain. Sunny and Rosie set about cleaning up the mess the Samulesons created after they ransacked the boardinghouse. They heard Annie talking in another room. The drug had taken effect. Her arm no longer ached and she was rambling aloud.

"Doan take 'em away, please doan take 'em away. Dey be children, dey done nothin' wrong. Please, sheriff, doan be takin' 'em away."

Sunny offered her a glass of water. Annie was confused, and wondered why her arm was wrapped. She continued talking.

"It ain't dem young people's fault. Dey had nuthin to do wit yer childs bein taken. Dey tryin' to help us by startin' a school. Ain't nuthin wrong with dem havin' sum money neither. Ya can't blame dem."

Rosie applied a wet cloh to Annie's forehead. "Sunny, she be talkin 'bout us."

Sunny nodded. "I'm sure people around here think we brought this trouble. Their children are gone, and we're still here."

Residents of Shantytown now considered Will, Sunny, Tom, and Rosie outsiders responsible for bringing the bounty hunters to their village. No one came to Will's Saturday class. Women looked away when Rosie and Sunny passed on the road. A week later, a group of angry parents went to the boardinghouse and demanded the four of them pack up and leave.

ᬛ   ᬛ   ᬛ

The rapidly expanding Western territories relied on the Riverboats to supply goods and materials. A pilot with the skill needed to navigate the Missouri River could name his price, and McGee wasn't bashful about requesting a high salary, especially after making almost nothing piloting a government snag boat.

At the end of September, the Polar Star docked in Council Bluffs. McGee went to the scruffy old harbormaster and inquired about Will and Tom.

"Ya mean the two Nigger bucks who moved here some time ago?

"I suppose. They were both sturdy young men, came here from St. Joseph."

"Yeah, I know who you're talking about. Bounty hunters went lookin for 'em a few weeks ago. They're holed up in Shantytown, bout a mile east a here."

McGee went to the livery, rented a horse, and headed east on Main Street. He passed a warehouse where two men engaged in an angry discussion. One of them cradled a shotgun and wore a badge. He glared at McGee when he rode past.

Will had closed his school and was carrying a desk Reverend Nate donated back to the church when he noticed a tall man on horseback riding into the village. Even from a distance he recognized McGee. Will ran toward his old friend.

"Captain McGee! What are you doing here? How did you find us?"

"Came to check on some old friends. Hear they've had some trouble."

"Yeah," said Will. "You're right about that. McGee got down from his horse and shook Will's hand. "Well, some things must be going pretty well. The man at the livery said you and Tom got married."

Will smiled. "That's right, come in and meet Sunny."

McGee found himself surprised by Sunny's beauty and happy to see Tom and Rosie again.

"Andrew said he knew you two would end up together. Wish I could tell him he was right."

Annie was all smiles when she met McGee. "Ain't never had no riverboad cap'tin in my house, I hopes ya think everything be ship-shape."

McGee laughed and looked around. "Annie, I think you could teach my crew a thing or two about putting things in good order."

McGee listened as Will explained all that had happened since they left the Williams' farm. The captain understood now why they were no longer welcome. Annie struggled to her feet.

"Captain, dis talk gettin' sad; evry'body be hap'ier if dey have a little food in 'em. I ain't got much, but would sure be pleased if ya stay an' have some vic'tuals wid us."

McGee remembered how the sheriff looked at him and wondered whether his visit had already caused more trouble.

"I'd like that Annie, but I had better get back and make sure my boat's still here. The sheriff didn't seem any too pleased to see me. Before I go, I wonder whether I might have a piece of that pie cooling on the window sill?"

Annie smiled. "Apple pie an' coffee comin' right up. Ya can't be leavin' jus yet." Annie went to slice the pie and heat the coffee. McGee's easy-going smile vanished, replaced by a new seriousness.

"I'll be leaving at five tomorrow. It would be best if all of you were on my boat."

This suggestion left the former slaves too stunned to respond.

"With the sheriff and locals helping the bounty hunters, you aren't safe here. This town will be known as an easy mark. You can bet those brothers, or a new group, will be back. I'll get you back on the Mississippi. You can head north, maybe go to Canada," McGee contended.

Tom rubbed his hands, troubled by the plan. "I doan know, Cap'an. You sure bout dis?"

"Yes, unless you want to try making your way north by land. You could team up with a wagon train in a few months, but these folks want you out of here now."

Annie came back into the room and noticed the solemn faces.

"Uh-oh, whad happin while I be gone?"

"I think we're leaving tomorrow, Annie."

"Leavin? Where ya be goin?"

Will tried to sound confident. "St. Louis, then Canada."

Annie's face displayed her concern. "Oh Lord, dat city be too big, an' Can'da be too far away. You be g'tting' caught an' sold fer sure."

69

THE GENTLEMEN'S CLUB OPENED AND was an immediate success, but without Harlan Chambers as a loyal patron. He had enjoyed many clandestine affairs during his political career, survived exciting encounters with jealous husbands, and reveled in liaisons with girlfriends in every city. But now Frieda received his undivided, devoted attention. The passing years had altered his sensual desires, and now he was ready for a permanent relationship. Harlan felt convinced he found the woman to whom he could be completely loyal.

Frieda sat in the lobby waiting for Harlan and thought about the first time she met him. His face was almost perfectly symmetrical, with a straight mouth, pointy nose, and dark hair mingled with traces of gray. He looked quite different from Charles or any other man she had found attractive. Frieda had known the politician for only two weeks, but in that short time had grown to love him. She tried to understand why everything happened so quickly.

Harlan arrived and flashed an adoring smile. He escorted Frieda to the hotel lounge, sat down next to her, and retrieved a small white box from his coat pocket. It was tied with a thin white satin ribbon. He presented it to her on the palm of his hand. "For you my love."

"Oh, Harlan, you shouldn't keep buying me presents."

"I suppose, but please accept this one."

Frieda carefully untied the ribbon and raised the hinged lid. Inside an exquisite diamond ring was nestled on a bed of white velvet.

Before she could respond, Harlan said, "Frieda, will you marry me?"

She began to cry. "Harlan, it's so sudden, maybe too sudden. Are you sure?"

"I am."

Frieda didn't hesitate. "Yes, yes! Harlan. I love you. I will be happy to marry you."

Harlan flashed a wide smile. "Then we must celebrate this special day."

After leaving the hotel they spent the day visiting Chicago's finest drinking and dining establishments. They returned to their room shortly after midnight. Frieda felt giddy from the drinks and day's excitement. She snuggled next to Harlan in the over-stuffed bed. Harlan proposed another toast. "Here's to Elizabeth for introducing us."

Frieda grew uneasy, and in a hesitant manner said, "Here's to Elizabeth."

Harlan propped himself up and said, "How did you two come to know each other?"

Frieda had worried this question would eventually surface. She struggled for an explanation.

"Harlan, if we are to be married then I must tell you the truth, just like when I told you my real name, and that I was taken in by another family after my parents died. Truth is essential in a relationship, isn't it?"

"Of course it is, my love." Harlan was sitting up in bed, sobering quickly. "What is it you have to tell me?"

Frieda had told Harlan that she was a house servant in St. Paul, but never revealed to him the complete story.

She started to cry after she divulged her role in Charles' death and Teeny's baby being taken away. Harlan was stunned. He was perched on the edge of the bed not quite sure he comprehended everything.

"My God, that's quite a chain of unfortunate events. That means Miss Douglas was, or still is, a slave. Does Arthur know this?"

"I don't think so. Please don't tell him."

"I have no choice, he works for the government. He could be embarrassed, maybe even arrested."

Frieda gave him a look of disbelief. "Embarrassed? He's opened a brothel for wealthy men, how can he be embarrassed?"

Harlan shook his head. "It's not the same. People will condemn him for cohabitating with a slave and demand he be removed from his government job."

"Harlan, after I left St. Paul, I thought I would never find love, or a safe place in the world. Now I have both. I don't want to spoil it, and I don't want to cause any more trouble. Please don't tell Arthur."

Harlan looked sympathetic, but did not respond. Both lay in bed for over an hour without saying anything. Finally they settled into a restless sleep.

In the morning Harlan dispatched a note to Arthur, requesting they meet for lunch. Arthur sent a courier back to Harlan's townhome with a swift response: he would meet him at noon.

When their meeting time arrived, Harlan sat in the café, feeling edgy as he sipped his coffee and waited. Arthur strode over to their table; the men exchanged greetings, ordered a sandwich, and followed up with a mug of ale. Arthur inquired about Frieda, and the conversation shifted to a discussion about their respective companions.

"I am enamored with Frieda. I have asked her to marry me."

"Harlan, you rascal, that's wonderful news! I often wondered whether you would ever settle down."

Harlan shot his friend an appreciative smile.

"Thank you, I'm glad you approve. And what about you? You reside with one of the most beautiful women in Chicago. Is marriage in your future?"

Arthur set his mug on the table and thought about the question. "I care about Elizabeth a great deal, but I'm not sure how she feels about marriage."

"But might you marry at some point?"

"You seem concerned, Harlan. Is there something you want to tell me?" Harlan took a sip of ale and began to reveal what Frieda had divulged.

"Arthur, are you aware that Frieda and Elizabeth were living on the same family estate in St. Paul? And that they left about the same time under very unusual circumstances?"

Arthur stared at his luncheon companion, looking perplexed.

"Please, go on. You certainly have my attention."

Harlan spent the next ten minutes relaying what Frieda told him the previous night. Arthur gazed at his drink and seldom looked up. He grew stony faced and silent when Harlan finished.

"Does Frieda know we are meeting?" Arthur asked.

"Yes, she begged me not to tell you, but I had to. You are living with a slave and violating the Illinois Black Codes. Your enemies would have a field day with that. You could lose your position, even be sent to prison. You don't have any choice but to end the relationship," Harlan advised.

Arthur shifted uncomfortably in his chair. He found Harlan's unfeeling suggestion that he cast Teeny aside vexing, but his diplomatic instincts took hold.

"Harlan, I appreciate the fact you are concerned about my professional well being, but I cannot abandon Elizabeth. I feel the same about her as you do about Frieda. And, I don't believe anyone is searching for her, so there is little danger of her past being revealed."

"But Arthur, you don't know that."

Arthur needed to be alone; he rose from the chair and left a few coins.

"Harlan, I need a little time to think this through. Please tell Frieda you did the right thing by telling me, and I will do my best to make sure Elizabeth is not hurt."

Arthur walked for several blocks, brooding, and then entered a store filled with trays of finely crafted bracelets, watches, and rings. Behind the display counter, a slender gray-haired man with an eye loupe attached to his spectacles stood attentively. He acted most amenably when the well-dressed customer entered.

"Good day, sir. What may I do to assist you?"

"I would like to see your wedding rings."

70

ARTHUR AND HARLAN MET FOR a drink in the hotel bar a few days later.

"Did you have a good weekend, Harlan?" Arthur asked.

"Excellent, mon ami, excellent. Frieda and I didn't leave our hotel room the entire time." Then he flashed a wicked smile, "Nothing but room service and convivial conversation. And you Mr. Irving?"

"Not too bad. Obviously you gave me a lot to think about after our last meeting."

"I know, and I apologize for taking such a hard line. I would like you and Elizabeth to remain together. What have you decided?"

"I would like to marry her. I purchased a ring, but haven't popped the question. I'm concerned about the issues you raised, and why she hasn't told me the whole story."

Harlan pursed his lips and raised his dark eyebrows. "Most understandable that you are concerned."

After they departed, Arthur walked briskly down Clark Street toward the *Daily Tribune*. The newspaper rented office space on the second floor of the Post Office. He climbed the stairs and paused. *The Tribune* salutatory was posted in large script outside the newspaper office:

WE SHALL AT ALL TIMES BE FAITHFUL TO HUMANITY—
TO THE WHOLE OF HUMANITY—

WITHOUT REGARD TO RACE,
SECTIONAL DIVISIONS, PARTY LINES,
OR PARALLELS OF LATITUDE AND LONGITUDE.

Below the greeting someone had scratched the word "Seditionists" into the pine paneling. The affront had been painted over, but indentations in the wood left the message legible. A young office worker greeted Arthur when he entered.

"How many I assist you, sir?"

"I would like to place an advertisement for a property my company wishes to sell."

"I would be happy to handle that for you, sir. Allow me to get the necessary information."

While relaying the contents of his advertisement, Arthur saw a police officer emerge from the back room. "Is something wrong?"

The young man looked back at the officer; "We've had a series of threatening letters. It seems people don't want a free press unless it supports their beliefs. They feel the newspaper has been taken over by the Whigs, who want an end to the wildcat currency."

Arthur looked surprised. "They're sending you threats over that?"

"Well, our paper also supports the abolitionists, and it has published positive things about a Springfield politician by the name of Abraham Lincoln."

Arthur had read Lincoln's speeches and knew the national debate over slavery was heating up. Death threats against a publisher or politician arguing against slavery were disturbing—especially to a government official who was cohabitating with a slave.

He paid the young man for the ad and began the long walk back to his apartment. After a few blocks his thoughts about a marriage proposal were interupted when he had the odd sensation he was being followed. He slowed and recognized a face in the crowd; it was Reverend Talbot. Arthur dismissed this as coincidence and continued walking. His thoughts returned to Elizabeth and the best way to approach her with his questions and concerns.

That evening Arthur and Teeny settled into a comfortable routine in the bedroom when Arthur heard a noise outside. He assumed it was rain spattering against the windowpanes. He closed the window and returned to bed. Teeny gently nibbled his ear, and moved her hands down his chest. Arthur demurred and said, "I need a moment." He took her hand and looked into her eyes, his face earnest.

"Liz, would you consider making our relationship permanent?"

"You don't have to talk about making things permanent, Arthur." She stroked his hair, and ran her fingers along his cheek and lips.

"I'm happy with our arrangement. When it runs its course, I will always be grateful to you."

Arthur hadn't anticipated this response. He moved to the side of the bed.

"Does it bother you when I talk about the possibility of our making a commitment to one another? You are always so evasive when I mention the subject."

"Arthur, I care about you a great deal, but I don't want things in my past to embarrass you or cause you to resent me."

"Well, I'd like to know what you are referring to. But no matter what you tell me, I feel certain we should remain together."

Teeny moved from the bed to a chair in the corner and began to relay parts of her past. She told him about the doctor who owned her, then explained how she eluded the detective and came to Chicago. She neglected to mention her child.

"The doctor hired someone to find me once before, and may try again."

"He already has your daughter, isn't that enough?" Arthur instantly regretted revealing everything Harlan told him.

Teeny felt betrayed. "You knew I had a child? You knew all along?"

"I didn't find out about this until a few days ago. Harlan proposed to Fredericka, and she felt she had to tell him about her past. That's when he felt obligated to tell me about yours."

Teeny leaned back in the chair and began shaking her head. "You found out, and didn't come to me, didn't give me a chance to explain? And you still want to talk about marriage?"

"Let's not be self righteous. You could have told me about your past and your baby. And yes, I still want to talk about marriage."

Before Teeny could respond, there was a loud pounding at the door.

"Damn it! Who's banging on the door this time of night?"

Arthur opened the door and discovered a sopping wet Reverend Talbot. He screamed at Arthur, spraying him with drops of rain and saliva.

"You are throwing me and my congregation out! Selling our place of worship without warning!"

Arthur tried to retain his composure.

"You have no right to come here at this time of night, Talbot. Arrange a proper meeting and I will discuss renting, or selling you the building."

"You know we can't meet your demands," Talbot screeched. "You're doing this because I publicly objected to your glorified whorehouse."

Arthur slammed the door on the irate preacher and bolted it.

Livid, Talbot continued to yell through the thick wood door.

"You haven't heard the last from me. You will be punished!"

Arthur returned to find Teeny curled up in bed.

"Was it Talbot?" she asked.

"Yes. That man's not right. I think he's been following me."

Arthur extinguished the lanterns, then reached over and took Teeny's hand.

"I love you, and I don't care about the past."

Teeny fought back tears. Softly, she whispered, "I'm so sorry I didn't tell you about all this sooner, Arthur."

Arthur had hoped to hear, "I love you too."

71

WILL LEFT THE BOARDINGHOUSE EARLY the next morning and sprinted down the dirt road. He was winded as he stood in the alley waiting for Dave Thomas. When his benefactor arrived, he invited Will to join him for a cup of coffee.

"Your coffee gives me the squirts."

Thomas laughed. They walked past mounds of wooden crates and merchandise to his office, where he handed Will a steaming mug of coffee. "Put some milk in it."

It was too early to start unloading supplies and stocking the shelves, so Thomas assumed Will had something to tell him.

"What's on your mind?"

"We're gonna have to leave Council Bluffs, Mr. Thomas. The people in Shantytown want us out of there."

Thomas strolled over and gazed out his office window toward the river.

"Ya gonna leave on that big boat that docked yesterday?"

"Yes, sir. The Captain of that boat helped Tom and me before, and he offered to help us again. He's going to take us back to St. Louis. From there we'll go north, maybe to Canada."

"I don't blame you for leaving, but be careful. Four of ya traveling on the river is risky; damned slave hunters are everywhere."

The boss returned to his desk. "I'm sorry things didn't work out better. Write me when you land, so I know where to send your money."

"I'll write you Mr. Thomas. You're the best friend we've had in this town. And, I'm not sorry we came here. I would never have met Sunny if we hadn't."

Thomas smiled when Will mentioned Sunny, but couldn't think of much else to say. Will laid the keys to the warehouse room on the desk.

"Good-bye Mr. Thomas. Thank you for everything."

When Will arrived back at the boardinghouse, he found Sunny sitting on the steps talking with Rosie. Both looked anxious. Rosie greeted Will, then hastily went inside. Sunny asked Will to sit next to her.

"Will," she said quietly, "Rosie's gonna have a baby."

He was pleased, but he could tell Sunny had more to tell him. She held his hand tightly.

"Rosie and Tom are not going with us. Tom wants to use some of his money to fix up the boarding house. Make it nicer before the baby comes."

"But the people don't want them here. And if they make the house nicer, the people in Shanty will become even meaner."

"Tom thinks that once people in town find out a baby's on the way, they'll be left alone."

Will looked down the dirt road at the ramshackle houses and whitewashed frame church. He shook his head and went inside. Rosie, Tom, and Annie were all in the parlor. Tom spoke first.

"We be sorry, Will, but it be best if we stay here. Rosie is carryin' our chile now, an' she should'n be trav'lin. Be'side dat, I see a haint in a dream las night. He look like Greef, an' he say he gonna kill me if I go on dat river."

Will didn't feel he should argue or try to change their minds.

Tom and Rosie began hugging their friends. Tom placed one arm around Will and the other around Sunny. Annie came forward and touched everyone's cheeks.

"You be fine young people, an' ya gonna have a good life. Sum day, we all be ta' gedder again."

"Annie, Tom's got some money. Some of it is here and some is in the bank. Mr. Thomas is gonna help him manage it. It's best that no one else knows about it." Annie knew what he meant and nodded in agreement.

Tom looked dejected.

"You been my bes frend, an' you always will be. Now dat I kin read a little, ya kin send me a letter, okay?"

Will nodded. "And you promise to write me. I want to know whether it's a boy or girl and how you're being treated."

They shared hugs all around one last time. Then Will picked up the two carpetbags and motioned to Sunny; they walked hand-in-hand through Shantytown toward the river.

McGee stood waiting. Once he heard the reason Tom and Rosie decided to stay behind, he said he agreed with their decision.

"Happy is the man who avoids trial and tribulation—especially with a baby on the way. How about you two, are you ready to make this trip?"

"Sunny's not sure she's gonna be welcome on the boat, Captain. Lotsa folks don't like coloreds, or Indians, an' she's both."

McGee waved his hand dismissively. "She'll be fine. She's so pretty nobody will care," he said with a wide grin. "Let's get aboard. I'll show you around."

McGee extended his arms. "Look at this boat. It's two hundred thirty feet long, has the finest saloon, and the best boilers on the Missouri."

"It's a beautiful boat," Will agreed. "It's sure different than the old snag boat."

McGee chuckled. "The old snagger had a crew of six. This one's got a crew of forty. I've got six officers, a cabin crew, deck hands, cooks, waiters, maids, wooders, roustabouts, and others I can't remember."

"Where do we fit in, Captain?"

"I think we'll start with Sunny working in the galley, and you waiting tables in the saloon. The staterooms will only be half full until we reach Kansas Village. That'll give you both enough time to learn the ropes. Once we leave the Village we'll be heading back to St. Louis with a full boat. You'll have to be on your toes by then."

On shore the sheriff looked angry as he stood on the post office porch, carefully watching the Polar Star. He had seen enough and called out to Charlie Timmers.

"Need ya ta send a telegram to St. Louis, Charlie."

"Sure thing, Sheriff, who's it goin to?"

"Lynch and Thompson."

"The slave sellers?"

"Yeah."

The Polar Star stopped at every town along the Missouri to pick up more cargo and passengers. McGee busied himself in the pilothouse, looking for suspicious ripples that would indicate a snag or sawyer. Before long, first officer Hobson entered with some disturbing news.

"Captain, we've got a problem. There's a sick family on the main deck tryin' to stay outa sight. Unless I miss my guess, they got the cholera."

McGee ordered Hobson to take over. On deck, he discovered a young couple and their child huddled behind several crates. The mother curled around her son, stroking his brow. McGee winced as he observed the boy's shriveled skin and sunken eyes.

"How long has he been like this?"

"A few days. We thought it was somethin' he ate, but he ain't gettin' no better."

McGee motioned for the parents to follow him. The couple staggered to their feet and followed McGee along the promenade deck to a small room. He told a steward to bring several pitchers of water.

"Make your son drink as much water as you can. That goes for the two of you as well."

In the meantime, black smoke billowed from the stacks of the Polar Star. The boat was now full and heavily laden with cargo. She left Kansas Village and steamed toward Jefferson City. In the saloon, first class passengers dined contentedly on roast chicken and fresh vegetables, unaware that seriously ill passengers rested in a small room close by.

Late the following afternoon the Polar Star prepared to dock. On shore, the local Oom-Pah band and town folk staged a rousing welcome for the big riverboat. With all the excitement and noise, no one heard faint wailing coming from the far end of the saloon.

Passengers made their way toward shops and restaurants, and McGee sent Hobson to summon the local doctor. When he arrived, he looked down at the emaciated boy and sadly shook his head. In a gentle, kind voice he said, "Please, let me take him." He placed the boy on a blanket and wrapped him carefully. The parents stared in silence at the bundle that held their lifeless child. The doctor put reddish-brown laudanum powder in two glasses of water and handed them to the grieving couple.

McGee pulled the doctor aside and said, "Doc, I've got a favor to ask. I'd like for these folks to bury their boy, and stay a while. They need to get their strength back before travelling any further. If I carry them back to St. Louis, there's a good chance they won't make it. And if the passengers find out their boy died of Cholera, it could start a panic."

The doctor wrote down an address. "Take them here, Captain, after dark."

"I owe you Doc," McGee replied, patting the doctor's back.

"A bottle or two of bourbon from the saloon would be a fine payment."

McGee signaled to the bartender. "Two bottles are going home with you right now."

McGee stood on the Hurricane deck, watching the doctor leave. Just then, a member of the crew approached holding a telegram.

"We received this while you were talking with the Doc, Captain, it's from St. Louis."

```
LYNCH AND THOMPSON CHECKING CARGO
STOP

PACKAGES MUST BE SECURED STOP

BIREMAN
```

McGee stroked his chin and watched lanterns being lit on shore. When his first officer returned he said, "Warren, send Seth to the pilothouse."

Seth Mathers, the boat's carpenter, had a wide girth and was winded by the time he climbed three flights of stairs. The last time he had been to the top was to repair a loose board in the pilothouse. Seth saw McGee waiting for him.

"Got another loose board, Captain?"

"No Seth, I've got a rather unusual job for you. I need two coffins."

Seth looked surprised. "Who they for?"

"Hopefully we won't need them. But I want them finished before we reach St. Louis. One other thing Seth, work on them when you're alone. We don't need to make anyone nervous."

72

WITH ATTRACTIVE WOMEN EMPLOYED AND Arthur and Harlan's wealthy friends in attendance, the Gentlemen's Club continued to thrive. Located in a quiet, respectable area of the city, most people weren't aware the Club existed. But Reverend Talbot made sure members of his congregation knew. Every Sunday he regaled them with sermons disparaging the "debauchery" taking taking place there.

Talbot used the pulpit to encourage his parishioners to do whatever necessary to stop the immoral behavior. Churchgoers petitioned authorities, sent letters of indignation to the *Tribune*, and even stood with placards at the Club's entryway. The Reverend believed God had selected him to preserve the virtues of hard work, honesty, and self-control. Corrupt businessmen and whores, who operated openly and without penalty, signaled the beginning of the end for Chicago, and the Republic. The Gentlemen's Club had to be shut down.

Daylight grew short in October; by seven o'clock the town lay swathed in darkness. Talbot had dressed in black from head to toe. He sauntered unseen past the main gate toward the wing of the Gentlemen's Club where Arthur and Teeny resided. He peered in a window and saw two couples dining.

"Are you working on a speech during dinner?" asked Arthur.

Harlan had been scribbling a few notes with his left hand, while holding a fork in his right.

"I apologize, but tell me what you think. It has to be perfect for the rally tomorrow."

"Let's hear what you have," Arthur responded, an amused look on his face.

"Citizens of Illinois, you deserve an elected official who is honorable; someone who has a political record that reflects the wisdom of the constituency and one who believes Manifest Destiny is in the best interest of our great country."

Frieda appeared more interested in the food than in the speech. Teeny sat bored and was none too pleased about hosting Frieda as a dinner guest.

Arthur listened and chuckled, "That's not very subtle, Harlan."

"Let me finish. You'll be pleasantly surprised at how I dance around the controversial issues."

Now, Arthur began laughing.

The discussion was interrupted when they heard a loud banging at the door. Everyone looked toward the entryway as the noise grew louder; it sounded as though someone was striking the door with a hard object. Arthur tossed his napkin and reached for the door's large brass handle. The door flew open, sending a basket of walking canes sliding across the floor. The enraged and twisted face of Jeremiah Talbot emerged. His eyes darted about wildly. His hair was tousled; veins along his neck seemed ready to burst.

He charged toward Arthur with a long knife, screaming, "You whore monger!"

Teeny yelled "No!" as Arthur staggered backwards. The front of his white shirt turned crimson.

Talbot glared at the stunned group.

He started toward the women with knife raised high. "Whores! Filthy whores!"

Harlan seemed immobilized, but suddenly he swung his fork across his chest and buried it in Talbot's thigh.

The enraged reverend gave a shrill yell, tugged at the fork, and threw it angrily against the wall. Then Talbot pointed his knife at Harlan.

Arthur, bleeding badly, grabbed a heavy walking stick and violently clubbed the Reverend's outstretched hand. The knife fell to the floor. Talbot moaned and curled up in a ball. He clutched his broken wrist.

"Harlan," Arthur said weakly, "Get the police, and find me a doctor."

At City Hospital Dr. Ellison addressed the diplomat's friends. "Fortunately, the knife missed the main artery. I stitched the wound, and the bleeding has stopped. With a few days rest, he should be fully recovered."

Teeny held Arthur's hand, and Harlan vowed he would make sure the Reverend "rotted in jail."

Before leaving the hospital, Teeny, Frieda, and Harlan, each gave an account of the night's events to a police officer. A *Tribune* reporter, standing nearby, scribbled everything he heard into a notebook. The story received a large space on the front-page the following day.

MINISTER STABS DIPLOMAT.
SENATOR PREVENTS ADDITIONAL MAYHEM.

The story developed into a topic of great interest. A follow-up story described the two women at the crime scene as "extremely attractive," one of whom was engaged to Senator Chambers, the other a companion of the diplomat. People clamored to know more about the people involved and the minute details of the event. The story grew even more intriguing when members of Talbot's congregation insisted their minister be regarded as, "a local hero" and not as "a mad man."

The congregation selected Edgar Blair to champion Talbot's cause. Blair served as an officer in the newly formed Railway Detective Agency (RDA). The RDA was created to deter criminal activity on the new train that would soon carry passengers and cargo between Galena and Chicago. Edgar had dedicated himself to both his religion and his profession; now the two came together in a fortuitous way.

Blair felt certain something occurred that triggered the Reverend's attack. He refused to think of his minister as a criminal who should be incarcerated. He eagerly volunteered his time and skills to prove Talbot's innocence.

Blair's plan was to prove the women lacked credibility and that Arthur Irving goaded the Reverend into a confrontation by selling his place of worship. He tried to uncover information about Teeny and Frieda, but no one seemed to know anything about them.

Late one Saturday night, as Blair returned from the Elgin run, a courier tracked him down as he checked out the last car of the train.

"This is for you Mr. Blair. It was sent to the *Tribune* office. They told me to give it to you as soon as you arrived."

Dear Mr. Blair

I am a clerk at the St. Paul hotel and I read the papers that are delivered here. The Chicago Tribune says you are looking for information

about the two women who were at that
diplomat's home. After reading the description
of them, I believe they used to live here in St.
Paul. The sheriff would know more about them.
His name is Earl Duncan. May God be with you
in your effort to free the good and righteous
Reverend Talbot.

Randall Simms

The letter energized Blair. With this information in hand, he went to see Judge Rutledge first thing the next morning. The judge was in his chambers getting ready to sign the order that would send Talbot to prison when Blair arrived.

"The women accusing Reverend Talbot have questionable pasts, and the diplomat provoked the Reverend on at least two occasions," he explained. "New evidence will, of course, be available soon."

Although Blair had very little information to work with, his argument somehow convinced Rutledge to provide a two-week delay before sending the Reverend away. The only thing Blair knew for sure was that Frieda was originally from St. Paul. He sent a telegram to the sheriff requesting more information.

```
NEED DETAILS ABOUT TWO WOMEN FROM YOUR
CITY STOP FREDERICKA SCHMIDT AND ELIZABETH
DOUGLAS STOP SEND DETAILS TO CHICAGO
TRIBUNE OFFICE STOP DETECTIVE

EDGAR BLAIR
```

ଔ ଔ ଔ

Earl Duncan went to the Granemann office with the telegram and a week old copy of the *Tribune* in hand. A small bell above the door tinkled. Robert emerged from the back room. "Hello, Earl. Haven't seen you for a while. Anything wrong?"

"I don't know, Robert. Look at this telegram, and read the story on the front page of this newspaper."

Robert handed Earl a mug of coffee and invited him to take a seat. Robert eased into his chair and read the telegram, then the newspaper story. He removed his glasses and stared out the window toward the old church. After pausing a moment he said, "So they both ended up in Chicago. What are you going to do, Earl?"

"I gotta respond. He's a law man."

Robert looked at the sheriff, who seemed to be waiting for advice.

"You could say Frieda Schmidt lived here for many years, but Elizabeth Douglas was not a resident. It's the truth."

The sheriff looked grateful. "You're right, Robert. It is the truth. Thanks."

73

ROBERT GRANEMANN'S REAL ESTATE BUSINESS was more successful than ever. Land and buildings were selling at a rapid pace. For Helen Granemann, however, life moved at a much slower, quieter pace. She found herself alone much of the time. Gabe left shortly after Frieda went to Chicago, and Robert's work required increasing amounts of his time. Robert knew Helen was unhappy and wanted to improve things for her.

After Sunday's evening meal, he took her hand.

"Helen, we have spent almost twenty years helping people find new lives, and I know we have paid a terrible price. But I think we should get involved with the cause again. It will be good for us, and I think Charles would have wanted us to continue our work."

She smiled and held Robert's hand tightly. "I think you're right."

Robert kissed her tenderly on the cheek.

"I'll be in the study. I'm going to write Mr. Bireman. Why don't you join me?"

Abe received Robert's letter a few weeks later. He anticipated reading about Robert's guilt and remorse. Instead, Robert praised Gar for "punishing a vile, mercenary human being;" he found the second half of the letter equally surprising.

I know it must seem like an unusual request, considering all that went wrong several months ago, but Helen and I still want to provide assistance to those trying to escape the oppression of slavery. Please be assured we have the resources and the will, and we can still be of value. Let us know when we can expect a new shipment.

Robert

Abe put the letter on his desk and slowly paced the perimeter of his office. He was lost in thought when there was a stern knock on the door. A formal looking courier greeted him once he opened the door.

"Telegram, Mr. Bireman."

He gave the young man a coin, thanked him, and glanced down at the message.

LEAVING JEFFERSON CITY STOP TWO
PACKAGES GOING NORTH FROM ST
LOUIS STOP

MCGEE

Bireman wondered who was on board McGee's boat. Then he thought about Robert's letter. He picked up a riverboat schedule and saw that Strickland's boat, the Adele, had left St. Paul two days ago and was returning to St. Louis. He went to the far wall and looked at a map of the river. Strickland would be pushing his boat twelve hours a day. Abe calculated its speed and determined he would have to take on wood in Dubuque. Abe decided to send a telegram soliciting his help right away. If Strickland rejected the request, Abe would still have time to make other arrangements.

Shortly after midnight, the Adele docked in the Iowa town. Strickland read the telegram.

GRANEMANN WANTS PACKAGES SHIPPED
TO ST PAUL ON NEXT TRIP STOP DO
YOU HAVE ROOM STOP

BIREMAN

Strickland's enthusiasm about transporting any more slaves had waned significantly as of late. Patrollers had stepped up their efforts all along the river. If the telegram hadn't been from Bireman, he would have ignored it, or responded "NO ROOM." Instead he stuffed the message in his pocket and walked back to his quarters.

Strickland poured a tumbler of bourbon. A few minutes later he pulled the crumpled telegram from his pocket and looked at it. His mind wandered… How was Elizabeth Douglas coping with the loss of her daughter? And what about Robert and Helen? The last time he got involved in transporting a runaway, bad luck dogged everyone. Could he really do this again?

He left his cabin, descended the stairs to the main deck, and walked slowly from the Adele toward the post office. He veered into a nearby bar and ordered a bourbon. He thought about what might happen if he were caught: Incarceration? Losing his Captain's license? Or, maybe some crazy bounty hunter coming aboard his boat and shooting him? He ordered another drink.

It was almost five when he entered the post office and spotted the telegraph operator sitting in a corner reading a newspaper. The captain handed a sheet of paper to he young man.

"Please send this to Abraham Bireman in St. Louis. His address is 108 Washington Street."

```
ROOM FOR TWO PACKAGES IN
NOVEMBER STOP PACK THEM
CAREFULLY STOP

STRICKLAND
```

74

THE POLAR STAR STEAMED SWIFTLY along. The day before docking, McGee called Will and Sunny to his quarters. He closed his cabin door and showed them the telegram from Bireman warning him patrollers were waiting.

"It seems somebody in Council Bluffs tipped off the slave traders in St. Louis that you and Sunny are aboard. They'll be waiting to search the boat when we reach the city tomorrow."

Will looked anxiously at Sunny, then back at McGee. "What are we gonna do, Captain?"

"I have a plan, but you're going to be…uncomfortable for a short time." He reached across his desk to retrieve the passenger manifest. "There was a young family on board when we left Kansas Village, the Dunbars. After their boy died, we left the parents in Jefferson City to bury him." Will and Sunny didn't see the connection.

"I asked the ship's carpenter to make two coffins. When the slave hunters come aboard, you and Sunny will be inside. I'll tell them the Dunbar's died of the Cholera after we left Jefferson City, and it's their bodies in the coffins."

Sunny squeezed her hands together and spoke in a strained manner, "I don't think I can do that captain."

"Sunny, those bounty hunters are going to search this ship from top to bottom, but they're not going to look inside coffins."

Sunny looked desperately at Will. "I can't stand the thought of being in a small box."

"Captain, how long before we get to St. Louis?"

"We spend the night in St. Charles. From there it's only a few hours."

"Could we practice? Let Sunny try? I'll be there to help her if she gets in trouble."

McGee thought about it. "Alright, let's meet after the evening card games begin."

Once passengers settled in for the evening's entertainment, Seth moved the coffins from his workshop to the stern. McGee told him to bore a few small holes on each side of the boxes. Then he lit up a cigar and waited. Will and Sunny arrived a few minutes later, slightly out of breath. "Sorry, Captain, we had to wait till the dining area was cleared."

"That's okay. Sunny, are you ready?"

Sunny gave a frightened nod. She knelt down next to the narrow tapered box. Will helped her inside. She lay on her back with arms folded across her chest. She let out a pitiful, soft whimper as he put the lid in place. Enveloped in darkness, with her elbows pressed against the sides, she bit her lip to keep from screaming. Seconds later she began kicking, and pushed the lid aside.

Breathing heavily, Sunny said, "I'm sorry, Will. I can't do this!"

She dabbed her eyes with the hem of her dress, clasped her hands behind her head, and took several deep breaths.

Will's demeanor remained calm, kind and encouraging. Sunny studied her husband's face, then looked over at the worried captain. She gazed up and contemplated the stars for several minutes. Finally, she said, "Let me try again."

Once again Sunny folded her arms and eased back down. Will heard her chanting very softly in a language he didn't understand. She closed her eyes and seemed to enter a trance. Will aligned the coffin lid. McGee pulled the time-piece from his coat pocket and wound the stem. Will and the captain stared intently at the coffin for several minutes.

Finally, McGee lifted the lid and slid it to the side.

"You lasted fifteen minutes, Sunny; that should be all the time I need."

Sunny sat up slowly and looked dazed. Will crawled over and hugged her.

McGee explained the plan. "After we dock I'll give two sharp blasts on the whistle. It will mean patrollers have boarded and you need to get inside these boxes."

Will and Sunny nodded grimly.

The Polar Star secured her berth just before noon. It was a warm day. Sunny and Will stood by the pine boxes, waiting for the signal. Officers shouted to one another and crewmembers rushed to secure mooring lines. On shore roustabouts secured the landing stage. In the pilothouse, McGee pressed the treadle and two sharp notes sounded. From their position on the stern, Will and Sunny moved the coffin lids aside. Lynch's men boarded the ship, passed the boilers, and moved steadily toward the back of the boat.

Sunny sat in the middle of the pine box, stretched out, and folded her arms across her chest. She began to softly chant. Will slid the lid over her and climbed inside the other box. Seconds later, two bounty hunters rounded the corner and spotted the coffins.

"Whadaya you got back here, Captain?" one of the men demanded harshly.

"Two deceased passengers," McGee replied in a calm, serious manner.

The tall bounty hunter looked dubious. "Who are they?"

"Ryan and Winnie Dunbar."

Let me see the passenger manifest," his partner ordered.

He studied the list and eyed the two coffins again, then added, "Where's their boy?"

"Jefferson City. They buried him and continued on," McGee explained. "Mrs. Dunbar died the day after we left, Ryan died last night in St. Charles. They hoped to make it to St. Louis so their relatives could take care of them."

The shorter but heavier bounty hunter mopped his brow with a handkerchief and sat down on top of Will's coffin. Will could see his pant leg through one of the tiny air holes; he clenched his fists and closed his eyes. He prayed neither he nor Sunny would make a sound!

"Don't seem right they just up and died after burying their son. Mind if we look inside these boxes?"

McGee scoffed. "I don't mind, but they died of the cholera."

The bounty hunter leaped away. "Why the hell didn't you say somethin' about the cholera, and why are you bringin' 'em ta shore? Why didn't you dump 'em in the river?"

"Their kin live here, and they deserve a decent burial. Here's the doctor's report, you want it?" McGee held out the sheet of paper he wrote the night before; he had signed it " Dr. Kyle Youngblood." The bounty hunter grabbed it and began reading.

McGee could feel the hot sun bearing down. "Are you gonna look inside those boxes or not?"

"No. Get some a your Nigger help to move them damn things. I want to look in the hold."

The Captain summoned two roustabouts. Will sensed he was being lifted. He didn't know his coffin had just been stacked on top of Sunny's.

Sunny lost her ability to mentally block out where she was. She dug her fingernails into the soft pine to keep from screaming. Splinters slid beneath her nails. Her throat became dry, her eyelids fluttered. Several minutes passed; one of the hunters surfaced from the hold and said, "Damn it's hot down there. Let's move on."

The bounty hunters left the stern and began their climb to the second deck. When he could no longer hear voices, Will crawled out and realized what had happened. He quickly moved his hiding place to one side and then lifted the lid on Sunny's. He was horrified; her hands were covered with blood, and she didn't appear to be breathing. Will carried her to a shaded area. He stripped his shirt away and dipped it in a bucket of water. He dabbed the wet cloth on her face. Sunny moaned and struggled to hold her head upright. She saw the fear in Will's face.

"I'm gonna be alright," she mumbled. "Where are those men?"

"They're still on board. We need to get away from here." He repositioned the coffins and guided Sunny to the tool shed. "I don't think they'll look in here again," Will whispered. He moved the ropes and chains to one side and they huddled in the dark. Ten minutes went by. They heard a patroller command, "Get all your Niggers down here. We wanna see who's missing."

Wooders, roustabouts, waiters, and kitchen help lined up opposite the stacked coffins. As names were read and shouted out, a man or woman would take a few steps forward. When they reached the end of the list, everyone was accounted for.

The bounty hunter scowled, wadded up the list, and threw it on the deck. He barked at McGee. "Did ya cut 'em loose in Jeff City? St. Charles? One a these days somebody's gonna kill you for helpin' them goddamned runaways."

McGee glared at the two men. "I have been patient and allowed you to search the boat, and now you need to leave. Should I summon my officers and the shore patrol?"

Lynch's patroller rested his hand on the butt of his gun. "That ain't necessary, but yer time's comin." He signaled to the other patroller. "Come on, we're leavin." When the two patrollers reached the gangplank the tall man yelled back, "Yer time's comin' McGee."

75

EDGAR BLAIR LEFT THE CHICAGO railroad station and walked to the *Tribune* office. As soon as he entered, a young man handed him a telegram.

"Here you are, Mr. Blair. They sent this over from the post office."

"Thank you. I appreciate the help you folks have provided."

"Glad to do it, Mr. Blair. Your investigation of the Talbot case has nearly doubled our readership."

Blair smiled, "I'll keep your reporter informed if there's any change." Blair read the message as he descended the stairs.

FRIEDA SCHMIDT LIVED IN ST. PAUL STOP
ELIZABETH DOUGLAS IS NOT FROM HERE STOP

EARL DUNCAN

The wording of the telegram miffed Blair, but he had a little more to work with. Frieda was definitely from St. Paul, and it seemed the other woman had stayed there at one time. He had a plan for using this new bit of information.

On Sunday, Harlan and Frieda returned from church to their town home. They sat on the sun porch and planned their afternoon: there was a political speech, dedication of a new three-masted schooner, and a late meal with Arthur and Elizabeth.

"Let's hope dinner is less exciting this time," Harlan said wryly.

"Harlan, would you mind if I rest up here before we join Arthur and Elizabeth? I'm not feeling all that well."

Ever since the *Tribune* had referred to Frieda as "The attractive blonde," she had received too much unwanted attention. Harlan knew she needed a break.

"I understand. I wish I could join you for a long afternoon nap, but duty calls."

"If you stayed for a nap, I would be even more exhausted," she replied coyly.

Harlan smiled, consulted the mirror, and adjusted his cravat. He took his hat and gave Frieda a sweet, lingering kiss. "See you in a few hours, my love."

"Harlan, will this thing with Talbot end soon?"

"I hope so, for everyone's sake. Be back around five."

Harlan left the building, crossed the street, and hailed a buggy. Edgar Blair watched from an alleyway. With Harlan gone, he pulled an envelope from his breast pocket. He slid it under the door of the townhome, knocked, and moved silently back to the alley.

Frieda picked up the envelope and was surprised to see it addressed to Frieda Schmidt. Only a handful of people in Chicago knew her by that name. Sensing a problem, she snatched the paper from the envelope.

> Miss Schmidt,
>
> I have corresponded with Sheriff Duncan in St. Paul. I would like to give you the opportunity to talk with me before I go to the authorities.
>
> Meet me at the Tremont Hotel at two this afternoon.
>
> Edgar Blair

Blair watched Frieda lock the front door and hail a carriage. He had his own carriage standing by and arrived at the hotel a few minutes before her.

Frieda scanned the hotel lobby, unsure how she would identify the detective.

A deep baritone voice reverberated behind her, "Miss Schmidt, I'm Edgar Blair." She turned to face a husky, curly haired man, with a red beard and mustache. He pointed toward a table in the back of the lounge.

"Miss Schmidt, I would like to get right to the point. You and Miss Douglas are in Chicago because of difficulties the two of you experienced in St. Paul, is that correct?"

"I have no idea what you are talking about Mr. Blair."

"Please, Miss Schmidt, don't drag this out longer than necessary. Earl Duncan made it clear you were a St. Paul resident. Why did you leave so suddenly? I know from various sources that when you came to Chicago you had no means of employment except for, shall we say, providing companionship?"

Frieda no longer made eye contact. She crossed her arms. Blair waited patiently for an answer. Frieda had concocted a story she believed would end the interrogation.

"I left because my services were no longer needed by my employer. I also left for personal reasons. My fiancé and I argued, and we separated. It felt uncomfortable being in the same town with him."

"Sorry, Miss Schmidt, I don't believe you. St. Paul is big enough that you could have avoided your fiancé. And someone as attractive as you could have found some type of employment."

Blair decided to bluff. "Sheriff Duncan said you left under duress without any explanation."

Frieda's wariness of Blair turned to fear. She began drumming her fingers on the table. Blair gambled again. "Since you and Miss Douglas left at the same time, did it have something to do with your fiancé?"

Frieda answered without thinking. "We didn't leave at the same time."

Blair's deception had worked; he now knew both women were in St. Paul together. He also knew there had to be a connection.

Frieda tried to backtrack. "I don't know where Miss Douglas is from or when she arrived in Chicago."

Blair continued, "Miss Schmidt, why don't you tell me about Miss Douglas. Is she a friend?"

"I am finished talking with you, Mr. Blair."

"Very well, I will go to St. Paul, or I will have Sheriff Duncan come here. Either way I will uncover the truth."

Frieda stood and responded in a firm manner, "Good day, Mr. Blair, don't bother getting up."

Blair didn't look at her as she started to walk away but said in a loud voice, "I'll be in touch with you and Miss Douglas shortly. Good day."

Harlan returned late in the afternoon to find Frieda staring out the parlor window. When she faced him her eyes were red and swollen.

"What is it my love? What's happened?"

Frieda showed Harlan the note that was slipped under the door and gave him the details about her meeting with Blair.

"Damn, this is getting out of hand." Harlan anxiously circled the room. "We have to tell Arthur and Elizabeth about this."

The evening turned morose after Frieda relayed the details to Arthur and Teeny.

Arthur couldn't hold back his frustration. "We should be celebrating your upcoming marriage, and now we are being investigated. A disturbed man attacked us, and we are the ones being investigated! This is shameful. It's wrong!"

Frieda believed she had made the situation worse by meeting with the detective. Harlan tried to reassure her the detective would have pursued his investigation, with or without their meeting.

"Arthur, I suggest you and Elizabeth leave Chicago. Take a trip until this blows over."

"Harlan, if we leave, this detective will become even more suspicious and more annoying." Harlan undid the top button of his shirt and rolled up his sleeves. In a firm voice and determined manner he said, "Then let's end this farce once and for all. We will tell the judge to release Talbot with the under-standing he never sets foot on any of your properties. That includes the old Mormon Temple."

"Harlan, this is going to look like we've got something to hide."

"We do, but we can make the public believe we are trying to do the noble thing. If this investigation continues, Teeny's real identity will be exposed, and Frieda humiliated." Everyone agreed it was the best thing to do.

Two days later Harlan presented the conditions for Talbot's release to Judge Rutledge.

"It would appear most unusual to simply release this man with all the pub-licity surrounding the event," said the Judge.

Rutledge suggested they end the investigation quietly and in stages. "I will propose Talbot's release when he signs a document agreeing to your terms. He can give a public apology a week later, and I'll have the charges dropped."

Harlan shared the judge's words with Arthur. Both felt relieved the mess with Talbot would soon be over. They planned a celebration for the following evening. Harlan ordered fresh flowers and champagne. Arthur slipped the wedding ring he had purchased into his coat pocket.

The couples sat enjoying their second bottle of champagne when a courier appeared at the front desk. "I have a message for Harlan Chambers."

"He's currently busy. Leave it, I'll give it to him later."

"Judge Rutledge told me to give it to him right away."

The clerk sighed, and in an exasperated tone said, "First room down the hall on the right. And be discreet."

The young man moved briskly down the hall and tapped on the partially open door. "Message for Mr. Chambers."

Harlan flipped the paper open, shook his head, and sat back down.

"What's wrong?" Arthur asked.

"Talbot rejected our offer."

76

A REPRESENTATIVE FROM REVEREND TALBOT'S congregation informed detective Blair that they had raised enough money to bring Earl Duncan to Chicago. Blair believed testimony from St. Paul's sheriff would reveal the two women lied about their past – rendering them unreliable witnesses. That alone would raise questions about the attempted murder charge. The congregation dubbed the detective's effort, "Reverend Talbot's Freedom Crusade." The editor at the *Tribune* could barely contain his delight with the new slogan.

Arthur read the newspaper and exclaimed, "What the hell did Elizabeth and Fredericka have to do with any of this?"

Harlan took the newspaper from his friend and said, "It's not about them. It's a tactic Blair devised to make the whole event seem like we are lying, and Talbot is the victim."

Arthur snorted, "Victim! The son of a bitch stabbed me!"

"People only know what they read, or hear, and what they read or hear is only a small part of the story."

Arthur remained indignant. "Newspapers have a responsibility to print the truth," he said angrily.

"They also have a responsibility to make money, and people love stories like this."

Arthur sighed and placed his coffee cup on the table. "I don't understand how everything became so twisted, Harlan. What would you suggest?"

"Get Elizabeth out of Chicago before her past is revealed and the bounty hunters come for her."

Arthur shook his head. "Harlan, I love her. I can't just send her away."

"Then go with her. Sell your share of the business to your partners."

"And my position with the government?"

Harlan shrugged. "It may be moot. If this unfortunate incident continues to gain notoriety, you will be replaced."

"And what about you? You are a public figure running for office. How will you get re-elected?"

Harlan gave his friend a cunning smile. "I can ride it out. Once this event is in the past, people will be more concerned about my position on manifest destiny and wildcat currency; I doubt they'll remember my association with Talbot."

Arthur slumped back in his chair. He pulled the gold fob from his vest pocket and checked his watch. "I promised Elizabeth I would meet her at the Club for lunch. We'll talk again tomorrow."

When Arthur arrived back at their living quarters he knew something was amiss. He entered the bedroom. An envelope with his name on it lay on the dresser. Before retrieving the letter, he went to the small closet where Teeny kept her clothes. Half of them were missing. Arthur sat on the edge of the bed and stared at the envelope. He felt he needed to talk to someone.

Arthur hailed a cab and returned to the Tremont, envelope in hand. Harlan was still sitting at a table in the lounge, engrossed in his newspaper. The politician looked up briefly but didn't notice Arthur's anxious demeanor.

"Glad you're back Arthur, listen to this story; last week a mob dumped a large block of marble into the Potomac. Seems the marble was a gift from the Pope to be used for the new Washington Memorial. Do you know why they threw it in the river?"

Arthur stood listlessly holding the envelope without responding.

"The Know-Nothings said it was a plot on the part of the Jesuits to undermine the American Republic. They think Catholic immigrants will take over the ballot box, then the Pope would run the country. Can you believe it? Stupidity isn't just in Chicago Arthur. It's everywhere!"

Arthur eased into a seat across from Harlan and slid the envelope toward him.

"What's this?" Harlan read the name on the front and carefully removed the hand written note. He looked up at his friend. "I have a feeling this isn't a love letter."

"In a way it is," Arthur replied.

Dearest Arthur,

If this detective reveals my past it will embarrass you, and lead to your arrest for violating the law and harboring me. Harlan will be judged guilty as well.

Please know how much I regret leaving this way. I hope you will be happy, you will love again, and you will remember me with affection and not anger. I am so sorry.

Elizabeth

"Arthur, we should try to find her. You and Elizabeth belong together. We can't let a *Bible* thumping fool and that boorish detective drive her away."

"It's already happened. She's been hunted before and feels she has no choice but to run."

Harlan looked morose. "I'm so sorry Arthur."

Arthur retrieved the note and solemnly rose from the table. "I'm going to the courthouse to see Judge Rutledge. I'll tell him this thing with Talbot is over. He can free the bastard."

Across town Teeny waited outside the livery for the next stage to the river port town of Ottawa. She watched a woman sitting on the front stoop of a tenement, gently brushing her young daughter's hair. She thought about Mary; was she crawling? How much had she grown? Did she still have red hair?

From behind a loud voice boomed, "All aboard!" The driver of the four-horse coach tied her bag to the top rack. Teeny glanced around at her fellow passengers and wondered whether they had read the stories in the *Tribune*. The absurdity of everything that happened with Talbot and the detective's investigation made her angry.

The whip cracked, and the stage lurched forward. Teeny stared out the window. Buildings began to slowly recede. Before closing the leather shade she looked back at the city one last time. "Good-bye Arthur," she whispered sadly.

77

MCGEE ENTERED THE LAW OFFICE and noticed his friend pacing back and forth.

"Morning Abe, you're looking particularly riled today."

Bireman nodded in the affirmative. "Getting too old for all this intrigue, Allen."

McGee leaned back in a chair and propped his feet on Bireman's desk. Jokingly he said, "Stop walking around like that, Abe, you're making me jumpy."

Bireman settled in behind his desk and clasped his hands together. He said to McGee, "Gordon Strickland heard about the slave hunters who searched your boat. He's worried his boat is next."

"Yeah, he should be. Those bastards came close to finding Will and Sunny, really close. I'm going to get them aboard Gordon's boat this afternoon." In a disbelieving tone he added, "I can't believe that family in St. Paul wants another delivery."

Abe let out a sigh and said, "I agree. Considering what happened, it's surprising they're willing to do this. But they seem to be looking forward to the young couple's arrival."

"Well," said McGee, "Past misfortunes cannot be mourned forever. The only cure for a broken heart is action."

Abe smiled. "That's a good one. Did you just make that up?"

McGee chuckled. "I don't know, maybe."

Will, Sunny, and two waiters from the Polar Star lined up on the bow and waited for McGee. On shore a group of roustabouts, arms and backs glistening in the sun, chanted:

"Fifty boxes we gots to load."

"Praise the Lord!"

"Now there's thirty."

"Praise the Lord!"

"Pile gettin' smaller,"

"Praise the Lord!"

"Rest be comin'."

"Praise the Lord!"

This soothing repetition of simple verse reminded Sunny of the mantra she used to ease her distress inside the coffin. She glanced over at Will who was standing on his toes, trying to locate the floating school.

"I wish I could see the boat and point her out to you."

"I know you've got some good memories from that riverboat."

"Better memories with you on this riverboat."

"Colonel Douglas, you're such a smooth talkin' scoundrel. What's an innocent girl like me to do?"

Will laughed and thought about how lucky he was to have Sunny in his life.

McGee arrived and made a hasty inspection of the four servants. All had dressed in the traditional black and white attire worn by saloon workers on board the fancy riverboats. McGee surveyed the crowd and plotted a course to Strickland's boat, then gave the order;

"Follow close behind me. Don't make eye contact, look as though you know exactly where you're going."

The group passed dockworkers, stevedores, cattle drivers, and police. Stacks of boxes, bales of cotton, and piles of produce made it difficult to see. Soon, Sunny spotted ADELE painted in large letters along the second deck of a large riverboat. A member of the crew sprinted down the gangplank and ushered them aboard. Strickland shook McGee's hand, and the four servants lined up for inspection.

"I'll take these two." Strickland pointed to Will and Sunny. "Don't think I can use all four." To anyone in the vicinity, it appeared a normal business transaction.

"Very well," said McGee. "The other two will return with me. How about a drink and dinner before you shove off? Say five, at the Bonton? I'll ask Abe to join us."

Strickland nodded, "See you there."

On the second deck of the Adele, a ship's officer had just introduced Sunny and Will to "Tommy the Troubadour." Tommy was a first-class songster and entertainer who performed every evening in the saloon. He took Will and Sunny on a tour of the kitchen and servant's quarters. Then he introduced Lars, the officer in charge of the saloon. Lars stood over six feet tall, had reddish blonde hair, neatly trimmed sideburns, and was dressed in a traditional starched white uniform. He explained to Will and Sunny the meal schedule and the pecking order used when seating first-class passengers.

Later that afternoon Will and Sunny looked around and found the boat almost deserted. Servants and roustabouts with passes visited friends, and most of the white crewmembers were taking advantage of various forms of entertainment in the city. Lars suggested the newcomers take leftovers from the kitchen and picnic on the top deck.

"You should have plenty of privacy there," he said in a friendly manner.

When Will and Sunny arrived on the top deck, the afternoon sun was slowly setting, and the air was pleasantly warm. A gentle breeze flowed, making it a perfect October day. Sunny spread a blanket where they could sit and watch river traffic. The couple unloaded the basket of food and the carafe of sweet tea spiked with a little bourbon the bar tender had kindly provided.

During their meal, Will entertained Sunny with tales of Big Lucy and the Reverend Meachum. He began a story about his first attempt at teaching, but stopped suddenly when two rough looking men appeared on the stairwell. For a few seconds, it seemed they were passing through, but they turned and began a slow edgy walk toward Will and Sunny. One man stood tall, with stringy straw-colored hair and watery blue eyes, the other was short and muscular, with deep-set eyes and black hair.

"Sunny, run! Get away from here!" Will whispered.

The tall man blocked her path. He sneered in a slow drawl, "Y'all got a little picnic goin on here?"

The short stocky man grabbed Will by the arm, "This man just asked you a question, boy. What you two doin' up here?"

Will knew he had to speak carefully. "Yes, sah, I was gonna tell ya. We jus' havin' a bite ta eat. Den we goes back ta our work."

The man squeezed his arm harder. "This here's a white man's boat, ain't it? Why are you two havin' a picnic here on a white man's boat?"

"We works on da boat. We ain't meanin' no dis'respec'. Me an' da missus jus' havin' some time ta'gedder."

The man smirked, "Yer missus? She's too pretty to be married to tha likes a you." He looked around. The boat appeared deserted. "Ya got papers?"

"Yes, sah, dey be in our cabin, we gets 'em fer ya."

"Don't matter if ya got 'em or not. Where I come from a nice spot like this is for white folk, an' you two ain't white."

Terrified, tears formed in Sunny's eyes. The tall man moved closer. He put a calloused hand on her chin and forced her to look directly at him. Will's fists tightened.

"You be right pretty for a half breed, ya know that?"

Sunny tried to turn away. The man grabbed her face with both hands and forced her to look at him.

"I asked you if ya knew you were pretty."

Scared and confused, Sunny couldn't find her voice. She didn't understand.

Will blurted out, "Yes, sah, she mean to say, Yes, sah!"

He glared at Will and commanded, "Then let's hear her say it."

"Yes, Sir," said Sunny. Tears were running down her cheeks.

"That's better. Now I think this little half-breed missus a yours wants to visit with my friend an' me fer awhile."

Before Will could move the shorter of the two men hit him on the back of the head with a lead pipe. He fell face down. Blood trickled slowly from the back of his head. The tall man threw Sunny down onto the deck. She kicked feverishly, but the short man grabbed her ankles. Sunny coiled and twisted in wild gyrations. She screamed. The man with the stringy blond hair put a hand over her mouth. She tore at his face and hair. He wrapped a muscular arm around her neck and punched her. She kept struggling. Two more rapid blows and she lay stunned.

The two waited a few seconds, then lifted her skirt and tore at her clothes until she was naked from the waist down. When the tall one pushed her legs apart Sunny tried to claw his face. The bearded man grabbed her arms and pulled them back over her head. She cried out. He landed another blow with his fist; Sunny groaned and stopped moving.

Will looked across the surface of the deck. Images seemed blurred and voices garbled. He wobbled and stood; slowly, things came into focus. He saw the tall man start to remove his trousers and lower himself between Sunny's legs. Will grabbed the Union flag from its bracket, wrapped the fabric around the pole, and ran toward him. The man emitted a shrill yell when the point of the shaft entered his rib cage.

Before the shorter man could reach his gun, Will hit his eye socket with the butt of the pole. While the two attackers writhed in pain, yelling foul curses, Will grabbed Sunny's hand and pulled her toward the stairs.

"Get away from here as fast as you can!"

Will stood in front of the stairs, watching Sunny run to safety on the deck below. A shot rang out, splintering wood above Will's head. Another shot rang out, louder, from the opposite side of the boat. Will was grateful it was Lars brandishing a double-barreled shotgun.

"Drop your weapons!" he ordered.

Then he leveled his shotgun at the man holding the pistol.

"I said, drop that weapon! Both of you get up against that wall!"

The straw-haired man could barely stand. He suffered several broken ribs, and blood oozed from the gash in his side. He slowly tugged at his trousers and then fell backward. Shouts rang out from below. Tommy bounded up the stairs leading two police officers to the top deck.

"Police! What's going on up here?"

"Robbery, and assault of a young lady. Come and arrest these two," said Lars.

The officers looked at the two men slumped against the wall and the bloody flag on the deck.

"Jesus, what the hell happened up here?" asked one officer. "Where's the girl who was attacked?"

Lars pointed to Sunny, who clung to Will near the stairwell. The officer motioned for her to come forward. Sunny's face had begun to swell, bruises had formed on her arms and legs, and her dress had been torn in half.

"The injuries to these men, how'd they get them?" the other officer asked.

Will stepped forward. The policemen looked at one another.

"We got a problem. You mean this Nigger attacked two white men?"

"No, officer, he was defending his wife and our boat. They're free coloreds and they work for me. These scum planned to rob the boat, and they attacked this lady and her husband."

"We're gonna have to sort this out down at the station. Where's the captain?" "He's having his dinner in town," Lars replied, becoming more annoyed.

"Get him. We'll file a report, and he'll have to sign off. You can put your gun away."

One officer nudged the men with his nightstick. "You two, come with us."

The other officer pointed to Tommy, "You, boy, go fetch the captain. Tell him to come to the precinct on Fifth."

Lars looked at Tommy and said, "Go on, Tommy, do what the man says. Captain Strickland's at the Bonton."

Tommy sprinted down the stairs and darted through traffic to the restaurant. The maître d' guided him past gawking diners to three men sitting at a corner table. After Tommy relayed what happened he was led back outside.

"Damn," said Strickland, "That poor girl."

Abe placed a hand next to his chin and sadly shook head. He looked at Gordon, then at McGee.

"Allen, why don't you come with me to the police station? You can tell them you're Captain Strickland, and we'll sign the paperwork. That'll give Gordon a chance to put things in order and get out of here on time."

McGee looked at his friend and said, "Okay, but don't you think somebody at the station might figure out I'm not Gordon Strickland?"

"No, I doubt they've ever met any of us."

The three vowed to meet again when Strickland returned from St. Paul. McGee and Bireman turned the corner on Fifth and approached the Precinct Station.

"I wonder whether Miss Douglas is fairing any better than Will and Sunny?" McGee mused.

"Hard to say, she seems to have disappeared."

McGee pointed toward the red brick building. Abe had his hands in his pockets and looked discouraged.

"This is a waste of time. They're not going to lock these two up for attacking a half-breed and a colored man."

"That's probably true," McGee agreed, "But we can't just ignore what they did."

"You're right," said Abe. "If we walk away, we're giving evil a free pass."

McGee gave Bireman a look of surprise. "That's a good one, Abe. Did you just make that up?"

"I don't know…maybe."

They solemnly entered the precinct. Bireman formally charged the two men with illegally boarding the Adele, attempted robbery, and attacking two crew-members. McGee signed Strickland's name to the paperwork. An officer on duty examined the document and placed it on the Chief of Police's desk.

"Says in the police report those two men were attacked by a colored man. Was he arrested?"

"He was not," said McGee. "He and his wife were attacked. They did nothing wrong."

The officer shook his head and appeared irritated. "This ain't gonna sit well with the chief when he gets here in the morning. A colored man attacking two white men and injuring them, it's not gonna sit well at all."

McGee sounded conciliatory when he said, "Have him come to my boat tomorrow afternoon. We can discuss it over a bottle of whiskey."

"I'll tell him. I'm sure he'll be there. He's gonna want to hear first hand what happened."

Bireman and McGee left the precinct and looked at one another with crooked grins. "Strickland should be in Alton by late tomorrow," said McGee, "That's a long way for the police chief to go for whiskey."

78

AFTER TAKING THE STAGECOACH TO Ottawa, Teeny boarded the steamboat Frontier. No one on board realized she was one of the women whose notorious story had recently appeared in the *Chicago Tribune*. She felt grateful to be inconspicuous, but she was still fuming about the bizarre events that ended her life in Chicago.

Several days later the Frontier docked in the bustling river town of Peoria. Teeny carried her bag through levee traffic to a hotel on the corner of Madison and Perry.

"Afternoon ma'am," said the desk clerk. "Are you looking for overnight accommodations or longer?"

"Just one night. I'm leaving tomorrow on the Governor Briggs."

"That's a very nice boat, ma'am. In the meantime, I'm putting ya up in the Jefferson room on the second floor. It's our second finest room and should be just what ya need for a good night's sleep."

Teeny signed the guest register and smiled benignly. She grew curious about the clerk's remark.

"Pardon me for being nosy, but who has the finest room in your hotel?"

The clerk seemed proud to announce the occupant: "That would be Mrs. Pelagie Lyons. She's in the Washington suite."

That evening Teeny entered the hotel dining room and waited to be seated. She noticed an elegant woman wearing a cream-colored moiré dress seated at a corner table. A waiter handed Teeny a card with the name Pelagie Lyons inscribed. "Lady Pelagie has asked that you be her guest at dinner this evening," he said.

"I don't know her. Are you sure you have the right person?"

"She seems to know you. May I escort you to her table?"

Teeny was reluctant, but the woman at the corner table flashed a winning smile and gestured to the empty chair.

"Please, dine with me," she said when Teeny approached. "Seldom do I have the opportunity to meet another woman traveling alone."

The waiter pulled the chair back and Teeny cautiously took a seat. He inquired whether he might bring her a beverage. Lady Pelagie answered in a kind, but abrupt manner for them both, "Water, and a bottle of your finest bourbon, so we can kill whatever might be living in that ghastly water."

Teeny glanced quizzically at her new companion. "How did you know I was alone?"

"I saw you check in this afternoon, and it certainly appeared you were."

Their conversation was momentarily interrupted, as the waiter had returned with a small pitcher of water and a bottle of bourbon. He put glasses and tumblers on the table and handed each woman a hand-written menu. Pelagie gave a gentle wave of her hand. "We'll order our meal after we chat awhile."

Teeny began to feel an unusual kinship with this woman and asked, "Mrs. Lyons, why are you traveling alone?"

"Because I can my dear. My last husband owned a great deal of property in St. Louis. Now I am able to travel and live as I please. Some of my uptown residences are quite nice. You might consider living in one until you sort things out."

Teeny was taken aback. "What do you mean, until I sort things out?"

"I was in Chicago when that nonsense with the minister occurred. I read the papers. I read as much as I can, Miss Douglas, it's how I stay a step or two ahead of the men I do business with. The *Tribune* has no audience in Peoria, so I doubt the residents here even know about the confrontation.

Teeny grew wary and uncertain of whether to continue the conversation. Pelagie sensed her concern; she reached across the table and gently touched Teeny's hand.

"You are safe with me, my dear, I assure you. Start from the beginning and tell me about yourself."

The lovely fugitive stared down at her drink, sighed, and tentatively began. Toward the end of her story Pelagie said, "So after you fled St. Paul, you ended up in Chicago?"

"Yes. After living there for several months I thought I might even marry the man I was living with. But then the investigation into my past began."

"Well, Miss Douglas, I will purchase a ticket for you, and for the time being, you will be my personal aide. There are no staterooms left on the Governor Briggs, so they will have to make accommodations for you in my room."

"But, you hardly know me, and I know nothing about you."

Pelagie paused and took another sip of bourbon. "Then I shall tell you. I am also from the south. After my first husband passed away I inherited his fur trading business. By the time my third husband passed away I was quite wealthy. My records in the city were, shall we say, reconstructed. I am now listed in the St. Louis directory, alongside several other notables, as a prominent white citizen."

Completely surprised, Teeny studied her dinner companion closely.

"You were a sla…" before she could finish Lady Pelagie raised a finger to her lips, and shook her head. She added bourbon and water to the glasses.

"I assume you are going to St. Louis to see your daughter?"

Haltingly, Teeny responded, "Yes."

"Then, by all means, take advantage of my offer. Now, I believe, we should have dinner." Pelagie signaled to the waiter.

By the time they finished their meal, other diners assumed the two women were the best of friends.

When Teeny retired to the Jefferson Room, her mind whirled with this latest turn of events. She turned down the wick of the lantern, wished she had known her mother, prayed for her daughter, and smiled when she thought about her new friend.

79

BEFORE THE ADELE DEPARTED, STRICKLAND brought a doctor aboard to examine Sunny. He rinsed her eye with a saline solution and applied red salve to her wounds. He finished, then spoke to the captain in private.

"Gordon, that girl is hurting. Her eye and scrapes will heal, but I'm worried about her jitteriness."

Strickland didn't seem to understand. "Her jitteriness?"

"Yes, she jumped a foot when I reached out to touch her. I'm not sure she's gonna be right in the head for some time. That must have been a brutal attack."

Strickland's face grew troubled. "Doc, should she be traveling, and working?"

"I think she'll be all right doing menial chores, but have her work in the kitchen or as a cabin maid. Put her somewhere she won't be noticed. She's upset by her appearance."

"Thanks, Jim. We're leaving soon, but let me buy you and your wife dinner when I get back. If there's no ice, I should be back in late December. Maybe we can celebrate the New Year."

"I look forward to it, Gordon. Have a safe trip." Strickland thought about the "safe trip" comment. He had never worried about security aboard his boat; now he and his officers constantly surveyed the decks, looking for anyone acting suspicious.

The Adele's steam whistle let out a low moaning sound as the big sternwheeler inched back into the main channel. Strickland gave the last tap of the bells, and the paddlewheel rotated faster. Sunny and Will emerged from their cabin and looked over the handrail.

"There she is, Sunny, my old floating school!"

Sunny regarded the drab steamboat and said, "Does it ever move?"

Will shook his head. "No, she's anchored there. You have to row a skiff out to get on board. Tom and I must have rowed out to that boat a hundred times."

Sunny was pleased Will could see the school one more time, but she didn't feel well and wanted to return to their quarters.

That evening she crawled into the berth and pulled the blanket over her head. In the darkness she tried to sleep, but her mind was unwilling to release the images of the men holding her down, hitting with closed fists, and tearing at her clothes. She squeezed her eyes tightly, tears rolling down the sides of her face.

Will held her tenderly, whispering "You're safe, everything is going to be all right." He caressed her and thought about how happy she was moments before the attack. Sunny clutched his arm and eventually drifted into a troubled sleep.

The following evening, the Adele made a brief stop in Hannibal. Passengers disembarked to visit shops and restaurants while roustabouts loaded wood for the boilers. Strickland went to the post office and sent a telegram to Robert Granemann.

ONE PACKAGE DAMAGED PRIOR TO
LEAVING STOP SHOULD ARRIVE IN
EIGHT DAYS STOP

STRICKLAND

Strickland returned to the boat, climbed the stairs, and approached Will and Sunny's cabin. He started to knock, but stopped when heard them talking . . .

"Will, I'm sorry I'm not the way I was before."

"I know, and I didn't mean to upset you. I just wanted us to be close again."

"It'll be like it once was, I promise, I just need more time. I want to get better. You know how much I love you."

Strickland turned away, embarrassed that he eavesdropped. He returned to his quarters and poured a tumbler of bourbon. He was supposed to be hob-nobbing with the first-class passengers, but decided to pass. Strickland gazed at the wide expanse of river, thought about the conversation he overheard, and poured another drink. He went to his desk, retrieved a sheet of paper, and began to write.

Will's breathing deepened and he fell into a sound sleep; but Sunny remained agitated and restless. She left the tiny cabin and walked barefoot toward the stern. Oiled planks beneath her feet were smooth and cool. Her pulse quickened as she approached the spot where she had been assaulted. Glints of moonlight reflected rhythmically on the swirling river currents. She stood by the rail and began reciting an Indian prayer her father taught her. Walking back to her cabin she heard Tommy singing in the saloon below. The lyrics surprised her.

> There's a good time coming, boys, a good time coming,
>
> The Pen shall supersede the sword,
>
> And right, not might, shall be the Lord,
>
> In the good time coming, In the good time coming.
>
> Worth, not birth, shall rule mankind,
>
> And be acknowledg'd stronger;
>
> The proper impulse has been giv'n.
>
> Wait a little longer,
>
> Wait a little longer.
>
> There's a good time coming, boys, a good time coming.

The audience had remained subdued during this serious song, but they turned raucous when Tommy strummed his banjo and launched into the lively "Camptown Races." Sunny listened to him sing about the bobtail nag and smiled. She touched her eye. The oozing had finally stopped. She slipped back into the berth next to Will. Sunny stretched out, and curled up next to him. Will held her close, and nuzzled her hair.

"I heard Tommy singing tonight," she whispered. Imitating Tommy's voice, she sang very softly, "Wait a little longer, wait a little longer. There's a good time comin' boys, a good time comin'."

Will laughed and said, "Miss Sunny, ya are indeed a mystery to the Colonel. I thought y'all was sad, and here y'all are singin'."

"I'm getting better, Will," and she sang the last verse again. "Good times a comin', wait a little longer."

Will gently stroked her hair. "Right now, being here with you is all the good times I need."

Tommy's music echoed through the cabin, and a few minutes later Will and Sunny drifted into sleep, bodies entwined.

ದ ದ ದ

Robert Granemann stood at the St. Paul post office reading the telegram from Gordon Strickland. "Damaged package," meant someone had been injured.

That evening he shared the telegram with Helen. "Oh my, there's trouble even before they arrive. Have we done the right thing by getting involved again?"

"Charles would have wanted us to, and we both want to help this young couple."

"I know, it's just that the people hunting the slaves seem so determined—and so violent."

Helen started to remove dishes from the table when she saw a rider approaching. "Robert, are you expecting someone?"

He rose from the table and looked out the window. "It's the sheriff."

The couple invited Earl Duncan inside. He joined Robert and Helen for coffee and started making small talk about the weather. Setting his cup down, Robert gave the sheriff a serious look. "I'm sure you didn't come out here to discuss the weather, Earl, what's going on?"

"I thought ya should know that Lynch and Thompson just hired two local patrollers to board the Adele when she arrives."

"Who are Lynch and Thompson?"

"Slave sellers. They think a couple runaways they're looking for are on that boat, the Adele."

Robert smiled wryly, "And you think the runaways are coming to meet me?"

"I'm not supposed to be talking about this with anyone, Robert. You do what you like with the information." He rose to leave. "Thanks for the coffee. You and Helen stay warm, it's getting real cold out there."

After Duncan left, Robert pulled a map from his desk. He followed the line of the Mississippi River with his finger and stopped on a river town in Iowa. Helen came up behind him, worry lines etched on her face. "What are we going to do?"

"Strickland will arrive in Davenport in a couple of days. I'm going to send a telegram and warn him, and let him know we're going to meet our guests at a new location."

80

TEENY STOOD IN A LINE of passengers waiting to board the Governor Briggs. The boat's first officer rushed over to greet her.

"Welcome, Miss Douglas. Lady Pelagie has your ticket and is waiting for you."

Teeny made her way up the gangway. She saw her benefactor waving to her from the deck. When Teeny reached her, they hugged, and Pelagie guided her down the hallway past the saloon and toward the cabins. The older woman looked like royalty as she approached the largest of the staterooms. A lanky cabin boy followed behind, toting several bags. He placed them inside the room and asked, "Will that be all, ma'am?"

Pelagie surveyed the interior. "No. We will need another bed, an additional chamber pot, and a pitcher of sweet tea." With that, she handed the young man two gold coins.

His face brightened. "Yes ma'am, I'll take care of that in two shakes!"

Teeny began arranging the suitcases so they were less conspicuous; one was extremely heavy, and she struggled to lift it.

"That contains books my dear. I forgot to ask, can you read?"

"Yes," her companion smiled, "thanks to a Quaker governess."

"Splendid, between the books and the card games, we should have plenty to keep us entertained."

Teeny picked up a few of the books and read the titles aloud, "*Gulliver's Travels, Pilgrims Progress, Uncle Tom's Cabin*. Have you read all these?"

"I'm working my way through them. All are about the trials and tribulations of the book's main character trying to get safely from one place to another. You should feel right at home reading any of them."

Early that evening, the two women travelers made their way to the saloon for a hearty meal of roast turkey, boiled rutabagas, and fresh green beans. A pianist, accompanied by two violinists, began playing a variety of up-tempo selections. Several couples lined up for a new dance called the Virginia Reel. The captain and first officer courteously invited Pelagie and Teeny to participate.

"Maybe tomorrow, Captain, after we've had a chance to rest. Tonight we're content to just sit and watch," Pelagie respectfully responded for them both.

Shortly before midnight a shift occurred in the saloon's activities.

"Come, dear, it's time for us to find a seat as close to the main poker table as women are allowed," Pelagie said.

She and Teeny sat on a raised platform and watched the dealer place chairs and spittoons around the table. The bartender arranged cigars, matches, ashtrays, glasses, and several bottles of bourbon.

Players for the high stakes poker game began to arrive. An elderly grey-haired gentleman in a beige suit, a rough looking trapper wearing a buckskin shirt and wool pants, a suave well-groomed gentleman dressed in a tailored charcoal suit, a sun-burned cowboy in chaps, plaid shirt and red bandana, and a meek looking man wearing an ill fitting blue suit and a black derby. All sought out their "lucky" seats. The dealer showed up sporting black trousers and a black vest that contrasted vividly with his crisp white cotton shirt. He stood deferentially when the captain arrived, and then rolled up his sleeves.

"Watch carefully," Pelagie advised. "See whether you can tell who has the winning hand."

The ladies watched as cards and bets flew. Although Teeny felt pretty sure she understood the game, she had no clue which player would collect the money. Pelagie gave her a knowing smile.

"Well, who do you think the winner will be?"

Teeny shook her head. "I have no idea."

"It's going to be the little man in the blue suit."

The player referred to had been sitting erectly throughout the hand, guiding his chips gently into the pot when bets and calls were made. When the first hand ended, he reached out, collected the chips, and stacked them neatly in front of him.

Teeny looked at Lady Pelagie. "How did you know he would win?"

"Watch the next hand, and I will try to explain."

The players anted up. The man in the beige suit, sitting on the right side of the dealer, cut the cards. Each player received five cards. While they examined their holdings, Pelagie began a droll analysis of each player.

"Beige suit just arched his eyebrows, blue suit already lifted two chips from one of his neat little stacks, and the fur trader leaned back and appears relaxed. Those three are quite pleased with the cards they have been dealt."

Teeny looked on while Pelagie continued. "The captain is rubbing the back of his neck, that's not a good sign. The cowboy just put his hand over his mouth; his cards are weak. Robert, the handsome man in the dark suit, is a professional gambler. His tells are almost impossible to detect."

Teeny grew curious. "You know him?"

"I've watched him play many times. His name is Robert Trudeau. He will not strike until the last hands are played, probably the night before we arrive in St. Louis. If you spot his tell, I will give you a ten dollar gold piece."

As the game unfolded, Teeny kept her eyes glued to Trudeau but detected nothing. Unexpectedly, Pelagie nudged her, "There it is." Teeny didn't notice anything.

"Robert's right hand moves toward the center of the table when he has a winning hand, then veers to the right toward his bourbon. He can win this hand if he wants," Pelagie whispered.

"If he wants…why wouldn't he want to?"

Pelagie smiled. "He will probably choose to fold and let others win small amounts. He is setting them up for the final game."

They watched for a while longer, but the night grew late, and they needed sleep. After the two women returned to their stateroom, Teeny gazed at her benefactor with admiration and wonder. "How did you learn those…those tells?"

"An excellent card dealer in St. Louis taught me the basics. Then I began to observe things on my own. A woman is constantly at a disadvantage doing business in a man's world. Knowing whether another person is truthful or not is a skill that has served me well."

"What did you learn about me when we first met?"

Without hesitating Pelagie said, "You didn't look at me, you kept your hands folded tightly in your lap, you hesitated when speaking to me, and your eyes searched the room as you spoke. You wondered whether someone would recognize you, and you didn't know whether you could trust me."

"That's…remarkable!"

Pelagie shot Teeny a kind smile. "You can be just as remarkable. Live and learn."

On the fourth day, the Captain addressed first-class passengers during their evening meal.

"We will be on the Mississippi River soon and arrive in St. Louis tomorrow morning. Please continue with your meal and enjoy the music. Poker games for the gentlemen will begin at nine."

Teeny looked at Pelagie and smiled, knowing she would have another chance to observe the games and learn as much as she could about the art of spotting tells. The two women sat and watched for almost three hours, with Pelagie providing commentary and guidance along the way.

Shortly after midnight, the captain made another announcement to the men remaining at the center table: "Final game gentlemen; I must put the ship and saloon in proper order prior to docking." Two of the players grumbled, thinking the game would continue until they decided it was time to quit. An elderly gentleman in a blue pin stripe suit lost a fair amount of money during the evening and he called for a fifty-dollar entry fee for the final game. The dealer bent his head and nodded in acknowledgement. The substantial amount surprised the players, but all remained seated and eased their money into the center of the table.

Pelagie rolled her eyes in disbelief and whispered, "That man intends to recoup his losses in one game, he's going to be played for a fool. Watch how Robert manipulates him. Mr. Trudeau is polishing his game before he heads down river."

Teeny asked her to explain.

"After we dock, he will look for the most luxurious boat leaving St. Louis for New Orleans and book passage. The bigger and more opulent the boat, the higher the stakes."

Bets and calls for the final game grew larger. Two players fidgeted uneasily. Pelagie told Teeny they were going to fold. A thousand dollars in chips and gold coins gilded the table. Trudeau bet another fifty dollars. The captain and two other players shook their heads and placed their cards face down on the table. They were finished. Only Robert and the elderly man in the pin stripe suit remained.

"Your bet," said Robert. He stared directly at his opponent.

"Seventy-five dollars," the man said, now perspiring heavily.

"I'll see that and raise you one hundred dollars."

The elderly man grimaced and stammered, "I, I can't match that bet. I'm tapped out."

"Then you are folding?"

The man looked around the room, and in a pleading manner said, "Will somebody here loan me a hundred dollars? I'll give you a promissory note and pay you back as soon as we reach St. Louis."

No one responded.

"Son-Of-A-Bitch!" the man shouted and threw his cards on the table.

Robert calmly reached out, encircled his winnings, and drew the money toward him.

"What were you holding?" The man demanded angrily.

Robert didn't look up. "It doesn't matter. You folded."

"What was Robert holding?" Teeny asked her mentor.

"Nothing," replied Pelagie. "It was a bluff, and Robert just walked away with a small fortune."

They sat a few more minutes and watched the players disperse. Trudeau gave a nod and a wink to the women who had been observing the game. He flashed a roguish smile at Teeny, then sauntered over to the bar and ordered a bourbon. Teeny looked at Pelagie.

"He appears to be a gentleman, but I believe we have spotted a tell that indicates he is the opposite."

Pelagie smiled. "Very good, my dear. Live and learn, live and learn."

81

SUNNY HAD JUST PROVIDED FRESH linens to the staterooms when a tall thin woman with a friendly smile approached.

"I's Bessie. Cap'in Stricklan ask me ta pay you a visit. He say to give ya a touch a color roun' dat eye so ya looks pretty."

Self conscious about her injuries, Sunny demurred, "I don't think it would help Bessie, but thank the captain for thinking of me."

"Bessie an' da cap'in know whad be best. Now sits an' lemme show ya whad I kin do."

Sunny thought it best not to cross this woman and took a seat. Bessie applied a bit of rouge and powder to the bruises around her eye, then held up a mirror.

"See? Now ain't dat better?"

Sunny nodded. "Yes, it does look better."

"I ain't done. Lemme see dat hair." Bessie untied the leather band and the unbundled hair cascaded down to Sunny's waist. "It be pretty, but it be too long." Bessie reached into her bag and pulled out a long, thin scissors.

"What are you doing?" Sunny cried out, panicked.

"I gonna do whad shu'da been done a long time ago; cuts dis so it can get sum air an' grow healthy. I's been doin dis fer forty years. Ya kin trust me. "

Bessie began lopping off strands of Sunny's hair. When she finished, Sunny was almost in tears. She reached for the mirror.

"My goodness!" She was astonished and pleased. "Will is going to be so surprised."

"He be su'prise aw right, an' den he be chasin ya all roun dis boat.

"Thank you, Bessie," Sunny smiled warmly.

Sunny found Will cleaning tables in the saloon. He couldn't get over how pretty his wife looked as she approached. He gently touched her cheek.

307

"It looks just like before." He asked her to turn, so he could admire her hair from all angles. Before Will could tell her how much he liked it, Tommy sprinted toward them.

"You're looking really beautiful Miss Sunny! I think I need to work you into my saloon act."

"You didn't run over here to tell me that Tommy, what's wrong?"

"Captain wants ta see ya both. Soon as I took a telegram up to him, he told me ta come get ya."

A few minutes later they stood outside the captain's cabin. Will knocked.

"Captain, it's Will and Sunny. Tommy said you wanted to see us."

"Come in, come in. Have a seat." He pulled up two chairs, and then took a closer look at Sunny. "My goodness, you look very pretty. Bessie did a fine job."

"You think Bessie could help me, Captain?"

Strickland shook his head and deadpanned, "No, Will, I'm sorry."

All three shared an unexpected laugh. Then Strickland turned serious again. He reached across his desk for the telegram and held it up.

"Got some news from your contact in St. Paul. Seems somebody in St. Louis tipped off the bounty hunters that you two are on board. We have a change in plans." He pointed to a map of the River on his desk. "A half-mile south of the city, there's a ferry landing. You're going to be dropped off there."

Sunny clutched Will's hand. Strickland saw the fear on her face.

"It'll be okay, Sunny, you'll both be safe. And, the Granemanns are looking forward to meeting you."

Will recognized the name. "Sir, aren't they the family who tried to help Teeny Douglas?"

"They are. They're courageous people, considering what happened to their son."

"Captain, what happened to their son?" Sunny asked.

"He was shot trying to prevent that St. Louis detective from taking Miss Douglas' baby. He died a short time later. I thought Captain McGee told you."

Sunny was startled. "He told us someone was killed, I didn't know it was their son."

"Yeah, he fell head over heels in love with that girl and wanted to marry her. Got shot by that detective and died a few hours later."

Sunny regarded Will and the captain with disbelief.

"Where is Miss Douglas now?"

"Don't really know. Some say she went to Canada, some say Chicago, but I haven't heard anything recently."

Will looked down, lost in thought.

When they got up to leave, Sunny said, "Thank you for all you've done for us, Captain. We're most grateful."

Will snapped back to the present. "Most grateful, Captain. I don't know what we can do to ever repay you."

Strickland escorted them to the door and replied, "Have a long and wonderful life together. That would be a fine payback."

"We're going to make that happen," Will assured him. "One last thing, Captain, how are we gonna get to that Ferry landing?"

"I'll hold the boat steady, and you'll row a skiff to shore. Once you're ashore we'll pull the boat back. No one will know you were ever aboard the Adele."

Will and Sunny walked back to their cabin. Strains of Tommy belting out 'Oh! Susanna' floated up from below. They couldn't help smiling.

In the tiny cabin, Sunny grew somber again. She sat motionless on their berth, gazing at the flickering lantern. Will knew something was troubling her. He sidled up next to her and took her hand.

"You're so beautiful. I love you so much."

"As beautiful as Teeny?"

Will now understood. "Yes, yes you are. And to me you're more beautiful."

"Did you love her, Will?"

"We grew up together. We were friends."

Sunny persisted. "Will, answer me. Did you love her?"

"No, it wasn't like that."

Sunny remained unconvinced.

"Please, Sunny, you know how much you mean to me and how much I love you."

"I know, but you also loved Teeny. And I'm pretty sure she loved you. And now you're stuck here with a one-eyed half breed who has no hair."

Will rolled on the bed and laughed. Sunny couldn't stay upset and punched him playfully. Will took her in his arms and kissed her, very gently.

"Is a good time comin, Mrs. Douglas?"

"Yes, boy, a good time's comin."

In the pitch black of three in the morning, the Adele's paddlewheel slowed, and the big boat stopped moving up river. Two deck hands carried the yawl to the stern and lowered it. Sunny and Will waited to get in. Sunny had two small bags. Will had his belt and the old satchel tied to his waist.

Lanterns illuminated black water swirling around the ship, but nothing was visible on shore. Sunny felt scared. Will waited for Strickland's final instructions.

"Just a bit longer; he'll give a signal when he's ready."

Finally, a dim light appeared. "Head toward that light. Once you're on shore, he's going to extinguish it, and we'll haul the boat back."

Will held out his hand. The Captain grasped and shook it. Strickland turned to Sunny, who was shivering and clutching her bag. Uncharacteristically, Strickland pulled Sunny gently toward him. He held her a moment.

"I'm so sorry about what happened to you on my boat. Please try not to let it hurt you any longer." He backed away and gave a final farewell, "Good luck. Have that fine life together."

Once in the yawl, Will locked the oars in place and helped Sunny into the boat. The dark swirls in the water frightened her.

"Will, if something happens, I want you to know how much I love you," she murmured tenderly.

"Sunny, nothing's going to happen. I need you to watch the light on shore and tell me if I veer off course. We'll be there in no time."

Crewmen untied the ropes, and the small boat moved toward the light. Two hundred feet from shore Will continued rowing hard, but the boat slowed. He pulled with greater determination; they heard a scraping sound. The boat stopped. Sunny saw fear in Will's face. "What is it? What's wrong?"

"Ice! We've hit ice."

Lanterns on board the Adele gave Robert an occasional glimpse of the yawl making its way toward him. When it stopped short, he walked to the water's edge and discovered the large patches of ice that had formed along the shore. He ran back to his carriage and grabbed a rope.

Will waved and yelled, "Over here! Over here!"

Granemann held up his lantern and could see the bow of the yawl stuck on a sheet of ice. He threw the rope. As the line unwound, it spun into the lantern, knocking it over. The flame went out.

Will was about to tie the loose end of the rope around Sunny's waist when the small boat jerked to the right. Both tumbled to the icy surface and watched the yawl being hauled back to the big riverboat. Will ran his hand across the hard surface and grasped the rope. They crawled toward the spot where they had last seen the lantern.

Suddenly there was a sickening cracking noise. River water slowly bubbled through a V-shaped opening. Within seconds the bitterly cold water soaked their clothes. Sunny screamed, her skirt weighing her down and her shawl tangled around her arms. The ice gave way, and Sunny slipped below the surface. She struggled, gasped for a breath of air, and disappeared again.

Will grabbed her arm and pulled her toward him. One hand held her and the other clung to the rope. Sunny's head slipped below the water surface again. Will shouted as loud as he could, "Pull us in! Please, pull us in!"

Robert heard the shouts and pulled the rope as hard as he could. The river current tugged firmly on Sunny's water-logged clothes. The rope tore the skin on Will's hand. Using all of his strength, Robert managed to drag the pair to thicker ice. They crawled toward him. He offered his hand and helped them up the slippery riverbank.

Will's teeth were chattering and Sunny was trembling violently. He held her close.

"We made it, Sunny! We made it!"

His wife could not respond. In her state of shock, images of ice and black water began swirling around her. . . her world turned surreal. She thought she heard Will's voice reading a passage from *Uncle Tom's Cabin*…

> "But she saw nothing, felt nothing till dimly, as in
> a dream, she saw the Ohio side, and a man helping
> her up the bank."

82

TWO MEN IN DARK BLUE suits stood on the St. Louis levee and waited in the drizzling rain. One held an umbrella and cloak. The other held the reigns of two horses harnessed to an enclosed carriage. The captain of the Governor Briggs escorted Lady Pelagie down the landing stage. One attendant enfolded a cloak around her while the other opened the carriage door.

"Please assist my friend, Miss Elizabeth Douglas. She is my new personal aide."

The man doffed his stovepipe hat, took Teeny's valise, and offered his hand to help her board. Before closing the door he looked inside. "Mrs. Lyons, shall we proceed home?"

"No, please take us to Madam Beauvais."

Teeny listened to the dull drumming sounds of rain on the carriage, looked out at the city, and wondered how long it would be before she saw her daughter. They rounded a corner and braked in front of a modest town home. A small sign next to the front door read "Madam Beauvais – Beautician and Hairdresser."

Pelagie opened a small window above her and said to the driver, "Please see whether Madam Beauvais is available for a consultation."

The driver spoke briefly to a slender black woman who opened the door. He signaled to the women in the carriage that they were welcome. The attendant on the back platform rushed to the side and provided umbrellas. Before they reached the entryway, Pelagie said, "How many people would recognize you in this city?"

"A few. I met several prominent men at the Silk Ribbon."

"Then we must take precautions to make sure they don't find out you have returned."

They entered the narrow two-story building, where the slim willowy woman who answered the door greeted them. Marie Beauvais introduced herself to Teeny, then turned to Lady Pelagie.

"Mrs. Lyons, how can I be of assistance?"

Pelagie looked mischievous. "Marie, I would like my assistant to have a new look. We want to be sure her old employer doesn't recognize her and want her back."

Marie gave a knowing nod. She directed Teeny to a seat in front of a dressing table with large mirrors on all three sides. Marie buzzed around the station, then delved into an armoire, bringing out a variety of hairpieces and wigs.

"Need a lighter color for the hair," she said to no one in particular. She placed an ashen blond wig on Teeny, then combed and adjusted it. Satisfied she had made the right selection, she proceeded to thin Teeny's eyebrows. She brushed on a bit of white powder, applied a small amount of rouge, and finally added a beauty mark.

"What do you think, Mrs. Lyons?" she said, triumphantly.

"Excellent, excellent! I think you have created a lovely new look for my friend."

Teeny glowed, pleasantly surprised, when she consulted the mirror. She picked up the bronze hand-mirror and viewed her new look from several angles. She turned to Lady Pelagie, "Do you think someone who met me a year ago would recognize me?"

"Always error on the side of caution. Now, we must go. Marie, you are truly an artist. Please bill me for your services."

Marie gave Teeny a small cloth bag containing tins of makeup. She escorted her to the door and whispered, "Be very careful my dear. Lovely as you are, you will not be spared if caught."

Teeny felt unsettled by the remark and wondered how Beauvais knew she was a fugitive.

The carriage came to a halt in front of an imposing three-story town home in the northwest part of the city. Pelagie handed each servant a package wrapped in decorative paper. They thanked her profusely, fawned over her new dress, and toted her bags away. Pelagie signaled for her personal servant, Letty, and told her to escort Teeny to the guest room.

"We'll have lunch in thirty minutes, Miss Douglas. We'll talk more then."

Pelagie disappeared into the library and began shuffling through correspondence. In the guestroom Letty opened curtains to a window that overlooked the city. Teeny surveyed the scene and said, "Letty, what is that steeple in the distance?"

"Catholic Church ma'am. Be where the money folks an' im'grants goes ta pray. One group be prayin ta get rich, da others prayin ta get even richer."

Teeny smiled. "Does Mrs. Lyons attend that church?"

"No, ma'am, no need. She got lotsa money."

Teeny found a mirror on the dresser and examined her wig and make-up. She took the powder and paint Marie had given her and arranged them in a neat row. After one last look in the mirror, she sighed and thought about how much time she spent looking like someone other than herself.

Pelagie had already taken her seat at the dining table when Teeny came down the stairs. She moved her chair closer to Teeny, leaned over, and spoke in low, hushed tones.

"It's best our conversation not be heard, not even by my servants."

Once she was sure everyone was busy, Pelagie said, "Do you have a plan my dear?"

Teeny hesitated. "No not yet. I have a little money and thought I could rent a room at a women's boardinghouse, then I want to see my daughter."

"Nonsense," said Pelagie vigorously, "You will reside here."

Then she sat with her elbows on the table, hands folded, and two fingers pointing toward the ceiling. After organizing her thoughts, she talked in a low, precise manner.

"Richard Walther, the father of your child, is the famous Cholera doctor, is that correct?"

Teeny nodded in the affirmative.

"Since the two of you were intimate, he knows your shape, your walk, your hands, and your facial gestures. I am telling you this because his office is only a few blocks from here, and you could accidentally meet." Teeny's heart was beating faster.

Pelagie scanned the dining area to see whether any servants had entered. Then in a barely audible whisper she said, "You must be very careful when you attempt to see your daughter. If you are recognized and caught, there is very little I could do to help."

Pelagie scooted her chair back to its original location, then rang a small bell. Within seconds a servant appeared with a tray of small sandwiches, fruit, and a pitcher of sweet tea. Teeny smiled at Pelagie through teary eyes. "Thank you for taking me in, thank you for…"

"That's enough, dear," Pelagie interjected kindly, "One thank you is sufficient."

In mid-December Pelagie asked Teeny to accompany her to the annual Christmas Charity Ball. Teeny was struck by how easily the well-groomed men and women moved about the large red and alabaster ballroom, making introductions and striking up conversation. Refined women strolled around bedecked in expensive jewelry and elegant gowns, their hair perfectly coiffed. She felt out of place.

Lady Pelagie sensed her protégé's anxiety. "Do not be intimidated by these people, my dear, most are mere hopefuls. They are here to meet the paragons of privilege and imitate their behavior. Their fondest hope is that someday they will be deemed worthy of being part of the ruling elite."

A tall handsome gentleman carrying a gold walking cane approached. His blonde hair showed light streaks of gray and he spoke in a confident, aristocratic manner. "Lady Pelagie, how lovely to see you again."

"Mr. LaSalle, it's been far too long."

He gazed at Teeny admiringly. "And who is your charming friend Mrs. Lyons?"

"Vincent, this is Miss Douglas."

Teeny immediately recognized him from the Silk Ribbon, where he and his son were regulars. Vincent studied Teeny, but seemed to make no connection to the past. He suggested to Lady Pelagie they arrange a meeting to discuss the purchase of a fur trading company that was turning a fine profit. They chatted a few more minutes. He flashed a wide smile and said, "I hope to see you both again, very soon."

As LaSalle walked away, Teeny said to Pelagie, "Well, Madam Beauvais' work has stood up to the first challenge."

Pelagie arched an eyebrow. "Vincent has seen you before?"

"Yes, at the Silk Ribbon."

"Very good. But don't become too confident, my dear."

The number of young men and women who came to seek counsel with Pelagie surprised Teeny. All seemed to ask a variation of the same question: Was the person they were with a suitable partner? After the last couple departed Teeny said, "Are you some type of matchmaker?"

Pelagie's face showed her amusement. "Some would say I am, but my advice has nothing to do with romance. These people are marrying for material wants and desires and to secure a position in society. I know the personal and financial histories of their families. I can predict, rather accurately, whether their expectations will be fulfilled."

"It all sounds…very unromantic."

Lady Pelagie gave her a benevolent smile and left for the powder room. Teeny surveyed the room and recognized a nattily attired figure standing by the staircase. She approached and stood before him.

"Mr. Bireman, do you remember me?"

Without hesitating he replied, "Miss Douglas, you look lovely."

Teeny smiled. "If I hadn't sent you a letter informing you I was coming, would you have known it was me?"

"No, I don't think so. I am surprised by your new appearance and that you are attending this event. How did you wangle an invitation?"

Teeny hastily explained. "It's all very complex, but Pelagie Lyons has taken me in and been very kind. I would never bring trouble to her door. But I would like to see my daughter. She is afraid someone will identify me if I try."

"I suggest you heed her advice."

Teeny saw Pelagie leave the powder room. "I must go, I hope to see you again, soon, Mr. Bireman."

"I look forward to it. Good night, Miss Douglas."

Teeny and Pelagie reunited and headed to the cloakroom.

"I saw you talking with Mr. Bireman. His legal assistance has been invaluable to me."

The two women assisted each other with coats. Pelagie looked inquisitively at Teeny once they were inside her carriage.

"Is Mr. Bireman going to assist you while you are in St. Louis?"

"I don't know. He did before, and I hope he will again."

Pelagie glanced out the carriage window and then gave a stern warning: "This city is divided on the issue of slavery, and the abolitionists have very little clout. As talented as Mr Bireman is, he could not save you if you are captured."

Teeny knew she was right, but she had to see her daughter, and Bireman was the only one she knew who might be able to help. As the carriage pulled to the front of Pelagie's townhome, she remembered the law office where Andrew took her a year ago.

When Social events of the holiday season began to wind down, Teeny ventured into the city alone. During the first week of the New Year, she took a carriage to 108 Washington Street. Abe looked pleasantly surprised to see her.

"Good morning, Miss Douglas. I hope you are well. From what I hear, you and Mrs. Lyons have been so busy, I'm surprised you're not exhausted."

Teeny laughed and took a seat next to Abe's desk. He retrieved an envelope, gently removed a letter, and placed it before her.

"You will never believe what this is."

Teeny glanced at it. "It looks like a child's letter," she observed.

"It's from Tom. He and his wife are living in Council Bluffs, Iowa. He asked whether I knew how to get in touch with Will and Sunny."

Teeny was shocked. "Tom can write? And read? I'm so proud of him and of Will for teaching him." Then she paused and asked, "Who is Sunny?"

"Will's wife. He and Sunny married while he was living in Council Bluffs."

Visibly she showed little emotion but internally she felt stunned. She had shown no loyalties to Will or tried to contact him, but she believed they still shared an emotional tie that seemed to bind.

"Where are they now?"

"They are in St. Paul. With the same family that helped you."

"Do they know I stayed there? And everything that happened?"

Abe nodded, "Yes, I'm sure by now they know." He removed his glasses and pointed them in her direction. "Right now though, you are faced with a more vexing question: how long do you plan to stay in St. Louis?"

"I would like to rescue my daughter, and then get away to a safe place." The words came out with such certainty that Teeny surprised herself.

Abe looked at her incredulously. "Trying to do that would be very dangerous." He stood up and clasped his hands behind his back. He looked as though he was going to scold as he approached her. Teeny could not have anticipated his response.

"If you are determined to take such a risk, you will need help. And you must never be seen by the Walthers."

Teeny heard the words and nodded. She was pleased the lawyer seemed willing to help, but worried her desire to see Mary would override his stern warning.

When she returned to Pelagie's residence, she came across Letty tidying up the drawing room.

"Letty, does Lady Pelagie own a spyglass?"

"Sure, she own jus' 'bout everything. It be on da man'tle in da library."

She pulled back the curtain in her room, focused the spyglass, and observed the street where Richard Walther had his medical office. Taller buildings in the foreground obscured the view. She was in the process of placing the long tube back on the mantle when Pelagie entered. Teeny looked embarrassed. "I'm sorry, I took this without asking. Letty didn't think you would mind."

"I don't mind. But if you insist on seeing your daughter, you will have to observe from a more advantageous location."

Teeny nodded. "Thank you for understanding. I feel I have to see her and know that she's all right. It's been almost a year." Teeny tried to remain in control, but tears sprang to her eyes. Lady Pelagie gave her a gentle hug.

"I know this is very difficult, my dear, but you must not weaken. I have an idea. Tomorrow we shall go shopping and afterward visit a small park not far from here." She gave Teeny a wink and added, "It's quite nice, and with that spyglass, you will get a much better view."

Across town Abe Bireman entered the police station where he filed charges against Sunny's assailants. He approached the front desk. Officer Ron Steiner was on duty. The man looked up and grinned. "Whadaya up to now you abolitionist weasel."

"Good day, Officer Steiner. I see the precinct captain allowed you to return to your old job. I am pleased, and I need a favor."

"Every time I see you, you want a favor, and then I get demoted."

"Nonsense, helping me has nothing to do with you getting demoted. The way you perform your duties is justification enough."

Steiner guffawed. "What do you want this time?"

"I would like to see the report on the two thugs arrested aboard the Adele last November. I signed off on it on the twenty-seventh."

Steiner gave him a skeptical look. "Why are you interested in scum like that?"

"I have been hired by the captain of the boat to prosecute the two and make them pay for damages."

Steiner chortled, "Bullshit, what's the real reason?"

"Really, Steiner, I need to earn a few dollars. Being an abolitionist weasel doesn't pay much."

Steiner laughed and shook his head. He went to a wood cabinet and thumbed through a stack of papers. He looked at the report before handing it over. "Says here they were jailed and then released the following morning."

"Hmmm," muttered Abe. He took the report from Steiner and began writing down the name, address, and occupation of the men who attacked Sunny. "They both work at Shaw's Emporium?"

"If that's what it says, it must be true. Two fine gentlemen like them would never lie."

Abe grinned and handed the report back. "Thanks, Steiner, I owe you."

83

SUNNY AND WILL MOVED INTO Granemanns' cottage with only a few belongings. The old satchel, the money belt, and a few other items were all they had. Clothes, Sunny's necklace, and books were lost when their bags disappeared into the icy water. Helen gave Will some of Charles' old clothes and let Sunny take what remained of Teeny's wardrobe. Will stood gazing out the cottage window watching the snow come down. He was wearing one of Charles's winter coats to ward off the frosty air. "Do you suppose it's always this cold here?" he groused.

"Will, we're lucky to be alive and to have this nice place to live."

"I didn't mean for it to sound like I was complaining. It just seems colder and snowier here than in Iowa."

"Tomorrow you should talk to Robert about finding a place to live. We can't stay in his cottage forever."

Will thought for a moment. "Helen seems to enjoy having you around to help with chores, and maybe I could farm some of Robert's land."

"Is farming what you want?"

"I'm not sure. I don't know how to do much except farm and wait on people."

Sunny frowned. "You are also a teacher."

Will nodded, but didn't respond. He had tried, but he didn't believe he ever had a chance to prove himself as a good teacher. Will walked to the stack of wood, placed a few more logs on the fire, and looked at Sunny curled up on the sofa. With a playful grin he said, "I must say, Mrs. Douglas, y'all look especially fetching in that dress. I think y'all should come sit by the Colonel on the veranda. I'll have the servants fetch us a couple'a mint juleps, and we can continue to discuss our future."

"You know very well Colonel Douglas that the dress I am wearing belonged to your old girlfriend, and no doubt it reminds you of her. At the moment, I am not interested in joining you on the veranda."

"The Colonel meant no disrespect ma'am. He meant the compliment for y'all, not the dress."

Sunny smiled, but felt curious. "Will," she said haltingly, "how pretty is she? As pretty as everyone says?"

"Yes, she is pretty."

Sunny stared at the fire for a few moments. "She had her baby here, and this is where the Granemanns' son fell in love with her. Does any of that bother you?"

Will sat down next to Sunny as they watched the flames dance around. The fresh logs made a popping sound, and shot a few embers to the floor. Will ground them out with his shoe.

"It was a long time ago, and it just isn't important anymore. I don't want things from the past to interfere with our life."

Sunny poked the fire and replied, "You're right, but it's not that easy. Seems I remember things that upset me and forget about the good times. I wish I didn't think that way."

"I'll bet most people are like that. We have to try harder to remember the good times. It keeps us going, gives us hope."

Sunny glanced lovingly at Will. "You mean like good times are a comin', just you wait?"

Will chuckled. "Yeah, I guess so. Tommy said it better in his song."

Sunny snuggled next to Will on the old sofa and gave his arm a gentle squeeze. She spent several minutes gazing pensively at the fire. She leaned over and kissed Will, first on the cheek, and then fully on the lips. She turned the wick of the lantern low, and stood in front of the fire. She slowly unbuttoned her dress.

Will watched the dress and other garments fall slowly to the floor. Sunny had her back to Will. The fire's glow accentuated the curves of her lithe figure. She turned, her arms crossed, hands covering her breasts. She dropped them and moved her hands slowly down her waist. She moaned, touched herself, and then touched Will's cheek and lips with moist fingers. Will reached up and pulled her toward him.

Their passion blazed so intensely that evening they never made it to the bedroom. They finished, exhausted. Will rose on his elbows and regarded Sunny, who lay sprawled out next to him. Both began to laugh. Will carried her in his arms, placed her on the bed, and hunted down as many blankets as he could find to cover them.

They slept soundly for several hours, until frigid air enveloped the room. Will opened one eye; moonlight illuminated his breath. He felt reluctant to face the cold, but knew it was necessary. He wrapped himself in a blanket and shuffled toward the fireplace. He lit small kindling and waited for flames to start burning the larger logs.

He stood shivering, glancing around the room. Questions about everything that happened in the cottage began to fill his head. When did Charles visit Teeny? How did they make love? What was the birth of the baby like? Did she ever think of him when she lived here?

The larger logs caught fire, and Will returned to bed. He snuggled beside Sunny, kissed her cheek, and felt so grateful she had come into his life. He supposed he would always have a place in his heart for Teeny; childhood memories seemed to keep them tethered to one another. He stroked Sunny's hair very gently so as not to wake her. She was his future.

The following evening Sunny and Will again relaxed in front of the fire. Will wore a silly grin. "Colonel Douglas can't wait for the lovely Lady Douglas to try on another fashionable garment. Y'all are gonna be the belle of all tha plantation balls."

"Now don't start up again, Colonel. I haven't recovered from last night." She eyed the dresses, ran her fingers across the scar on Will's cheek, and gave him a tender kiss. "Time for bed, Colonel, to sleep."

Will smiled. "Y'all know the Colonel is always respectful of the Lady Douglas' wishes."

Once in bed he pulled her closer. The two lay entwined in a familiar manner. Both felt happy and hopeful, and on this night, thought only about the good times.

84

ABE SAT ALONE IN THE small dimly lit room at the back of Rusty's tavern. A year ago he had sat in the same spot, arranging a meeting between a vengeful Robert Granemann and Gar. Rusty stuck his head through the curtain, "Abe, he's here."

Gar lumbered into the small room and sat across from Bireman. Abe moved the whiskey bottle across the table. Gar picked it up, pulled the cork, and began to drink.

Bireman watched, astounded by the amount the man consumed so quickly. "Would you like a glass?"

"Naw, I'm fine. Whadaya want this time, Mr. B?"

Abe handed Gar a slip of paper. "Here are the names of two men and an address. I need to know whether they're still living at this location and whether they are employed. There will be more later. That's all I need right now."

"Twenty dollars."

"Twenty dollars just to find out whether these two are living at the address I gave you?"

"Twenty-five dollars."

Abe looked annoyed, but reached into his pocket. "Fine, fine, twenty it is."

Gar finished the bourbon and let out a low rumbling belch. "I'll meet you here next week at tha same time. Gu'night Beermun." Gar plucked Abe's twenty dollar gold piece from the table and ambled away.

Abe thought about where he found himself and the conversation he just had. He looked at the empty bottle and shook his head. His life vacillated between societal events with the wealthy, literate, and respectable, and backroom meetings with a huge brute who would frighten the most hardened criminal.

The next day Abe boarded the Polar Star looking for McGee. The captain was in his quarters, sitting next to a small pot bellied stove, examining a list

323

of supplies being hauled aboard. He set his paperwork aside when he heard a knock and gave out a loud yell, "Enter!"

Abe opened the cabin door. "Nice greeting, Allen. Did you think I was losing my hearing?"

"Abe, good to see you. I thought it might be Seth here to fix the flue on this damn stove. He's getting up in years and doesn't hear very well."

"Losing one's hearing is an unfortunate part of getting older. Speaking of getting older, Allen, how are you holding up?"

McGee wondered why Abe was asking. "I'm good, Abe, but time seems to fly by. I'm gonna be fifty-eight next month. I think it's time to retire and pursue my true passion."

"Transporting slaves on the river?" quipped Abe.

McGee chuckled, "That's number two. Number one is gambling."

Abe looked at his friend and smiled. "Allen, have you ever thought about taking a brief vacation, say to New Orleans, aboard one of the fine new Mississippi riverboats? A fellow captain would give you first class treatment, and poker games go on all hours of the day and night."

"What are you fishing for, Abe?"

Bireman pulled up a chair next to McGee and eyed the bottle of bourbon sitting on the desk. "You going to drink that whiskey alone?"

McGee pulled out two tumblers, handed one to Bireman, and filled the glasses. Bireman ignored McGee's earlier query and said, "When's the last time you shaved that beard Allen? I'll bet if you did, you'd look ten years younger and feel even younger than that."

McGee shot Bireman a devilish grin. "Are you going to make me look younger so I can court your sister? I thought she was dead."

"That's my brother. My sister lives in Boston, and she's happily married. No, Allen, I have devised a plan that only a man wishing to add excitement to his life would be interested in. Since you are content sitting here watching the fire go out in your stove, that eliminates you."

McGee shook his head and laughed. "I'll bite. What kind of scheme have you devised that will brighten my dull life?"

Abe explained his plan. McGee shook his head in disbelief. When he finished, McGee poured another drink. "You can't be serious. We'll be hung, or put in jail for the rest of our lives."

"You just said you didn't have much time left, why not go out in a blaze of glory?"

They heard a loud rap on the door.

"Captain, it's Seth."

Bireman opened the door. "Thank goodness you're here, Seth. The stove isn't working properly, and the captain is getting cold feet."

McGee set his tumbler of bourbon down. "All right, Abe, set up the meeting and I'll start writing my epitaph."

Abe shook his friend's hand. "See you in my office next Friday, ten o'clock."

Abe returned to Rusty's the following week. When the curtain parted Gar said, "Hello, Beermun. How come there's no whiskey?"

Rusty walked up right behind Gar and set a bottle and two glasses on the table. Gar unceremoniously pushed the glasses aside and twisted off the cork. After several swigs he wiped his chin. "Well, Beermun, those two men you asked about are small-time crooks, stealin' or pullin' cons on immi'grunts. They don't stay anywhere long, but right now they spend most nights inna back room of a warehouse onna south side."

"Do you have an address?"

"Yeah, St. Louis Cotton Mill on Menard. Warehouse is in back. They give the night watchman a cup'la bucks to let 'em sleep there."

"Do they keep any of their personal items there? Clothes, shoes, anything like that?"

Gar took another long swig until only one-quarter of the bottle remained. "Yeah, they gotta big wood box they keep their stuff in. There's sumthin' else. One guy, the tall one, has some kinda wound that bothers him. Walks funny and holds his arm close to his side."

Abe was pleased to hear the man who attacked Sunny was still hurting.

"Nice work Gar. Can you meet me here same time next week?"

Gar drained the bottle and signaled Rusty for another.

"Sure, ten bucks."

Abe reached into his pocket and placed a small coin on the table. Gar's fingers were too big to pick up the tiny coin; he slid it to the edge of the table and into the pouch attached to his belt. "Dainty little thing ain't it? Beermun, are you gonna want these guys worked over?"

"No, that's not why we're meeting. I'll see you next week."

"See ya, Beermun." Gar grabbed the fresh bottle and shuffled into the night.

Lady Pelagie sat in her parlor reviewing a schedule of social events taking place in the coming months. She checked off the ones she planned to attend.

Teeny sat across from her reading *Pilgrim's Progress*. She sighed loudly. "Does Christian ever make it to the Celestial City? I hope he does, because I don't think I can make it to the end of this book."

"Give it time, dear, it's a difficult book. Why not put it aside and come back to it when you're refreshed?"

After a brief silence Pelagie said, "Vincent asked whether you might accompany him to the dance at the Missouri Hotel next month. I told him you were quite busy, but that I would deliver the invitation."

"I think it would be dangerous for me to attend, don't you?"

"Yes, but we must handle these invitations in a kind and discreet manner. There will be more invitations the longer you are here. You are a very attractive woman."

"I appreciate your guidance on these matters."

The conversation lagged and Teeny fidgeted in her chair. Finally, she spoke. "I saw him this afternoon, with the spyglass. Mary wasn't with him but Louise was. Who takes care of my baby while they're away?"

"Like many wealthy couples, they probably have a nanny who lives in their home." Pelagie looked at Teeny and smiled. "When you decide to leave, I want you to know you will be missed. I'm sorry I can't be of more assistance with your daughter."

"You have done so much already. I am so fortunate to have met you."

Pelagie raised her hand and pointed at her in a kind way. "Don't get carried away with compliments again my dear. You and I are not that different."

Teeny set the book aside and said, "Pelagie, I could never be the grand lady you are."

Pelagie turned serious. "Teeny, it's a mistake to think you are not worthy because of how you were branded at birth. You have to work harder, be smarter."

"I try to think that way but…"

"Ah, ah, no excuses; just say yes, Pelagie."

Teeny smiled. "Yes, Pelagie."

85

ON A BLUSTERY FEBRUARY DAY, Teeny arrived at 108 Washington Street. Abe welcomed her. "Miss Douglas please come in and let me introduce you to Captain McGee."

Teeny gave him a warm smile. "Captain McGee, I'm pleased to finally meet you. Gordon Strickland spoke highly of you." She took a closer look and said, "I'm a little confused, I thought you were…much older."

McGee chuckled. "Abe convinced me that with a shave and a little boot black in my hair some of those years would disappear. And what about you, Miss Douglas, you look much different than the young lady Abe described."

"This is the result of Madam Beauvais' skill. She did it as a favor for Lady Pelagie."

McGee's face bore a questioning look. "Pelagie Lyons? My, my, Miss Douglas, you travel in some fancy company."

Bireman, anxious to proceed, politely interrupted. "Well, thanks to barbers, hairdressers, and make-up artists, we may be presented with an unusual opportunity. But we must get to the task at hand. The longer Miss Douglas is in the city, the greater the risk." He produced a sheet of paper from his desk. "I have prepared a list of tasks that must be performed in the next few weeks. We should think about an April departure."

A week after meeting in Bireman's office Teeny sat on the edge of a park bench looking through the spyglass. A young lady emerged carrying a child covered with a pink blanket. Without thinking Teeny started to move quickly in the direction of Walther's office. Suddenly, Bireman's warning came back to her. She stopped, adjusted the spyglass, and saw Louise and Richard join the nanny. Louise took the child and Mary's face was visible. Tears caused the image to blur. She stood, holding the spyglass by her side, and watched the carriage pull away.

When she arrived home a brief note for her lay waiting in the entryway.

> *Our meeting will be Wednesday at*
> *the Cathedral. Ten o'clock.*
> *Abe*

Teeny placed the spyglass back on the mantle and started to climb the stairs to her room. Letty approached from behind and tapped her on the shoulder.

"Pardon, Miss Eliz'beth, but Mrs. Lyons would like to see ya…in her room."

Teeny nodded and made her way to Pelagie's room. She knocked gently on the door.

Pelagie greeted her, "Come in my dear, come in. I have a gift for you."

"A gift? My goodness, what's the occasion?"

"There is something I want to give you before you leave. Please have a seat at my dressing table…and close your eyes."

From her jewelry box Pelagie withdrew a necklace, cradled it on her fingers, and gently lowered it around Teeny's neck. She took a few steps back and said, "Now you may open your eyes."

Teeny gasped when she looked in the mirror. A necklace with gold links encircling red rubies led downward to a large cut diamond. Overwhelmed, she turned to face her patron.

"It's so beautiful! How can you part with it?"

"It's been sitting in that jewelry box for years," Pelagie said with a wave of her arm. "I think it's a fine going away present. Even if you don't have the opportunity to wear it, it will provide you with a measure of financial security."

Teeny stood and hugged her benefactor. "Thank you, thank you. I shall always treasure this." She sighed and said, "This has been a most remarkable day. I saw Mary this afternoon. I saw her face. I almost ran to her."

Pelagie put her arm around the young woman and looked sympathetic. "My, my. You've had quite a few surprises in one day. I suggest we retire to the parlor and we shall have a toddy or two, so that you will be able to sleep."

Bireman, McGee, and Teeny met in the Cathedral; it was empty and smelled of burned incense. Abe looked around and in a hushed tone said to McGee, "Have you made arrangements with Captain Bouchard?"

"Yes, the Julia Dee leaves for New Orleans on April fifth. He provided me with tickets for two staterooms."

Abe pulled a small calendar from his vest pocket. "A Friday. I'm assuming an afternoon departure."

Then Abe turned to Teeny, "And, you have more news about the Walthers?"

"Yes, there's a regular pattern in the family visits to his medical office. Louise, Mary, and the nanny meet there every Thursday afternoon. The nanny walks with Mary for a few minutes, and then Louise and Richard join her. They all leave in a city carriage. I assume they visit friends."

"Most likely they're going to see Walther's mother," said Abe. "She now resides on the western edge of the city." He jotted a few notes in a small book, slid it into his vest pocket, then looked at Teeny. "Now, for the most important part, how do we secure Mary and get you away from the city? The next time we meet I will have devised a plan for executing this delicate task."

McGee had a suggestion. "Let's make it next Sunday aboard the Polar Star. There's less chance anyone will see the three of us together."

Sunday arrived as the type of warm, sunny March day that deceived people into believing spring had arrived. A variety of birds circled and swooped down on fallen bits of straw, grain, and seeds on the levee. Aboard the Polar Star, Teeny, Bireman, and McGee huddled around a desk. They examined a city map that had a circle drawn around Walther's medical office.

"That's the plan, are we comfortable with it?" Bireman asked.

"What do we do if we're caught?" asked Teeny.

"Say nothing. The best thing to do is say it's all a mistake, and don't answer any questions. You will spend one night at the Planter's Hotel, then take a carriage early the next morning to the riverboat Julia Dee. Board as discreetly as possible."

McGee began to stare out the window at the riverboat Adele; he remained only partially connected to the conversation.

"Allen, do you agree?" asked Abe.

"I'm sorry, Abe, I kind of drifted away. I couldn't help but wonder how Gordon's doing, and whether he's feeling well enough to enjoy this fine day."

The Adele's first officer had informed McGee earlier in the week that Gordon Strickland was extremely ill. He had been diagnosed with a condition known as apoplexy, and the right side of his body was paralyzed. The doctor made regular visits, but he seemed unable to offer any successful remedy. He provided Gordon with laudanum, and offered to do bloodlettings, but Strickland refused both.

"Why don't we visit him when we're finished?" Abe suggested.

"May I go with you?" Teeny asked. "It's been a year since I've seen him. He was very kind to me."

Abe considered this for a moment. "I don't think that's a good idea. Members of his crew have seen you. We can't risk having you recognized."

"I'll let him know you're thinking of him," McGee offered, "and that you are beguiled by riverboat captains. That should perk him up."

Teeny asked McGee if she could send him a note. McGee slid a tray toward her laden with an inkwell, quill, and sheet of parchment. Teeny hastily wrote the message. She looked apprehensive when she handed it to McGee.

"Are you okay?" he asked.

"I'm worried. I feel so sad about Captain Strickland, and I'm scared about what will happen on the fifth."

McGee nodded. "Doubt and fear are the heaviest of all burdens, Miss Douglas. Do your best to ignore them." He tucked Teeny's note in his pocket. The two men escorted her to a cab, then walked solemnly toward the Adele.

At the landing stage McGee surveyed the boat. "I can always tell when something is wrong by the way the crew goes about their work. There is no doubt that this is a troubled boat."

As they boarded, First officer Daniel Curtis gave a polite greeting and escorted the men to the stairwell. Before they began the climb to the Captain's quarters, Curtis said, "Thank you both for coming. Captain Strickland is not doing well. His speech is slurred, he cannot stand, and he hasn't bathed for several days. I just wanted you to be prepared."

McGee walked down the narrow corridor with his hands in his pockets, shaking his head. "A proud man should be allowed to die proudly, not in ignominy."

Abe nodded in agreement.

They observed the first mate leaving Strickland's cabin as they approached. The man looked dejected. "I hope the captain recognizes you," he said sadly.

McGee slowly opened the door and looked across the dimly lit quarters. Gordon was propped up in bed with pillows, and holding an empty glass tumbler in his left hand. "Do you need that glass filled with bourbon?" said McGee.

Strickland's eyes had a dull hue and he struggled to see who had spoken. The white uniform he always wore so proudly was stained and wrinkled, and the uneven stubble on his beard exaggerated the paralyzed portion of his face.

McGee grasped his hand and reached over for Abe's. Strickland's eyes began to water as the three men locked hands. Gordon struggled to speak. "Thand yu for coming." He pointed to the chairs and said, "Sit."

"Aye Captain," said McGee. Strickland tried to smile, but could only move his head to one side and make a gurgling noise. He gathered what little strength he had, shifted his body, and pointed to his desk. "Middle drawer." Abe picked up an envelope with 'Last Will and Testament' written on the front. He held it up for Gordon to see. "Yes. Abe...please do whad it says for me." Bireman nodded. "I'll be glad to do that, Captain."

Strickland slumped to his side. His breathing became labored. McGee rushed to the door and told the first mate, "Go quickly and fetch the doctor." While they waited McGee slipped the note Teeny had written into Gordon's hand. "It's from Elizabeth Douglas." Gordon's eyes shifted to McGee and he seemed to recognize the name. He tried to open his hand and see the note. McGee gently took it. "Here, let me read it."

> Captain Strickland, Thank you for helping me and treating me with such kindness aboard the Adele. You are a good man, and I am fortunate to know you. I hope you recover soon. Please write me when you do.
>
> Your friend,
> Elizabeth Douglas

Abe wasn't positive, but he thought he saw a glimmer of a smile. At least that's what he told Teeny when he delivered the news that Captain Strickland had passed away.

86

WILL CARRIED A LOAD OF wood back to the cottage. Sunny was waiting for him and opened the door. He stacked wood next to the fireplace and glanced over to where she was standing. Her hands were clasped in front of her waist and she had a radiant smile. "Thought I'd better let you put those logs down before I tell you the news. I don't want you to drop one on your foot."

Will looked at her with a puzzled expression. "The Colonel, being the wise man we both know him to be, can tell by the lovely Lady Douglas's smile, that ya'all must have good news ta tell me," he drawled.

"Well, how does the Colonel feel about having a little recruit join his regiment?" He paused for a moment, then grinned. "We're gonna have a baby?" Will grabbed Sunny, hugged her tightly, and lifted her off the ground. "Easy Colonel, easy."

"My oh my, I can't believe it. What are we going to name him?"

"Or her. The Colonel needs to put me down now."

"Let's tell the Granemanns," said Will eagerly.

"We should tell them both at the same time. Mr. Granemann's not going to be home until late."

That evening they hurried down the path from the cottage to the Granemann home. Robert invited them to the parlor, but Will's excitement to share news of the baby quickly faded when he saw the look on Helen's face. Robert sat down next to her, then he asked Will and Sunny to take a seat. "When I was at the post office this afternoon there was a letter waiting for me." Robert paused and looked down at the paper he was holding. "Mr. Bireman sent me word that Gordon Strickland passed away."

"No! How can that be? He was fine just a couple months ago." Will appeared shocked as he spoke.

"I don't know the details Will, but there's something else. He left you and Sunny a portion of his estate." The young couple gawked at one another, surprised and confused.

Robert knew they wanted details and said, "I wish I could tell you more but we'll have to wait. Mr. Bireman is going to write and provide me with the particulars in a day or two."

An odd mix of emotions raced through Will and Sunny. After a long pause, Will decided to speak up. "Mr. and Mrs. Granemann, even though one of our friends passed away, a new one, a new friend is going to be joining us. Sunny and me, we're going to have a baby."

The mood suddenly brightened and within minutes they were discussing names, when the baby was due, and where Will, Sunny, and the baby would live. Robert and Helen insisted they remain in the cottage.

"That's very kind of you," said Will gratefully, "but at some point we're gonna need a place of our own."

Robert shook his head and started to explain how difficult it was for coloreds to lease or buy property. He paused when he saw Earl Duncan riding up to the front of the house. Robert hurried to open the door and asked, "What brings you out here this late Earl?"

"Thought I'd better give ya a heads up Robert." He pointed toward Will and Sunny before continuing. "Your colored guests over there, are gonna have to have them manumission papers with em whenever they step off your property." The couple looked at Earl, distraught and confused.

Robert asked Earl to take a seat. The sheriff nodded, removed his hat, and continued. Ever since that doughface Pierce got elected president, southerners have been riding rough shod over him. Now he says all the new territories ain't gonna be free, they're gonna be governed by popular sovereignty. There are a lot of pro-slavery folks head'in this way to stake a claim on them lands out West. And, they ain't gonna be shy about takin any coloreds they can round up with 'em."

Earl paused and gestured toward Will and Sunny again. "If they got their papers they got a chance of bein left alone, at least in St. Paul."

Robert shook his head in disbelief. "When's all this going to end Earl?"

"Don't look like it is. It's gettin worse. That's why your coloreds got to be careful." He paused for a moment, then appeared sad when he looked up. "By the way, Robert, did you know Captain Strickland passed away?"

Robert nodded. "Yes, we just got the news. He was a good man."

"He was. I feel bad. The last time he docked in St. Paul, bounty hunters roughed him up real good. They were looking for runners on his boat and couldn't find 'em. They said he was hiding 'em and started to whale the tar outta him." Earl held his hat by the brim, rotated it slowly, then continued. "Some of his crew finally showed up and chased the bastards away. He was lucky to be alive…at least for a while longer."

"Can't we get rid of those goddamned ruffians?"

"It's me an' my son and a few volunteers, that's all the law we got. An' I don't see people lining up to help."

"I know…I know," said Robert sadly. "Thanks Earl, for coming out here and bringing us this information. I'll see you in town next week, and we'll have a drink."

Earl gave a tip of his hat, "Good night Robert, Helen." He looked back to where Will and Sunny were standing. "You two keep your papers with you at all times," he said bluntly, then turned and departed.

Will looked troubled as he watched the sheriff ride away. "Did those men punish Captain Strickland because they couldn't find Sunny and me?"

Robert sighed and said, "Most likely they heard stories about Gordon transporting slaves. That's the only excuse they needed to search his boat and harass him." Will was still upset. "Did that cause his illness?"

"Hard to say. I think everybody gets a certain number of ticks on the clock after they're born, and when your times up, it's up."

Will asked politely, "Mr. Granemann, do you believe that's what happened with your son?"

"I don't know; poor Charles didn't get many ticks, that's for sure." He squeezed Helen's hand. "Maybe the clock changes when you put yourself in danger. But don't go blaming yourselves for what happened to Strickland. He died working for what he believed in…as did Charles…as might any of us."

"Thanks for saying that Mr. Granemann, but I can't help thinking that maybe…"

"Will, you and Sunny are going to have a baby. Don't start fretting over maybe. We have to celebrate the good times when they come our way. The older you get the more you realize how important they are." Will put his arm around Sunny and gave her a gentle hug. "Yes Sir, you're right about that, an' right now we've got plenty to celebrate."

After drinks with the sheriff at Harry's bar the following week, Robert went to the post office. He picked up two letters, both sent from Abe Bireman. Before leaving the building, he opened the one addressed to him. He looked surprised, and then smiled. He snapped the whip and urged his horses to pull the carriage home at a rapid clip.

When Will and Sunny finished their chores, Robert asked them to join him and Helen. "Please, have a seat. I've got two letters here. One is from Abe, it's about Gordon Strickland's last request, and the other is for you and Sunny. It's from Tom Douglas in Council Bluffs."

"Tom wrote us a letter?" Robert nodded and smiled. "Yes. After you read it, maybe you would like to share it with us."

Will and Sunny began to read the letter and simultaneously grinned. When they finished reading Will looked up. "I think Tom would be proud if I shared his first letter with you.

> Deer Will an Sunny
>
> Mr. Thomas help me with this letter, but I write most of it my self. Rosie an I has a new baby. He be a boy an We name him Will. Annie be actin' like she a granma. Revern Nate say we gonna Chrissen him on Sunday. I Wish you an Sunny could meet him. He be a hanful. Sherrif tell Mr Thomas and Mr Bowers dat we shood never been allow to put money in dat bank cause it make white peeple angry. Mr Thomas give me an Rosie keys to da secret room if there be more truble. Most folks in Shanty have forgivin us now dat da baby be here. Some are still mad. Rosie send ya both her luv an so do I. You always be my bes frend. Please write me back.
>
> Tom Douglas

Helen smiled. "Tom sounds like a good man. Did you teach him to read and write?"

Will looked proud and nodded. "Yes ma'am. He's only been at it a couple years; he's come a long way."

Robert stood up. "I have more news. This letter's from Mr. Bierman, and I would like to read it." He cleared his throat and began.

> Dear Robert,
>
> I want to inform you that Gordon Strickland left a portion of his estate to Will and Sunny. It is a considerable sum—two thousand dollars to be exact. I will be sending you a federal bank note for that amount. Please keep it safe for them. If it is revealed a white man left them this money, the gift will be rescinded and distributed to his other heirs. My best to all,
>
> Abe

Robert smiled after he finished reading, but Will and Sunny sat motionless on the sofa. They stared at Robert and the letter in his hand.

Will finally spoke up, "I can't believe it, why would Captain Strickland leave us that much money."

"I guess something in you two touched him. You should be pleased, and I think it's time to celebrate."

Robert walked over to the liquor cabinet and pulled out a bottle of Madeira. Helen brought four fluted glasses from the breakfront. Robert poured and asked everyone to raise a glass.

"Here's to a fine new beginning for Will, Sunny, and the baby that's on its way. And to all the good people, some who are no longer with us, who made this day possible."

Will spent a lot of time during the next few weeks thinking about the inheritance: part of it he would keep for Sunny and the baby, but some he wanted to use to help others. He discussed the possibility of donating to an abolitionist newspaper, or the Liberty Party, but Robert convinced him he couldn't do either without raising suspicion.

Robert thought about Will's desire to help others and one day asked him, "Will, how did Berry Meachum run his operation in St. Louis?"

"Mr. Meachum would go to the slave auctions and bid on slaves, just like the whites. If he had the high bid, he owned the slave. That slave would work in his business and pay him back. Meachem would sign some papers and the man was free. Then Meachum would head back to the auction and buy somebody else."

Robert listened and shook his head. "A colored man going to an auction and bidding against whites…I can't imagine. That takes a great deal of courage."

"Yes, Sir. He is courageous, and smart. I am blessed to know him."

"Have you thought about doing something similar? What if you helped slaves find a place to live, and gave them a little money to get started, or helped them buy their freedom. They could pay you back, and you could use that money to help someone else. Maybe someday even start a school."

Will mulled this over and reflected on his experience in Council Bluffs. He didn't want to offend Robert but was wary of his suggestion. "Mr. Granemann, maybe I could share your thoughts with Mr. Taylor and hear what he has to say."

Will and Sunny were lying in bed sharing their day when Will relayed to Sunny his discussion with Robert.

"You be careful Colonel Douglas, Lady Douglas wants to live peacefully. We're having a baby and don't need to stir up any trouble."

Will smiled. "Lady Douglas seems to think the Colonel is quite powerful." He pulled Sunny close and kissed her cheek. "Y'all seem to have forgotten the Colonel's regiment is very small. It would be hard to start a major uprisin' with one tiny recruit."

87

ONCE AGAIN ABE FOUND HIMSELF in the small back room of Rusty's bar. This time he was waiting for Gar and one of his contacts, an unseemly fellow named Scrovis. Scrovis arrived early. He was short and potbellied. His thinning blonde hair was tied in back with a dirty leather strap. His small hands didn't seem to match his muscular tattooed arms, and his partially closed pale blue eyes made him appear half asleep.

"Are you certain you understand what it is you are to do?"

"Yes, I do." Scrovis appeared annoyed to have his ability called into question. Nevertheless, Abe wanted reassurance.

"Let's go over it one more time."

"I go to the Second District Police Station, tell officer Steiner I overheard two low lifes talkin' about stealin' a baby. I tell him they're holed up in the St. Louis Cotton Mill's warehouse. And then I disappear. When do I get my money?"

"When the job is done. And I'll see you get an extra ten dollars if you do it exactly the way you just said."

"Ya got yerself a deal, Mr. Bergerman, ya hired the right man."

The two shook hands and Scrovis departed. Abe sat in the dimly lit room, thought about how his name was just mispronounced, and wondered whether Scrovis could be trusted. Rusty parted the curtain and brought Abe a bottle of whiskey. Just as he consulted his timepiece, Gar entered the room.

"Sorry I'm late, Beermun. Took me a little while to collect some money. I can't move as fast as I used to."

Abe noticed dried blood on the knuckles of Gar's right hand. He cringed at the thought of that giant fist hitting someone. He pushed the whiskey bottle forward and pointed to the blood. "Looks like you collected."

"Yeah, he shouldn't a run. That just makes me mad."

"I'll be sure to pay you on time."

Gar picked up the bottle. "I know ya will, Beermun, yer a stand up guy. Want any of this whiskey?"

"No thanks, maybe later." Gar poured a small amount of bourbon on his right hand to wash the blood away without even a shudder from the sting, then he downed the remainder. He looked at a burlap bag Bireman retrieved from under the table. "

Whatcha got, Beermun, a present?"

"This is what you're going to put in the box where those two men are staying. Make sure no one sees you."

Gar told Rusty to bring another bottle, then he said to Abe, "Nobody's gonna see me cause I know what I'm doin'. Can you say the same?"

"Point well taken. I guess we'll find out soon enough." Abe reached inside his vest pocket and produced two twenty dollar gold pieces. "Here's forty dollars; I'll pay you the other half when we're done."

"Eighty bucks for droppin' off this bag an' makin' sure Scrovis keeps his mouth shut. Wasn't there somethin else?"

"Yes, I will need a city cab for a few hours on the fourth."

Gar smiled. "That's an extra twenty."

Bireman sighed and produced another coin.

"Good doin' business with ya, Beermun. How about a drink for the road?"

Abe remained skeptical about drinking from a bottle with no label, but impulsively, he pulled the cork and took a swig.

Slowly he set the bottle down on the table. Gar watched Bireman turn red and cough. It took another minute before he was able to speak. "I've had many bourbons," he said hoarsely, "but never anything that tasted like this. Don't know why this stuff hasn't killed you."

"Somethin's gonna kill us all. I'm hopin' fer me it's tha whiskey." Gar drained the bottle and started to leave. He hesitated, and looked back. "Ya gonna be alright?"

"Yeah, I'm okay."

Gar chuckled, "Thanks fer tryin' to have a drink with me."

Ↄ Ↄ Ↄ

April third, Teeny and Lady Pelagie sat in Jackson Park watching pigeons chase down scraps of bread Letty tossed on the ground. The companionship the two women enjoyed was coming to an end. Teeny finally broke the silence and in a quiet voice said, "I'll be leaving tomorrow morning, Pelagie."

"I'm sorry to hear that." She looked around to make sure Letty couldn't hear.

"Do you think you have a good chance of rescuing your daughter?"

"I hope so…I'm scared. Acting in such a devious manner frightens me."

Pelagie arched her eyebrows and replied, "Devious practices are a part of our life. It's what we do to survive."

"But this seems much different."

"It is, and it is very risky. When it comes to a child being abducted by a slave, even though you are the mother, the authorities will be merciless."

Teeny watched the birds pecking the ground. She sighed. Letty came up to the women and motioned with her hand that it was time to leave.

"Time we be off. I gots to get supper cookin' or we be eatin' stale bread wif dese pigeons."

The three climbed inside the carriage. Pelagie tapped the front panel with her walking stick. After dinner, Pelagie asked Teeny to follow her to a small room filled with shoes, dresses, coats, and a wide assortment of fashionable attire. Pelagie reached for a small box and withdrew a suede pouch with a thin cloth belt attached.

"This goes around your waist, and the pouch rests in front of your undergarments. Put the necklace and anything of value in there." She handed it to Teeny and added, "Have you finished packing?"

Teeny nodded. "Yes, my bags are at Mr. Bireman's office."

"Very well. I suggest we retire to the parlor now for a farewell sherry, or two."

The next morning Pelagie did not descend the stairs for coffee as she customarily did. Letty relayed a message. "Lady Pelagie say she not feelin' well but maybe she be join'n ya later."

Teeny set an envelope on the parlor mantle. In addition to the farewell letter, she placed the elegant card that Pelagie sent her inviting her to dinner at the Peoria Hotel. On the back Teeny had written,

december 3, 1853, first dinner with my dearest friend

ભ   ભ   ભ

Teeny arrived at Bireman's office early in the afternoon on April fourth. McGee had dressed in black pants, a black vest, a white shirt, a black top hat, and black boots.

Teeny scrutinized him. "You look like a city cabby! And what happened to your hair?"

McGee feigned a look of surprise. "What do you mean?"

"It's yellow."

McGee removed the top hat to expose the entire wig. "Yes, Abe says I look quite handsome," he winked and chuckled.

"I didn't say you looked handsome; I said that wig makes you look like one of the thugs that attacked Will and Sunny."

Teeny forced a smile, but felt troubled inside. "Have either of you heard from Will?"

Abe shook his head. "Not recently, but we should receive a letter soon. Sunny will be having her baby in a few months."

"I always thought he would be a wonderful father," Teeny said wistfully.

Abe excused himself to put on his disguise. He returned wearing brown wool pants, a checkered flannel shirt, suspenders, dark brown boots, and a black wig.

Teeny shook her head. "You both look like you should be running some type of scheme to steal money from immigrants!"

"That's good," Abe chuckled. "Let's hope anyone who sees us thinks the same thing."

While Abe spread out a city map on his desk, McGee looked at Teeny's valise. He noticed a small pewter pot with a tiny heart shaped knob on the end sticking out. McGee picked it up and asked, "What's this little coffee pot for?"

"That's a bubby-pot." She pointed to the spout. "These tiny holes allow Mary to get milk. If she doesn't need it, I can spoon feed her." She was talking about something McGee knew nothing about, or would ever experience… there were times he regretted never marrying and having a family. He looked again at the tiny pot, cradled it gently, and placed it back in the valise.

Teeny took a deep breath. "You both are risking so much, are you sure you want to go through with this?"

McGee gave a somber expression. "Good deeds remain, Miss Douglas, all else will vanish once we are gone."

"Is that from the *Bible*?"

Abe looked at her and smiled, "We're never sure where those sayings come from." Then he motioned for them to come to his desk. "We need to look at this map one last time." Abe traced the route the carriage would take with his finger. "That's the plan, do you have any questions?"

"Yes," said McGee, "What if the nanny refuses to cooperate?"

"Then you have no choice but to pull your gun." McGee reached around and adjusted the pistol tucked inside his belt.

Abe folded the map, looked at his watch, and in a resolute manner said, "It's time for us to go."

McGee inspected the rig Gar left in front of Bireman's office. He climbed to the driver's bench and took the reigns. Abe and Teeny ducked inside. McGee cracked the whip and announced, "First stop is St. Patrick's." They travelled north on Sixth, then turned on Biddle Street. McGee stopped the carriage in front of a massive gothic structure topped with a 200-foot spire.

Teeny stepped down with her bag. "Wait by the church entrance until we return," said Abe. "If we're not back in one hour, take a cab back to Pelagie's."

Then his cab turned and headed back to Seventh Street. A few blocks later McGee pulled the carriage into a side street. Walther's office was now only a half block away. Abe checked his timepiece. "Give me five minutes to get to the front, then pull the rig up."

McGee watched Abe shuffle down the street, doing his best to impersonate a menial worker. When he reached a row of stores and offices, he stood off to the side where he wouldn't be noticed. McGee waited, then guided the carriage slowly forward.

Annie exited Walther's office carrying Mary. She stopped in front of Murdoch's Variety Store and pointed to different objects in the window. McGee eased the carriage to the curb. Abe headed toward the nanny.

"Miss! Miss!" He shuffled up to where she was standing. "Dr. Walther fetched me an' asked me ta give ya this here note."

The nanny looked at the oddly dressed man, switched Mary to her other arm, and opened the folded piece of paper.

Annie,

Louise and I are going to be detained for a short time. Take the cab we reserved, and we will meet you at mother's house.

Richard

Abe signaled for the carriage. McGee tipped his hat, exposing his yellow hair. Annie hesitated, and looked back at Walther's office. Abe gave a kind smile and opened the carriage door. Annie thought the change in plans unusual, but sensed nothing threatening. She accepted Abe's hand as he assisted her into the cab.

Bireman gave a signal and the carriage slowly pulled away. Abe hurried to the servant's platform. He sat on the back facing Walther's office. Richard and Louise could emerge from the front door at any moment. The buggy picked up speed and rounded the corner. Abe breathed a sigh of relief.

Three blocks south McGee pulled the cab into a narrow alley. The carriage slowed and ground to a halt. McGee applied the brake and climbed down. Abe circled from the back and opened the carriage door. Annie was startled to see the man who handed her the note now confronting her.

"Why are you here, why have we stopped?"

"Please step out of the cab," said Abe.

Annie grew frightened. Suddenly she began yelling, "Someone, please help me!"

"We'll have none a that." McGee brandished his pistol. "My partner and I are gonna wait here with the little one, an' your gonna deliver this note to Dr. Walther."

"I'm not going to leave this child with you."

"Ya got no choice, ma'am. Now please give the little girl to my partner and step out of the carriage. The quicker ya deliver this to tha doctor, the quicker this'll all be over."

The nanny clutched Mary tightly. An incredulous look spread across her face when McGee forced her arms apart and Abe took the child. McGee pulled her from the carriage and jammed the note in her hand. "Now get goin. The sooner ya get back to the Walther's, the better it'll be for this sweet little girl."

Instinctively, Annie reached for Mary. McGee grabbed her arms and directed her away from the child.

"There's the street," he barked harshly, "now get movin! An' don't go yellin fer help the minute ya leave, or the Walthers might never see this child again."

Annie began running down the alley and stumbled on to Seventh Street. She looked in all directions for a police officer, but found only strangers. She sobbed and struggled to catch her breath. Not knowing what else to do, she ran as fast as she could toward Walther's office.

Back at the carriage, McGee snapped the whip. "We need to get out of here!" The cab rumbled down the alley to Eighth Street and back to Biddle.

As soon as Teeny spotted the carriage she flew down the steps. She pulled the door open. "Oh Mary!" she cried as she climbed into the carriage. "Here, here, my baby, everything is all right." She cradled the crying child and kissed her cheeks and forehead, while tears of joy rolled slowly down her own face.

McGee tightened his grip on the reigns and headed back to 108 Washington. They arrived moments later. Bireman stepped out, looked around, and signaled for Teeny to bring her daughter.

Inside the law office McGee changed back into his captain's uniform, Abe donned a pinstriped suit, and Teeny held and rocked Mary, she and her baby were oblivious to everything going on around them. Abe walked to the window and watched one of Gar's accomplices guide the city carriage away. McGee peered over Abe's shoulder and said, "Well, so far, so good, although I feel bad about the way we treated that poor nanny."

"I know, but we didn't have much choice. Let's hope the Walthers aren't too hard on her." McGee nodded and took another look outside. "It's almost dark. We need to get to the hotel and away from this part of town. I'm going to hail a cab. As soon as it arrives, bring everyone down."

McGee secured a two-horse enclosed rig. Teeny entered with Mary, and McGee slid in next to her. The carriage driver tied the bags to the rear platform and climbed back to his perch. From the carriage door, Abe said to McGee, "Take care, my friend. If all goes well we will dine once again at the Bonton. I'll send correspondence to the St. Charles Hotel until you advise me differently."

Teeny reached over and grasped Abe's arm, "Thank you, Mr. Bireman, thank you for everything!"

Abe smiled and backed away. "You still have a long way to go, Miss Douglas. Good luck to you and your daughter." The cab pulled away. Abe watched until the lantern hanging on back became a small glowing speck.

"Good evening, Captain," said the front desk clerk. "Good evening. My name is Allen McGee, and I have two reservations: one for myself and the other for my niece and her baby."

The clerk rifled through a stack of small cards and with a flourish pulled one out. "Here we are, Captain McGee and Elizabeth Douglas." He tapped the bell on his desk and a skinny bellhop appeared. "James, please take the Captain to room 42, and his niece and her baby to 44."

Shortly after being shown to their respective rooms, McGee headed back to the lobby to see whether any news had begun to circulate about the kidnapping. He found nothing posted on the resident's information board. He watched the hotel's plainclothes officer meander about in a relaxed manner. For the moment, everything seemed quiet.

McGee entered the bar, ordered bourbon, and watched a well-heeled group of poker players anteing up. McGee recognized one of the men wearing a dark charcoal suit and gold cravat, but couldn't think of his name or remember where he had last seen him. He finished his drink and went back up the stairs. He tapped gently on Teeny's door. She opened it slowly and looked apprehensive. "Is everything okay?"

"So far, so good." He smiled at Mary, "How's our little passenger?"

Teeny looked back at the infant sitting on the bed and playing with a rag doll. "She's a sweet little girl. We're getting reacquainted. She ate a few crackers and drank some milk. I think we're going to be fine. Is anything going on outside?"

"Nothing yet, but word of the kidnapping will be all over the streets by tomorrow. The sooner we get aboard the Julia Dee, the better. Captain Bouchard will make sure no one bothers us once we're on board."

"We'll be ready bright and early." Before closing the door she said, "Good night, Captain, and thank you." Mary's large blue eyes watched her mother's every move, and now she let out a cooing sound. "I believe Mary just thanked you as well."

88

AT THE POLICE STATION ANNIE sat nervously at a small square table. Richard, Louise, and the Chief of Police hovered.

"Tell me again what these two men looked like," the chief insisted.

The nanny described them: "One was fairly tall, with blonde hair, the other was average height, and had black hair. One was dressed like a regular cabby, the other, I don't know, just ordinary work clothes, brown pants and a checkered shirt."

"And they told you the child would be safe?"

"Yes, that's what they said."

Richard and Louise looked grim. The officer continued, "The note they gave you, what did they say about it?"

Annie could scarcely hold back her tears. "Give it to Doctor Walther, and this whole thing will be over quickly."

The Chief of Police took the note from Richard and looked at it one more time. "I never seen anything like this, a bunch of words glued to a sheet of paper." The chief thought for a moment and said to the nanny, "What happened to the other note they gave you, the one that said the doctor would be detained?"

"The shorter man kept it."

The chief shook his head and looked again at the ransom note. He turned to Richard, "Do you have the money they're asking for?"

Richard nodded. "I can get it as soon as the bank opens."

"Get it and come back here first thing. This note says they want it by noon and left in a sack next to the Lyon Park monument. We'll be waiting for 'em."

Louise appeared perturbed. "What are you and your men doing right now to find her?" The chief tried to calm her. "I've spread the word and sent out notices to all the precincts. Every man on the force is looking for those two men. We'll find 'em and your baby."

At nine o'clock in the morning, Richard withdrew five thousand dollars from the First Missouri Bank and took the money to the central precinct. Not far from the police station McGee, Teeny, and the baby boarded an enclosed coach. Eight blocks south Scrovis appeared at the second district's front desk and asked for Steiner.

Steiner emerged from the back and scowled at the scruffy looking man. He felt certain he had arrested the n'er do well before. What could the man be doing back here?

"What the hell are you doing in here?" Steiner called out.

Scrovis spoke haltingly. "I heard two men, at Winstead's Tavern, two nights ago, talkin' about takin' a child—fer money. One of 'em had blonde hair and a bum arm, the other had dark hair and was kinda short."

Steiner knew that a wealthy doctor's baby had been kidnapped, and the description matched those of the two kidnappers. He began treating Scrovis with a little more respect and scribbled a few notes while they talked. Scrovis told Steiner the two men were living in a small room behind the St. Louis Cotton Mill.

Steiner looked sternly at the informant. "Wait here," he ordered, while he hurried down the hallway to get the captain. When Steiner and the captain returned, however, Scrovis was gone. Steiner's eyes darted around the room, and he yelled to the other policemen milling about, "Where'd that ratty lookin' guy go that was just standin' here?" The officers looked around and shrugged. Steiner ran to the entryway and looked in all directions. "Son of a bitch!" he snorted.

The captain glared. "Well, wha'd he tell ya that's so damn important?"

"He said he thinks the two men who stole that doctor's baby are holed up behind the St. Louis Cotton Mill." He showed the captain the notes he had jotted down. "See here, the description he gave me matches the one in the police bulletin."

Within minutes the captain assembled half a dozen men and proceeded with his entourage down Columbus Avenue. When they reached the mill, the police fanned out and located the night watchman. The thin, mustached man pointed toward a small room that jutted out from the back of a warehouse. "That's where they sleep durin' the day, but they ain't back yet. I don't know where they work."

"Do you have a key to that door?"

"Yep," replied the watchman, "I sure do." He stared at the small room. Then he said, "Ya want I should open it fer ya?"

The captain couldn't believe the discussion was dragging on. "Yes, do so quickly." To the others, he barked instructions, "Sergeant, you'll come with me. The rest of you search the area for two men, one tall with blond hair, the other short with black hair."

Inside, the sergeant began a quick search of the room's contents. The captain rifled through a wood trunk containing clothes and shoes. He pulled a burlap bag from the trunk. The contents were astonishing: cut up newspapers, a small pot of glue, and a child's doll. The captain shouted to his sergeant, "Look at this! These bastards took that baby!"

Friday afternoon, April fifth. McGee, Teeny, and Mary were aboard the Julia Dee anxiously waiting to get underway. McGee spotted a young paperboy hawking newspapers and yelling out the latest news. "Kidnappers Captured! Baby still Missing! Read the story!" His stack of papers was just about gone. McGee hurried down the landing stage and handed the young man two pennies and began reading,

> Two men were arrested by St. Louis Police and charged with kidnapping the daughter of Richard and Louise Walther. Randy Haragan and Tony Camarata were captured when they returned to a room in back of the St. Louis Cotton Mill warehouse. A child's toy and materials used to create the ransom note were discovered on the premises, along with a pistol and large carving knife.
>
> The men denied any knowledge of the kidnapping and said they never heard of Richard or Louise Walther. The chief of police said the evidence was clear...

The low thundering sound of the Julia Dee's whistle interrupted McGee's reading. He sprinted to the landing stage. The crew untied the lines, and roustabouts used long poles to maneuver the ship past other vessels. McGee stood in the shadows of the main deck and scanned the levee for police. The large steamboat glided slowly into the main channel. Seconds later a loud rumbling note bellowed forth, and they were underway. The journey down river toward New Orleans had begun.

89

WILL SAT IN TAYLOR'S BARBERSHOP and watched a large, pleasant looking black man, trim the hair of a middle aged white man. "Be with you in a moment son," Taylor said.

The man in the barber chair looked in the mirror and said, "I'm looking forward to hearing you and your boys play in St. Anthony next weekend. It should be quite the party."

"Yas, sah," said Taylor, "We're gonna scrape them fiddles till everybody in that hall is kickin' up their heels."

The man chuckled and handed over a few coins.

Taylor grinned, "Thank ya kindly Sir." He escorted his customer to the door, opened it for him, and then looked over at Will. "Hop in the chair son, an' I'll neaten ya up while we talk."

While Will sat in the chair, Taylor trimming away, he explained to the barber that he had come into a little money and would like to lend a helping hand to others. His plan was fairly simple: give a small sum of money to Negroes arriving in St. Paul and help them find a place to live and work. Maybe someday even start a school.

Taylor's scissors hovered in the air for a moment. "You're thinking of a Freedman's Village, like they have in Canada? Where colored folk could live and work and get a fresh start?" he said politely.

Taylor's phrasing gave Will the answer. Meekly he said, "Yes, sir, that was my plan. I need someone who has more experience to tell me what my chances are."

"Well, son, the problem is we don't get many families comin' here ta get a fresh start. We get some who are desperate, and some who have escaped. Often we hide the runners, or move 'em further north until the slave hunters or their owners give up. If you were to start a Freedman's community, then slave hunters would know exactly where to look."

Will grew quiet. Taylor's busy scissors paused again; the barber circled around to the front and faced the young man. "Son, I don't know how you came into money, but if you wanna help, ya have to do it a little at a time. Ya can't be thinkin' in terms of helping lots of people or setting up a school."

Will felt embarrassed. He got up from the chair and started to leave.

"Just a minute, son. I appreciate what you're tryin to do, and if you want ta help, you can start right now. There's three young women chained together on board the riverboat Ben Campbell. She's docked a few blocks from here. A good bribe will get 'em off that boat."

Before Will could ask how much, Taylor said, "It's gonna take thirty dollars… each.

These last few words led Will to understand Taylor had handled escapes like this before.

"Yes, sir, I'll get the money for you."

"Ya best hurry son. They're gonna be shipped out ta'morrow. We don't have much time." He looked out his shop window as Will started to leave. "Is that Robert Granemann waitin' for you?"

"Yes, sir, he's been kind enough to put me and my wife up at his place until our baby's born."

Taylor walked out of the shop with Will and up to the carriage. "How ya doin' Robert?"

"Pretty good, Bill, and you?" The friendly manner in which the two men greeted each other surprised Will. He remained at a respectful distance and waited for Robert to let him know when he was ready to leave. He noticed an exchange of money between the two men. Later, Robert told Will he had given Taylor the ninety dollars. "I thought we had better speed things up."

In bed that night Will gazed at the ceiling and explained to Sunny what happened in Taylor's shop. "Turns out the things Robert and I dreamed up didn't make much sense, but now I feel I'm using some of our money the right way—at least I hope so."

"Imagine how good you'll feel if those girls get off that boat and get away."

Will rolled on his side toward Sunny and gently placed a hand on Sunny's stomach. "I love you, Mrs. Douglas. How's our little recruit doing?"

She smiled. "I think that tiny kick just now was a signal that he, or she, wants you to know things are just fine, thank you."

Early the next morning a flat bed wagon pulled up to the front of the Granemann home. Two roustabouts from the Ben Campbell gently removed three barrels, placed them upright in the yard, and looked over to the front porch. They gave a wave, pointed to the barrels, and climbed back on the wagon. A few seconds later Robert and Will realized what was happening. They pried the lids off the casks. Three extremely thin disheveled young women, wearing nothing but rags, crawled out. Frightened, they huddled together and stared at the two men.

Helen and Sunny gathered blankets, towels and a pitcher of water. They wrapped the girls, and began wiping mud and blood away from their faces and hands. The oldest girl had several scars on her back. She spoke first and tried to explain how they ended up chained together on the boat.

"We be bought couple a years ago by a widow man in Memphis. I be sixteen, Sissy be fourteen, and Dee Ann be twelve. The ole man beat me cuz I try ta run. He always makin' Dee or Sissy lay wif him so he kin pump away on 'em. After he shrink up an' die of da gypsy sickness, a paddyroller come an' take us ta auction. Da man who buy us say he takin' us to work in his camp."

In the midst of her story Sheriff Duncan arrived. The three girls saw the gun and badge and began quaking. Helen tried to reassure them they were safe. The girls held each other and trembled as the sheriff came closer.

Earl's face registered his shock as he observed the three skinny bedraggled girls who appeared only half alive. "My God, they're a mess!" he commented to Helen.

"The owner of them girls hired a couple bounty hunters to find 'em," he explained to Robert, "they're looking everywhere."

"Couldn't we offer to buy the girls from him?" Robert asked.

"I doubt it. He's a lead miner from Plateville and plans on rentin' 'em out to other miners by the hour. He could make a boatload of money doing that."

Robert looked disgusted. He told Will to hitch up the horses and asked Helen to pack some food. "Sheriff, I'm gonna take them to the Brown Bear outpost. I'll leave them with that French farmer who helped us before. If that miner or the bounty hunters show up, tell them I'm on the other side of the river looking to buy property."

"Ya better hurry, Robert. He's already searched the levee and been to Taylor's. A few dollars of bribe money, and somebody's gonna spill the beans. They could be on their way here right now."

That night Helen and Sunny sat on the front porch, two oil lanterns glowing, and watched for the Granemann carriage. It was almost midnight when they heard the hoof beats and the creaking wheels as the men returned from Brown Bear. Will and Robert climbed down and began brushing mud and dirt from their clothes. Both were exhausted from moving rocks and tree limbs from a narrow back road.

Helen held up a lantern and looked at the scratches on the side of the coach. "Goodness," she said, "Did ya take them all the way to Canada?"

"Slid into a tree," explained Robert. "I didn't want to risk running into bounty hunters on the main road so we took the Old Soldiers Trail. Did that miner come here looking for the girls?"

"No, Earl came back late this afternoon an' told us he's offering a reward for their capture, but decided not to hang around St. Paul. He's going back to buy three or four new girls, then head back to Plateville. Too bad he won't give up that terrible idea."

Will took the horses to the barn, wiped each one down, and gave them water and a bucket of oats. He returned to where Robert was inspecting damage to the carriage door.

"I can't believe we took that damn cow path home when nobody was looking for us," he sighed in frustration.

"We thought we were doing the right thing at the time, Mr. Granemann. And ya know what folks always say, everything happens for a reason."

Robert looked exasperated and responded harshly. "I lost my son for no reason, Will, so I don't believe that nonsense. And these girls, what's the reason for the way they've been treated?"

His harshness came as a surprise to Will. "Sorry Mr. Granemann, I didn't mean to upset you."

"Yeah, I know. I'm tired, and I'm just blowing off steam."

Helen invited Will and Sunny to stay for sandwiches and coffee. The four sat around the kitchen table discussing details of the Brown Bear trip. Sunny asked, "What's going to happen to those girls?"

"They might get someone to help them go further north, possibly to Canada. Or, they might split up an' work for different farm families in St. Cloud. Nobody knows for sure how these things will play out," Robert said, getting up from the table.

"Thank you, Mr. Granemann, for helping those girls." Will tried to determine if Robert was still upset.

Robert looked back at him. "You and Sunny deserve the thanks; it was your money that got them off that boat." He left the kitchen without saying anything more.

While getting ready for bed, Sunny looked out the cottage window toward the big house. "Mr. Granemann didn't seem himself tonight. Is everything okay?"

"I'm not sure. We were talking earlier, and I said something about how lots of people believe everything happens for a reason. He didn't like hearing that. He believes things just happen, like his son being killed."

Sunny thought about that for a moment. "Will, what do you think?"

"I don't know. A lot of bad things seem to happen to good people, and I don't understand why...I wonder whether it really is all part of God's plan. What about you?"

"I was brought up by Indians. They don't see the world the same way you and a lot of other people do."

Will looked at her quizzically. "Don't they believe there's a God that watches over us, controls things, and makes things happen?"

Sunny remained pensive as she tried to explain. "They believe all life comes from the earth and returns to the earth. The Great Spirit is in all things, but I don't ever remember hearing that the Great Spirit had a plan, or made things happen to us for a reason. Indians believe there are things that can never be explained. They accept that."

Sunny grew concerned that she and Will had never discussed this. "Will, what should we teach our children to believe?"

It was late, and Will was tired. He took Sunny's hand and smiled. "Teach them that questions like this should be talked about by people who don't have chores to do the next day."

Sunny grinned, "Doesn't the colonel have something to say that will inspire his tiny recruit."

"I do." He moved close to Sunny's stomach and whispered, "Little recruit, the Colonel would like y'all to know that if you're a slave trying to escape, y'all don't wanna get caught."

Sunny rolled to her side and faced him. Trying not to laugh, she responded, "The Colonel is so wise." Then she turned down the wick on the lantern and snuggled in. She felt grateful for their current situation. She thanked the Great Spirit, then prayed that Will's God didn't have other plans.

90

THE JULIA DEE STEAMED ALONG, two days downriver from St. Louis. McGee volunteered to keep an eye on Mary while Teeny stretched her legs and looked around. She stood in the bright sunshine, took deep breaths, and felt joy that her daughter was with her. It seemed they had escaped the city undetected.

She strolled along the promenade deck and observed the variety of people milling about on the main deck: Indians, immigrants, Quakers, fur traders, farmers, and workers brought from China to lay track for the new railroads. She entered the saloon and noticed a totally different group of passengers. Here, wealthy planters, ladies dressed in finery, high-ranking soldiers, ministers, Northern businessmen, and Southern crop brokers mingled.

Except for the Quakers and ministers, the only thing the passengers had in common—no matter how much money they had—was a preoccupation with gambling. If passengers and crew weren't rolling dice or playing some type of card game, they would bet on arrival times at the next town. Some even wagered on the depth of the water before the leadsman yelled out his measurement.

Teeny wandered to the front of the saloon and saw a group of men playing poker. It reminded her of the evenings spent with Lady Pelagie when the grande dame taught her to spot tells. She was about to return to her room when she recognized one of the players that had been aboard the Governor Briggs months ago—it was Robert Trudeau. Pelagie told her that Trudeau would book passage on one of the large boats headed to New Orleans.

He looked much as she remembered: his mustache was neatly trimmed and waxed to blend in a fashionable manner with his angular sideburns, and he wore a tailored charcoal suit accented by a gold cravat. He retained the same calm and self-assured façade.

She returned and told McGee there was a professional gambler on board who she had watched play cards when she traveled with Lady Pelagie several months ago. She described him, and McGee realized this was the same man he saw in the Planter Hotel bar.

"I knew I had seen him before. I watched him walk off with over two thousand dollars in a poker game at the Missouri Hotel."

"Pelagie says he's one of the best, but she spotted a tell that no one playing against him seems to have noticed."

McGee grew intrigued, "Is that right? Go on..."

"I'm convinced she spotted a very slight movement when he holds a winning hand."

McGee began to pace back and forth. Teeny sat on the bed holding Mary; both watched the captain walk in circles. Then he stopped. "I'm sorry, I was just thinking, is there a way you could demonstrate the tell that Pelagie spotted?"

"I'm sure I can. Do you have a deck of cards?" He pulled a deck from his coat pocket. "Do you need to be sitting at a table?"

"That would help, I also need a glass of water."

McGee removed a washbasin and pitcher from a small table. He set a glass of water on the table and moved a chair next to it. "May I hold Mary while you demonstrate?"

"You can try. She's a little skittish today."

McGee lifted the little girl carefully. He held her, and they both watched. Teeny placed five cards face down in front of her, and then positioned the glass of water to her right.

"Okay, this water is Trudeau's bourbon. He picks up his cards, looks at them, and there's no reaction. He discards three and is dealt three new cards. Now he has a good hand, but still reveals nothing. After everyone places bets he reaches for his drink. But his hand is slowly moving toward the center of the table. His hand then veers to the right, and he picks up his drink."

"Is there anything else?"

"No, that's all. The movement is very slight. Pelagie insists he's not aware of it. I watched him do this even when he lost a few hands. Pelagie says he will often lose intentionally. He wants to keep everyone in the game until the stakes are higher."

Mary had fallen asleep in McGee's arms. He gently handed her back to Teeny and smiled. "I'll bet you didn't know I had that effect on women did you?"

"What effect is that?"

"Putting them to sleep."

Teeny laughed. "That's good to know; the next time she's restless I'll pay you a visit."

He looked back at the table and glass of water. "I'm going to play a few hands of poker and see whether Lady Pelagie is correct."

McGee went back to the saloon and casually approached the main table. He asked the dealer if he might join the game, "Should someone decide to leave or need a break."

"Certainly," he replied. "I'm sure this hospitable group of gentlemen would welcome a riverboat captain to the table."

The men nodded, but no one appeared ready to leave. McGee sat nearby and watched several games play out. By the end of the fifth game he hadn't noticed any unusual movement. During the next game Trudeau made a very slight move toward the money before picking up his bourbon. After the final bets were made Trudeau revealed three aces and feigned surprise that he won.

One of the players decided to retire. McGee was invited to take his place. He concentrated on Trudeau and didn't pay much attention to his own cards. Trudeau assumed that the captain's failure to win a hand made him an easy mark.

By day seven, the Julia Dee was approaching New Orleans. Trudeau asked the first officer to assemble a high stakes poker game for the final evening. Five people received invitations; one of them was McGee.

McGee and Teeny comiserated in her stateroom; they discussed possible strategies and what he should do if the stakes grew exorbitant. Teeny went to the side of the bed, turned her back, and raised the front of her dress. She untied the cloth pouch wrapped around her waist and placed it on the bed. She carefully removed the necklace.

"If Trudeau doesn't have the cards he needs to win, he will force everyone out of the game by raising the stakes. I've seen him do this. This should keep you in the game."

McGee was awed by the quality of jewels and craftsmanship. He let out a low, soft whistle. "This is incredible, it must be worth four or five thousand dollars. May I take a guess as to who gave you this? And, are you sure you want to risk it?"

"Your guess would be correct, and yes, I'm willing to risk it. If you win, we'll share the profits. My daughter and I will have some financial security."

McGee massaged the back of his neck. "You know, Miss Douglas, fortune makes friends, and misfortune ends them. We have to accept the fact that Trudeau, or someone else, may win."

Teeny nodded. "I am willing to take that chance, and after all you have done for me, we will still be friends."

Twelve bells sounded. McGee, Trudeau, Colonel Jordan from Georgia, Andrew Hunter from New York, and Randall Cranston from Virginia, gathered at the center table. The men introduced themselves, placed their drink orders, and purchased poker chips from the banker. A crowd of curious onlookers gathered behind the main table. The audience began making side wagers, betting on who would win, who would lose, and who would be the first to drop out.

Finally, everyone was ready, and the dealer announced, "The game will be five card draw. The initial ante is two hundred dollars."

The colonel mumbled an obscenity, letting everyone know what he thought of such a high stake.

After everyone received five cards, the dealer looked left. "Your bet Mr. Cranston."

"Two hundred dollars." He tossed in two chips.

Hunter was next. "Call and raise that two hundred more."

"Anyone else?" asked the dealer.

McGee had been quiet, then spoke up. "Call and raise two hundred more," he said confidently.

Astonished whispers arose from the spectators. A military officer observing the game exclaimed, "Four thousand dollars on the table, and nobody's drawn a card! That's more money than I make in two years."

McGee watched the colonel massage his forehead. Cranston squinted and leaned forward. Trudeau and Hunter seemed unfazed by the betting and tossed in their chips. McGee slid his chips to the center of the table. He was surprised everyone had remained in the game. The draw proceeded; everyone took three cards except Trudeau. He took one. The dealer looked around the table to make sure everyone was ready. "Betting will again proceed from my left gentlemen."

Cranston suddenly grew timid. "One hundred dollars," he said, tossing in a chip.

"Call and raise that five hundred," said Hunter.

Colonel Jordan mumbled an obscenity and dropped out. Cranston thought about it a minute longer. "Too rich for me," he said, and folded.

"Three still standing," announced the dealer. "Anyone care to wager?"

McGee studied Trudeau, but failed to detect any subtle movements. He looked at his cards and continued the betting. "One thousand."

A loud murmur surfaced from the crowd. Trudeau shoved his chips to the center and calmly said, "Call and raise one thousand more."

The audience watching had doubled in size. A collective gasp emerged. Hunter's discomfort showed. Though he rolled his eyes in disbelief, he believed his hand was good enough to win. He remained in the game, slowly pushing his money forward.

People hooted, hollered, and slapped one another on the back. They were watching a once in a lifetime poker game. McGee asked for a pause, and told Trudeau and Hunter he needed to purchase additional chips. He pulled the necklace from his coat pocket and showed it to Captain Bouchard. "How much will you give for this?"

Bouchard inspected the jewel encrusted gold necklace. "Four thousand."

He relayed his appraisal to the banker. McGee collected forty one-hundred-dollar chips and returned to the table. The dealer looked to see whether everyone was ready. "Let us resume, gentlemen. Do we have additional bets?"

"One thousand," said McGee.

An elderly woman, overcome while watching such large sums being wagered, was helped to a lounge chair in the far corner of the saloon. A heavy silence filled the room. Hunter shifted uncomfortably in his chair and said, "Gentlemen, I am sorry to say I cannot match that last bet, I'm low on funds so I will fold."

Trudeau asked for a pause in the game so he might purchase additional chips. He returned to the table and moved a stack of chips to the center. "Call and raise another thousand." Stunned, the crowd held its collective breath waiting to find out what McGee would do.

The dealer waited. "Has the betting ended gentlemen?"

"No, call and raise another thousand."

Sullen, Trudeau glared at McGee. He rose slowly from his chair and said, "Pause, once again." He walked over and whispered something to the Captain that was inaudible to bystanders. Captain Bouchard looked down and shook his head. "I'm sorry Mr. Trudeau, but I could lose my license for violating the regulations set forth by the owners of this boat. They have a strict rule against making loans without proper collateral. You can see the signs posted in the bar, and elsewhere, stating that."

Trudeau tried to conceal his embarrassment at finding himself in this situation. He returned to the table. The words exploded from him like an angry growl, "I can no longer continue, the game is yours." A raucous cheer erupted from onlookers. Trudeau sneered and slumped dejectedly in his chair. He finished his bourbon in one swallow and looked angrily at McGee. "Care to tell me what you're holding?"

McGee raked in the chips from the center and said, "You know as well as I that at this point it doesn't matter." He handed his cards to the dealer. With a quick shuffle McGee's cards were merged with the others. The dealer looked around the table. Everyone appeared exhausted. "I assume we are finished here gentlemen."

Three of the players stood and congratulated McGee; Trudeau remained seated. Finally he stood, but didn't look at McGee. He went to the bar and ordered a bottle of bourbon. McGee took his chips to the banker, and asked to receive his money when the boat docked. Before leaving he told Bouchard he would like to buy back the necklace. The captain nodded.

McGee knocked on Teeny's stateroom door. She tried to judge by his expression what had happened. "I heard yelling and cheering but was afraid to open the door."

"Well, said McGee," without showing much emotion, "I had a rather poor hand, and I'm pretty sure Trudeau could have won."

"Could have won? Does that mean you won?" McGee flashed a broad smile. "Yes, thanks to the necklace, Trudeau couldn't match my final bet."

Teeny gently put Mary on the bed, and hugged McGee. She felt giddy. "You won. You beat a professional gambler."

McGee corrected her. "No, *we* beat a professional. And you have a nice endowment to begin your life in New Orleans."

Teeny cried, hugged McGee again, and then kissed him on the cheek.

"We're not finished yet," he said. "Abe will send us news in the next few days, I'm hoping no one is looking for us." He paused, looked over at the little girl and said, I'll see you and Mary in the morning."

Before leaving he stood by the door and gave Teeny a concise salute and a kind look. "Dame fortune seldom knocks more than once in a lifetime...Thank you for helping me prepare for her arrival. Good night, Miss Douglas."

McGee paused outside Teeny's cabin and noticed Trudeau lingering at the bar.

In a surly manner Trudeau called to him, "Captain, how about a game or two before you retire? I would like a chance to recoup some of my loss."

"I'm sorry, Mr. Trudeau. If we were to play, you wouldn't have enough money to cover my first bet."

"You bastard!" snarled Trudeau.

McGee cocked his head and frowned. "An honest man is none the worse because a mad dog barks at him. Good night, Mr. Trudeau."

91

AFTER SUNDAY SERVICES, DAVE THOMAS made a trip to Shantytown to deliver a letter to Tom and Rosie. He applied the brake to his buggy and walked up the porch steps. Before he could knock Tom opened the door and welcomed him. Thomas held an envelope for him to see. "Got a letter here; it's from Will."

Rosie stood next to Tom, holding baby Will. Annie yelled out from the kitchen, "Tell Mr. Thomas to come in here an' grab some biscuits an' coffee. Jus caus he own da place doan mean I gonna wait on him."

Thomas laughed when he heard her. He greeted Rosie with a hug, tugged on Will's tiny hand, and made his way to the kitchen. Annie gave him a big smile as she poured the coffee.

"You're looking good, Annie. How's that arm feeling?"

"I be doin' preddy good, Mr. Thomas, how bout you?"

"Not bad. I guess Tom told you about all the nonsense going on in town?"

"He say it always busy, lotsa folks movin' west, an' dey all seem upset bout one thing or another."

"Yeah, every day those free state an' popular sovereignty folks are hangin' around my store, spouting their views an' wanting me and my customers to sign their damn petitions. I just want to sell my wares."

Thomas took a sip of coffee. "What do you think, Annie?"

Annie laughed. "Ain't important what I think. Nobody gonna care. Let's get to da parlor an' read dat ledder."

Everyone watched Tom open the envelope. There were three pages written in longhand. Tom was overwhelmed and handed the letter back to Thomas. "Mr. Thomas, could you be doin' tha readin'? It'd take me all day ta get dis read."

They took a seat as Dave began. There was news of Sunny's pregnancy, a description of the farm and cottage where they were living, surprise at being left money from Captain Strickland, and how they used some of that money to help three young slave girls escape. Thomas paused and wiped his brow. "My goodness, there ain't time for grass to grow under that boy's feet. Something's always happening."

He arched his eyebrows and smiled as he read the next part. "Will concludes his letter by saying, "If our baby's a boy, he will be named Tom." After the last line was read all three clapped, and begged him to read the letter again. "Specially dat las part a'bout name'n dat baby."

After he finished reading the letter a second time, Thomas handed the letter to Tom. Tom folded the papers carefully and said to Rosie, "Seem like all I gots left a my fren be dis ledder."

Annie gave him a kind but stern look. "Dat ain't true Tom. He always be wif you. And as long as you keep writin' each other, you always be ta'gedder."

Dave Thomas was putting on his hat, getting ready to leave.

"Mistah Thomas, I'd like ta write Will again, real soon," Tom said.

Thomas nodded. "You start writing, and bring the letter to work. I'll make sure we get it mailed."

Thomas returned to the town center. The sheriff and two deputies roamed the City Park, picking up scraps of torn placards and righting benches that had been knocked over. He spotted the Elliot sisters standing off to the side, shaking their heads, and looking perturbed. "What happened?" Thomas asked.

Emma glared at him. "Once again, those abolitionist Nigger lovers attacked the good people who are supporting popular sovereignty. Thank God none of the sovereignty people were hurt."

Thomas looked at the two elderly women and thought about serving up a rebuttal, but decided it would serve no purpose. "Nice seeing you ladies. You're both looking well." He turned and began a brisk walk back to his store.

Emma looked at her sister, "He didn't mean that. He knows we don't look well. I don't trust him. I think he might be part Indian." Gertrude nodded. "Or part Nigger. We know he's not one of us."

CB   CB   CB

Robert and Will sat at the kitchen table reading different newspapers. Robert remained engrossed in a month-old copy of the *New York Weekly Sun*. Will was reading a two- week-old copy of the *Missouri Democrat*. Both papers had been delivered by stagecoach earlier that day.

"Listen to this, Will. It says here a minister and his wife just founded a college for the education of coloreds in Pennsylvania. It's called the Ashmun Institute. Do you think you might like to visit that school?"

Will stared at the paper in front of him and didn't respond.

"Will, is everything okay?"

"Sorry, Mr. Granemann. I just read here that Berry Meachum passed away." Visibly upset, Will had trouble relaying the rest of the story. "He…died while preaching…they say the Freedom School is going to close."

"I'm sorry, Will. I know Mr. Meachum and his school meant a lot to you."

"He seemed so full of life, so healthy. I can't believe he's gone."

Robert searched for the right words to comfort his friend. "Be grateful he was in your life, if only for a brief time." After he said this, however, he realized it was as much for his own benefit as for Will's.

Will nodded and slowly got to his feet. "I think I'll head back to the cottage now. Good-night Mr. Granemann."

Will was in a melancholy mood when he greeted Sunny. He went to the back room and took out the old leather satchel. All that was left inside was Teeny's torn letter and Granda's brightly colored beads. He sat on the bed holding the letter and staring at the beads resting in the palm of his hand.

Sunny sat down next to him. "What's the matter Will?

Will fought back tears. "Berry Meachum's dead, and they're gonna close the school."

Sunny slipped in next to her husband, put her arm around him, and rested her head against his shoulder. "I'm sorry, Will." They sat like that for several minutes before she noticed the beads. "Did Mr. Meachum give you those beads?"

Will gave her a sad smile. "No, Granda, the old voodoo woman at Mary Dale gave them to me. She said they would bring me luck." Will rubbed the back of his head and wiped his eyes with his sleeve. "Back in St. Louis, Big Mama Lucy said these beads worked because I had some money and was alive, and for a black man that's as good as it gets."

Sunny gave him another hug. "You have a lot of good memories about those times. Maybe that's part of the luck from those beads." Then she noticed something else. "What's the scrap of paper?"

Will handed it to her. "It's part of a letter that Teeny slipped to me before she was sold…"

> Will,
>
> I have taken the moneybox
> Master Douglas
> kept papers
> and put them
> look in the cook
> Pritchard knows
> miss
>
> please dont forge

Sunny read the words that had meant so much to Will and had changed his life. "Will, what does it mean?"

"She was trying to tell me she put the money and the Douglas' will in an apron in the cook shed and that Pritchard was looking for it too. I found the money and the last request, but never did figure out what I wasn't supposed to forge."

Sunny arched one eyebrow and gave him a sweet smile. "I'm pretty sure that last line says please don't forget me."

Will looked at the paper again. "Oh…yeah. I think you may be right," he said, slightly embarrassed.

They sat silent for a few moments, until Sunny said, "Have you, forgotten her?"

"No. I don't think you ever forget someone you grew up with."

Sunny had to ask, "Or loved?"

Will shook his head. "I wasn't in love the way I am now. I couldn't love anyone more than I do you."

Sunny moved closer. She kissed him on the cheek. "The colonel is honest and given the closest thing he can to a perfect answer. Therefore, Lady Douglas and our tiny recruit are pleased."

Will smiled for the first time since he returned to the cottage. "The colonel is pleased as well and anxious to meet his new recruit."

He put the beads in his pocket, and looked again at the remains of the letter. He touched the corner of the note to a flame in the fireplace and dropped the burning paper inside. He walked back to where Sunny sat watching him. He gently stroked her cheek, and looked at her lovingly. "The colonel is a lucky man."

92

TWO WEEKS AFTER THE KIDNAPPING, the Walther's baby remained missing. The police ruthlessly interrogated the two men arrested, but couldn't make them reveal the child's whereabouts. Richard and Louise believed that if she was alive, any chance of finding her was slipping away. Richard decided to take matters into his own hands; he dispatched a courier to Martin Lunt and requested a meeting that afternoon.

Lunt arrived promptly and followed the housekeeper into the parlor. He appeared calm and confident. He knew why he had been summoned. Lunt politely requested they dispense with small talk. "I wish you had contacted me sooner. The people who have taken your child are likely hundreds of miles away by now."

Richard and Louise looked astonished. "What are you saying? The men who took her are in captivity."

"No, those two didn't take her. I interrogated them, and they aren't smart enough to pull off a kidnapping. They could barely write their names, which means it's highly unlikely they created the ransom note."

"What about Annie's description of the men?"

"Not conclusive."

"What does that mean?" Louise asked, chagrined.

Lunt's lips stretched and formed a disturbing smile. "Mrs. Walther, your nanny acted under duress and is most likely mistaken about her identification. We need additional facts and new information."

"I see," said Richard. He knew what was coming. "And exactly how much do you need to begin your search for additional facts and new information?"

"Three hundred dollars. I'll let you know whether I need more, depending on what I uncover and how long this investigation takes."

"Mr. Lunt, we would like for you to begin your work immediately," said Louise, "We will have the money delivered to your office tomorrow." There was a sense of urgency in her voice.

"Very well, I need a letter from you informing the Chief of Police that I will be assisting in the search and that you would like him to cooperate and share all evidence."

Richard walked over to the roll-top desk, picked up pen and paper, and wrote the letter. He handed it to Lunt. "What do you plan to do first?"

Without hesitating the detective responded. "There was an informant who led police to the alleged kidnappers. I need to find him."

Late that afternoon Lunt took a carriage to the second precinct and asked for Officer Steiner. A tall mustached officer behind the front desk acted as though he didn't know the detective. "Who wants him?"

"Martin Lunt." The officer smirked. "Is Steiner gonna give ya lessons on how ta catch criminals?"

Lunt responded in a sardonic manner, "Yes, I hear he's the best."

The officer stopped his joking and went to find Steiner, who was preparing to leave for the day. "Tell Lunt I'm off duty and to come back tomorrow," he said.

The officer delivered Steiner's message, but a moment later he returned. "Wait up, Steiner. Lunt has a letter from the Chief; it says we're supposed to cooperate," the officer explained.

"Shit!" Steiner returned to the front desk where Lunt stood waiting.

"Thank you, Officer Steiner for seeing me. I just have one or two questions." Steiner grunted. He motioned to Lunt to follow him to a spot where they would have a little privacy. "Is this about that kidnapping?"

"Yes. I understand an informant relayed to you the whereabouts of the kidnappers?"

Steiner looked annoyed. "Yeah, you know that already, so what do you want?"

"I want you to describe him."

Steiner started gesturing. "Short, big arms, a bunch of tattoos, yellow hair tied behind his head. He didn't tell me his name."

"His name is Scrovis," said Lunt. He turned and abruptly left the precinct.

By ten o'clock the next morning one of Lunt's associates had apprehended Scrovis in a seedy tenement house and hauled him into the detective's office. Lunt's colleague forcibly seated Scrovis across from the detective and stood behind him.

Lunt began his interrogation. "Please tell me again how you obtained information about the kidnappers."

Lunt's man held Scrovis immobile in his chair. He had no choice but to respond. "I already told the police, I overheard these two talkin' in Winstead's bar about stealin' a doctor's child," he explained.

Lunt reached across the desk, grabbed Scrovis's right hand, and deftly snapped his index finger.

Scrovis howled and cradled his right hand with his left. "You son of a bitch! You're a bastard, just like everyone says!"

Lunt paid no attention to the insult; he looked calmly at his prey. "Perhaps you didn't understand the question. How did you obtain the information you gave the police?"

Beads of sweat formed on Scrovis' forehead. "I overheard them two talking…" before he could continue Lunt reached across and grabbed his hand.

"No!" screamed Scrovis, "No!"

Lunt snarled, "Answer me, or I will break all of them."

Scrovis pleaded, "Lawyer! A lawyer gave me their names. Bergermun, his name's Bergermun!"

"Bireman?'

"Yeah!"

Lunt was astonished. He was aware of the lawyer's abolitionist activity but couldn't understand why a well-respected lawyer would get involved in a kidnapping. He said to his associate, "Get this scum out of my office, and get me a carriage." The associate grabbed Scrovis by the collar and escorted him to the street. He rudely deposited Scrovis on the curb and hailed a buggy for his boss.

Half an hour later Lunt arrived in the central precinct and sat down to wait for the Chief of Police.

Shortly, the Chief walked in and gestured for Lunt to come to his office. Lunt handed him Walther's letter and sat on the edge of a chair while the officer read.

"I won't take much of your time, Chief. I just need to ask you a few questions. These two men you're holding for the kidnapping, were they arrested before?"

The chief rifled through documents piled on his desk, then pulled out paperwork related to the two men. Attached to it was an arrest warrant filed in November. "Says here they were arrested and charged with robbery and assault a few months ago."

Though Lunt felt reasonably sure he knew the answer to his next question, he asked anyway. "Who filed the charges?"

"Captain Gordon Strickland and his lawyer, Abraham Bireman."

A narrow slit of a grin formed on Lunt's face. "Thank you for your time. You've been most helpful."

Lunt's next stop was the riverboat dispatcher's office, where he inspected records of all arrivals and departures for the month of November. While examining the paperwork he noticed one of the boats he was investigating was moored on the levee. Lunt approached the Adele's landing platform and introduced himself. He asked First Officer Daniel Curtis for permission to speak to Captain Strickland.

"The captain passed away a short time ago, Mr. Lunt. The Adele has a new captain," the officer answered politely.

"My condolences, officer. I wonder if you might remember whether Captain Strickland received any regular visitors prior to his death?"

"Not regular, but the day he died Captain McGee and another gentleman were with him."

Lunt calmly led him to the next question and answer. "Was the other man's name Abraham Bireman?"

"Yes, he agreed to handle the Captain's final request." Lunt thanked the officer and returned to his office. He drafted a letter informing Richard and Louise he had new information. He would send a complete report in a few days.

When Abe Bireman arrived at his office the next morning, he received an unpleasant surprise: Martin Lunt stood waiting outside his office. Lunt acted superficially congenial as he greeted the lawyer. "Good morning, Mr. Bireman, I wonder whether I might have a few moments of your time."

"Certainly, it's an honor to have the city's foremost detective pay me a visit." Bireman invited Lunt to take a seat.

"No, thank you. I just have a couple of questions; this will only take a moment."

Abe felt uneasy about Lunt's unannounced visit. He took a seat behind his desk, shuffled a few papers, and gathered his thoughts.

Lunt stood in front of Bireman's desk. "I understand you were kind enough to handle the last will and testament of Captain Strickland. And, that you and Captain McGee were present when he passed away," the detective said cloyingly.

The tips of Abe's fingers came together; he placed them next to his chin, almost as if he were hoping for divine guidance. "Both of those statements are correct. I assume you are sharing these thoughts because you are leading to a more important question?"

Lunt's demeanor became menacing. He leaned forward. "Yes, I believe you were involved in the kidnapping of Dr. Walther's child. I assume others were involved as well...maybe Captain McGee...and maybe the slave woman who bore the child."

"Surely you are experienced enough to know that slander is a criminal offense. Your reputation and livelihood are in jeopardy by making such an absurd accusation."

"As is yours, Mr. Bireman, if I am correct," Lunt swiftly rejoined.

"If you have evidence supporting this preposterous theory of yours, please share it with the authorities. I bid you good day."

Lunt wasn't finished. He glared across the desk. "Does the testimony of a man named Scrovis seem like evidence?"

Abe was momentarily caught off guard, but then responded evenly. "No, I believe the man you are referring to is a common hooligan. His testimony can be bought and sold. Therefore, it has no credence in a court of law."

"I will gather the facts needed to prove my allegation. You and Captain McGee should have known better than to assist an escaped slave. Good day, Mr. Bireman."

Abe sat behind his desk, unsettled by the gut-wrenching blow just delivered. After pondering the situation for several minutes, he jotted a short note and sent it by courier to Rusty's Tavern.

Lunt returned to the Adele once again. He told a member of the crew he needed to speak with First Officer Daniel Curtis. In his hand, he held the letter Walther drafted instructing the police to share information. He presented it to Curtis.

"What is this?" asked Officer Curtis.

"It's a request from Dr. Walther to share information."

Curtis grew uneasy. "I don't understand. What does the letter have to do with me or the late captain?"

"I believe there was correspondence between Captain Strickland and Mr. Bireman that might contain information about an escaped slave. I would like to see any documents or letters that might have been saved."

Curtis's discomfort increased, as did his suspicion. He looked at Walther's letter again. "This letter isn't addressed to me. You'll have to bring a letter from the Chief of Police to see the captain's personal effects. Good-day, sir."

"I will do that. Thank you for your time, officer."

Lunt's bluff wasn't a complete failure; the officer's response indicated there were items of Strickland's still on board. Lunt stood on shore and planned his next move.

93

THE NEXT EVENING BIREMAN APPEARED once again in the back room of Rusty's Tavern nervously waiting for Gar. Rusty set a bottle of bourbon in front of him along with two glasses. "Is this the same stuff you always serve?"

"Right, my finest bourbon."

Abe felt reluctant to take another chance with the pale brown liquid but decided to pour a small amount in the glass tumbler. He swallowed, felt the burning in his throat, and started to sputter. After the second drink, he decided the brew wasn't so bad. Gar sauntered in and noticed Bireman's glass, then the bottle.

"Beermun, ya got a head start on me. It's my turn to have a go with that whiskey." Gar finished the bottle in several noisy gulps and signaled Rusty for another. Rusty placed the bottle on the table and pulled the curtain closed.

The second drink had Abe feeling lightheaded and belligerent. "That bastard Scrovis sold us out." Abe started to pour himself another tumbler of bourbon.

"Hold on there, my little friend. I think ya had enough for now. What happened with Scrovis?"

In a mocking tone Bireman answered. "Martin Lunt, St. Louis' finest detective, got him to talk. Scrovis told Lunt I gave him the information about the two men charged with the kidnapping. That's not all. Lunt came to my office, and let me know I was a dumb ass for helping a slave woman get her child back."

"He's right…you are a dumb ass."

Bireman laughed and nodded. Gar took a healthy swig from the bottle and mumbled a few curse words. "I shoulda never trusted that weasel Scrovis."

"I'm sure Lunt had ways to make him talk." Abe reached for the bottle and filled his glass. "Now we have to decide our next move."

"We?" Gar retrieved the bottle, polished it off, and ordered another.

"I need someone to tail Lunt and make sure he doesn't uncover any more information. Are you willing?"

"Well Beermun, ya got yerself backed in a corner. I'm glad to help, but I need a little extra for this job."

Bireman rolled his eyes knowingly. No doubt this was going to be expensive. "How much extra?"

"Five hundred." Abe picked up the tumbler of bourbon and swallowed the contents. This time he didn't cough or hesitate to respond. "Five hundred it is."

At three in the morning Lunt sat on a drayman's wagon, waiting for lights to be extinguished aboard the Adele. There was still activity: supplies being loaded and unloaded, a dice game taking place nearby, and occasionally a yell pierced the night air. He adjusted the two Bowie knives tucked inside his belt and released the safety on his pistol.

A half hour later he strode casually toward the Adele, looked around, and walked silently up the landing stage. He lingered near the bow for several minutes and waited to hear sounds that would indicate someone on board was awake. All he heard was the creaking and groaning of the large wooden structure and the occasional squawking of birds.

He removed his boots so they wouldn't resonate on the wood deck and ascended the central stairs that led to the saloon. The air smelled of stale cigars and bourbon. Stairs to the third level were narrow, and the passageway was dark. Halfway up he stepped on something sharp. He winced and reached down to feel the bottom of his foot. A shard of glass from a broken bottle now lay embedded in his foot. He silently cursed, pulled the glass out, and continued his climb to the third deck.

He looked to his right; no lights came from the small cabins assigned to waiters and kitchen help. The officer's quarters to the left also remained dark, except for a faint light in the last room. He proceeded along the outer passageway to the captain's cabin. Inside a lantern was still burning. Lunt could see the captain sprawled out on the bed, asleep. He surveyed the interior but saw nothing that resembled stored material. If Strickland's personal items were on board, they were elsewhere.

Lunt circled the captain's quarters and found the stairwell leading to the pilothouse. The stairs were steep, his foot was bleeding, and he had no light to guide him. He reached the top deck, relieved to see the outline of the pilothouse against the dark sky. He limped to the entrance and found a lantern and matches. He lit the wick and inspected the cut on his foot. He pulled another sliver of glass from the wound and wrapped his foot with a handkerchief. Lunt looked around. Three wooden crates with the letters G S painted on them stood stacked in the corner.

He crawled over and began to examine the contents of each box. At the bottom of the third crate he found two telegrams and a letter from Abraham Bireman. Lunt started to read but stopped when he heard a loud creaking noise. He stuffed the letter and telegrams in his pocket and crawled toward the stairs. He backed down carefully, trying to keep pressure off his injured foot.

He reached the third deck and hobbled to the stairwell leading to the staterooms and saloon. Out of the darkness came a deep voice, "With all the money you got, Lunt, how come ya don't hire sum'body to snoop around for ya?"

Lunt recognized the voice. It was the same man who attacked him once before. He reached behind and pulled the two knives from his belt He limped slowly backward toward the stairwell. He tried to make a run for the stairs, but blood oozing from his foot caused him to slip and fall. Two large hands grabbed him around the shoulders and yanked him upright. Lunt turned quickly. He used all of his strength to force the knives into Gar's mid section. Then yanked them upward, trying to do as much damage to the big man's internal organs as possible.

Gar was stunned by the swiftness of Lunt's retaliation. The acrid taste of blood rose from his throat to his mouth. He wrapped his massive arms around the detective and dragged him to the stern. Lunt kicked violently and tried to free himself. Gar had a vice like grip on Lunt. He stumbled; both men crashed through the railing. They tumbled through darkness and landed on a paddlewheel blade. The wheel had been hoisted above the surface for repairs, and now the added weight caused it to slowly turn. Lunt and Gar dangled on the edge... then slid silently into the dark water.

94

WILL AND SUNNY LOOKED FORWARD to the Granemann's weekly shopping trip into town. First stop, the Farmer's Market. Sunny and Helen exited the carriage to shop for coffee, salt, and fresh meat. Robert and Will continued on to the post office to pick up mail and newspapers. They had just secured the brake on the carriage when two well-dressed gentlemen from the International Hotel approached. One of them said to Robert, "Pardon me, sir, do you know which of the riverboats is likely to have a good card game on board?"

"The riverboat Nominee is your best choice. The games are honest and the drinks are good."

"Thank you, sir," the man replied politely. "We just arrived and really don't know our way around. May we pay you a reasonable fee to have your Nigger secure us a carriage and take us to the boat?"

"Will Douglas is a free man, gentlemen. If you would like to procure his services, you should ask him and discuss compensation with him."

The man responded with a rude laugh, "I can't do that, sir. Where I come from, there ain't no such thing as negotiatin' with a Nigger, and I'm sure he doesn't know what compensation means."

Will spoke up, "It's just as well you not hire me, sir. You would be as unwelcome in my company as I would be in yours."

The man turned to his friend. "Well I'll be damned. Did you hear that, James? This Nigger talks just like a white man. Next you'll be tellin' us he can read and write."

Will raised one corner of his upper lip and forced a crooked smile. Robert felt uneasy. "Good day, gentlemen, and good luck with your card games."

The man who had been doing the talking made a slight bow, then snidely said, "And good luck to you, Mr. Abolitionist." He waved a finger in Robert's face. "It's folks like you who kowtow to these Niggers that are gonna split this country apart."

Will gave a retort he quickly regretted. "This country's already split apart, and you're gonna make sure it stays that way. Otherwise you'd have to pick your own damned cotton."

"You come back home with me boy, and I'll show you how an uppity Nigger gets his due for talkin' to a white man like that. In fact I'm thinkin' about blowin' your Nigger brains out right here!"

Earl Duncan heard the shouting and approached the group. The man yelling at Will placed his hand on his pistol.

"Keep that gun holstered, sir; we'll not have any shooting in my town. What's the problem here?" said the sheriff.

"We were just asking where to find a good poker game, and this Nigger started cursing us, then he threatened to attack us."

Robert rolled his eyes in disbelief. Duncan looked at the sky, then at the ground, and measured his words. "Gentlemen, this is Robert Granemann, one of St. Paul's finest citizens. And this is Will Douglas, a free man. Now, there's no need for more yelling. Let's all move on.

"You're all a bunch a goddamned abolitionists, an' y'all ain't gonna be happy until there's a full scale battle, are you? Well after that happens, you'll be singin' a different tune."

"I'm sure we'll all be singing 'Hail Columbia,'" replied Robert.

The two men grew even more incensed and began mumbling loud obscenities. Duncan shouted, "Stop! Everyone move on!"

That evening at dinner, the story of what happened outside the hotel was told and re-told. Everyone laughed when Robert said, "I should have threatened those men with my sixty-five year old haymaker. That would have shut them up."

"Does that haymaker still work?" joked Will.

Robert pointed to his flexed right arm. "Of course! Lucky for those two Earl arrived in the nick of time and saved them."

Sunny and Helen were grateful the confrontation ended without anyone getting hurt, and the laughter around the kitchen table put everyone in a good mood. Sunny grabbed a handful of plates, getting ready to clear the table, when Robert held up his hand and signaled for everyone to wait a moment. He looked serious. "I hope you don't mind that Helen and I discussed your future earlier today." Robert began, solemnly. Will and Sunny grew suddenly apprehensive.

"We consider you both part of our family, and we're worried about the undercurrent of ugliness that seems to be taking over this country. There's the ongoing blight of slavery. Our government is fighting with Indians and Mexicans. The Know Nothings hate the Irish and the Germans. Protestants and Catholics don't respect each other. It goes on and on and never seems to end," he continued.

Sunny gave Will a worried look. Helen moved closer to Sunny and put a hand on her shoulder. "Everything will be fine, just give him a moment to finish his tirade."

"Anyway, Helen and I are concerned about your safety. We think you should continue to live in the cottage.

Will looked at Sunny, who was smiling and nodding.

"We are happy to accept your offer Mr. and Mrs. Granemann, but we can pay you. We have the money from Captain Strickland."

Robert kindly demurred. "Let's wait, Will, and see how things work out. See if you can use some of that money to help others, the way you intended."

While Helen and Sunny bustled around in the kitchen, Robert and Will relaxed on the front porch reading newspapers. Robert reached into his pocket and handed Will a small booklet. "Take a look at this, Will. It's a speech by Frederick Douglass that they were selling at the bookstore."

Will started reading a reprint of Frederick Douglass' "Fourth of July" speech that he gave several months ago. Robert sat down and waited for a reaction. Will had nearly finished, when he pointed to a passage and started to read it aloud.

> What, to the American slave, is your 4th of July?
> I answer; a day that reveals to him, more than
> all other days in the year, the gross injustice and
> cruelty to which he is the constant victim. To
> him, your celebration is a sham; your boasted
> liberty, an unholy license; your national greatness,
> swelling vanity; your sounds of rejoicing are
> empty and heartless; your denunciation of tyrants,
> brass fronted impudence; your shouts of liberty

and equality, hollow mockery; your prayers and
hymns, your sermons and thanksgivings, with all
your religious parade and solemnity, are, to him,
mere bombast, fraud, deception, impiety, and
hypocrisy—a thin veil to cover up crimes which
would disgrace a nation of savages. There is not
a nation on the earth guilty of practices more
shocking and bloody than are the people of the
United States, at this very hour.

"What's going to happen to him for saying this?" Will asked, incredulous.

Robert shook his head. "I'm not sure; he's very cautious wherever he goes. Some say it's one of the greatest speeches ever. Others say he's a rabble-rousing traitor who should be hanged."

Will handed the pamphlet back to Robert. "Do you know where he is now?"

"From what I've heard, he still speaks at abolitionist rallies, but I suspect with all the death threats, he's making his way to Canada."

Just then, Helen approached, interrupting Will's thoughts on the Douglass speech. She looked concerned. "Robert, I think it would be good for Sunny to pay Doctor Becker a visit. Will, has Sunny been sleeping through the night?"

"No, she get's up one or two times, why?"

"I think this baby is coming early; we should ask the doctor."

The next morning Will pulled the Granemann carriage to the back of the Becker residence. Two days earlier a tribe of Dakota Sioux raided a military camp on the Minnesota River, killing four soldiers. Since that attack, people in St. Paul looked at all Indians with suspicion, even those who were living in St. Paul before the attack. Robert stepped down from the carriage and looked to see whether anyone noticed his arrival. Sunny waited for a signal. When the doctor waved, she hurried to the back door and went inside.

After the examination, Becker seemed pleased. "Everything is fine, but I would expect this baby in September, not October."

"Will you be there to help when the baby arrives?"

The doctor nodded. "I'll be there, Robert. I'm not like Englehart."

Becker was referring to a doctor in Galena who refused to treat an injured Indian chief who had been attacked by a drunken mob outside a saloon.

Englehart defended his actions by saying, "I only treat American citizens—no Niggers, no Indians." After the Indian died many people criticized the doctor for violating his medical oath. Others hailed him as a true American.

Will escorted Sunny back to the carriage. Before they left, Robert said, "Helen and I appreciate your helping us Doc. Sunny's a fine young lady; she doesn't deserve to be treated like an outcast."

Becker looked toward the carriage and sighed. "It's the world we're living in Robert. Nothing's as it should be."

August was one of the most peaceful months Will had ever known. He admired the stacks of giant white clouds that formed in the blue summer sky and marveled at rows of perfectly formed stalks of corn in the fields. On the last day of the month, Robert returned from the post office with a letter from Abe Bireman.

That evening he read it aloud. The last part of the letter took everyone by surprise.

> The enclosed newspaper story explains the altercation that occurred, and the death of Gar and Lunt. The good news is that Miss Douglas is reunited with her child and has left the city. I will write with more details as soon as I hear from Captain McGee. My Best to everyone and congratulations on the new baby when he or she arrives.
>
> Abe

Everyone glanced from face to face. "Where do you suppose she went with her baby?" Helen asked.

Robert placed the letter on the table and looked at it thoughtfully. "Knowing Abe, I'll bet he booked passage to a place no one would suspect."

Sunny grimaced. She felt a sharp pain in her abdomen; she clutched Will's arm. "Seems all this talk about babies has aroused our little recruit. That was a pretty good kick." The tranquility of late summer was over.

95

ONE TUESDAY MORNING IN EARLY September, Helen called out to Robert, "It's time to fetch Doc Becker."

Will and Robert quickly climbed aboard the carriage, while Helen gathered up towels and a washbasin. Shortly after the men returned, the doctor realized something about this baby's birth was different.

Will and Robert paced in the front of the cottage for what seemed like hours. They heard screams of pain, what sounded like a gasp of horror, and finally the wail of a tiny infant. "Do you think something's wrong?" said Will.

"I'm sure everything's okay. Doc should be out in a minute."

Helen, all smiles, entered the room where the men sat waiting.

"Congratulations, Will! It's a boy, and he's beautiful! But wait here and talk with Doctor Becker before you go and see him."

Becker came from the back room. He didn't look or sound as cheerful as Helen.

"Congratulations, Will, your baby boy is healthy." He paused a moment and began to explain what had transpired. "The baby's birth was unusual, very unusual. Your child was born behind the veil."

Both men looked at Becker, confused and apprehensive. "What does that mean?"

"I've only seen it once before, Robert. It's a thin skin that surrounds the baby at birth. I cut it away and the baby looks normal." He paused again, and then gave a blunt directive. "But, you must keep the details of this birth to yourselves. Tell no one." Becker rubbed his forehead and appeared troubled. "Some people believe babies born this way have special powers. They believe he will be able to predict the future, even heal others. You must bury the skin and never mention it again. If people who believe these superstitions find out about it, they will never leave you, or your baby, alone."

Will couldn't wait any longer; he rushed to the backroom, followed by Robert and Helen. Sunny was cradling the baby and nursing him. Will bent over and kissed her sweetly on the lips. "How's Lady Douglas and our little man?"

"We're perfect."

Will smiled at them and said, "I agree." He stroked his son's cheek and in a gentle voice said, "Hello, little Tom. Welcome to the world." Will reached in his pocket and pulled out Granda's brightly colored beads. He showed them to Sunny and said, "Seems like the beads are still working."

A few weeks after the baby was born, Will and Robert took the carriage to the city to gather newspapers and correspondence. After they left the post office, Robert pulled the carriage to a halt on a steep grade. The two men looked down at the construction of a new building. "What's goin' on down there, Mr. Granemann?"

"A new church is going up. It's being built on the same spot where the old one stood…where Charles was shot by that detective."

Will couldn't help but wonder, "Does it upset you to visit here?"

"Not like it used to. Time does heal a lot of sad memories."

"Mr. Granemann, do you know where Teeny went after she left the church?"

"She went to Taylor's home, and from there to the levee where the Excelsior was moored. It's only a short distance. I'll show you."

Robert guided the carriage down two more streets and pointed to a spot where the riverboat had tied up that fateful day.

"I'm not really sure how she managed to elude that detective and get away. I know Taylor helped, and another fellow by the name of Claibourne."

Will was transfixed and tried to imagine everything that occurred. He said a silent prayer for Teeny and her daughter. Robert looked at the dark clouds forming in the northwest and thought it best they head home. "Storm's coming; we're going to get our first snow." Robert released the brake and started to turn the carriage when a familiar figure approached.

"Congratulations, Will; I hear ya have a brand new baby boy."

"Thank you, Mr. Taylor. Yes, sir, I sure do, and he's keeping us busy."

Taylor grinned. "How are you and Helen holdin' up Robert? Been a long time since you had a baby on yer place."

"Everyone's fine, Bill. What's new in town? We haven't heard much about the movement. Are new shipments arriving?"

Taylor looked toward the river. "Big news is comin' from the East. Fellow by the name of John Brown in Massachusetts is trying to form a colored militia to fight the slave catchers and help the runaways."

Robert was astounded. "They'll hang him for that."

"Yes, sir, they probably will, but so far he seems to be gittin' away with it."

"Does Mr. Douglass know him?" asked Will.

"Yeah, they've met, even talked a couple a times. Douglass thinks Brown is smart, but a very strange man. Besides, using weapons ain't his style. He thinks words are more powerful."

The conversation lulled for a moment. Then Robert said, "Thanks for keeping us informed, Bill. Can I give you a lift?"

"Thanks for the offer, Robert, but Adie says I'm gettin' fat and need to walk more. I tell her there's just more of me ta love, but she ain't thinkin' I'm very funny."

"You take care, Bill." Taylor nodded. "You take care too, Robert. An' Will, you take care of that pretty wife and baby." Then Robert flicked the reigns and guided the carriage from the levee to First Street. Will turned and took one final look at the Excelsior's mooring spot. So much had happened since he last saw Teeny…a lifetime ago it seemed. A cold wind from the north became stronger and snow began to fall. The two men huddled together and headed home.

96

NEW ORLEANS WAS BEAUTIFUL, DIRTY, violent, genteel, and raucous. Civic leaders had created wards and precincts that divided the city into sections, where social prominence and business interests received preference. Immigrants coming to New Orleans had little respect for these artificial boundaries and resented being told where they should live. That resentment often resulted in violence. In the midst of this cultural potpourri, Dr. John and Marie Laveau openly practiced voodoo and the black arts with the rich and poor, as well as old and new residents. The spiritual and social mix made New Orleans the most interesting and most violent of all southern cities.

Sugarcane, tobacco, and cotton fueled the city's wealth. To keep the economy booming, slaves were sold every day, even on the church steps. The ever-present slave trade and chaos made Teeny quite uncomfortable, but this was her new home. Now she had to find a place to live and raise her daughter.

While returning from a shopping trip at the boisterous levee market, she spotted a row house for sale in the French Quarter. A small park was nearby, the neighborhood was safe, and the house was built on high enough ground that it escaped the constant flooding. The location seemed ideal. She rushed back to the hotel and asked McGee if he would handle the negotiations.

McGee agreed and found that he enjoyed the process of haggling with the owner over the sale price. To him it was like a poker game with wagering, bluffing, and calling for the final bet. He felt giddy when his last offer was accepted and eager to tell Teeny she had a place of her own. He weaved along crowded streets toward the St. Charles Hotel.

While ascending the ornate staircase, an elaborately festooned servant beckoned. "Sorry to interrupt yer day, Captain, but this letter was delivered by messenger for ya." McGee saw Abe's return address and hastily opened the envelope. A letter and newspaper clipping lay inside. He read the letter and clipping, then sat on the stair step and read them both again. He shook his head.

McGee knocked on Teeny's door. She could tell by his odd expression that something happened. "Are you okay? You look like something's wrong."

"Ah, never judge by appearance. I have much news to share." He noticed Mary sleeping on the bed. "I don't want to wake her, should we talk elsewhere?"

Teeny shook her head. "She sleeps soundly. Please tell me what has happened."

"First, the good news. I have agreed with the owner of the townhome to purchase it for a fair price, and the place is yours."

"Oh, McGee! Oh my!" She gave him a hug. "That's wonderful news."

Then McGee pulled the letter from his coat pocket and said, "There's more. I have a letter from Abe. You won't believe what happened in St. Louis."

Her cheery demeanor faded. "Oh, no," said Teeny. "Please tell me it's not bad news."

McGee unfolded the letter and gave Teeny a brief summary: "Richard and Louise hired Martin Lunt to investigate your baby's disappearance. Somehow he pieced together information that tied Abe and me to the rescue of your daughter."

Teeny nervously wrung her hands. "No, no! Not after we've made it this far. Is he coming after us?"

There was no remorse in McGee's voice as he answered. "No, he's dead."

"Oh, my god! Is Mr. Bireman okay?"

"Yes," McGee replied, handing her the newspaper clipping.

> The body of St. Louis detective Martin Lunt and an unidentified dockworker were found on the east shore of the Mississippi River at 10:00 a.m. Wednesday morning. Police believe the two men had a violent altercation aboard the riverboat Adele and fell overboard. Precinct Captain Tim Donnelly said that two knives and a great deal of blood where found on the top deck of said riverboat.
>
> The doctor conducting the examination speculates that the river current carried the men to the location where the bodies were discovered.

Wounds on both men were severe, and the doctor
believes they may have been dead before entering
the water.

Teeny wore a blank look and stared at the newspaper clipping. She walked slowly to McGee and put her arms around him. She rested her head on his chest, and sobbed softly. "Is it finally over?"

He nodded. "I believe so. Either way, it's time you made a new life without living in fear of being discovered."

"You're right, but I know I'll always be looking over my shoulder."

McGee thought about that for a moment and said, "You are aware, Miss Douglas, that a smooth sea never made a skillful mariner. You have endured many difficulties, and it has given you the ability to navigate a safe course for you and your daughter."

Teeny smiled. She thought about McGee's sayings and realized she was going to miss them. She walked to the bed, placed her hand gently on Mary, and stroked her daughter's hair. "What are your plans, Captain?"

"I'm not sure. I might visit my sister in St. Joe, or pilot a few more years, or maybe retire. The first thing I'll do is visit Abe, make sure he's okay, and buy him the dinner I promised."

"Would you consider residing in New Orleans? Mary and I would love for you to stay; there's plenty of room in our new home…no obligations…no strings attached."

He gave Teeny a sly smile. "Youth looks forward, and age looks backward, Miss Douglas. You have much to give and much to look forward to." McGee paused and gave Teeny a tender smile. "I will write. And if I decide to partake of southern hospitality, or need a partner in a high stakes poker game, I will call on you."

Teeny tiptoed over and kissed him gently on the lips. "Please do that, Captain."

97

WILL, SUNNY, AND BABY TOM snuggled together on blankets in front of the fire. Will watched flames dance around the logs; occasionally he glanced out the window at the falling snow. Little Tom slept soundly, and Sunny was about to nod off. He adjusted the wick on the lantern and quietly lifted a newspaper. He began reading a section of the *Times* that collected news stories from different parts of the country.

> Riot — A bloody riot occurred in New Orleans last Monday night between large parties of Americans and Irishmen. Fire arms were freely used on both sides, and a great many were wounded and several killed. The military were called out and the mob dispersed. On Tuesday night the fight was renewed, when two persons were killed. Again the military assembled, and this time effectually quelled the disturbance.

> Massacre — We have received full particulars of the massacre by the Sioux Indians of Lieutenant Grattan and the detachment of troops under his command near Fort Laramie. Upon the death of Grattan the troops became panic stricken, and the Sioux tomahawked every man but one, who effected his escape through the assistance of one of the hostile savages. The Indians refused to allow the dead bodies to be buried.

California — Persons having one half or more of Indian blood in their veins shall not be competent witnesses in a case where a white person is a party. Under this statute, the Supreme Court has decided that a Chinese—an Asiatic—belongs to the Indian race, and is, therefore, not competent to testify against a white person. Judge Wells dissented from the opinion.

Fugitive Slave — A dispatch from Chicago, dated Sept 12th, says: Much excitement prevails here in consequence of the attempted arrest of a fugitive slave by three slave hunters from St. Louis. The cries of the fugitive speedily drew together a large crowd, and in the confusion, he was torn from his captors. The three hunters instantly made an attack on the crowd and recaptured the fugitive. During the mêlée, one of the slave hunters fired a pistol, killing a prominent Chicago citizen. The slain man was identified as Arthur Irving, a government diplomat.

Virginia — At a meeting of the Democratic National Committee it was determined to hold a mass meeting at Tammany Hall to second the efforts of those in Congress who are endeavoring to pass the Nebraska Bill—mandating popular sovereignty in all the new states. Senator Stephen Douglas, of Illinois, introduced the bill.

New York — a general call for a Grand Mass Meeting of citizens opposed to the passage of the Nebraska Bill now under advisement in the Congress of the United States, resulted in an immense throng

gathered near the corner of Grand and Elizabeth
Street. It was estimated that over three thousand
assembled peacefully to protest the actions of
Senator Douglas.

Oregon — We commend the perusal of this letter
to the patriotic men of Oregon and ask them why
they have wept in a corner and silently allowed so
much time to pass to strike a blow to exterminate
the Indians who killed twelve white pioneers?
To prevent further wholesale butcheries by these
worthless peoples resembling the human form
they should all be eliminated.

Will slumped back into the couch. He found the news disturbing and wondered whether the country would ever offer his son a better life. Little Tom
lay peacefully asleep, his head resting on Sunny's stomach. Will eased a few
logs from the pile and gently placed them on the fire. He reached for another
newspaper and picked up a copy of the *Tribune*. Abraham Lincoln's "Peoria"
speech received space on the front page. He read bits and pieces, but one section captivated him.

Nearly eighty years ago, we began by declaring
that all men are created equal; but now from
that beginning we have run down to the other
declaration, that for some men to enslave others is
a 'sacred right of self-government.' These principles
cannot stand together. They are as opposite as God
and Mammon; and whoever holds to the one must
despise the other.

Will noticed little Tom stirring. The baby woke; his large bright eyes stared
up at his father. Will thought about Doc Willis' words: "People believe a baby
born behind the veil has the ability to predict the future." Will bent forward and
kissed his son gently on the forehead. "Little man, I'm gonna teach you to read.

And when you read stories like these…you will be able to predict the future. But, I warn you, you may not like it."

Will felt Granda's beads in his pocket and smiled. He turned the lantern low, arranged the quilts and blankets, and watched snow pile silently on the sill. Will fell asleep with his family. For a brief moment in time, all were at peace.

ABOUT THE AUTHOR

PAUL STEINMANN is a native of St. Louis. Retired from teaching at Webster University after forty years, Professor Steinmann also taught in elementary and secondary classrooms early in his career. He is an avid Cardinal fan, mediocre golfer, and aspiring sous-chef, and lives in St. Louis with his wife, Stephenie, and two small dogs that may or may not be Yorkies. *Will* is Steinmann's first novel.

www.ingramcontent.com/pod-product-compliance
Lightning Source LLC
Chambersburg PA
CBHW020508260626
47156CB00006B/1918